THE ONLY CITY

Praise for *The Only City*

'Lovers and hustlers, migrants and dreamers—each carries a piece of Bombay. Together, their voices form a portrait of a city that is merciless, beautiful, and always alive.'

—Sonia Faleiro

'Bombay can be your soulmate and friend. This city of plurality addresses everyone in the singular—"*tere ko*", "*mere ko*" are levellers. Everyone here is on the edge, and the balancing act becomes the dance of survival. *The Only City*, thoughtfully put together by Anindita Ghose, has eighteen strikingly restless Bombay stories, each with a distinct voice amidst the layered noise; each striving for a moment of change.

Some of the images that live on are: redeveloped apartments named after Italian islands, money-plant chawls, the vanishing sea, private nurses in their crisp uniforms, the grille between the first- and second-class local train compartments, the Bombil-scented breeze, sacks of khadi sakhar, yawning mansions, maharajas posing as tamed cats on the walls, electric-blue fingernails ... Characters move from one story to another as if from one train compartment to another. They are bound to this insomniac dream city and its lights in their own ways. A line from Shanta Gokhale's story says it all: "Being everybody is the best thing for a storyteller. But being everybody is always not being everybody."'

—Jayant Kaikini

'*The Only City* showcases contemporary Mumbai at its best and worst, with Chirodeep Chaudhuri's quiet photographs serving as a counterpoint to the hectic lives in the stories. A literary exploration of Mumbai circa 2025 (with one fabulous futuristic tale), which will also serve as a historical record for future generations.'

—Sooni Taraporevala

'If you're longing to read one new work of fiction about Bombay, *The Only City* is the only book you need to read. It gathers eighteen of the city's best writers in a Queen's Necklace of stories that celebrate and castigate the city in all its dazzling complexity. For Bombayites spread out all over the world like me, this marvellous anthology is the cheapest ticket home.'

—Suketu Mehta

THE ONLY CITY

BOMBAY IN EIGHTEEN STORIES

edited by

ANINDITA GHOSE

FOURTH ESTATE • *New Delhi*

First published in India by Fourth Estate 2025
An imprint of HarperCollins *Publishers*
HarperCollins *Publishers* India, Cyber City,
Building 10-A, Gurugram, Haryana – 122002, India
www.harpercollins.co.in

2 4 6 8 10 9 7 5 3 1

P-ISBN: 978-93-6989-325-6
E-ISBN: 978-93-6989-783-4

Typeset in 11/15.4 Sabon LT Std
by HarperCollins *Publishers* India Pvt. Ltd

Printed and bound at
Replika Press Pvt. Ltd.

MIX
Paper | Supporting
responsible forestry
FSC™ C016779

This book is produced from independently certified FSC® paper to ensure responsible forest management.

*

HarperCollins *Publishers*, Macken House, 39/40 Mayor Street Upper,
Dublin 1, D01 C9W8, Ireland

For the fools who leave.
But more for the fools who return.

कसे तुम्ही; काय वर्णू थोरवी! तुम्ही पोलाद, तुम्ही अलवार
फुले टपकन पडताच; जखमा होतात हृदयावर

—

How shall I speak of your glory? You're steel, you're soft:
Your flowers, falling, leave wounds on my heart.

—Narayan Surve, 'Mumbai'
Translated from the Marathi by Ranjit Hoskote, 2025

Contents

HOMECOMING

Editor's Note

I had been covering a jalebi competition between small eateries run by immigrants in New York City's Jackson Heights neighbourhood, when my journalism school classmates started to text me: 'You are in my thoughts' and 'How are you, Anindita?' Alarmed by the comma in a text message, I called one of them back.

Did I know there had been a terror attack on Bombay, my British classmate asked me. No, I had rushed out of bed, been in the subway system for an hour, and then been consumed by fried flour and sugar syrup. I had barely checked my phone. As I heard his voice on speaker phone, while frantically reading the news in parallel, I remember breaking a sweat under layers of winter clothing. This was November 2008.

I was never meant to come home for the short Christmas break the month after—I had a thesis to work on, a new romance to attend to, and last-minute flight tickets were imprudent on a student budget—but I did. I took a train to see the Taj; to see the bullet holes on the walls of the cafés I had never liked the food in. When I did, I knew I could never leave the city again. Though I went back to finish my master's degree, though I worked with a newspaper in Delhi for three years after that, though I continue to have fantasies of moving (to the mountains, to a farmhouse, to Auroville, to New York), I have never really been able to leave. Call it the narcissism of the cricket fan who believes they have to wear a lucky T-shirt for their team to win, but I believe terrible things happen to Bombay in my periods of absence.

It's not just the 2008 terror attack—the December 1992 riots happened in the one year my father decided to move the family to Bangalore. On the day of the July 2005 floods, I was in the city, but had chosen randomly not to go to university at Kalina that morning. So it is that I can never leave, I must always be present, and I must be out and about.

When people say Bombay smells of garbage and rotting fish, the homes are too small, there are too few green spaces, the traffic is unbearable, the roads are riddled, the poor have been unfairly moved near toxic landfills, the city still isn't rain-ready, I know it's all true—except that the fish are drying, not rotting. I'm a romantic, but I'm not wholly delusional. I spend reams of time wondering what it is that I love. *That I love* is irrefutable.

It is hard not to love. Even my Bengali parents, who moved here from Kolkata and Delhi, and tried steadfastly to keep the city out of our home through my childhood and teenage years—no Hindi movies, river fish over sea fish, Darjeeling tea over chai—now love. They have finally left behind the mangoes of their childhood and become besotted by the Alphonso.

Admittedly, Bombay is no city of joy, of lights, lakes, hills—those trifling things from which other metropolises draw their names. It is not a place of aching beauty. But it carries a quality of everyday pageantry: a sea laps at its edges all the way from the north to the south. It is Dolby digital thunder and torrential rain pelting down. It is a film shoot in that chalk-blue cottage in Bandra. It is Dadar flower market at dawn, a diaphanous pink dupatta fluttering out of the ladies compartment, the soundtrack of Mohammed Ali Road at noon, the TV actor pretending to shield their face from paparazzi they've paid, the family of four savouring kala-khatta golas at Juhu beach on a Sunday evening.

Is it any coincidence that Bombay is shaped like a continent? This city holds countries. In the Andheri building where I grew up, each of the four flats on our floor housed a different word for mother. So there it is: one thing I love about Bombay is the people who make it up. If all the people of the city were replaced with people from another city, it would not be Mumbai as it stands now. One could argue, that would be true for most cities, but it is truer for some cities more than others.

This is what I had in mind when I invited contributions for the anthology. *The Only City* is a collection of vignettes, a city painted in media res, anchored not on nostalgia or landmarks, but on a cast of Bombay characters. In Diksha Basu's 'Bollywood, Baby', we have an aspiring actress who wears designer clothing but lives in her building's upscaled servant quarters; in Amrita Mahale's 'Aai-Tai', a girl who is the first in her family to pass class twelve does data annotation in an AI firm; in my own story 'Normal Neighbours', a couple drawn from two unassuming steel towns have metamorphosed into the city's avocado-eating elite. For all of them, as well as for the ad filmmaker in Prayaag Akbar's 'Hoodbhoy House'—who wants to mine his daughter's school to expand his professional network—Bombay is the only city that can give them dimension.

The eighteen stories in this anthology are new and previously unpublished. The presence of stalwarts and celebrated peers is thrilling, and it gives me particular joy that this is the first time that Ranjit Hoskote, Raghu Karnad, Jairaj Singh and Prathyush Parasuraman are publishing fiction. I didn't set out to have a certain style of story, though with many writers, I had an inkling of what to expect: I expected, for instance, that Shubhangi Swarup would have zoomorphic elements in her narrative. That Kersi Khambatta would bring levity to his tale of petty politics in a Nepean Sea Road co-op society. I hoped Shanta Gokhale would invite us into domestic spaces in Shivaji Park in the unaffected way only she can. But I did not know that Jeet Thayil would give this anthology a whole new genre with his ominous 'Your Meat in My Hands'—a stand-out even within his vast oeuvre. Or that Yogesh Maitreya, in 'The Sound of Silence', would present the musings of his deep-thinking Dalit protagonist in a form I cannot quite describe. As a reader, this mix of the familiar and the surprising is what makes an anthology sing for me. It's why I listen to the radio.

The poet Arvind Krishna Mehrotra's declaration that there is no such thing as an objective anthology is incontestable. While eighteen writers is by no means a comprehensive list, and there are many others I would have liked to include, each writer in these pages is here for a critical reason. Several of the Bombay-born writers have set their stories in the neighbourhoods they spent their childhoods in. And while not all writers are Bombay/Mumbai 'born and brought up', each has a singular connection to the city, almost alchemic. Manu Joseph wasn't born here, but this is the city that made him a journalist and then a novelist: his writing has always provided a sardonic view as an outsider-insider, a gaze that asserts itself in 'Sufficient Magic'.

A short story is tasked with doing many difficult things, but most importantly, it frames a moment of change. This city, with its determined indeterminateness, fosters epiphanies of all kinds. What we have here, in these pages, is a collection of Bombay moments. Sometimes, it is a slow buildup leading to a moment that fizzes, like in Raghu Karnad's opening story, 'Speedboat'. The 'moment' in each of the stories is clear to me, but I don't intend to spoil your fun. Look out for the tiny strokes too: a girl chancing upon a balloon animal, a child stealing a useless key, lost young men being handed bundles of twenty-rupee notes at a dance bar, a mother rolling a hundred puran polis.

The stories span relatively vast spatial and temporal schemes. There is Marine Drive and Malabar Hill, Kamathipura and the streets of Bandra as one might expect; but there's also Sion and Saki Naka and the bylanes of Khar. The action in Prathyush Parasuraman's 'Two Bi Two' is set on a local train between Dadar and Mulund stations. Ranjit Hoskote's 'A Painter's Last Stop' captures the clip-clop of time over ... a century! Some themes emerged too strongly not to see patterns—immigrant nurses, vanishing women, marital ennui, thwarted desire. I began to see this as many anthologies in one, whorls of petals that must unfurl to reveal some kind of sacred pollen. However, no theme was as ubiquitous as the people's desire to claw their way up—a Bombay trope often exploited in literature and cinema. This brand of covetousness doesn't exist in cities that lean on the assumption that your birth determines all. Bombay promises the possibility of climbing a ladder, driving characters to do things they would never have pictured themselves doing. It makes them seek more—though the definition of more keeps shifting. For the screenwriters in Jairaj Singh's 'Where the Lights Never Go Out', the hunger for more takes them to dark alleys. For Shibani, in Dharini Bhaskar's 'Silver Clouds', it is the unspoken appeal of marrying a boy who lives in a Marine Drive home with 'mahogany doors and bubble-glass windows'. For Nurse Shanti in Tejaswini Apte-Rahm's eponymous story, first it's a better job in the city, and then it is a better city than the city itself.

Not all the stories are celebratory. For love is about looking deeply even when the light isn't soft and warm. In 'Strays', which cleaves the anthology in two, Lindsay Pereira's street urchin has mastered the art of expecting nothing from Bombay despite its relentless promise of everything. Namita Devidayal's 'The Girls of Visty Villa' brings in dark whimsy, ripe for Tim Burton. The city itself morphs through each story. Sometimes it is a third wheel in a romance, sometimes a site of abuse, sometimes a playground for unlikely friendships. It is Bombay and Mumbai, or both, based on what the story or each author called for. For me, it could not be anything other than Bombay. Because in my dreams, and in my phone calls, I call it Bombay. And if I were to be honest, the city I live in continues to be Bombay, even though it changed to Mumbai on paper thirty years ago.

One of the favourite parts of the week for me, as a magazine editor, was when we set the pagination, or ordered the pages for the reader. Though focus groups always concluded that most people read magazines backwards or haphazardly, we took this stage of publication very seriously. In this book, photographs by Chirodeep Chaudhuri—who is a virtuoso documentarian of the city—group the narratives in broad clusters. We start with arrival, we meet characters at various stages of settling in, we witness them reaching for more, we venture into the speculative, and we end with leaving—both literally and metaphorically.

I learnt from Chaudhuri, who has been photographing the city's clock towers for three decades, that while the British favoured Madras Time and Indian Standard Time (IST), the city's residents held on fiercely to Bombay Time, a local solar time that reflected the rhythms of the city. For almost a century, what appeared to be a technical debate over minutes and meridians became a deeply political act. Bombay Time, 39 minutes behind IST, was in effect till as late as 1955. The city's Parsi fire temples still follow Bombay Time! Indeed, this city of many stories is a city of many histories, a city built over and over by succeeding visitors who have come and gone, while the Kolis who were here before anyone else are, thankfully, still here.

And how many names this city bears: at various points Galajunkja (land covered in water), Manbai, Bombaim and Ilha de Boa Vida (island of good life), this amalgamation of seven small islands has gone from being undervalued in a Portuguese princess's dowry to being India's most populous and prosperous city. How does one begin to parse a city that once followed three clocks? How does one write of a city that has to live up to so many names?

In seventeenth-century Japan, the haiku master Matsuo Basho wrote that he longed for Kyoto even in Kyoto. When Imtiaz Dharker wrote 'Hiraeth, Old Bombay', her poem about wanting to take her husband—no longer alive—to Café Naaz—no longer there—she leaned on the old Welsh word that spells a deep longing for home, of a time passed, a place lost, or perhaps never been to. There are so many Bombays that are lost to me. And so many new Bombays I might never inhabit. For now, I live in my Bombay, and that is enough.

Anindita Ghose
Khar, Bombay
June 2025

Speedboat

RAGHU KARNAD

I

Now back to the city, while it was still light.

Red eyes at rest behind reflective sunglasses, shoulders cooling under layers of lotion, cotton and now the bay breeze, they flip-flopped down towards the end of the pier. Som led the way. His party straggled behind him. He turned to watch them, hoping they would see him answering the phone.

'The ferry is reaching now,' the man's voice said. 'You have to wait.'

'How long?'

'Just, you have to wait.'

The pier was where the public ferry embarked, and where their private boat would pick them up in between the ferry schedule. But they were late. The guy on the phone was testy. 'Just be there, on the side,' he said and hung up.

Som went on ahead, entering the shade beneath the roof at the end of the pier. There were many people here. Low cement walls ran around the area, and down one side, a chain of wheeled metal barricades were set up to force ferry passengers into a queue. The barricades divided the end of the pier lengthwise—into the wide expanse where Som now stood; and a narrow channel along the wall, filled with a restless mass of bodies silhouetted in the false dusk under the roof.

In the empty space on his side, Som was alone. The breeze ran through his hair and over his scalp. He patted it without thinking, a habit he had acquired when his hair began thinning; encouraging it to stay put, as if it might just rise off his head one day and float away into the world. He took off his sunglasses.

His party had closed in together at the sight of all the ordinary people. It cut into their buzz, and Som was glad. He had suggested—but not forcefully enough to take credit now—that they get to the pier an hour ago. That would have been just after the previous ferry went out; this place would have been empty. But, well, they were all trapped in the prism of the poolside, stupefied by sun and water. After lunch, which was late as always, the girls had gone off to the terrace to get high. When they came back, they gave up any conversation, or even speech, and it was best just to let them move from deck to pool and back, dousing hot skin or drying slippery shanks on the tile and wood. They even ignored their phones, which were placed safely away from puddles of beer and the water running down their arms. Then evening laid its cool hand over them, and someone brought out cups of espresso, and the girls rose to go shower and moisturize.

Sadiqa was at his elbow. 'Boat here?'

Som shook his head. 'Sorry. You see this queue? We're at the end of it.'

'Meaning? They don't look like they're waiting for a speedboat.'

'No. But our speedboat is waiting for them to be gone.'

'You're not serious.' Her lips thinned. She looked for a moment as if she might throw open her arms and appeal to the hundreds to step back for a minute, so they could squeeze past.

'It won't be long,' Som said. 'It's past six as it is. Are we all here?'

They turned to count their party. Sadiqa's husband Leo came strolling into the shade, the black swallowing up his pale legs and blue cotton shorts. Behind him, the kids lingered together in the sunlight. Their group lengthened as one fell back to take a photo, then compressed together again for selfies. They were all knees and shoulders and lengths of bare skin tipped with candy-coloured accessories.

Som's daughter Zia moved with a lolling gait, and even when she stood in one place, she swung her arms around, pushed the brim of her baseball cap from side to side, front to back, mimicking a graceless child. His son Yash carried the icebox.

There was a flicker and a flash, a grid of tubes lit up in the tin roof overhead. The silhouettes were banished and the crowd bathed in sudden, shock-white fluorescence. At once, Som was aware of the eyes in the ferry queue, scrutinizing his family without the benefit of reflective sunglasses.

'Zia,' Som said, as his daughter arrived. 'Put something on please, it's getting cold.' Even in this light, she had the afterglow of a day spent exquisitely and expensively bored. Not least of her entitlement, he thought, was her ability to just stand here, in front of a hundred men, in what people no longer even bothered to call short-shorts.

She tilted her chin at him. 'You're cold?'

Som was in shorts too, and flip-flops. A crumpled linen shirt.

'That's not ... it's going to be cold on the speedboat.'

'I'll wear something when we're on the boat. Anyway, what boat? Where boat?'

'Well, actually, if we had …' he managed to say, before her phone produced a chorus of bubbling, like a goldfish acapella.

'If we had left …' he continued.

She punched at her phone with both thumbs.

'Darling,' Som said. 'That's a nice message tone. It's also the sound your phone will make when I throw it in the bay.'

She looked up at him as if he was a madman preparing to attack her and turned away very slowly. Som was left feeling the sting of the implication that this was his fault, and not theirs, when he had told them—and he should remind them, he had said it twice …

But then Zia turned back to him and pulled an idiot face of remorse. She went back over to Sadiqa's girls.

'Go Team Speed!' she said.

'Speed*boat*!' whooped Yash, as he caught up.

'Much speed, no boat,' replied the younger Peerbhoy girl, and she and Zia smacked palms together.

The lights going on must have meant that the ferry was arriving. The passengers began to push forward within the barricaded area. Feet shuffled over discarded foil packets, and a tea flask fell, bouncing a melody against the cement. At the front, the ticket-men were making an announcement; faces strained to hear them. A few other faces were still turned on Som's family.

'They're not staring at me, you know,' Zia said. 'They're staring at you. You're the Big Man here with a private boat waiting, Pa. You and Leo. We're just the zenana.' She tugged an imaginary veil over her eyes.

Som dug into his satchel. 'Right,' he said, and held out her balled-up windcheater.

She put it on, tugging it down to her thighs. It fell an inch below her shorts. How easy it had once been to wrap her up in any fabric or in his arms—in a time that he no longer recalled very often, and she never did. It was easier now to put his arms around Yash, but even that took justifying. They never reached out for him, and any touch that lasted longer than an instant released a low throb of awkwardness between them.

Som examined his own bare ankles and calves. Experimentally, he inflated his chest and pulled his stomach flat. He knew his waist was leaving him again, this time probably for good. What scared him was a softening deeper inside, the mushy middle of his once-firm belief in himself and his own necessity to the world. When he was younger, he had moved through the city feeling both ready and capable, like a man who has just caught a ball. It was a magnanimous attitude, and extended to everyone. Then he had kids and learned afresh what he was needed for; city life became a contact sport. Later, with their mother gone, Som thought he would be everything for them, provide them with heroic affection. But their ages made it all wrong.

He frowned and patted his hair. He should see his hairdresser, maybe even this evening if they were back in time. Zia would say, do you really need a haircut? And circle a finger over the crown of her head. She didn't know that when you're losing hair, a good haircut is more important than ever. Barbers understand. When a barber looks down at a head of thinning hair, his touch is filled with tenderness, the way you hold a dying animal.

Som had gone to the same barbershop forever and he valued it more and more as a place outside the ordinary run of things. His thoughts went quiet in there and his senses were heightened—which was exactly unlike this afternoon, or most occasions when he went through the motions of relaxing with friends. In the barbershop, the air was always bright with mingled, inexpensive fragrances. It was sensuous, even though it was rare to ever see a woman there. It was the only place where anyone ever touched him and lingered at it. They handled his hair, stroked his chin. The callused fingertips moving from his scalp to his cheek would send a feathery current through the length of his body, the one sensation he felt anymore that could be described as a thrill.

When it ended and the shaving cream was wiped off his face, he would think about what else he could ask for—but there was nothing, really, besides a cut and shave to keep him in the chair. Then it was back to handshakes, and social cheek-to-cheeks, and his children's there-and-gone embrace.

'There she blows,' said Zia.

The ferry was coming, heaving itself over the water. It appeared as a gaily painted pavilion on a hull that displaced hardly any water, though it would sit lower on its way back. It closed in and swung its rump up toward the boarding platform. A few men had already pushed past the ticket collectors and down the stairs.

Anxiety was spoiling the air. The people in the queue crowded hard against the ticket gate. Heads were raised high on their neck muscles, teeth visible. A conductor cursed aloud as he was pushed off balance. From the back of the line, a young man gave up on waiting, and came loping up along the empty side of the pier. Som watched as the man ran past him, grabbed the barricade and swung himself over, straight into the front of the queue. His slippers clipped a young woman in the cheek. He landed low, burrowed into the crush of bodies and through the gate.

'Whoa,' said Yash. 'That's not cool.'

The young woman, with her hand on her cheek, reached her other arm back to an older woman in a sari. It was a frenzy at the gate now, and the two women stood still, unable to enter. The first queue-jumper was gone but others had followed. A boy vaulted, his hands on the crossbar; an older man clambered over. The iron barriers rocked on their wheels.

'Okay, guys, get back a bit please,' said Som. He reached for Zia's arm, which rotated out from under his hand as smoothly as if she was warming up at the gym.

'What the hell is going on there?' Sadiqa was on her toes, peering into the mess.

'I think they cancelled the last ferry,' said Leo.

'What?'

'Guard says they cancelled the next ferry. So, this is the last one going tonight.'

More men had run up from the back. A small throng had now gathered on Som's side of the barricade, waiting to climb over. The next man who tried lost his balance and fell forward, right on top of the two women by the ferry gate. They disappeared from sight.

'Stop that!' Sadiqa shouted. The other men turned back to her with pitying eyes; they could not hope for the rich lady to understand. Skinny backsides in dyed jeans rose and fell, dropping into the space where the two women had just been standing.

'Someone help those women!'

Som tensed but did not move. The right thing to do was hopelessly complicated. He shifted his weight, testing his inertia. He had been pretty tipsy that afternoon.

Sadiqa turned to him. 'For god's sake, get those two out of there,' she said. 'They'll be trampled to death.'

'I'll go,' said Yash, the beautiful boy.

'No. Stay here,' said Som, then took his son's arm. 'Or come behind me.'

They stepped up to the throng of men and got in among them. Som summoned every advantage of height, build, language and class, and swung them all before him. 'Move,' he said. 'Out of the way!'

What he needed was to be wearing actual shoes. 'Out of the way, fuckers.'

Who the hell are you, motherfucker? someone said.

Who am I—he turned, then thought twice. These men were too close, and they were desperate. Yash could get hurt. Strange fingertips were pulling on his shoulder. Som pulled himself upright and, pointing over the barrier, shouted: 'My daughter! That's my daughter there!'

All at once, there was space. Inches opened up around them, bodies repelled by an instinct about rich men, daughters and troubles worse than missing the last ferry. Reaching the barricade, Som looked down through all the legs and feet. Something twitched on the ground. A hand? No, it wasn't a hand; it was a cloth bag.

The two women were there as well, backed up against the pier wall. The girl's arms were around her mother, and her face was turned into her mother's hair, her eyes closed, and she was very still. A Pieta on the Pier. The crowd moved over them, tripping and stamping. Som, absorbed by the sight, didn't think of his hands on the barricade, or of anything, until her eyes reopened wide with shock and anger, staring straight at him.

For a moment, they held each other's gaze. Then her face formed a wordless appeal. Her lips moved. What was she trying to tell him?

'My bag,' she said. 'Can you get my bag?'

Som looked down to where the beat-up sneakers, rubber slippers and knock-off Crocs trampled past the zippered bag. He bent to reach for it, then stood back up fast with a catch in his back. 'God,' he said, 'fuck,' as pain ballooned under his shoulder blade. For a long minute he was immobilized, gripping the crossbar and whispering at the pain to go away. When he looked down again, Yash was there, crouched low under the arch of his body, reaching for the bag. Scarlet toenails in a braided leather sandal caught the strap and kicked it away. The slender arm darted out again, caught the bag and pulled it back and through. Som had just stood there the whole time, as if rusted to the barricade. The girl had watched all of it.

A minute later, it was over. The ferry was full, then more than full, and the operators slammed the accordion gate shut. It pulled away from its mooring, wobbled a bit on the swell and moved off into the open bay. Suddenly the pier was empty.

Breeze pulled at empty snack packets. A single slipper lay on its back. Som lifted his son to his feet, just as the young woman got to hers, her mother still in her arms. The two women steadied themselves by smoothing down each other's clothes. The only sounds were of the fizzing tube lights and the security guard's laments as Sadiqa tore into him. 'Madam,' he cried, 'I only work here ...'

The two women checked each other's faces and feet for bruises. Then the younger one turned.

'Thank you,' she said, as she took the battered bag. 'I'm so sorry. But thank you.'

'It's fine,' said Som and Yash together.

'Oh my god!' Zia approached, her fists bunched together over her mouth. 'Are you okay?'

'Just let me ...'

'Come and sit down here, please,' Sadiqa insisted. The guard was behind her, holding out his heat-warped plastic stool. 'Put it here,' she told him, 'and go call your supervisor.' He put down the stool and strode away to hide.

The young woman led the older one around the barrier, to where the family was waiting. The older woman was not as old as she had seemed—maybe in her sixties—and the other one not as young. Som turned away, the pain receding from his shoulder and the shame rising in his chest. Sadiqa introduced herself as the older woman sat down.

'Thank you for this help,' the younger one said. 'My name is Nitila. This is my mother. Ma?'

The mother brought her hands together, without letting go of the bag. 'Namaste,' she said. 'Thank you. Yes, I am her mother.'

With her hands back in her lap, she resumed checking the bag's contents by touch.

'Is your bag okay?' said Sadiqa, and parallel conversations began.

'Do you know ... I'm sorry ... but do you know how we can get back to the city?' said Nitila. 'Today, I mean? If there is a bus?'

The older woman reached into the bag and produced a round, paper-brown chikoo.

'Ah! God, I thought it must be jewellery, from the way ...'

'Uhh, you can't take a bus now,' Zia said. 'That's insane!'

Som's phone was buzzing in his pocket.

'Lovely, is this from your farm?'

'Not exactly ...' Nitila turned to regard the chikoo. 'You could say, my father grew them.'

'Where do you live?' Som wanted to know.

'He grew them?'

'You know, I cultivate fruit too,' said Leo, warmly but implausibly.

'He just passed away,' said the mother.

Nitila reached for her mother's hand, which was inside the bag.

'He planted them at a farmhouse here. He was the gardener.'

'You know what I love? Chikoo ice cream.'

'There's a bus stop back in the village,' Leo said, now in consultant mode. 'From there, it's about two and a half hours by road. Depending on traffic. Maybe three. But that's from when the bus leaves.'

'We'll be fine,' Nitila said, nodding to herself. A furrow formed on her forehead, straight up between her eyebrows. 'We came for the day. We don't have a place here.'

'Where do you live?' Som asked again.

'Leo!' Sadiqa said, gesturing at the obvious.

Som felt a tap on his arm. Behind him was a short, weather-beaten man with gelled hair and huge pecs under his V-neck. He moved his finger over the group, counting silently.

'Nine. You said seven, sir.' He shook his head at the fickle outcomes of all his best planning. 'Okay. Come on, the boat is waiting since long.'

II

'My god, is it safe?' her mother said, as they climbed into the speedboat one by one. Everyone thought that was funny, after she had nearly been killed in a stampede. They laughed together. Whatever it was going to do, the show-off speedboat with its big sharky nose, it was not going to sink. It might burst into flames. It might turn on its end and become a rocket.

The man, Som, had gone down the steps first, to where the boat was waiting. He carried the icebox, then moved up to the front, looking like he wanted privacy. The others took their time to settle in, indulged by the speedboat guys, who had just figured out what was up with the extra passengers.

The girls debated the best options for each of their guests. They seated Nitila's mother behind the pilot, in the shelter of the wheelhouse. Nitila was about to sit next to her, when Zia put out a hand. 'You've never done this before, right?' she said, not waiting for an answer. 'You have to sit up front.'

In the bow, up front, there were seats for four—foam-pads on moulded plastic chairs, two to each side. Som was already there.

'Oh no, no.'

'You *have* to be up front. Otherwise you might as well be on the ferry. This is where you get to feel it.'

'To feel what?'

Zia rolled her eyes sideways and up, as if considering. 'The speed?' she said. 'And don't worry about getting splashed. It's just fresh Bombay seawater.'

By then, they were turning away from the pier. Nitila steadied herself over the nodding of the bow and sat down next to Zia. Som was across from them, looking away over the water. Iridescent tones were beginning to show on the backs of the oily swells that separated Alibag from home. The boat pointed its nose out at the bay. It began to shred the smooth burls of the water, and the bay spat back.

'Hang on ti-i-ight,' someone trilled from the back.

The bow of the speedboat cleared each swell, lifted them weightless, then hit the next one. Nitila was conscious of being lifted above her seat, until she had only skin contact with it, then coming back down. In the distance, the whole city jumped, dropped and jumped again.

Nitila turned over her shoulder to check on her mother. Her mother had both hands on the rail, and her shoulders raised almost to her ears. She unfurled the fingers of one hand to wave.

'Ma, hold the bag,' Nitila said. She couldn't shout in front of these people.

The boat sped up, smashing at the water.

Her mother shook her head, *what?*

Up, *smash*, back.

'The bag!' Nitila made a grabbing motion in the air. The bag was on the seat. Her mother smiled and nodded. Zia tapped her shoulder for her attention: they were overtaking the ferry.

There was always a point, Nitila thought, during the ferry crossing, when a speedboat shot past, raising the sleepy tempo of the bay. Those aboard each vessel had to observe each other, or choose not to. For the speedboaters, the overtake usually entailed raising one hand, to convey a blushing apology: Yes! We're all crossing today, sorry to cut ahead! We too believe in a more equal world—really! Goodbye!

Just that morning, Nitila had been on the other side of it, while she leaned on the ferry's railing, throwing chips to the seagulls, and watched an ivory arrowhead fly by. She was used to coming out to Alibag on Sundays, with the college kids on day trips and salaried families who carried their own lunches to eat and leave on the beach. Nitila would visit the big house, where her father stayed and tended the gardens. It was one of those compounds built and preserved for the owners to party in, three or four times a year. Sometimes the owners would be there and would emerge disheveled to greet her. They would shake her hand and marvel at her qualities and at their own part in producing the fine, smart creature before them. The men enjoyed looking at her, and felt good about themselves for enjoying it.

Nitila took for granted a yearly increment in her dignity, her ease in that world. The economics of the Alibag house were beyond her, but she had crossed its moral terrain often enough to know that, for the family, benevolence was the best part of pride. She only had to learn to play along, to take a seat in the sitting room, where her father had never sat, and put a hand on the armrest as she talked about college. 'Come,' they would say, and invite her to try a new thing, 'Come and taste this, it's lemon soufflé,' or 'Come, see if these fit you, yes, they're pedal pushers, they're meant to look like that.' It was always an invitation in, and Nitila went, never setting a foot wrong nor staying too long. She gave a performance of poise, good diction, eye contact, and with each visit it was less an act and more like an exercise of her own self. Once, she had wine pressed upon her in a frosty, long-necked glass.

She was careful not to grow too used to it. But there was no place else to explore this side of herself, besides the Alibag house, where nothing made the family happier than to watch her become someone more like them. And it was well after her father fell from the ladder, and got his diagnosis, and came back home to them in the city, that his salary stopped coming.

Things changed after her father died. They let go of their flat and took a single room, but there was debt and now only that was growing. The day her mother told her about the loans, Nitila found a job at the mall—on her feet behind a counter eight hours a day. Mornings, she squeezed into a staff changing room along with forty other women, all attempting to dress and to step out fresh, uncreased, made up. On the daily train, in the sharing auto, in the canteen and behind the counter, she was trapped in a cage of strangers' shoulders. In the city, as you lost money, people squeezed in around you, not in support, but in an orgy of indifferent touch. They squeezed, she shrank, they squeezed further. She went home too tired to even start thinking about a way out.

Her friends praised her resilience, making a virtue of her circumstance, which was that she had nobody she could depend on. Then they stopped texting. Relatives gossiped because being poor is sad, but becoming poor is a scandal. Nitila had known that she would always be a ferry-person. But while her father had been alive, she had thought that, maybe, she'd do well enough that one day, for example, a richer friend might invite her to some other, even richer person's party at their beach-house or luxe bungalow in Alibag. It had always been a stretch. Now it wasn't even a lie worth telling herself. She was going to miss out on everything.

Then, last week, the lady of the Alibag house had sent a voice note saying that the trees had fruited, a compliment to her father; would Nitila and her mother like to take some chikoos home? When they got there, only the lady of the house came out, looking in a hurry. She called out for tea but wasn't having any herself, so Nitila and her mother took their cups into the kitchen and chatted with the cook. Then they took their chikoos and left, going to the public beach to walk there.

By the time they got back to the pier, Nitila's mother was moving the way she did when her feet hurt. They were at the front of the queue, but the announcement came, and people grew unruly. Boys started jumping over the barricade right next to her. Nitila watched the crowd close around the gate, like a fist, and she couldn't bear it. She hated the gate, the ferry, the hour of the crossing, and she hated all the hours beyond. She could not bring herself to squeeze in again.

On the empty side of the pier, the rich man was looking in her direction. Earlier, Nitila had been watching him. She had never seen him before, of course, but still she knew: the type of house he had come from, the kind of boat he was waiting to board. And she knew something else about him besides. Watching him watch her, inside the commotion, Nitila took hold of her mother's shoulders. She pulled her close, pressed a knee into the back of her mother's knee, and guided her soft body down onto the floor of the pier, to wait for him.

They were now among the lights on the oil rigs and tankers lying at deep anchor, red and green over the darkening water. Above, the sky was still dressing for the night, throwing on one colour after the other behind a screen of clouds. Ahead, the city sparked to life. Bright pixels bunched along the skyline. She felt as if her pupils had widened for the first time since she was a child, to admit the effect of sheer wonder.

Air pummelled at her face, her teeth and the glistening surface of her eyes. Zia whooped. It was an instinct, or a partial syllable overheard through the wind that made Nitila turn and see her mother's head hanging low behind the pilot's chair. Others in the back were bending over as well.

The fucking bag. The fucking bag was on the floor. Each time the boat jumped and landed, a chikoo had bounced out and gone skittering across the deck. Her mother had grabbed the wrong corner of the bag, which set loose more fruit. The bag was back in her lap now. But the freed fruit bounced and rolled like ping pong balls, capering around the deck and underfoot.

From his seat in the back, Yash held up two chikoos.

Nitila moaned. How many others were out? She held the rail and lurched to her feet.

'What's ha—ing?' Zia asked, voice snatched off by the wind.

'The chikoos,' Nitila said, knowing she couldn't be heard, or possibly understood.

Som was looking over, motioning to her to sit down.

'I'll just—' she said, and the speedboat jumped. The deck was gone from under her feet. The bow struck the water, and the deck came back up, hard. She stumbled but landed mostly on her feet, in a crouch.

'—' Som said, holding out his hand. 'Care—'

The boat jumped, and again the deck was gone. This time she crashed down on all fours. It hurt, but the shame came faster. She tried to get herself up; if she could grab just one chikoo, that would explain—

The boat jumped again. Up she floated, like a cat, and banged back down onto her hands and knees. Horror. Panic. She couldn't get up. A siren in her head was screaming: her kneecaps would break on the rivets of the deck if the boat didn't slow down, and her heart would break from embarrassment if it did.

She lifted off again.

Two arms closed around her mid-air. This time she landed half on the foam-pad and half against Som's thigh and chest. He kept his arms around her for a moment, while she held the rail and put her feet down on the floor. Then he let go and shifted a little into his own seat. Nitila's heart was punching into her throat. The shock, the affront, the indignity. Falling like a rag doll in front of these strangers.

He cupped his hand by her ear.

'Don't worry,' he said, 'It always happens the first time.'

He raised a bare knee, circled his palm over it. Her own knees throbbed but it was subsiding. She winced in reply, and her honest shame bled through her expression. He gave a small nod. She dropped her face into the crook of her elbow. Warm drops ran out of her eyes and were lifted away by the rushing air. When she looked up, a change had come over him, his face was calm.

She wondered if she should move back over to Zia, but she stayed as she was, attentive to the spot where her triceps pressed against his. For the rest of the ride, as the city grew near and the pitch of the boat began to slow, Nitila turned her head and took in the bruised sky, an occasional rogue fruit dancing past her feet, the southern horizon lined with the lamps of fishing boats. The grand hotel approached with all its bulbs on. Her upper arm stayed pressed against his, and her right hand lay close to his left hand, both very still except for a moment when they held each other.

Aai–Tai

AMRITA MAHALE

When she was seven years old, Sayli had asked a young neighbour where his father was, even though she knew that the boy's father had been crushed by a dumper a month before he was born. 'Aai says he has gone for a tour ...' the four-year-old had replied. 'Somewhere far away.'

'But where?' she had pressed. 'Didn't she say when he is coming back?'

The boy shook his head and bit his lip sadly. 'I'll ask her again,' he said.

She remembered the boy's voice as he said this, a small leaf in the wind. A week later, Sayli's father left home, never to return.

'*Aai–Tai?* You mean Aai–Baba, right?' the tattoo artist asked her. 'No, Aai–Tai,' she repeated. 'It's for my mother and two older sisters, they are my world.' Artist Amol did not ask her why her father had been left out; he only shrugged his shoulders and made a sound like 'tcha'. What would Sayli have told him anyway—that he was a drunkard who had abandoned the family over a decade ago?

Something like that.

'You are over eighteen, pakka?'

She nodded and put her right hand out, making a 'C' with her thumb and fingers. She tapped on the middle of the curve, the fleshy part between the knuckles of her forefinger and thumb. 'Right here.'

'Right on Marine Drive,' he said.

'Huh?'

'Your hand, it looks like the Mumbai Back Bay,' he explained, tracing his finger along her hand. 'Look. Your thumb is Nariman Point, then Marine Drive, Chowpatty'—he tapped on the nail of her index finger—'and here, Malabar Hill.'

'Good,' she said, grinning. 'All three of them love Marine Drive.'

'And how about you? You don't like it?' the tattoo artist asked.

'It's nothing special,' she said with a toss of the head. 'I go every day. My office is right there, at Nariman Point.'

'Office?' he remarked. 'You look like a student.'

She shook her head. 'I do computer work. Have you heard of artificial intelligence? I work in that line.'

Artist Amol nodded in admiration.

Sayli had found the tattoo artist online and had already seen the insides of his shop on Instagram. The walls of his establishment, which he called his studio, were all black, with large pictures of gods and fairies painted in neon. The massive portrait of Shiva next to the entrance was inked on his arm, too.

'I want it to be written in the same style ...' She pointed at one of his tattoos that said 'Priyanka'. Sister? Girlfriend? Wife? She did not care or dare to ask. 'But smaller and in Marathi.'

Kanchan would have asked.

'Where do you live?' he said as he pulled on his work gloves.

'Sai Wadi,' she replied.

'Where is that?'

'Andheri East, near the station,' she said.

'Oh, you mean near the world-famous Gokhale Bridge?' Artist Amol guffawed.

She smiled and nodded. The bridge had been in the news for many months—it had collapsed a few years ago, severing a key east–west artery, and when it was rebuilt and reopened after much fanfare, it turned out that it was six feet higher than the flyover that connected to it.

'You know what, the whole fiasco with the bridge is their way of reminding us that they will always keep us dangling,' he said.

'Who *they*?'

'Arre baba, the system, the system. Ready?' Artist Amol used a stencil to place the purple words on her hand—Aai–Tai—with heartbeats at either end.

'Take a deep breath,' he said and put the needle to her skin. It's not as bad as Kanchan said it would be, she thought, but when the needle touched her knuckle, she cried out *Aai!* Then she pursed her lips and looked down. She knew that Kanchan would laugh at her tattoo the next day. At our age, we should be getting the names of our boyfriends inked, Kanchan would say, not of our parents or brothers-sisters.

But Kanchan had not been raised by a single mother with three daughters, she had not been the first in her family to pass twelfth standard or touch a computer or open a bank account in her teens. Nor had Kanchan been the first in her family to not be married at eighteen (and that too, without a fight). It had been no harder for Sayli to get here than it had been for Kanchan, and for that small but radical turn of fate, she had her mother and sisters to thank. With her first salary, she wanted to etch her gratitude on her skin for the world to see.

Her mother smiled and patted her cheek when she saw the tattoo. 'What was the need, babudi?'

At work, the next day, it was not Kanchan but the supervisor Shyam who made fun of her tattoo. He saw her showing it off to Gauri and immediately grabbed her hand. 'Show me, show me. Aai–Tai? Wow. So, in Hindi, that's Maa–Behen? Bold, very bold.' All the girls giggled. Shyam kept holding her hand, which she did not like at all. Sayli looked towards Madam. She had her headphones on, but the din reached her sharp ears anyway. Or perhaps it was Sayli's helpless stare that caught her eye.

'Come on, team. Remember our goal for today. We need to complete a hundred videos. We only got to ninety-two on Saturday.' Madam clapped her hands to get the team back to work.

Shyam let go of Sayli's hand and started looking over the girls' computer screens. 'Good work, Gauri. Very good, Kanchan, keep it up. Fatima, the red shoulder dots should be right at the shoulder joint, not in the armpit. Here, shoulder ...' He tapped her first on the shoulder and then under her arm, 'Not here! And where do you think the hip joint is, huh?' Fatima flinched, but Shyam did not try to get over-smart this time, not with Madam watching.

Safe under Madam's gaze, Sayli returned to her tasks. On her screen was a baby on its back, placed on a white sheet. She selected the blue dot in the menu, then clicked on the centre of the baby's forehead to place the dot there. Next, the green dot on the baby's neck. With her mouse, she went on to mark the shoulders, the elbows and palms, the belly button, the hips, the knees and feet. It took her less than a minute to place all fifteen dots, despite the pain that shot through her right hand every few seconds and made her suck air. Artist Amol had warned her about the pain. The naked baby was now covered in blue, green, red, yellow, brown and rani pink spots. She hit the submit button, and the next frame appeared. The same baby, a bare canvas of brown skin again, one hand across its face, the palm covering the forehead. The yellow dot for the palm would have to go exactly where the blue dot for the forehead also needed to be. She had never encountered this before—newborns did not usually move so much—but she knew what to do. This is why the dots were of different colours, Madam had explained on the first day. So that the computer knows what is what, even when one body part covers another. Sayli clicked the submit button again, and the next frame of the video came up. After about forty frames, the video was completely marked. It had taken her just under half an hour, a personal best. She pressed the button that said 'Compile', and the newborn came to life. But in this new video, the baby remained concealed by a many-coloured stick figure—the sticks connecting the dots she had placed so painstakingly—that mimicked its movements seamlessly. Perfect, she thought. Finalize. Submit.

The next baby was a chubby one, little rolls of fat around her belly and thighs. 'Oooh, little doll,' Sayli put her hands on her cheeks and sighed. Kanchan looked over and cooed at the baby as well. But the work had to go on. Click, click, click, click.

'There should be a small black dot for the face, too, Madam. These babies are too cute,' Sayli had declared on the first day of work at the ShishuAI office. Madam had laughed and asked her her name. 'Sayli Suresh Shigwan.'

'What we are building here will have the same effect, Sayli,' Madam had explained. 'It will protect babies and children—not from nazar but from real illnesses and disorders. The work all of you will do here is very important. The dots mark the most important joints of the baby's body, so you are actually teaching a computer the shape of a baby's body. You are teaching it to see the baby. Once it can see the baby, it will also be able to understand the baby—its weight, its height, if it is moving normally or not, if it is healthy or not. You are the ones who will give AI its intelligence, you are the ones who will make this computer a mini-doctor.'

If the computer is so smart, Sayli had wanted to ask, why does it need the dots to do something as simple as seeing that a baby is right there? And how can mere dots make this blind computer a healer, when people need to go to college for many years to become doctors? But she did not ask Madam anything. If she did not know how ATMs or bank accounts worked, or why tattoos did not get washed off, she did not need to know this either. Besides, as a woman she understood that to see or not see, to be seen or not be seen, these were not always simple matters; perhaps it was similar with computers.

After the first day of work, Sayli had gone home with a numbing ache in her head and shoulders, a throb in her wrist, but also what felt like the fizz and jump of cola all through her body. She had had to repeat the name for this new kind of work many times before her mother and sisters could say it. Ann-no-tay-shun. They did not care what the work was for; it was computer work and she worked with seven other women. They could not think of a better job for a young woman. Sayli did not mention the male supervisor who had been contracted to ShishuAI along with the band of eight data annotators, nor did she speak of his roving fingers.

Kanchan, who had started data entry work right after the board exams, had got her the job. It was Kanchan who had convinced Sayli's sister to pay for a three-month computer course for her. After just two months, Kanchan had asked her to come to her office in Marine Drive to interview for a new kind of data entry work, called data annotation. Sayli was ready. Keyboard, mouse, monitor, Q-W-E-R-T-Y, save, delete, undo—she had absorbed these new ideas like an old sponge, and oozed them just as easily when pressed. She had got the job within ten minutes.

A week later, she was on the second floor of the glass matchbox that was ShishuAI's office, with the promise of thirteen thousand rupees a month and the possibility of a few thousand more if she clicked and dragged fast enough.

Sayli took to the work easily. Within two weeks, she was almost as good as Shyam, their supervisor. She was the first to meet the target of marking ten videos per day, and as soon as she got there, the target was increased to twelve, then fifteen. Four days ago, she had got to fourteen, but when the other girls had groaned, she had slowed herself down. After all, anything over twelve would still earn her a bonus, so why make things harder for everyone?

It almost seemed too easy, which made her feel guilty. She did not fully understand where the feeling came from. She started waking up at six in the morning, without her mother asking, so she could finish the cooking and cleaning for the day, before leaving for the station at 7.45. The first of the pressure cooker whistles in the building went off long before theirs—other working women had many tiffins to pack before they set off for their own jobs. Her mother, too, had to wake at 5 a.m. to fill the buckets when the municipal water came, but she'd go back to sleep for an hour before heading to work. It was only a fifteen-minute walk to Andheri station from their home. On most days, Sayli took a fast train, but if she was tired, she would take an Andheri local—where she would find a seat reliably—and catch a forty-minute nap. Twice she had seen Madam in the same train, the 8.11 Churchgate fast; once Madam had had her earphones on, another time they had smiled at each other across the grille that separated the first-class section from the second. Both times, neither had found a seat; they stood resting their backs against the partitions near their respective doors. Over their heads, unclaimed grab handles kept swinging—not unlike a row of dangling handcuffs—too high for many women, including Sayli. At Churchgate, Madam made her way to the shared taxi stand, and Sayli to the bus stop.

Occasionally, Sayli let herself dream. On the cusp of sleep, her mind's film projector would cast upon her closed eyes a mix of memories, real and desired. More reels than films, fragments bereft of logic—a fight with Kanchan, showing Shyam his place, Sayli picking up a dotted baby and bringing it to her bosom, Sayli in Madam's chair announcing the targets for the day. One day, why not? Sometimes, she nearly dozed off at work, too. Frame after frame, dot after dot, every minute was an invocation to the God of Sleep. When this happened, Kanchan would poke her in the ribs. She would sit up straight and slap herself once or twice for good measure.

Sayli clicked on 'Next' and shrieked. Madam walked over to Sayli's station—'What the hell!' She clicked on the video view—'Fuck. How did this get here?'

The girls looked at Madam all at once—they had never seen her lose her composure before—then they turned to look at Sayli's screen. Before them was a six-limbed creature, not unlike a flailing insect on its back, a sleepy newborn jerking and moving her limbs slowly, two legs and two arms, and then two more reed-like arms that grew out of her shoulders. Madam bolted out of the room and came back with a grey-haired man who wore a grave expression.

'I am 100 per cent sure the protocol specified that no children with deformities or major illnesses should be included,' Madam said. 'I trained the hospital supervisors myself. They should not have recorded this baby. I don't know how it happened.'

'Have you checked the consent forms? Did her parents agree to this?' said the grey-haired man.

Madam tapped Sayli on the shoulder and asked her to get up. She began to type furiously at the keyboard, and folders and forms flashed on the screen amidst the clatter of keys. 'Nothing. It's missing. I'll call the hospital supervisor and double-check. Should I delete the videos and records right away? We won't get into trouble, right?' But the way she said the words, it was clear to everybody that what she meant was, 'I won't get into trouble, right?'

Madam's boss dismissed her fears. 'Of course not, Ananya. Get into trouble for what? This is no big deal. Please don't delete anything. Guys, please get back to work.'

It was impossible to focus after that. The day's tally stood at only seventy-eight videos—Sayli herself had completed just eleven—but neither the girls nor Shyam could be wrested from the grip of the four-armed baby. They knew nothing about her, not her name, not even the hospital where she had been recorded. Only ShishuAI employees had access to those details, not the contractors.

'I am going to call her Charulata. Our four-armed little goddess, Charu,' said Gauri.

'Charu … very clever!'

'But how is this not in the paper? It should be a big story, no?'

'Maybe the parents want to keep it a secret?'

'Then why did they agree to let their baby be recorded?'

'Do you think they will know if we take a video of the screen?'

'Don't even think about it! Madam strictly forbade it. Remember the first day?'

'Arre, how will they know?'

'We signed that contract too, remember? To not take photos or save any videos. The DNA.'

'NDA, it's called NDA. Non-Disclosure Agreement.'

'Please, Kanchan, be sensible.'

'Arre baba, it was a joke. I thought you would know by now not to believe everything I say.'

Charu—Sayli learnt that evening—was already in the newspaper. When she was walking home from the train station, she got a message from Gauri on WhatsApp—a picture of a clipping from an English newspaper. *Baby Born with Four Arms, Mom Dies in Childbirth*. The text was a little blurred, but Gauri understood the gist. The baby's mother had been rushed to KEM Hospital from a maternity home in Mankhurd for an emergency operation. The father said he could not afford to look after a fourth daughter, let alone the cost of the surgeries needed to fix her. He begged the hospital to keep the deformed girl and then disappeared. There was no date on the clipping. People lied on the Internet, this much Sayli knew. And WhatsApp forwards could not be trusted.

Maybe their Charu was fast asleep in her mother's arms, with her sisters playing around her. And her father, who had already made the arrangements for the surgeries she needed, was reminding the girls to be gentle with their baby sister. It was certainly possible. Sayli found herself staring at her tattoo, wishing and praying.

When she reached her building, Sayli heard someone call her name. A hand waved at her from the passenger seat of a rickshaw. She craned her neck to see—it was Madam!

'Madam! How come you are here?'

'I live here ... right there!' Madam got out of the auto and pointed at one of the brown towers next to Sayli's building. 'Do you live around here too, Sayli?' There was a note of surprise in the question.

Sayli nodded and pointed to her own building. From where they stood, the open window of her fifth floor kholi was visible.

'Oh, the SRA building. I see,' said Madam.

Sayli thought she sounded a little relieved.

'Have you grown up here, Sayli?'

'I was born here, but it was a chawl back then. Then the redevelopment happened. We only got the flat when I was seven years old.' Three months before her father left. 'How about you, Madam?'

'I have lived here since I was ten. Except four years in between when I was in college. How funny that we have never seen each other here despite being neighbours for over ten years.'

Sayli thought about what Kanchan might say in this situation, and this time, she decided to say it. 'Madam, is it really that funny or surprising? Do you have any friends from the SRA building?'

Madam blinked slowly, taken aback. 'No, no, I mean, I … yes, you are right, I don't. And listen, you don't need to call me Madam, please call me Ananya.'

'It's okay, Madam,' Sayli protested.

'No, really, I am not that old. Tell me, how old are you?'

'Almost nineteen.'

'I am only twenty-three, yaar, just a year and a half out of college.'

'I'll call you Ananya Madam, is that better?'

'How about Ananya Didi?'

Sayli nodded. 'But Madam in the office.'

Ananya Didi smiled and said, 'Done,' before she turned towards her gate.

'Madam … Didi, one minute!' Sayli opened the newspaper clipping on her phone. 'Do you think this is our Charu?'

'Who?'

'The baby with four arms … the one whose video we saw in the office today.'

Madam looked more closely at Sayli's phone and gasped. 'Her mom died giving birth? That is horrible.'

'So it is her, pakka?'

'You know what, the video was from KEM Hospital too, so yes, I am pretty sure it is the same baby. But don't tell anyone I told you. I am not supposed to reveal any PII.'

'What?'

'Personally identifiable information. Personal information about the babies.'

'Why?'

'For ethical reasons. Privacy, you know? Never mind, you will not understand. But yes, it's a very sad situation.'

'Didi, can we do something for her?'

'You mean the company? I don't know ...' And after a pause, she added, 'Like what?'

'She will need an operation.'

'I am sure the hospital will take care of it. It's a government hospital. All treatment is free there.' Again, after a pause, with a flicker of doubt in her voice, 'Isn't it?'

'You know better, Didi.' But no, why would she know better? Sayli was certain that she had never stepped into a government hospital. 'Will you at least ask if there is something the company can do to help?'

Ananya Didi made a vague sound to suggest she would.

The next day, Sayli eagerly waited to talk to Ananya Didi. 'Didi, did you ask?'

'Ask what?'

'Whether the company is willing to help with Charu's treatment?'

'How will we even find her? Or know what she needs?'

'We can just go the hospital, no? I can come with you.'

'I have a lot of work to do today. I can't think about this now. But I will try and go tomorrow, okay?'

The following day, Sayli cornered Ananya Didi again.

This time, Ananya Didi was firm. 'Sayli, look, the company cannot get involved in all this. It's a sad situation, no doubt, but we have nothing to do with it.'

'But Didi, the company's work is to save babies, no?'

'It doesn't work like that. We are a start-up, not an NGO.'

'Didi, can't you try just one time?'

Ananya Didi sighed and looked away. 'Sayli, please let it go. And get back to your work.'

For the rest of the day, Ananya Didi avoided Sayli. She did not come into the annotators' room for more than a minute at a time, and averted Sayli's gaze each time Sayli tried to look at her. When Shyam tried to ask for an extension on the target for the week, she snapped at him. 'Get your team to focus on work and not on gossip and social service.'

Sayli knew what she had to do.

The next morning, she headed to the hospital instead of making her way to work. She hadn't informed Shyam or Kanchan, but she would deal with that later. From Parel station, she had to ask around to find the right bus to KEM. Asking for directions made her feel like a grown-up. For most of her life, her mother or sisters had led the way, or a more fearless friend like Kanchan. By the time questions occurred to her, they already had answers.

At the hospital, there were so many people everywhere that Sayli's heart began hammering. In the biscuit-brown corridors, she had to step over the outstretched legs of patients and family members to move forward. Every minute or two, her hand would reach for the top of her bag, to make sure the zip was fastened. Her savings from two months of work, about nine thousand rupees, were in an envelope in a compartment inside. Past Infectious Diseases, and ENT, and Cardiology, she found the labour ward and the NICU. She asked for the staff nurse. She took a chance, introduced herself as Sayli from ShishuAI. The staff nurse did not know anything about the company. 'What is ShishuAI?'

'We do research at the hospital,' Sayli explained quickly. 'But that is not why I am here. I have come to check about the girl who was born last week with four arms.'

The nurse frowned. 'What about her?'

'Do the doctors know what treatment she needs? How much will it cost?'

'The doctors know everything, don't they?'

'I ... I mean, we ... the company wanted to see if there is anything we can do to help.'

'That you'll have to check with her father. He took her home yesterday.'

'What? Did he not say he could not afford the treatment?'

'Yes. But what do you do even if you can't afford? You cannot abandon a child like that.'

'How will he look after her?'

'She is with her family ... why are you asking so many questions? Do you want to adopt her? How old are you? Sixteen?'

'I just want to help her. Do you have the father's phone number?'

'I am not a social worker, baba. I need to get back to work now.'

With her heart limp like a two-day old balloon, Sayli left the hospital. If only she had come two days ago, she might have been able to help Charu. She had made the journey for nothing. But at least the day was young, it was only 9.30 a.m. She could still go to work.

'You are over an hour late, Sayli. Where were you?' asked Shyam.

'I was not feeling well.'

'And you didn't message anyone?'

'I felt better, so I decided to come.'

'Good. But if you don't complete at least ten videos, I will cut half a day's pay.'

Sayli couldn't keep the morning's happenings to herself for long; she told Kanchan everything. Kanchan couldn't keep it to herself either. Over lunchbreak, she made Sayli repeat the story to everyone. 'Do you think the father will get the operation done? How will he get the money?' She wanted to hear what her friends thought. She wanted to feel hope.

'There are so many ways now,' offered Fatima, the optimist. 'Haven't you seen the advertisements where families ask for money for their children's treatment?'

'Arre baba, don't remind me of those scary ads. Children with terrifying-looking tumours the size of my fist, they give me nightmares,' said Kanchan.

Shyam had a different take. 'Maybe the father will keep her as is. He could make money off her. Perhaps we'll find her begging at a signal in a few years. Such things happen.'

'Don't say such depressing stuff, please. I keep thinking about what it would be like to have four arms, what all I could do with two extra hands,' Kanchan declared.

'I can think of a few things, should I tell you?' said Shyam in a teasing tone.

'Get lost,' Kanchan snapped back, but also in a teasing way.

'If you had four arms, you could cook twice as fast. Good for your man.'

'If I had four arms, I would make my man buy me four sets of bangles.'

'That's all? Done.'

Kanchan giggled, then punched Shyam on his arm. He pretended to fall out of his chair.

'Lunch break is over, team. Get back to work. Quick, quick.' It was Ananya Didi. She cast a glance at Sayli, and immediately turned her face away. 'We need to focus, okay? We are very close to the target of the three thousand videos we need to launch. We must work faster. Think about the babies whose lives the product will save.'

Sayli could not take it anymore. She turned the computer off, picked up her bag and walked out.

'Oh, hello! Where are you going? It's not even 3. Hey, stop! I'll mark you absent!'

Sayli paid no heed to Shyam and started to walk faster. No one came after her, not even Ananya Didi. She got into the lift and pressed 'G'. Before she left the building, she turned around one last time, but there was nobody.

She had nowhere to go, so she walked towards the Marine Drive promenade. Even at three in the afternoon, life buzzed around the sea. Students from the colleges in the area bunking classes, lovers, beggars and urchins, office workers on smoke breaks, mothers and ayahs with babies in strollers. And to serve them, chaiwalas and chanawalas, and a balloon seller with a zoo of twisted animals. Sayli watched two little girls in torn oversized frocks pursue the mothers, with mixed success. One of the girls, about six years old, tried her luck with the balloon seller, but he shooed her away. Inches away from the bustle, men with their faces covered with cotton kerchiefs took naps on iron benches.

It was not fair, it was not right. Somewhere in the city, a baby needed help, but nobody seemed to care. And worse, there was nothing Sayli could do, nothing but forego a few hundred rupees as a form of protest. Her hand went to her bag again; the money was still inside. The money had made the journey from her bank account to her purse, but hadn't moved an inch further.

When she reached the parapet that ran along the promenade, she was reminded of what Artist Amol had said about the Back

Bay. She held up her right hand against the outline of the sea. The skin around the tattoo was still a little pink, still raw. Was she a good sister, she wondered. Would she, one day, be a good mother?

Sayli felt something squeak under her foot. It was a balloon animal, a pink dog that had probably been discarded by a bored child. She kicked it to the side of the promenade, away from the footsteps of others wandering the city, lost in their thoughts.

Why did she spend so much time in her head, people asked her. But where else could she go? If she were a boy, she would have taken off on an adventure with her buddies to feel better, to Lonavala or Matheran. Or set her eyes on a cricket trophy, or on the highest dahi handi in Sai Wadi, or in all of Andheri, perhaps even in all of Mumbai. If she were a boy, she might have shed her clothes right there and jumped into the sea, let the waves take her far from the shore, far from the city, so far that all its people—the couples entwined on the parapet by the sea, the joggers, the walkers, the hopeful and the desperate, the balloon seller and his balloon animals, the unwanted daughters—would appear as no more than colourful dots against the outline of the metropolis. And then, perhaps, she would learn to see what was what.

Then, perhaps, the world would make sense.

A breeze blew the pink puppy back to her feet. This time, Sayli picked it up. Immediately, a beggar girl ran towards her. 'Tai, please can I have the balloon? Please, tai?' She handed the balloon to the girl, who grabbed it and hopped over to her friend—or older sister—who squealed when she saw the new acquisition. As she watched the girls pet and cuddle the pink dog, Sayli smiled. How much joy the silly balloon had brought them, a joy that would not stand up to the prick of a safety pin, and yet so precious.

'Listen, come here!' she called out to the girls. 'Are you hungry? Will you eat something?'

'Yes!'

'What will you eat? Chana? Vada pav? Pav bhaji? Tell me.'

The girls looked at each other, their eyes brimming with mischief.

'Go on, tell me.'

'Pizza!' they cried out together. 'From that shop,' said the little girl with the balloon, pointing at the fancy corner restaurant across the street.

'Nice try,' Sayli said, laughing. 'Come.'

Bollywood, Baby

DIKSHA BASU

Sister Josie angrily shushed Sneha before Sneha had even stepped out of the lift. Sneha wished she had the confidence to say something, to tell Sister Josie this was shared space, that Sister Josie should rock the baby inside the flat instead of always being rude to Sneha, but instead Sneha just nodded and walked on the tips of her toes so her heels wouldn't make a sound.

Sister Josie stood, shaking her head disapprovingly. These young girls all flocked to Bombay with the same dreams—of what? Being on Page 3? Dating some ageing hero who had gone to Turkey to get hair plugs? These girls were a tale as old as time. Not her. Sister Josie had come with the noble intention of being a nurse, and that was exactly what she was now. She had always earned more money than her husband, Joseph, that good-for-nothing, and she could always hold her head high that she helped take care of people and would not be seen going hither and tither with half her breasts hanging out, no thank you. Sister Josie had been doing the night shift here for six months, starting the day the baby was born at Hinduja Hospital, and she must have seen this girl next door at least three-four dozen times, but the girl wouldn't so much as say good evening.

'It's wide awake, why do I have to be quiet?' Sneha finally turned around to say. It had been months of this. Months and months and months. Sneha didn't complain about the fact that she could hear the baby cry all day and all night, but surely, she could walk to her doorstep in peace. She knew this baby nurse looked at her and judged her and probably whispered about her when she swapped with the day nurse each morning, but Sneha didn't care. Or tried not to care anyway. She wasn't doing anything wrong, and she had always been determined not to care about what people said. *Log kya kahenge* was no concern of hers, she was far too progressive for that. But still, she avoided eye contact because not everybody could be as modern as her, and sometimes it was just easier to hunch your shoulders a bit and look away.

'She,' Sister Josie said. 'It's a girl. And her name is Zara.'

Sister Josie was always wearing a crisp white nursing uniform that gave her a sense of intimidating authority. Sneha had spent four nights at Lilavati once when she had had dengue, surrounded by women in similar uniforms. She had messaged her friends, and everyone sent her nice messages back, but nobody came to visit. Nora sent some magazines with her driver, that was nice.

'This baby just won't sleep,' Sister Josie said. 'I rock her and rock her, but she won't sleep. Thirty-seven years I've been a nurse, and never had one who keeps me awake all night.'

'Do you sleep during the day?' Sneha asked. She was surprised by her own question, surprised by her curiosity, but she had spent yet another evening being talked to by Vikas, and she was desperate for conversation.

Sister Josie was suspicious about the question, and the interaction. She wondered if this little wisp of a girl, barely a woman, was going to complain, was going to tell her not to rock the baby in the hallway. Zara was quite loud, this woman would be well within her rights to ask Sister Josie to take the baby inside, but the problem was that inside, Zara's parents had screaming-shouting fights most of the night. It wasn't uncommon for parents of small babies to go through such phases, but it certainly did not make things easy in such a small flat. Big fights need big homes, Sister Josie always said. She told Joseph the same thing once when he had raised his voice at her for caring more about her clients than him. You want to raise your voice at me, she had told him, you had better make enough money to buy me a bigger house, so the neighbours don't hear. Joseph had never shouted after that, and their marriage had been much nicer. Also because Joseph slept on the sofa each night.

'I'm coming from a party at Olive,' Sneha continued. She wanted to explain where she had been. She felt she needed the nurse's approval. She was certain that Sister Josie thought she was a prostitute. 'I'm Sneha, by the way. There was a party for a film I have a small role in. It's called *My Mother and I*. Have you heard of it? Releasing tomorrow. I play one of Sonakshi Sinha's friends.'

Sister Josie sort of wobbled her head in response, still saying nothing.

'I thought it would be a big deal, this role, but I didn't even get to meet Sonakshi Sinha while we were shooting. They just edited all our sections to make it seem like we were in frame together. And I tried to introduce myself to her tonight, but someone from her team thought I was just some fan, and I got pushed to the side.' Sneha waved her arm down at her expensive outfit to show Sister Josie how pathetic she felt. She had spent half the money she had made for the movie on tonight's ensemble, a slinky pre-stitched silver sari with a bedazzled bra for a blouse. Not only was this stupid outfit expensive, it was also identical to what nearly a dozen other women at Olive were wearing that evening. If Sister Josie didn't reply, she would cry, of this Sneha was sure.

'I used to like her father's acting,' Sister Josie said. 'But now, why do all actors go about joining politics? Actually, why not? That's also acting only I suppose.'

It was the kind of thing Sneha's father would say, expecting people to laugh. Her poor father sitting in Delhi, waiting for her to give up, to come home, to do something respectable. If he had been the one who had died while her mother lived, Sneha would have had to fight for the whole Bollywood dream more passionately, arguing that she wanted to do things her own way, try and fail if needed, and so on. Instead, it was her father, her sad, quiet father, who sat at home in Mayur Vihar in his perfectly ironed khakis and short-sleeve, collared shirts and ended every phone call with some version of, 'You come back here any time you want. We can work everything else out.'

'Would you like to come in for a cup of tea?' Sneha asked Sister Josie. 'Maybe the baby will like the change of scene.'

Sister Josie looked down at the baby who suddenly seemed perfectly content and calm and wide awake against her cushiony bosom. She looked over her shoulder at Zara's flat. She wondered if the parents would come out and have qualms over where Sister Josie had taken the child. Would they worry? Unlikely, she decided. She had been a family friend's baby nurse also; they all trusted her. The friend had a four BHK in Pali Hill and used to send a car and driver to pick up and drop off Sister Josie and give her non-veg for dinner every night. Not like this family that left a few chapatis and a bowl of vegetable each night and made her have only poha for breakfast, with so few peanuts sometimes you wouldn't even know they were in there. Sister Josie brought along at least two packets of makhana each night. The nights got lonely and long sometimes, with just this baby for company. In the bigger houses, she would spend the whole shift chatting in a different room with friends doing the same job in different parts of the city, the country, some even abroad—but now what to do? It was just her and this baby and her packets of makhana. She would go, she would see how this girl lived, see what other lives people lived, she always enjoyed that.

'Chalo, why not.'

'You have nice skin,' Sneha said.

'Mushroom supplements,' Sister Josie said.

Sneha unlocked the door to her flat and led Sister Josie in. Sneha was horrified to see it through someone else's eyes and apologized and apologized and quickly rushed to pick up heaps of clothes and toss them on her bed. She moved filled ashtrays out of sight and cleared out the empty and half-empty glasses that were scattered around the floor. A bottle of Sula drained of wine had also turned into an ashtray at some point before she had left for the party. It all looked so pathetic, and after hours left in this state, the whole flat now smelled the way the inside of that Sula bottle did.

Sneha had caught glimpses into the home next door, the one where Sister Josie worked, and it was always perfect.

'What do they do, her parents?' Sneha asked.

'Father works at a bank, mother runs a catering company,' Sister Josie said. 'Nice couple. They said they've barely even spoken to you. How long have you lived here?'

Sneha opened the balcony windows and stared at the other buildings around her, all with rooms with cozy lighting. It wasn't the most expensive part of Bandra West, but it was nice, comfortable, safe. She often stood at this window and looked out at the other homes, wondering who the inhabitants were and what they did. The building across the back lane, Little Flower 3, reminded her too much of her father's home. There was an uncle there who sat around all day in a lungi in the balcony, drinking cups of tea, reading the newspaper, scrolling on his phone. They made eye contact often, and Sneha would always rush back in and shut the window when that happened.

'Two years,' Sneha said. 'I suppose our schedules don't really match.'

Sister Josie rocked the baby and walked around the flat, looking at things.

'Not everything here is mine,' Sneha said as Sister Josie stopped in front of a bong on a shelf. 'The owners left it furnished, quite literally even with their things on the shelves—which works well for me because I don't really have that much.'

Sneha handed Sister Josie a cup of tea—just boiling hot water with a tea bag—and asked, 'Do you … would you like me to hold the baby while you have your tea?'

Sister Josie looked her up and down, clearly not planning to trust Sneha with a small baby, and picked up the cup and sipped out of it with her head turned away from the baby's head. Sneha nodded at her.

'Do you have children?' Sneha asked.

'One son,' Sister Josie said. 'He died when he was fifteen. Car accident.'

'Oh my god,' Sneha said. 'I'm so sorry. I … did he … was he … were you … I'm so sorry.'

Sneha was hoping Sister Josie would say something to ease her out of her awkwardness, to free her and let them change the topic. That was what Sneha had learned to do whenever she told people that her mother had died when she was in class ten.

'My mother died when I was in class ten,' Sneha said. 'I was fourteen.'

Sister Josie nodded. This girl seemed motherless. Sister Josie could sense those things. Not that having a mother would change much. These days girls knew what they wanted, and maybe it was for the best. But motherlessness was a state Sister Josie could identify. Some babies were motherless even with their mothers in the next bedroom. Sister Josie had seen it many times—the day nurse handing over the baby's log to Sister Josie in the nursery, mother nowhere in sight. Sometimes the mothers would just be in a state of shock, and eventually they'd come back to their children, nervously at first, kissing the child while Sister Josie held them close, or falling asleep near the infant but shouting for Sister Josie at the first sound of a cry. Those mothers left a different kind of mark on the children. These days, everyone went on and on saying: What about the fathers? But the fathers were never around and the fathers were anyway useless, Sister Josie always said, no amount of feminism was going to change that.

'You should make friends with Zara's mother. She's a lovely person, would be a good friend for you to have,' Sister Josie said. 'She's from Bangalore, doesn't know too many people here.'

'I have a lot of friends.'

There was a loud knock on the door. Then someone rattled the doorknob and shouted for Sneha.

Vikas.

Sneha could tell his voice was slurred, and she could hear him clawing against her door. She wondered if he had knocked at other homes before finding hers, if Zara's mother had opened the door in an elegant kaftan from Kilol and looked at him and his red eyes with disgust and said Sneha lives next door, before slamming the door shut and returning to her comfortable bed and whispering to her husband that it was some drunk man trying to find that odd girl in the flat next door. Sneha didn't want to open the door, but she also didn't want the neighbours to all wake up.

None of them except Sharma auntie downstairs liked her one bit. And Sneha was pretty sure Sharma auntie had dementia, so that wasn't saying much. She always stood behind the wrought iron gate, with the wooden inside door wide open, watching everyone passing by. Sometimes she would sit on a little mooda and peel oranges and eat them with the sticky juice running down her spindly arms. She always called Sneha 'heroine' and stopped her to ask if she had met Amitabh Bachchan yet. Sometimes she would hold a piece of fruit out to Sneha through the bars of the gate. Nobody else in the building said much to Sneha.

Sneha looked from the door to Sister Josie and back to the door. Vikas knocked again, shouting, saying, open, baby, open the door, darling Sneha, open na, come on, Sneha.

Sneha had recently accepted a lakh from Vikas. She had reasoned that it was additional payment for her role in the film and it was better than the heartbreak of having to ask her father for money.

Sneha lifted her finger to her lips and motioned for Sister Josie to stay quiet. Sister Josie did, but the baby in her arms wailed loudly. Sneha heard Vikas outside say, 'Oh shit. Sneha? Sneha, open, baby, I need to piss. Come on, man.'

'Pretend it's the wrong flat,' Sneha whispered to Sister Josie and slipped into the bedroom and shut the door, pressing her ear against it. She heard Sister Josie throw open the main door and scold Vikas and tell him that he would wake up the baby.

'That baby looks awake,' Vikas said. 'Damn, I didn't know she had a baby. I don't know how I feel about that.'

'You don't need to feel any which way about anything,' Sister Josie said. 'I don't know who you are or what you're doing going around blind drunk rapping-banging on doors at this hour … but get lost from here or I'll call up the police.'

'Is the baby mine?' Vikas said. 'Is the kid mine?'

'Listen, you good-for-nothing loafer,' Sister Josie said. 'Go. Stop disturbing people. I'm shutting the door now. And what for do you have curly hair? Men shouldn't have curly hair. Is that why you drink so much? Curly hair is meant for babies and ladies.'

Sneha laughed in the bedroom. She imagined Vikas standing there with his bloodshot eyes, thinking that baby might be his, accepting Sister Josie's insults about his hair.

'Wait. Don't close the door. Where is Sneha?'

'Who is Sneha?' Sister Josie said.

'Sneha!' Vikas shouted now. 'SNEHA! Listen, man, you can't ignore me after taking money from me.'

He was going to wake up everyone else in the building, Sneha thought to herself. Sister Josie was handling him well, but Sneha knew how determined he could be, how nasty. She would have to step out.

'SNEHA,' he shouted again.

Sneha could hear Sister Josie shushing the baby who was starting to fuss about all the chaos. Sneha looked around the small room. It was so tiny, her bed folded up into the wall when needed. She never put the bed up, she never even made the bed, and this made the room feel smaller still. The watchman downstairs had said this flat was meant to be the servants' quarters, but nowadays people would pay twenty thousand rupees a month to sleep in a cupboard in Bandra, so the landlord had decided to put in the folding bed and rent it out separately. The flat next door, the baby's flat, that was the real one. In this flat, the toilet door was actually two small double doors that directly faced the commode, and there was a full half-inch gap between them, so even when Sneha was home alone, she hated sitting on the toilet and looking out of that gap and being able to see the bedroom.

'Sneha,' Vikas said, barging in and knocking on the bedroom door. The entrance door closed with a bang. 'Sneha, man, open na? I didn't even know you left the party. Nora had to tell me when I was looking all over for you, and it was damn embarrassing.'

Sneha opened the bedroom door and said, 'Sorry, I wasn't feeling well, had to go home.'

Sneha looked past him at Sister Josie, still standing in her drawing room with the baby. Sister Josie was making no motion to leave and putting up no performance of not listening.

'Is that my baby?' Vikas said.

'I really need to get some sleep,' Sneha said. 'I have dance class in the morning.'

'Did you just take a rickshaw home? Sneh, that's ridiculous. I would have driven you,' Vikas said. He leaned forward and placed his hand on her hip. Sneha stepped back.

'Please don't call me Sneh,' she said. 'I really do need to sleep.'

'Fuck, man, don't be such a killjoy,' Vikas said. 'You aren't even cast in anything that needs dancing for god's sake. Let's have another drink.'

'Right,' Sneha said.

'You know it's rich,' Vikas said, his tone shifting. Sneha knew when his tone made this shift towards cruelty. She had heard it directed at her before, directed at other women, at writers, at bartenders, at his driver. 'When you need me, you're all friendly-pally, calling me up, getting a lift, getting papped on the way to the party, posing-posing for their cameras, hand on my elbow. No? But now you need to sleep. Got what you wanted, fucked off from the party without even telling me, and then you hide in the bedroom. Nice. Imagine if this was all reversed—imagine if I treated you like that? Huh? Then? Don't act like there's no transaction here.'

'Vikas, you're drunk, and you're being a cliché,' Sneha said. 'Don't do that. Go home, we'll talk in the morning.'

'Why didn't you tell me you had a baby?' Vikas said.

Sneha glanced out at the baby nearly asleep now and felt protected by its presence.

'I didn't want you to know,' Sneha said. 'I wasn't sure how you would handle it.'

Vikas shrugged.

'I think it's cool,' he said. 'Motherhood is kind of sexy. How do you pay for all its shit though? Babies are damn expensive.'

'That's why I need work,' Sneha said. 'And it's why I need to get to kathak in the morning … so I can get better roles.'

Vikas turned and looked at the baby. Sister Josie stared back at him. Sneha still stood by the doorway to the bedroom and said nothing.

'She said she needs to sleep,' Sister Josie said.

'It's …' Sneha said. 'It's okay, Sister. Just make sure Zara baby doesn't get disturbed.'

'No,' Sister Josie said. 'It's not okay. You need to sleep. She needs to sleep.'

Vikas turned to face Sister Josie and the baby, and Sneha wanted to step in-between. She didn't want Vikas's alcoholic breath anywhere near that perfect baby's face.

'That's not mine,' Vikas said, looking down at Zara's face now. 'That's definitely not mine. Wait, it couldn't be mine. We haven't even ...'

Sister Josie walked to the door and held it open for Vikas.

'Young man, get yourself home and to bed, and I suggest you drink a lot of water before you sleep,' Sister Josie said. 'And consider mushroom supplements. This is no way to live.'

'No, Sister,' Sneha said. 'Vikas, just crash here, go to bed. I'll get you some water.' Sneha avoided looking in Sister Josie's direction as she said this.

'I'm out,' Vikas said. 'This is all too messy for me. It's not worth any amount of money. Sneha, as a friend, I'm suggesting you take the money and get yourself and that baby out of this city. Honestly, I'm saying this kindly. Don't stay here. It isn't going to happen for you, but good things still can happen for you.'

'Vikas, please,' Sneha said. 'Just stay, please, let's calm down and talk. I don't have to go to kathak tomorrow. Anyway, I want to be focusing more on serious roles like you were mentioning last week. Some indie stuff.'

'Sneha, no,' Sister Josie said. 'You don't need to placate him. Stand up for yourself, for god's sake, let this curly-haired man go home where he belongs. Probably has a poor wife and kids tucked away somewhere. I know his type.'

'Auntie, you don't know anything,' Vikas said and walked out the door, surprisingly pulling it gently shut behind him.

'Good riddance,' Sister Josie said. 'A dime a dozen, those men are. I've worked in god knows how many homes of men just like him. You don't need him.'

'Why would you do that?' Sneha said. 'Why would you do that? I absolutely do need him. I knew what I was doing.'

'Hain?' Sister Josie said. 'You've gone mad or what?'

The sound of a metal bowl hitting the floor and circling a dozen times before coming to a rest in the flat upstairs interrupted the silence. People were starting to wake up while Sneha still had not gone to sleep. Homes were going to soon come alive with cups of tea and moong dal chillas for breakfast. Air conditioning would be switched off to let in the humid heat. Babies would have their diapers changed, women would look at themselves in the mirror and wonder if their faces had changed overnight. Autos would grumble past, lifting dust into the air. The dust from yesterday would be swept out of corners, vegetables would be bought, lunch and dinner menus would be discussed. Sneha had nothing to do today except go to kathak and then meet Nora for lunch and send a few texts around to see if there might be castings she could attend. She was supposed to go to Sun-n-Sand with Vikas, but she suspected that invitation no longer stood. Sneha could vanish, use the money and book a ticket back to Delhi just like Vikas had suggested, and nobody would notice. She would text Nora that she had to cancel, and Nora would probably be relieved. Everything in this city would continue uninterrupted if she left.

Sneha sat down on the sofa next to where Sister Josie was standing with a sleeping Zara. 'I needed him,' Sneha said. 'He was going to put me in his next film, and I was handling it how I wanted to handle it. The world has changed, men don't have this blind power anymore. I was in control.'

'Some things stay the same,' Sister Josie said, swaying back and forth.

'Not this,' Sneha said. 'Not this.'

Sneha lay down on the sofa, close enough to Sister Josie to see the crisp creases in her white pants. She watched Sister

Josie's legs sway back and forth, back and forth, and felt a deep exhaustion come over her. Sneha closed her eyes.

Sister Josie watched her, and for the first time in her entire professional career, Sister Josie's own legs also felt heavy with tiredness. She sat down on the sofa next to Sneha, Zara fast asleep in her arms. She moved Zara to just one arm and used her free hand to stroke Sneha's hair as Sneha's breathing softened and deepened into sleep.

Normal Neighbours

ANINDITA GHOSE

Even before they were married, they had decided never to live in one of those new apartment complexes with identical towers named after Italian islands and foreign flowers.

They chose, instead, the top floor of a four-storeyed building in the neighbourhood where almost all their friends lived. The building did not have a lift; introducing a lift in the sixty-year-old structure would ruin its charm. And their neighbourhood was all charm. Cafés that served twice-baked croissants were tucked away in streets that still bore the name of Koli villages. Lilies and tuberoses were sold out of plastic buckets on sidewalks. Dense bougainvillea that looked like it had feasted on the wealth of generations spilled over tall boundary walls. They recognized charm because they had, over a decade and a half, learnt its ways in this city.

Aparna and Mahesh were both from steel townships—it was a fact that had lifted their first conversation at the Goafest gala dinner. They had studied in Ahmedabad and Pune and made their way to Bombay for their first jobs. Now its sounds and smells were home. The beauty of this city was that when they met new people at the weekend farmer's market, dressed in crushed linen like everybody else, nobody asked where they were from.

They were a happy couple. Their happiness was in the small details that unhappy couples would surely notice: when they threw large parties, they did not hover next to each other all evening. And they were friends with each other's cousins.

After eight years of living together, they did move to a building named after an Italian island. It had been barely two weeks. They had moved, somewhat reluctantly, because they believed it was time. The last few times Aparna's mother had come to visit them in their old home, she had asked when they would shift to a place where they could settle down. Aparna knew she meant a building without paparazzi at the gate; a building with a lobby and guard desk, lifts, a playground, and normal neighbours. She hadn't insisted on vegetarian neighbours—her daughter now ate chicken and eggs—but she meant neighbours who were not Sach, the celebrity physiotherapist to movie stars, who spent each of his mornings raking the miniature Zen garden outside his door. Or Paloma and Kabir, the divorced architects who continued to live together to co-parent their two rescue beagles.

The new building complex was not far from the neighbourhood they had left behind, but it was a different world—it even had its own movie theatre. From the window of her eleventh-floor bedroom, she could see cars move in orderly lanes on the Bandra–Worli Sea Link, their true speed distorted by distance, the beeps and honks entirely eliminated.

The new home also happened to be a shorter drive to his workplace. Until recently, it was also her workplace. But she could afford to take a sabbatical now. They could afford it.

'What will you do but? You'll sit around and scroll?' a colleague had admonished. 'You're going to balloon up.' Years of smoking, a habit she had picked up in her first month in an advertising agency, had countered that fear so far. Breakfast used to be coffee, accompanied by a banana at best. Lunch was something quick from the canteen. Dinner was usually roti-sabzi in front of the screen, unless they went out, which meant dinner was four cocktails and maybe some salted nuts. But she wanted all of this to change. She wanted to sleep before midnight and make her own vegetable juices in the morning—green and red on alternate days. She wanted to get in some exercise every day; it helped that the new building complex had a gym, pool and courts for racquet sports.

As part of her new routine, after she made breakfast for the two of them, she would water the plants and sometimes sing to them, scan the newsletters, follow the markets and move some money around. And then, after Mahesh left home, she would go for a swim. She went at the same time every day, met the same women in the changing rooms and spent the same amount of time avoiding eye contact with the children's coach, who never failed to ask if she wanted help improving her backstroke.

The lift would take her down eleven storeys to the lobby level. She would have to cross the courtyard to get to the sports club. The courtyard was landscaped with identical dwarf palms, which the broker told them had been imported. Low bushes dropped day-old white blooms on the walkway, reminding her of her walk back home from school in Bhilai. As a little girl, she would pick up the flowers and give them to her grandmother. Dadi would put them at the altar even though they were picked from the ground. She said they were pure because her Appu had brought them for her. Aparna hadn't visited Bhilai since Dadi had passed.

Each day, the walk across the courtyard took enough time for Aparna to think about what she would tell the cook to make for lunch and dinner, the groceries that needed to be bought, which carton still had to be unpacked. She liked to replay the resignation conversation with her boss, too. 'I don't understand ... why don't you quit when you actually need to,' Lulu had said, stubbing her slims in the bar's ashtray, her electric-blue fingernails like lightning against the dull metal. Aparna couldn't recall exactly what she had said in response, but she felt more and more convinced by herself with each retelling. She frequently thought about how she had everything she wanted at that moment. That was what had led to the prescription for the melatonin supplements—the anxiety that it was all falling into place.

For a time, life is soft clay, it can go any way. But now things were starting to set in shape.

On one side of the courtyard was a children's playground with seesaws, swings, monkey bars and other things she didn't know the names of. On weekday mornings, it was usually occupied by toddlers and young nannies in jeans. On weekends, Aparna saw parents there as well. The fathers were so attractive these days—she wondered if her own father had been as attractive to women of her age. The mothers usually sat on steel benches, speaking conspiratorially to each other. She wondered what they spoke about. Her advertising colleagues with children were always talking about the Waldorf method and hidden sugars. So much of what she did in her years in advertising was determining archetypes. She was certain those women on the benches were in banking or consulting.

The people here seemed so unlike the neighbours they had left behind. What would the women on the benches make of Sach, Paloma, Kabir? Or her and Mahesh? They hadn't had a chance to get to know their new neighbours yet, beyond enquiries on the building WhatsApp group. Aparna wanted to have the house ready before they invited anyone over; and the frames for the dining area were yet to arrive.

Her first interaction with someone from the building had taken place just that morning. She had entered the lift with her swim bag and pressed the button for the lobby. She was wearing a long T-shirt over her swimwear. When the man stepped in on the eighth floor, she felt aware of her bare legs. All of a sudden, she was covered in gooseflesh.

His shirt was hanging out of his trousers and he was holding formal work shoes in one hand, smoothing his hair down with the other. His feet were very fair. He had no hair on his toes. 'Shoot, shoot, I have to go up first,' he said, fumbling with his hands in his pockets till he produced a wristwatch.

'Okay … but this lift is going down,' said Aparna. 'Everything okay?'

'The time … no, no, no, if you don't mind … I can't go all the way down and then up. I'm on the twenty-eighth floor. I'm 2802. I have a call starting soon.' He banged a fist gently on the lift wall like someone who had never done it before.

Before Aparna could nod her assent, he had already leaned across her. He pressed a series of buttons—the lift came to a halt, changed direction, and they were now going up. As he pulled back, she could smell his musk. Not his cologne. She could smell him.

'Sorry,' he said.

'It's okay, I was just going down to the pool.'

He nodded.

'I like to go before it gets too sunny, but five minutes here and there won't make a difference,' said Aparna. 'I'm 1101.' She put her bag on the floor, holding it in place with her feet, and waited for him to thank her.

But he wasn't looking at her. He was looking at his phone, strapping on his watch, rotating his neck, staring at the lift buttons lighting up floor by floor as if to will the lift to move faster. She registered that his forearms were muscular. He probably played tennis.

As the lift neared the twenty-eighth floor, he became less agitated. He turned to Aparna and extended his hands, which she shook tentatively. His palms were cool and dry.

'I'm Abhay. I've made a terrible first impression. I'll make it up to you sometime. Nice T-shirt by the way ... Stones fan here too. See you around.'

When Mahesh returned that evening, she started to tell him about Abhay of 2802.

He held her by the shoulders to interrupt her. 'Appu, you've been wanting to meet the neighbours. Mustafa introduced me to his B-school batchmate, some guy called Aravind in 902. Called us over for drinks at eight today.'

An evening of wine and conversation seemed appealing to Aparna, even if it was going to be with the B-school crowd. In their old building, they got together often—for drinks, joints, poker, Catan, or to watch a movie on Paloma and Kabir's projector.

She was surprised nobody had told her that one had to actively prepare for a sabbatical. People were otherwise so eager to give advice on all matters. But no one had said that she couldn't go from deciding how to dress each day, soaking in the city during the commute, working ten hours a day, and carrying that feeling of being indispensable, to days stretching ahead where nobody needed anything from her. That the fantasy of unfettered reading time would ultimately be disappointing.

That face yoga got boring. She had signed up for two online workshops. She also watched YouTube videos—this week she was doing a deep dive into plant fungus. But late afternoons were a blank canvas, one indistinguishable from the other. Most days she had packages to receive, open, return. Some days, she sent Mahesh a selfie, and he replied with a heart emoji a few hours later.

A few months ago, before she had quit her job or planned the move, her therapist had told her she was mildly depressed. The guidance was to regulate her circadian rhythm, get daily exercise, engage in stimulating activities and meet people she enjoyed meeting. She had emerged from that appointment to go to the salon across the road and ask the head stylist to cut her waist-length hair into a textured, spiky bob. When Mahesh had seen it, there hadn't been any exclamations. He had said he liked the new bob. But, yes, yes, he liked the old Appu too. No, he meant he loved them both.

'Should we take something?' Aparna said, as she browsed through the hangers in her cupboard for something that would make her look interesting, and not just pretty. She settled on a green silk kaftan that was knotted in the front, and green ballerina shoes. 'We should take something along. We have that saké. And a sparkling.'

'We're not giving the saké we carried back all the way to people we don't know,' Mahesh said, poking his head into the room. 'And who knows if they'll even appreciate it?'

'Is this Mustafa fun?' she asked while they were getting into the lift, wine bag in hand.

'He's good at his job. Why?'

'Aravind and his wife will be interesting if Mustafa is interesting.'

'No, Appu. There is never a guarantee on that. Think about all the uninteresting friends we have and love.'

'If they talk about real estate and half-marathons, I'm leaving!'

'We'll see. Whoever lasts longer gets to pick the next show.'

They laughed till they reached the door. They were the only ones there. Aravind told them a few others from the building were coming later. His voice reminded Aparna of her father's younger brother. The living room had a colour palette of beige and tan, set off by a large piece of contemporary art with concentric circles of colourful bindis by an artist that Aparna recognized. She took a step back to take it in, and then went closer to look.

'We bought it for our last anniversary. I have wanted her for a while,' said Aravind's wife, introducing herself as Smita. She had just emerged through sliding doors that closed off the rest of the house.

'Beer? Wine? Or up for something stronger for a Friday evening? Smita's margaritas are famous,' said Aravind.

'I will have to try it some other time then. It's a working weekend for me. Wine is good,' said Mahesh, which made Aparna smile. She admired his monastic discipline. It wasn't tattoos and the new sports car that had got him promoted to national creative director.

'Oh yes, Mustafa told me he's been working weekends. But I didn't know the creatives *also* worked. I thought you guys sat around rolling and discussing Herzog, and the campaigns just appeared.'

Mahesh shot him a friendly grin. He didn't need rescuing, but Aparna interposed anyway. 'I'd love a dry white if that's not trouble,' she said. 'And where did Smita go?'

'Checking on our younger one,' said Aravind, filling three wine glasses and passing them around. The glasses had flat bottoms and very thin, amber-coloured stems. They looked Nordic.

Aparna and Mahesh went through two glasses of Pinot Grigio each. More than a decade of drinking together had given them the gift of synchronicity. Aravind was taking his girls to an organic farmstay in Bali next month and they swapped travel stories. He headed his firm's risk assessment vertical and fellow partners had insisted he use up his leaves. Smita was in marketing but was considering moving to pro-bono work. After about an hour and a half of conversation, which Smita joined only in waves, Aravind asked if they'd like mint tea. Aparna took this as a cue to leave, but her husband could be a bit thick sometimes. He said yes, then no, and then yes again to the offer of tea. By the time the tea arrived, the doorbell rang and Smita emerged from the sliding doors again to let people in. She had put up her hair, and added on a chunky necklace of acrylic chain links, and suddenly looked glamorous. She left the door ajar and people poured into the living room in a steady stream. The new entrants parked themselves on the sofa and dining table chairs in cosy knots. A few went straight to the kitchen to unload things they had brought along. Two men helped Smita carry out a glass beverage dispenser. The air was filled with perfume and the heady whirr of conversation, with an occasional, 'Where have you been!' and 'Look at you!' sparking through.

A woman with a complicated silver nose stud refilled Aparna and Mahesh's empty wine glasses. Another woman tore the cling wrap off a salami board and offered its contents to Aparna, adding that it was vegan. Aparna glanced at her phone and around the room—it was close to ten, and there were eighteen people in the living room. She hoped to see Abhay of 2802 among them, and she did. When they made eye contact, he left his group by the dining table and walked over to where she was standing, but as she and Mahesh were amidst rapid introductions with several of the new arrivals, he became part of the cursory introductions with the group.

Aparna made conversation with the vegan salami woman who worked in climate change consulting. On learning that Aparna was an advertising strategist, she started soliciting her thoughts on a campaign, when Mahesh came and whispered into Aparna's ear, 'Have to drive to Pune early tomorrow morning.'

Aparna would have liked to stay, but she was fading. She could not understand how she was more tired during her sabbatical than all the years she had worked long hours and done the cross-city commute.

Smita was missing again, so they took their leave from Aravind, who said it was good to have had them over. He said he would be in touch.

'Fun people,' said Mahesh, once they were out of the door.

'You don't think it's odd he didn't insist we stay?'

'Did you want to stay? You never want to stay these days. Oh, Appu. We can go back in.'

He called for the lift.

'No, I didn't want to stay. But he should have asked us. They should have asked us a few times.'

'They don't have the Aparna Gupta rule book yet.'

'And why did he call us at eight?'

'So we could chat. That's a good thing, isn't it?'

'They should have asked us to stay.'

'Come here. Stay here.' He crooked his left arm as he stepped into the lift.

She smiled, settled into the cave of his arm, and leaned her head on his shoulder. She liked that he was a full foot taller than her. 'Emmy ...' she said, looking up, 'Smita said they get together a couple of times a month. Do you think they play high-stakes poker?'

'I think they call spirits. Planchette. Séance.'

'These corporate types are also really into mushrooms these days.'

'My bet is on spirits.'

Two weeks later, Smita messaged Aparna for them to come over that Friday night. Aparna made pots of mushroom pâté through the afternoon. In the evening, she got dressed and inaugurated a lipstick called Coral Ecstasy. This time, she and Mahesh knew better than to be the first ones.

The door was slightly ajar when they reached 902. The furniture in the TV area had been moved around, the tower speakers played afro-jazz, and two women wearing Wonder Woman tiaras were pulling people to the area to sway with them.

Abhay from 2802 found her and plied her with a pill and a glass of water. 'Well, hello there. Is this ok? I said I'd make it up to you.'

Aparna was taken aback. She took the pill out of the tiny ziplock bag and flipped it on her palm—it had been a while. She looked at Abhay and raised her eyebrows. He gestured to her with his finger to look around the room. She put it on her tongue and swallowed. She drank the glass of water that Abhay had handed her, and then joined the Wonder Women on the dance floor for what felt like hours. At some point, she found Mahesh, and he told her, yes, he would pop a pill, too. She felt on the brink of something. After a while, she couldn't hear the music, only the beats. The air conditioning didn't feel sufficient, but that was alright. All her energy was pulsating in the centre of her body, in her stomach. No, she was not on the brink of something, she was at the centre. She was at the centre of her own life. One of the Wonder Women placed her tiara on Aparna's head. Aravind passed around bottles of water with mint leaves floating in them—these people were just so friendly, so considerate, so full of surprises. Where was Mahesh in all this? Even the serious-looking man with the moustache—Aparna had seen him on Page 1 of *The Economic Times*—was on the dance floor. He was surprisingly good. Actually, they were all good. Afro-jazz had given way to '90s Bollywood. When *'Chaiyya Chaiyya'* played, everybody dropped to their knees at the right time, even the vegan salami woman.

Aparna needed to sit for a while. The silver nose stud woman turned out to be Abhay's partner. It was hard to remember all the names; hers sounded like a Bengali sweet. The two of them drew her into a conversation about capitalism and nuclear families. They sat beside each other on the sofa.

'We are not capitalists,' Abhay said.

'You absolutely are,' said Aparna. She could feel her voice grow louder even though all these people were sitting close to her and listening intently. She saw Mahesh across the room and waved at him. He came and handed her a glass of iced water, gave her shoulder a squeeze, and went back to where he had been standing near the bookshelf.

'You are capitalists. You work in wealth management. You literally count money everyday.'

'Getting paid to count money doesn't sound bad,' said a man in a shimmering yellow shirt, sitting on the armchair across from her. 'I wish that was all we needed to do.'

A woman came and sat on his lap. She was also shimmering. Aparna narrowed her eyes. The woman looked like Smita.

'You're right in a way,' said the woman. 'But we are not capitalists when we come home. We share.'

Aparna got engrossed in the cube of ice in her water. The ice cube was so large, it touched the walls of the glass. She had to swirl it really slowly, and very carefully, to produce a rhythmic clinking. By the time she looked up from her glass, she had lost her attentive audience. Abhay and silver nose stud woman were gone. Shimmering yellow shirt and shimmering woman were gone. The music had gone low and everyone was looking at the TV screen. She looked at the TV screen too. Numbers were popping up on it one by one. They were three and four digits; she recognized them as apartment numbers. Aravind was controlling the screen with his mobile. Suddenly, he made the numbers jumble.

'Do I have everyone who is in for this fortnight?' asked Aravind.

'Not us. We have college applications in 403.'

'Aparna, Mahesh, do you need a briefing? I sent the playbook to your phones earlier in the evening. Have you downloaded the app?'

Aparna had no idea where her phone was. She was staring at the screen, and now her head was throbbing. She looked towards the bookshelf and saw that Mahesh was walking towards her. His neck seemed peculiarly long. He looked like the giraffes they'd seen in Tanzania.

'Take your time,' said the shimmering woman, who was now definitely Smita. Mahesh came to sit beside Aparna. She could feel everyone's eyes on them.

'Appu?' said Mahesh.

'It's rude of these guys to spring this on us,' Aparna said in a low whisper.

'I thought you understood when we came here the last time. And you wanted to come today.'

'No … I'm still not clear on what's happening.'

'You've been wanting to try things.'

'What about you? You're okay with how things are?'

'I'm okay either way.'

'Well, it's a no from me.'

'No being "I want to think about it"? Or no-no?'

'Why is this on me? You make a show about asking me what I want. In the end, we always do what you want.'

'That's not fair Aparna. We are having a discussion.'

'I can't have a discussion with twenty people around us.'

'I can't put up with this right now. What would you like to do?'

They went to their own bedrooms when they reached home. The next day, she woke up at noon to Mahesh arguing with the cook about why kadi patta made its way into every dal and curry, about how he had not grown up eating kadi patta, about how he wanted the dal to be made just the way his mother made it. They spoke little the rest of the week. They ended up watching three full movies.

At the end of the week, Smita asked them in a group chat if they had downloaded the app and wanted to join the next Friday. Aparna replied immediately to say they would come. Then, she spent the afternoon crying. That evening, she met

Paloma in the old neighbourhood for dinner and told her how fantastic the new building society was.

The app was called 'Apartment Shuffle'. When you opened it, candy-coloured letters and numbers fell into a jumble to the tune of the viral Korean song about apartments. It seemed almost parodic.

When Friday evening arrived, they went down to 902 even later this time, closer to when Aravind was jumbling numbers on the screen. She wanted the 2802 male icon to appear beside the 1101 female icon. It didn't. But when the 2802 female icon appeared beside the 1101 male icon, she felt like she had swallowed a fidgety bird. The silver nose stud woman was attractive in the way rehabilitated hippies are. She was from Delhi.

Aparna paired with Aravind. He came up to talk to her after he was done with his screen duties, asking if she'd like another margarita. 'We only need to decide where and when we are meeting tomorrow. Any preferences?'

The next evening, Mahesh left home before her. Aparna and Aravind had agreed to meet at the P2 level at 6 p.m. The plan was to drive to a boutique hotel in Worli, across the Sea Link. She saw Aravind just as his driver was handing over the keys to him. When she was seated and belted in the front seat beside him, she put her hands up and broke into a laugh.

'You're not sure,' said Aravind, adjusting the rearview mirror.

'What gave it away?'

'The flip-flops.'

'I'm sorry.'

'I understand … well, I can't speak for everyone, but this has been great for our marriage.'

'Come on.'

'You know "Apartment Shuffle" was Smita's brainchild, right? Brilliant woman, my wife.'

'I don't get it. You both seem …'

'Look, we are left-brain folk. There are no surprises here. It's fair play.'

'But it's like a game.'

'You get the point, Aparna. It is play.'

'But for us …'

'Don't worry about it.'

'I really am sorry.'

'Don't be sorry. But you will have to do something Smita doesn't do with me—the mango cream at Haji Ali.'

At that moment, as the car spiralled up from the parking level to exit to the road, Aparna was happy to be there with Aravind. The week had been too unpleasant, too quiet.

The queue for a mango cream at Haji Ali Juice Centre wasn't as long as the ones to enter the dargah. But there was always the risk that they'd run out. And then you'd have to wait while they whipped up a fresh batch. So, when it was his turn, Aravind bought three servings.

They sat on the Worli seawall with their plastic containers and spoons, at first facing the water. The construction work made both the air and the view unpalatable. Aparna followed the sluggish movement of the foam lines on the water's surface.

'Do you come here often?' she asked.

'I lived around here when I first moved to the city. The flat I shared with two others was so small, if one of the guys cooked methi in the evening—is it methi?—we'd come sit here till the flat aired out,' he laughed.

'But what did you look at? There is nothing to see here,' said Aparna.

'It was new then. I had never lived in a city with a sea,' said Aravind. 'I met Smita in my first month. She used to live in a PG in Colaba, and I had to bribe my flatmates if we wanted the space to ourselves for even an hour. We would go over B-school case studies. I would hold her hand.'

She let Aravind believe that they were sharing the third mango cream, but let him eat most of it. He said she should use the hotel they had booked, because going back to an empty home might be unpleasant. He would go to a friend's home for a drink.

'It's just seven though. Is there anything else you want to do?' he asked.

'Actually, there is.'

Aravind waited.

'I want to walk across the Sea Link,' said Aparna.

'You know you can't.'

'I know. But I want to.'

Aravind contemplated this for a few seconds. 'I'll give you a head start and follow in the car. If you get caught, just act disoriented.'

Aparna swung her legs over and landed on the promenade with a spring. She held her palm up for a high-five. Her face was flushed.

'Okay, okay, you should be able to get away with a couple of minutes. Don't get us both arrested. That would definitely make your Emmy jealous.'

Aparna managed to walk on the side of the eight-lane bridge for what seemed like five minutes, keeping one hand on the concrete edge throughout. The salty sea breeze washed over her face, made her hair fly wild. Sweat trickled down the backs of her legs, and the fabric of her flimsy summer dress flapped about. The sun was a perfect circle—it would dip into the water any moment now. In photographs, Aparna could never tell the difference between a sunrise and sunset. The same wrinkled tender pinkness seemed to mark beginnings and endings.

When a police car came up to her with lights flashing, she motioned to say that she was feeling nauseous. She pointed at Aravind's car and got into it without protest. Aravind dropped her to the hotel, which wasn't very boutique, but at least it didn't smell of artificial lemongrass. She asked the kitchen to make her a dal khichdi; she slept well that night.

The next morning, she called for a taxi before she left the room. All she needed to do was get out of the hotel bathrobe and back into her clothes from the previous night.

As she waited on the road for her ride, she wondered if she should text him, and what she could say. She couldn't really ask her husband how his evening was. What had the playbook said? Then just as the taxi she had booked cancelled, a kaali-peeli stopped before her. The driver said she was his first customer for the day, and so he couldn't refuse the ride even though the distance was short. His taxi smelled of soap and sandalwood. Half-burnt sticks of incense were hooked into the AC ducts in front of the idols of Ganesh and Lakshmi on the dashboard. When she settled into the backseat, she texted Mahesh to tell him to keep the laundry bundle outside the door if he was home.

The three dots in their chat window came and went. 'How are you Aparna?' he finally wrote back.

'I walked across the sea link last night!' she wrote. Then she edited out the exclamation. After a minute, she added: 'When did you get back?'

'About an hour after I left.'

Aparna rolled down her window, and breathed in the morning. There were oversized cement sunflowers on the road divider. The roads were a mess, but the sunflowers seemed to have a fresh coat of paint. They were a brighter yellow than she remembered.

'Have you eaten?' Mahesh wrote.

'No. Hungry.'

'I'm making breakfast. Come home.'

It must have rained in the night. Drops of water clung to the surface of the cement flowers. They looked almost real.

She leaned her head on the side of the taxi.

Two Bi Two

PRATHYUSH PARASURAMAN

'I sink back into my hard wooden
Third-class seat, buffered by
This odour, as by a divine cushion.
And do not suspect that this ride
Will be for me the beginning of a meditation
On the nature of truth and beauty.'

—Gieve Patel, 'Bombay Central'

I do not need a handjob, I do not, no I don't, I think, ravenous and reluctant, both. His hands—*his* hands—graze my bulge, *his* fingers flirt with the metal zip, which slips down easily, smoothened by wear, and now fly open, the button at my bulging waist intact, sweat soaked into the waistband, my pant is like a lip, a gaping mouth on my unwashed jeans—three weeks since it was last touched by detergent, I think, maybe a month. I should just toss it in the laundry, finally, tonight.

I should have swatted *his* hands off, wilted my posture away, but those fingers—I see a wedding ring—found their way under my kurta, into my pants, searching for the sleeve of the boxer. *He* rubs the soft underbelly of *his* finger over the seam of my sleeve, the fingers folding deeper, cautiously, confidently touching the skin of my cock, a dexterous patience with my foreskin, I want to pat *him* on the head and bend over. I should not make eye contact; I do not make eye contact; *he* should not know that I want it. I do. I should not want it. *His* fingers find one of the many holes in my boxer, gaping, the threads widening with every harsh tumble spin, *his* fingers further boring the hole. I should just toss them out, finally, tonight.

A small evening breeze ruptures the brimming train compartment, exhausted men hanging like laundry from the footboard. *He* tickles my balls. I staunch a giggle and my body shakes, finally turning to *his* face, barely inches away from mine.

Those eyes, so kind, big and intense, those lashes like thick fringes, curling towards god. The small bead of sweat collecting at the edge of *his* nose flutters. The thoughts pile. Perhaps, it is not a breeze as much as the pre-monsoon wet, saturated, hanging, heavy air that is rammed into, disturbed by the rattling train, gathering crowds from the South of Bombay—VT first, then Byculla—spitting them, and swallowing some along the suburbs up north—Dadar, say, from where I was picked up today—swaying east—Kurla, say, from where *he* was picked up today, then Ghatkopar, Mulund, Thane, Dombivli, and on it goes, limning the Central line.

There is a crowd cartel, standing in line, clogging one half of the entrance to the compartment, also the exit from the compartment. These men will get off at Dombivli, many stations away, but a nerve centre of crowd recklessness, that to leave the compartment here as the crowds at that station enter, is to put your body at the risk of a tailspin.

I would know.

I was caught in the eye of one such maelstrom in my debut year in this city, spinning around as one crowd leaked out the train and spinning faster as another flooded in, my body in between, torqued like a lopsided wave between shore and shoal. You learn. That's what the city is for, its citizens bearing the burden of being here, perhaps bearing it not as a burden, but as air, holding secrets as though scents, and you, the babe in the woods, being schooled by either experience or quick lovers—no, you do not do that, you stand at an angle, you go here, have you not been touched at the urinals of Churchgate, been fucked by the glance of wary men as the portland stone of Flora Fountain glistens in the night; you let them stare, you let them know that you like being stared at, not by smiling, but by staring back, by allowing their gaze the gift of yours.

The men are resilient, these Dombivli squirts, for they won't let anyone entering from earlier stations push them deep into the compartment, nor will they let those exiting at earlier stations wriggle their way into their line. They are like a pillar—you do not engage with it, you navigate around it.

He is one among them, this Dombivli cartel, and I am standing next to *him*, trying to strategically carve a path out of this cocoon in time for my station, Mulund, two stops before *his*. *His* other hand holding the grab handle above, I lodge my face under *his* armpit, its rotten, spiced secretions, the deposits of his workday, currying under a bicep that has been stretched into shaped sculpture through the years. I rub the bridge of my nose against its contours. I want to wear *him*. Mouth closed, *he* breathes out heavily through the nose, that warm exhale on my temples, my face looking away. *His* jaws are in a rhythmic loop, chewing gum, perhaps, sweeping away the day's unwashed flavours with synthetic mint, his cheekbones looking polished. I steal a look. He smiles, all teeth, the shrivelled pellet of gum caught in the enamel guillotine.

The day's collapse perfumes the train—in the pits, in the breath, and, most perceptibly, most deceptively, in the small grotto behind the ear. Walking out of the shower as a child, dad used to stop me in my leaking step and ask if I scrubbed that skin, because the scents sediment most strongly in this depression, he warned kindly always, but firmly—there, and the inner lining of the foreskin, pull it all the way back, slowly, all that gunk lodged, white powder that tastes stale, smells rancid, and settles into a grainy paste if not dusted. I promised myself if I had a son, I would circumcise him, because that shrivelled skin flaps around when flaccid, makes you come faster, and if *he* was not being so gentle with it just now, as the erection pushes the skin back, as *he* helps push the skin back, there might have been pain. There is no pain. *He* is good. A goodness that makes you ask how much that finger has felt and feathered to make this goodness feel so easy. A jealousy enters my heart, and I have to remind myself that we locked eyes, and emerged into existence in each other's lives but a few minutes ago.

His eyes look tired; the eyes of the man behind *him* are shut; the man behind him has dug his gaze into the phone. I move closer. *His* grip tightens. I wince. *He* slacks, and this time, builds the pressure slowly. We breathe together.

The wind ruffles the widow's peak of men by the footboard, pushing it further every year, like a mountain's height weathering down, and weary feet stand on two handfuls of space, sometimes less, sometimes lesser still; the harsh white tube light; the humming fan; the sour metal of the congested grab handle, five, maybe six hands pooling on one anchor, the metal polished by touch, so much touch, rippling the light.

Will the handle ever give way, its screws unbuckle? Sometimes the very act of travelling in these trains feels like faith. That the whole damn thing has not collapsed so far. That we are still standing, somewhat squandered. That I am still standing, somewhat, leaning against *his* flexed arms so thoroughly, my body in diagonal rest, my bag hung from the front, my chin resting on its worn out leather—waterproof, I was lied to, when

I bought it; a lie, I realized, while holding my notebook whose edges had been smudged so thoroughly, all my framed thoughts were now a blur—and my hands under this bag, holding *his* wrist, guiding *his* speed, then floating my fingers through the air, trying to reach *his* pants. *He* is hard, the erection bent so tautly against the tight underwear and pants, as though bursting. Must be hung. Eight inches? I can feel a wetness under my tongue, saliva pooling. I should be on my knees.

Slowly, perceptibly, *he* takes my cock out of my pants for some air, and I freeze. The gesture is so brazen. It can feel the soft wind sieved through the crowd. My hands back with me, I look at *his* face, and think again, why am I here? *He* smiles, raising *his* eyebrow, coming closer, whispering in my ears, 'Dombivli?', and I shake, no, 'Mulund'. The strokes are more and more bold, the pressure hardening but also producing a slight sharpness of pain. This, I am used to.

Another man, close by, but not too close, looks at me, looks down at the hands disappearing under my bag, and looks back up at me, eye contact that is knowing, fully furnished. His face refuses to let up more—no judgement, no jealousy. But he won't stop staring. I let him. For how many years has he been travelling these compartments, I ask his silence, assuming a history to deepen the present through the past, to insist on meaning, to give that empty gaze purpose, or better yet, pathos; how he could have been an archivist of queer pleasure, elsewhere, elsewhen, but how, instead, his desperation, his circumstances, his resignation turned him to stone.

'You have place?' Hands in my pants, lips to my ears, *he* asks.

I shake my head, no. I live by myself; I could have nodded, yes.

This past month I have been abstaining, refusing to ride this 2x2 compartment, the second door of the second last compartment, this cauldron of desire, where men know, know that men also want men. I have had my fill, I reasoned, and now I must retreat from my longings.

Sex often had a painful aftermath, my asshole ripped one month, a numbing injection along the walls of my bowels in another—to harvest the HPV warts—by the steady hands of the skin doctor recommended by my proctologist. It was strange, that moment with the dermatologist, who moved around hospitals and shared this particular office with a paediatrician—the ceiling was scratched with cartoons, the fan's blades covered with stickers of Winnie-the-Pooh, and I was sleeping on my side, pants down, foetal posture, limp dick, a stuffed toy of Peppa Pig in my direct eyeline.

No sex, I told myself, giving the sample of my warts for a biopsy, hoping it was not cancerous, dreaming that I would not, would never need to, wilt in the waiting room of an oncologist. Do I even enjoy sex? I promised to not be touched, to not smoke, never smoke (I whispered) as I smoked. The last one, this is the last. A promise kept is deferred indiscipline, I learned, and my life is a string of promises. No sex, never sex.

A friend asked if I had lodged in me a death drive, and it sounded so chic, I smoked into her face. 'In a city like Bombay? Whoever wants to live?' She flicked my cheeks, annoyed, and I turned over her Freudian accusation in my head, less for its intended effect than for its meaning—do I really want to die?

How else can I explain to myself the willingness—or say, ambivalence—to follow a stranger into a public toilet, close the door behind us, and swallow what he has to offer, stick whatever he wants, wherever he wants, not even insisting on a condom, not even the formality of a whimper, not even the expectation of pleasure. 'I really think you need a therapist,' she sighed, knowing her concern fell on deaf ears, knowing I cannot stand therapists, the mined meaning they impose, reducing me into a trope, and my life into a narrative, using words I will cling to—I *will* cling to—for these words are so seductive, their implications so easy.

I want to live, I am sure of that. How could I have a death drive when I wear sunscreen so diligently? Washing my face every night—a gentle cleanser, mind you—scrubbing off the city from my skin, where does that come from?

No sex, then.

Today is different.

My promise has been put to test by an old flame, flickering, who texted me a disappearing photo of his horse dick in the afternoon. I swallowed my saliva, scratching my crotch. I would not reply; he had made me cry, does he not remember? I forget there are men for whom memory is not warning but ammunition, whose relationship to their past is not as charged, not littered with minefields. I did not leave work early as I usually do. I waited for rush hour, instead, descending into the crowds, the bodies pooled together in Dadar—where hordes from both the Central and Western line erupt in overlapping chaos—thinking of that image he sent, a blurring chorus of my weeping fading out.

Why am I here, I whispered into my throat, trying and, miserably at sea, failing to place intention next to action—they floated in opposite directions. I walked all the way to the end of the platform, past the waiting area for first-class passengers—where I should have waited, I did have the quarterly pass, I did pay for it—past a crowd waiting for their train to Mysore, a family deciding what to eat from the stall—samosa pav and rose milk, always, I ordered as though them—to get to this part of the platform where this compartment, this specific 2x2 compartment, would align as the train rested for its twenty seconds.

I looked for the familiar markers, the pillars I had made a mental note of years earlier, to locate this area, where the second door of the second last compartment would halt, picking up the lower middle class and the queers—though, I must clarify, many would be offended by this description of them as queer; imagine a man, his dick up my ass, telling me he is not gay, and me saying, no, no, of course not, just plunge deeper, be a man, his hypocrisy and my desperation finding common ground, both of us giving up something central to us—to be together. Men, who had also made note of the pillars, the familiar markers, were waiting, eyeing me as I eyed them, ricocheting glances which can fall on one's skin as either accusation or longing.

As the train arrived at the platform, I swivelled my backpack to the front, and slipped my watch out of my wrist, and along with my phone, my spectacles, and earplugs blaring some know-it-all four-hour podcast, dumped it into my bag, tightening my first two toes over the grip of my chappal. A crowd rushed in as a crowd rushed out, heads knocking, arms both creating and filling space, pushing into every crevice, heads cutting arms, hips shoving bodies, thrust, thrust, make more space, let more men in, bodies helping you carve a path into the compartment, pushed from behind, pushing from the front. Strange how, in the midst of so many people, so little of you is cared for, looked at, that it almost offers the promise of privacy. Would you believe me if I told you that I had kissed a man here once, in this crowd, our faces hidden by both, our arms holding on to the handrail, and the general public's disinterest in and indifference to us?

At the next station, Kurla, *he* was flung in. Our eyes first met, then parted, *his* eyes hovering around the compartment, scoping the prospects a bit more to meet again as he filed into the Dombivli cartel, and this time, the gaze stuck. I had been summoned. I looked down, looked up, *his* eyes had not wavered. *He* raised both eyebrows suggestively, for a second, and I found my way, through that crowd, towards *him*, making space in order to occupy it, contorting my body as the train rattled, and we held our stretch of space, like a thread that could snap, but that never did, and *he* held that thread and pulled, tugging till I could feel *his* breath on my ears.

It is so rehearsed, the rhythms of this recklessness. Another world emerges in this disappearing twilight. Men press up against each other, dicks—some hard, most softened by labour, by cigarettes, by time—tucked between the butt cheeks of the men in front. Some swat this invasion, turning around with a sour expression. Others welcome it. The bags offer a buffer—some press their canvas bags against the arch of the back of the person in front. If that man can feel something sharp against his back—your metal bottle, perhaps, or the hard edges of the perfume you always keep inside, or the small bottle of lubricant or poppers—he sneers and you rearrange yourself, your bag, whichever is easier. Under it, hands swarm till they find skin. Often, I have found a thickening hardness, an emerging erectness against my back, and I do not know from whom, and I do not care of whom, refusing to look back, wriggling myself making that cock comfortable, as he presses harder and I allow myself to be pressed against, a willing tablet of wet clay, emboss yourself, I think, leave your trace, and let it recede, and let there be more.

Over the balding heads, and others full of swept hair, I can see the city blur past, all impressionist renderings, even when the train stops, the sense of a city smudged remains—all the lights from apartments rupturing the skies, all the tenements, built one over the other, shrouded by the blue tarpaulin that is out in preparation for the incoming monsoon. The clouds collect moisture to douse a city so choked, it sprouts upwards, towards space. Some days, when I am unable to get inside the compartment, hanging by the footboard, the city at my disposal, my life hanging by the strength of my wrist, I wonder how many million people and their lives I glide by on this train. Now that it is summer in wane, I notice flowers blooming haphazardly at the edges of every station, in colours pulled from the brightest pastels. On other days, I have desire.

An older man who had snoozed off in his seat jolts awake by the rhythms of his body—it knows. Ghatkopar, the next station, his destination. A ripple in this pond, the crowd eddies slightly, with murmurs of complaint, the bag of frail bones turning this way and that, huffing, humming. I do not move, though, stopping the ripple, staring at *him*. Space is made around us for the man to edge through, as though our togetherness is assumed, respected as a sacred singularity, and as he is chucked off the train at the station, a fresh wave of embodied scents pour in. I am next, one more station, five more minutes.

I can feel the wetness of *his* breath, *his* hands under my bag, *his* eyes at, on, onto, into me, and mine wandering here and there, trying not to be conspicuous, knowing fully well that many, if not most, men in this compartment, looking at me, looking at *his* hands, would know, have surmised, the fondling of the cock, a fondling of a cock. Some stare, and I do not know if it is curiosity or competition or yearning. Boredom, too, perhaps. It was, after all, a long journey for most, travelling all the way from the bowels of Colaba, to be hacked off, as part of the crowd, at Kasara, hours away—a distance sutured by the fast train rattling by stations that only the slow train would, otherwise, pause to take a break, a breath in.

I disturb my body, shaking it, clearing my throat, looking *him* in the eye, a blink longer, and *he* understands; we must part. Smiling, *he* tucks my dick back into my pants, carefully—it is still quite hard—zips me up, smooths my kurta over my body, passing *his* hands over the creases, retracing and reversing my dishevelled state, making sure I look presentable to the world outside, and moves aside to make space for me to squeeze through, me asking the man in front, if he, too, has to get off at Mulund, hmm hmm, he says annoyed, and I wait behind his head full of unwashed hair, and the station arrives, and I am spat out, and I straighten myself, almost tripping over a man who shoves himself into the compartment forcefully without making a sound nor turning his face into a pained expression of displeasure. This is all unexceptional.

The train pauses, then leaves; and I, leave, then pause, look back. I cannot find *him*, swallowed as *he* is by a new crowd, their overlapping frames. *He* might find another man. I think of *his* ring. Something in my stomach tightens.

Walking home, I stop at the thela at the corner, smoking an ice burst under a shedding tree of copper pods, those yellow blossoms clogging the windshields of parked cars under it. A breeze dislodges a clump of these papery blooms from the branches, and the thick, heated air holds them suspended for a moment longer. As I rest my beaten body against a parked scooter, the kurta stuck against my back, sweat as glue, my underarms a marshy pit, and each fold of fat oiling a paste of dirt, some petals settle on my head. I can feel their weightlessness. I do not dust them off, I do not, no I don't.

I let *it* be.

The Storyteller's Tale

SHANTA GOKHALE

Ketaki has been stealing my stories since our schooldays. Ketaki Ghosalkar. From Gangadhar Niwas down the road. No, not Bole Road. The main road. Where we stay, that is Mehta Mahal, stands at the corner of Bole Road and the main road. Bole Road's the one with all those hardware and timber shops, and the Puratan Vatavriksha Shri Hanuman Mandir at one end, and the Portuguese Church at the other.

Ketaki was named Ketaki because she was born fair-skinned. What's the connection? Oh, so you've never seen a ketaki flower? It is cream-coloured. Ketaki was born cream-coloured. That's the connection. Her hair is brown and curly. Call it frizzy. She wears it in a ponytail, though I never saw a pony with a tail like that. But she tosses her head quite a bit when she talks, which you might say is pony-like. 'When she talks' sounds like there are times when she doesn't. Actually, there is no time when she doesn't. A boy in our class, I think it was Sridhar, once said, 'Here's a riddle. What does Ketaki look like with her mouth shut?' The other boys guffawed. The girls were very angry. As far as we were concerned, Ketaki was not to be teased. She had lost her mother when she was three.

Despite this, the truth is, when Ketaki is in the room, she alone talks. Others listen. It is not that she always has something of substance to say, but she says it emphatically, aided by a booming voice that leaves others with no option but silence. Aai says it is all very well being fair-skinned, but a woman should sound like a woman. By which she means a woman should have a melodious, honeyed voice, failing which, at least a soft excuse-me-but-may-I-say-something voice. When Ketaki visits, and Aai can't hold her irritation any longer, she comes out to the balcony where we sit and shouts at me, 'You want the whole of Bole Road to hear you?' In keeping with the Marathi saying, tell off the daughter and the daughter-in-law gets the message, Ketaki lowers her voice for a couple of minutes. Then she is back to 100 decibels.

Ketaki is an actress. Directors tell her that the theatres these days come equipped with a sophisticated sound system, so she must learn to modulate her voice. But modulating her voice is beyond Ketaki's actorly capacities. Perhaps that is why she gets only bit parts in over-the-top comedies where everyone is expected to shout in order to be funny.

Once, only once, was Ketaki offered a lead role, and she played it with gusto. We had finished college, and all of us had started on our various careers as bank clerks and primary schoolteachers and hospital counsellors. I was working towards my master's in German, and Ketaki had landed her first bit role on the stage. This was the late eighties. The mills had shut down one by one. Mill workers had lost their livelihood. Their sons were all over the place, some depressed and drinking, some skilling themselves as welders and joiners, some working in malls and some taking to crime. Kashiram Gawande, famous for writing and directing plays when the mills were thriving and millworkers had a strong cultural tradition going, decided that theatre would give these lost young men an identity and some hope for the future. He wrote a play for them which he planned to enter for the state drama competition. Back in the glory days of the mills, if women couldn't be found to play female characters, young boys played them. Gawande's boys, being modern, refused to audition for female roles. The play was about Shivaji and only one actress was required to play Saibai, Shivaji's eldest and most beloved wife. Desperate to find her, Gawande scoured the middle-class mainstream stage and found Ketaki. She was not only fair-skinned but had plenty of time on hand for rehearsals.

Our school gang of four K's—the fifth being on stage—went to see the grand rehearsal of the play at Damodar Hall in Parel. What a prize ham Ketaki turned out to be. Nobody said so, of course. You can't say you are a prize ham to a school benchmate. Particularly not to Ketaki, who lost her mother when she was three. So, I was deputed to say something vague like, you looked smashing in those gorgeous nine-yard saris, or, take it from us, the play is going to win the first prize. But I thought we owed Ketaki something more complimentary about her acting. So, I said, 'Well, well! Hidden talents and all, hunh?' Standing beside me, Kaveri, Kasturi and Kirti nodded till their heads almost fell off.

Why have I spoken at such length about Ketaki's acting? Because it has a bearing on the present story. Actresses take other people's lines and make them their own. That is what they are trained to do. When they declaim the playwright's lines and manage to sound like the words are theirs, the thoughts are theirs and the feelings are theirs, they are applauded for 'getting into the skin of' or 'actually becoming' the character. When Ketaki steals my stories, she is using her actorly skills to make them her own and to retell them with such conviction that listeners believe the words are hers, the thoughts are hers and the feelings are hers.

I think it is time I clarified what I mean by stories. I don't mean once-upon-a-time type fictions. Mine are yarns spun from snatches of overheard conversations or things that I have seen or experienced. In short, something small made big with colour and spice. I told stories all through school, and Ketaki stole them all through school. Nobody ever challenged her. Nobody ever said: 'But didn't Kinnari tell us something like that last week?' People don't. Nobody told the emperor he wasn't wearing clothes. A little kid did and probably got boxed on the ear for it. Moreover, Ketaki's mother had died when she was three.

Perhaps an example of how she stole my stories may be pertinent at this point. I once told the girls a story of which I will relate only the bare bones here. We were in the ninth class and had a massive crush on Mrs Nadkar, the French teacher. She was slim, had alabaster skin, jet-black, wavy hair and big eyes. We were always looking for excuses to waylay her in the corridor or go to the staff room with 'difficulties'. One day, I went during lunch break, pretending to find the pluperfect tense confusing. I knew how it was formed, of course—add the past participle of the main verb to the imperfect tense of the auxiliary verb, and voila, there you had it! The idea was not to have the tense explained, but to sit close to Mrs Nadkar and watch her lips form a *moue* around *plus* each time she said *plus-que-parfait*. 'Come in,' she said when I knocked, and, thrill of thrills, she was alone in the room. She was standing by the matka. '*Assieds-toi, s'il te plaît*, Kinnari,' she said. 'I'll be with you in a moment.' She turned around and bent low to draw herself a glass of water. Then, even as I sat admiring the perfect curves of her bum under the stretch of her sari, she ... oh dear ... how do I put it ... after all these years I still ... she ... well ... broke wind. I was so embarrassed for her that I wanted to get up and scoot. In fact, I was in the act of rising from my chair, when she straightened up. Turning around, she looked straight at me and said with a half-smile, 'Too much bean curry at lunch.' Cool as cool can be, she spent the next ten minutes explaining the *plus-que-parfait* tense to me. But all I heard was a long-drawn-out piping sound that seemed to have lodged in my ears as an aural keepsake.

'Is it clear now?' she asked.

'Oh, yes, miss. Very clear. Thank you so much,' I said, my ears going *peeeee* non-stop as I fled from the room.

There was total silence when I finished telling the girls this story.

Ketaki broke the spell. 'It was something else. A bird,' she said.

'No. It was her,' I replied sadly.

'How can you be so sure?' Kaveri asked.

'Because there was nobody else in the room, and it came from where she was bending,' I said, sadly again.

Another silence followed, during which Kasturi let out a long, quivering sigh, and five young hearts plummeted to the earth's womb.

'I guess she's only human,' I said at last. The others nodded, not one bit consoled.

That was the end of our crush on Mrs Nadkar. But not the end of the story. The story was repurposed a decade later to serve a leading lady right for having told Ketaki that she sounded like a megaphone. The location was the green room, where the leading lady was touching up her makeup between acts. Present in the room were the makeup man, the costume girl and Ketaki. The leading lady dropped her lipstick accidentally and bent to pick it up. It rolled away. She bent further to get it. The extra pressure on the abdomen sent a long unscripted rumble of wind through her alimentary canal, ending in an explosive thunderclap.

'The makeup man and the costume girl rushed out of the room to laugh,' Ketaki chortled. 'I stood watching the great lady's futile attempts at covering up the sound with a fluster of fabricated noise. "You know what?" I said to her with deep sympathy. "What is done is done. What is heard is heard. But I promise not to tell." With that, I walked out straight into a gale of laughter. The actors and crew now wanted to hear the details. But I was in saint mode. "Why do you laugh?" I said. "She's only human."'

Having delivered my punchline with elan, Ketaki tossed her head and bellowed with laughter.

Itsy-bitsy stories like these are for general consumption. The real ones, the ones with imaginary people and events, I reserve for myself. When I'm spinning one of these in my mind, people ask me why I am smiling. Am I? I ask back. Don't be mysterious, they retort. Me, mysterious? A mysterious woman wears slinky purple dresses and gold eyeshadow, and paints fish tails by the corners of her eyes. I am in saris all day and every season, on account of which the vegetable-sellers in the wholesale market down the bridge from Plaza Cinema call me Auntie. I'm okay with that. No, really. Except that they call Aai Auntie, too.

Incidentally, Aai has serious objections to my 'fad', as she calls it, of telling myself stories. What are these stories? Why can't you tell them to me? Or write them down like sensible people do? Publish a collection. It will add a shine to your name.

How do I explain to her that stories are gossamer things. Words pin them down like butterflies on a display board. Like butterflies, they keep the same shape and colour forever, they don't shape-shift as they do in my mind. Aai isn't interested in all this. She is busy leading up to a hoary fear. If I go around smiling to myself because I'm telling myself stories, how do I think my in-laws will react? And more importantly, my poor husband? I don't answer. Merely smile. I have stopped reminding her that I am thirty-five and single by choice precisely because I want freedom to tell myself stories and smile when I so wish. But Aai is not done yet. She is still harping about my life: 'Now, if you wrote down your stories and brought out a collection, your in-laws would have something to be proud of ...'

Frankly, I don't like the word 'collection'. It reminds me, yet again, of pinned butterflies. I recall buying a collection once from Jaico—Jaico, the bookshop, near Rhythm House, the music shop. Oh ok. What I mean is, Jaico, the bookshop, which used to be next to where Rhythm House, the music shop, used to be, across the road from Jehangir Art Gallery. You've heard of that? Seen it even? Yes, that is where the festival happens. Why is it called the Kala Ghoda Festival? Because King Edward VII (VIII? VI?) used to sit on a black horse there. No, not the real king. The statue king. On a statue horse. Where have they gone? I don't know. Why should I know everything about everything just because I tell stories? Queen Victoria is somewhere in Jijamata Udyaan. So, I suppose, Edward and his horse are there, too—him being her son.

Wait. Now I've lost the link. How did I get to British royalty? Oh, yes, Jaico and the Kala Ghoda Festival and ... well, anyway,

I bought this collection of stories because everybody was reading it and raving about it, and I am emphatically everybody and was looking forward to reading and raving about it, too. By the way, there is an enormous advantage to being everybody. People don't notice you in a crowd. Forget crowd. People don't notice you in a room. Forget room. People don't notice you one-on-one. They look at the space behind you, wondering if that's where your voice is coming from. Being everybody is the best thing for a storyteller. You're the fly on the wall. But you know what, being everybody is not always being everybody. Take this collection, for instance. I opened it the moment I settled down in the bus; and despite being everybody, I could not read beyond page three. At page three, I yawned. It was, if I remember right, a wide, lengthy, noiseless yawn, a strong indication of boredom. The story was about a company executive who battered his wife on a regular basis. The blurb praised the author for the delicacy of observation she brought to human relationships. What delicacy? My father hammered Aai every payday because he'd drink up half his salary and didn't want to feel guilty about it. When he died, Aai cried like she had the Arabian Sea in her lacrimal sacs. Now, explain the delicacy here. In my grandmother's chawl, when you heard a woman scream, you knew her husband was kicking her around like a football. When the screaming stopped, you knew she was serving dinner to the footballer-husband and the children. Delicacy of observation, my foot. I yawned again and slid the collection into my handbag.

But I have another story about a story collection that you might find amusing. It's a short one. You know Yashwant Dubey, our minister of culture. I don't mean know-know. I mean you've seen his pictures in the papers. Round chubby face, handlebar moustache. Looks a bit like Bade Ghulam Ali Khan in his later years. Apparently, Dubeyji spent his childhood in Mumbai. It was Bombay then. He says he has fond memories of eating bhelpuri at Juhu. Naturally, he was keen to have his fifth collection of poetry, inspired by Marine Drive and Chowpatty and Juhu, released in this city. For some reason, he writes in English, but never mind that. Dubeyji announced that he was going to have what he called a modest get-together for the launch of the book, and the city's most famous poet, the Jnanpith award-winner Bhau Bhalerao, would 'do the honours'. The news was in all the papers. Now, you know what Bhau is like. You don't? Well, you will.

My brother Dinkar Rangnekar—yes, I'm a Saraswat, if you must know, and I'm not asking you why you must know—is a journalist of renown. You wouldn't know? Ah, you don't read newspapers? Of course, you don't. You get all the news on WhatsApp. Well, then, you'll just have to take my word for it. My brother is a well-regarded journalist. He had an invitation for two for the book launch. His wife couldn't make it, so I went along. It was a huge, opulently modest do, with a great variety of snacks and pastries and dips and sandwiches flying around. No alcohol, of course, but fresh watermelon juice and something called a Kiwi Float. In the middle of the eating and the drinking, Dubeyji stood up very modestly and very humbly requested Bhau to honour him by releasing the book. Bhau uncoiled his legs and stood up, slipping his hip flask into his waistcoat pocket. Dubeyji averted his eyes tactfully, then waited for Bhau to join him. Bhau didn't budge. So Dubeyji gestured majestically for the wrapped and ribboned book to be carried to where Bhau stood. He himself, laughing modestly all the while, joined Bhau, saying, 'There are times when Mahomet must go to the mountain,' and made as if to slap Bhau on the back. But Bhau stepped aside, forcing Dubeyji to shove his floating hand into his trouser pocket. Bhau undid the red ribbon around the gold wrapper, tore open the wrapper and looked curiously at the title of the book.

The photographers waited.

'*Lost Horizon*,' Bhau intoned. 'Intriguing,' he added, as he turned the pages. Then, unbidden, he began to read out the first poem.

The photographers waited.

The poem was about sea sounds. After a few lines, Bhau looked up, said, 'And so on.' He closed the book.

'Thank you so very much,' said Dubeyji, doubled up with modesty. 'To hear my poem in your august voice is ... oh, I can't describe it ...'

'An unbelievable honour?' Bhau prompted.

'You have taken the words out of my mouth,' said Dubeyji. 'Please read the full poem if you will be so kind. It is my favourite.'

'Certainly,' said Bhau obligingly and read on.

The photographers waited.

When I got home, I memorized the last lines of the poem from the copy Dinkar bought, for future narrations of the story. This is how they went:

From the conch at my ear
A blessing did I hear
There is your destiny
That horizon is for thee
Stretch your hand that far
Oh, young boy from Bihar
You weep sad tears today
Salt in the salt of the Bay
But have faith and you will see
The dawn of a radiant destiny.

Dubeyji had sobbed into his handkerchief when Bhau had finished reading the poem. People had murmured, 'What a moving poem. So poetic.'

The photographers had waited.

Looking up at the gathering, Bhau had said, 'It is not often that we hear verse like this. I wish Dubeyji the very best for his future writing journey. Five collections of poetry are no mean achievement. I have only three to my name. With such a track record as his, I feel confident that one of these days our illustrious minister may even write a poem.'

The audience nodded vigorously and clapped hard. Dubeyji took both of Bhau's hands in his, lifted them to his closed eyes and said, 'I will, I will. With your blessing, sir, I will.' Then he plucked the book smartly out of Bhau's hands, turned it around to face the audience and planted it back. The photographers sprang to their task. Keeping a firm hand on the book, Dubeyji grinned at all the waiting camera lenses, and only then did he let go of Bhau's hands.

I remember the day I told Ketaki this story. We had just finished our final BA exams, she with psychology and I with German. We sat in the balcony, looking at the church, its conical domes washed with the late afternoon sunlight. The warm sweet smell of puran polis came wafting out to us from the kitchen, where Aai was rolling them faster than a machine. She had an order for a hundred to be delivered by the evening to some place in Prabhadevi for somebody's engagement. I was the delivery girl, and Ketaki, who had nothing else to do, was coming with me. Even as I told her the story, trudging to Prabhadevi, I had a feeling she was not getting the point. My suspicion was confirmed when the story came back to me a year later.

'I must tell you what happened yesterday,' Ketaki began excitedly. 'You know our education minister, Shrikant Pandey.'

I sighed.

'So, I was at this party held to launch his poetry collection ...'

Her director—being Pandeyji's cousin—had been invited and took her along. Amitabh Bachchan launched the book, read out a poem and said, '*Wah! Kya baat hai!*' People wept to hear him read. Then Amitabh made a speech about the infinite richness of nature. 'Pandeyji has written about the sea,' he said. 'One day, he will write about the hills, the trees, the birds and the clouds.'

Ketaki turned to me, and her voice did the impossible. It dropped to a worshipful whisper. 'The icing on the cake, Kinnari, the icing on the cake! Amitabh recited his father's poem ... something about clouds ...'

'*Aaj Mujhse Bol Baadal*?'

'That's the one. After the recitation he said ... you must hear this Kinnari ... it's a line I will never forget ... he said, "Nature is infinite. Nature is god incarnate."'

Ketaki looked at me with wide open, expectant eyes. I did my moved-by-emotion look. But I was saddened. She had done my story a great injustice. Where was the irony in her retelling?

Ketaki lacks subtlety. Take this example. We had been for a walk along Dadar beach. We had had bhelpuri. Our Dadar bhelwalas were once the best. Where are they now? When the state road development people started reclaiming the land at Bandra for the Sea Link, the sea got pushed up our beach till there wasn't enough sand left for half a bhelpuri cart to stand on. Anyway, going past Narli Baug on our way home, we saw a woman with a rag wrapped around her waist, bare boobs drooping, face cobwebbed with lines, sitting under a coconut tree, muttering to herself.

'That tree will fall,' I said.

'Why?' asked Ketaki and Kirti in one voice. 'There's no wind.'

'It will fall because of the story she is telling it.'

Ketaki and Kaveri looked mystified. So, I told them the story about the old woman who was ill-treated by her sons and their wives. With nobody to pour her woes out to, they accumulated in her stomach, making it bloat till it was near to bursting. Utterly miserable, she walked out of the hut one day, when her sons and their wives were away, and kept walking until she reached the forest. There, she spotted a ruined, roofless cottage. Exhausted, she stumbled into it and collapsed against a wall. Looking up at the blue sky, she began to talk about her suffering. Her voice grew louder as her story surged out in wave upon wave of pain. When the walls heard the story, they collapsed one by one. And as they collapsed, her stomach contracted till it got back to its original size. The cottage was now all rubble. She sat in the midst of the rubble, amazed at how light she felt. The sun was dipping westwards. It would soon be dark. So, she struggled up and began her long walk home.

'Back home? To that hell?' Kirti asked.

'I don't see the point of the story,' Ketaki said.

'No?' I asked.

'No,' she boomed. And that was that.

But not quite. A few days later, she said, 'Why did you say the coconut tree in Narli Baug would fall?'

'Because the walls in the folktale fell.'

'Why did the walls in the folktale fall?'

'Because they found the old woman's story unbearably painful. The author seems to suggest that stones are more human than human beings like the old woman's sons. The moral is implied, not spelt out. You are free to interpret the story as you like. That's the beauty of folktales.'

Ketaki looked doubtful and said a dismissive 'hrrmph'.

More than a little annoyed, I suggested we change the subject.

'Sure,' she said enthusiastically. 'Actually, I've been waiting to tell you what happened last week. But let me get us some tea first.'

Coming back, she took her seat, tossed her head and settled into storytelling mode. 'It was sensational,' she began. 'Just shows what fools even educated women can be.'

I tried looking interested, though I was still bugged by her 'hrrmph'.

'There was this woman sitting next to me in the train, fancily dressed in a salwar-kameez outfit, with a lot of bling, smelling of sandalwood, if you please. Not one of the train regulars. Plump, wheat-coloured, curly hair. After a while—I think we must have just passed Mumbai Central—she opened her handbag and took out her mobile. She dialled a number and said excitedly, 'It's true, darling. We've got the tickets. They're here, in my handbag. No, there is no catch. You're so suspicious ...'

I groaned inwardly. I knew how the story was going to proceed. Although the concerned woman—whom my colleague, Netra and I had met at the bus stop—had straight hair and was dressed in pants and a top, she had also called someone on her mobile phone and told him that she had the tickets in her handbag and that there was no catch. Then, she had said, 'What? What do you mean we can't go? Oh no ... can't you tell them not to come ... put them off for just four days ... imagine, four days in Goa ... and I went through so much trouble buying that stuff first, then going to the place by cab ... flog them? Who to? I know my colleagues would be only too happy to pay a measly 500 rupees for a trip for two to Goa, but how do you think I would look asking? Like I can't afford to let 500 rupees go down the drain? They're my colleagues, yaar. Anyway, I'm on my way home. We can at least gaze on the tickets before we tear them up.'

'At that point,' Ketaki said, her face aglow with the sensational line that was coming, 'Rashmi, who gets off at Lower Parel, said to the woman, "Excuse me, but I overheard your conversation ... when is this trip to Goa? If the dates suit us, my husband and I would love to go." The woman with the curly hair looked embarrassed, so Rashmi said, "No, no, not for free. I'll pay you 500." To which, the woman said, "My husband thinks it was 500. But it was actually 2,000. When I got to the shop that announced the scheme, they said that I would have to become a member first, and the membership cost 1,500. I didn't tell my husband because he's a big kanjoos. But personally, I thought even 2,000 was nothing for four days in a three-star hotel in Goa." Rashmi agreed that it was nothing and promptly parted with 2,000 rupees. When I met her the next day on the train, her face was all squeezed up like a squirrel's. What happened, I asked. And guess what she said ...'

I didn't have to guess. I knew.

'When she looked at the tickets in the morning, there was nothing on them. No word, no number. Innocent of all print. Blank as a dead man's face.'

The last line was a straight lift. I was now expected to gasp and make a horrified face. But I had still not forgotten her 'hrrmph'. So, I simply shrugged and said, 'People can be so gullible.' My response offended her deeply. Her reproachful look and the clatter with which she cleared the tea things made that quite obvious. But, come on. There's only so much you can do to contribute to a friend's happiness. Even one who lost her mother when she was three.

Nurse Shanti

TEJASWINI APTE-RAHM

I

On the first day of her new job, Nurse Shanti wrapped a white sari around herself and donned a nurse's cap. She drove stiff black bobby pins around the edges of the cap, scraping her scalp but taking care not to break any hairs. She wore sturdy black shoes over white socks, picked up her small suitcase and left her quarters without a glance back.

'Do you want to check the inventory?' she asked the warden downstairs.

'Not unless you've managed to pack the bed and cupboard into your suitcase,' the woman replied.

Nurse Shanti pretended to smile.

'Where are you going?' asked the woman, curious. 'What happened at the nursing home?'

'I'm joining private service,' said Shanti, half answering the first question and choosing to ignore the second.

'You'll come back,' said the warden. 'Where's the security in private?'

'I don't want security,' said Shanti. 'I want money.'

The warden gave a raucous laugh, and her small eyes grew keen, calculating the young nurse as if she were a column of numbers.

Two bus changes later, Shanti stood in front of her new employer's building near Shivaji Park. It was two storeys high. It faced a small and noisy traffic circle, on a road lined with cramped shops and low residential buildings. On the ground floor was a board painted in multicoloured letters: 'Tiny Treasures Day Care'. The place will be deserted at night, she thought. She climbed the old, dimly-lit wooden staircase. On the first floor she passed two doors—one with a cobwebbed padlock hanging from a rusty latch; the other displaying a bright red nameplate that said, 'Sushil & Sandy', above a peacock blue door mat.

There was only one apartment on the second floor and the nameplate was broken in a jagged slant, so the initials were missing. She could only make out the surname: 'Maneckshaw'. Nurse Shanti pressed the bell and heard a short, muffled ring. A well-dressed woman in trousers opened the door. She wore a small dangling pearl on each ear, and her grey hair was like a perfect wiry helmet.

'Hello, ma'am, I am Nurse Shanti.'

'Yes, come in,' said the woman, appraising Nurse Shanti's appearance with a stare. There was nothing to disapprove of, Shanti knew, and so she stepped confidently through the door into a small corridor. 'Feroze uncle is in the living room. I'm Mrs Presswala.'

'Yes, ma'am,' said Nurse Shanti. Mrs Presswala seemed to relax at this demure answer and took in a small breath that she held in her lungs for a second before exhaling. 'Feroze uncle is my husband's uncle. I will stay here with you for two days, so that you know everything. After that, I will have to join my husband in Delhi, I can't stay any longer,' she said, shaking her head as if to blame Nurse Shanti and other people for unreasonably trying to detain her. 'Here he is.'

Nurse Shanti looked in at the door to a spacious living room. It was so large that it needed two sofa sets to fill it, one at this end of the room, one at the other end. On a chair sat Maneckshaw, a frail man with shoulders that hunched a little, dressed in a crisp cream shirt and brown trousers that had turned baggy on his frame. His thin, grey hair was brushed straight back over his scalp. He wore a striped tie and his walking stick stood upright between his knees. He was the picture of neatness. There was a benign expression in his eyes and a half-smile on his lips.

Mrs Presswala bent over him and said in a loud, slow voice, 'Feroze uncle, this is your new nurse … okay?'

Maneckshaw nodded and turned his head slightly to look at Nurse Shanti in a sidelong, upward glance. Then he looked at his nephew's wife and said in a quiet, rasping voice, 'I'm not deaf, my dear.'

Mrs Presswala appeared not to hear. 'He forgets everything,' she said to Nurse Shanti. 'You'll have to keep reminding him of your name.'

She then led the way out of the living room. She showed Nurse Shanti the kitchen and the two bedrooms with attached bathrooms. One bedroom was strewn with Mrs Presswala's clothes and bits of silver jewellery on the dressing table. The other was a large, sparse chamber containing a low bed with a thin white pillow, and a bottle of water on a bedside table.

Shanti's bed was in a small, box-like room.

Maneckshaw's tremulous voice called out from the living room. Mrs Presswala sighed and hurried there, trailed by Shanti.

'I seem to have misplaced my pistol, my dear,' said Maneckshaw, blinking up at her. 'Have you taken it?'

Mrs Presswala spoke in the slow, scolding voice apparently reserved for him. 'Uncle, you said that yesterday, and I told you I found it.'

'Where is it? I want to see it,' he insisted.

'Don't worry, it's safe. I've put it away,' she said, with barely restrained impatience.

Maneckshaw shook his head, looking argumentative, but Mrs Presswala had already turned away. Seeing Shanti's wide-eyed expression, she rolled her eyes, saying in a low voice, 'He keeps saying he's lost his pistol. He was in the army. Some memory stuck in his head, god knows what. I've never seen a pistol here.'

Mrs Presswala now launched into a catalogue of instructions and explanations. She was precise, like a teacher scratching out orders on a blackboard with a stick of chalk. 'There is a woman who comes twice a week to sweep and to wash the clothes. A tiffin will come every day from Wadia Home Care. The bill is pre-paid. Feroze uncle eats only once a day, at lunch time. If he goes to the club in the evening, he has a toast and coffee there. If you need to call the doctor or anyone else, here are the numbers.' Mrs Presswala produced a small handwritten sheet of numbers. 'My number in Delhi is there. And please ... no using the phone for your personal calls. The last nurse ran up a huge bill calling god-alone-knows-who. There is also the number of Feroze uncle's son who lives in America.' She opened a cabinet to reveal an array of syrup bottles and capsule strips. 'Here are the medicines. Go to Dr Dastur's clinic once a month to get more—this is the address—and there is no need to pay for them, the bill will be settled directly. He will also give you your salary.'

Clearly, the previous nurse had fiddled more than the phone bill, hence this cast-iron system of the giving and spending of money. Certainly, there was not much scope here for fiddling.

In two days' time, Mrs Presswala swept out of the apartment and left for the airport in a taxi, and Nurse Shanti's private service began in earnest. She found that Maneckshaw was used to a rigid schedule that consisted primarily of sleeping. His bedroom opened onto a long balcony, open to the sky and lined with withered potted plants. Every morning, he woke at 6 a.m. and hobbled up and down this balcony in his yellow shorts for ten minutes, on thin liver-spotted legs. Nurse Shanti then gave him tea and a digestive biscuit, after which he slept till 10 a.m. Afterwards, he had a slow and tottering shower, leaving the door slightly ajar while she waited outside for him. By 11 a.m., he was dressed in a newly washed set of loose white pyjamas and read the newspaper till it was time for lunch. He lunched in front of the television in the living room, eating his bread and cutlet or fried fish and rice on a tray covered with a white napkin and correctly laid out cutlery. If Nurse Shanti set the fork and knife the wrong way around, he would move the fork to the left and lay the knife on the right and look at the new arrangement for a moment, before picking up the cutlery again and commencing his lunch. After lunch, he slept till 4 p.m., when it was time to go to the club, for which a set of freshly ironed clothes—shirt, trouser and tie—was required. The club was a short taxi ride away.

Every day he demanded, in his frail, reedy voice, to know where his pistol was, speaking to Shanti in a mixture of English and broken Hindi. 'I had it before Mrs Presswala came,' he would frown. 'She must have hidden it somewhere.' To quieten him down, Shanti would make a show of rummaging through his wardrobe, bending over to look into the lower shelves, stretching up to slap her palm noisily on the things on the top shelf. The only item of interest she saw was Maneckshaw's old army uniform, neatly folded in a sturdy wooden chest at the foot of his bed, amid sheets and old saris, presumably his wife's.

'Nothing, sir,' she would say, shaking her head in disappointment, as if she'd fully expected to find the pistol. This little charade usually took place as he dressed for the club after his nap. Once they set off in a taxi, with the salty sea breeze washing over them, he forgot all about it.

The club was a small, red-roofed building, consisting of a lawn scattered with cane chairs and tables, a table-tennis room with peeling wall paint, a musty library-cum-card room and a cavernous badminton court under renovation. Waiters in faded uniforms didn't bother asking Maneckshaw what he wanted but simply brought him his toast and coffee. He sat with a group of old men on the lawn, with Nurse Shanti sitting on a chair behind him, helping to pour out the coffee and butter the toast, and handing him a tablet that had to be taken at exactly 6 p.m. every day. He would sign a faint, shaky signature on the bill and busy himself talking with the circle of seven or eight elderly men in Parsi–Gujarati, with a smattering of English. Shanti understood a good amount of English thanks to the nuns who had educated her. She did not understand a word of Parsi–Gujarati but gathered that several of the men could not hear very well. Maneckshaw could hear perfectly but often did not bother to repeat himself when someone said, 'Hm?' or leaned in towards him. They sat there every evening, on the green grass, watching each other and their coffee cups, apparently content. They looked like a circle of fragile, hook-nosed birds with curved backs and cloudy eyes, a creeping layer of white ceramic slowly coating their pupils. As if in uniform, they dressed in subdued cottons—light lemon trousers, pastel polo shirts. The wives of the old men stayed in the card room, emerging only at the end of the evening to collect their men and go home.

By 8 p.m. every night, Maneckshaw was in bed, watching the evening news, sometimes with a small shot of rum by his side, but in ten minutes he was inevitably asleep, and Nurse Shanti would turn off the television and the lights. She then prepared and ate her dinner. By 9 p.m. she had nothing whatsoever to do.

After 9 p.m., she thought. She raked over her past, and felt the fat, ugly welts on her calves. She thought about the uncle who wanted her to get on a bus with a man who had bought him a glass of tea earlier that day; the aunt who hit her calves with a ladle still hot from the frying pan when she had refused to go with the man; the terror-filled bus journey to Mumbai when she ran away, after her younger sister disappeared overnight; and, above all, the comfort of feeling the stolid bundle of money, stolen from her uncle, in the purse on her lap all through the long drive. Maneckshaw's clean and quiet flat had the peculiar effect of making her feel that she simply wanted to lie down and sleep. As if, after the years of constant moving and struggling, the bribes given and taken, the men who had tried—one, successfully—to force themselves on her, her tired self had found a place where it could rest.

But there was no time to rest. She thought, now, about what she could extract from the situation in which she found herself. Her aim was to go to Dubai—an expensive proposition according to the agent who would arrange her passport, visa and nursing job. It would take a long time to save that kind of cash. How much for Germany, she'd asked. He gave her an appraising glance and said, 'Too much. For you, Dubai or Abu Dhabi.'

There had been a few offers to give herself to men in order to gain favours; to the man who sold her the nursing diploma, for instance, or to the agent who got her the nursing home job. But she was not prepared to give. She only meant to take. She considered various petty options as a starting point towards bigger plans: moonlighting elsewhere for a few hours every day and leaving the old man locked up while he was asleep; or slowly selling off some of the items in the flat.

But something far better happened before she could put any of these tentative ideas into motion.

One night, she loitered by the gate of the building, staring into the city. The sky was black, the pavement was black, and sandwiched between the two was dim white streetlight which made every face appear grey. The road had started emptying out, but the wider clamour of the city rumbled on in the sky, dotted with starbursts of beeps and honks. Bored, she barely noticed the dwindling passers-by or the young men leaning on parked cars and smoking, one occasionally revving his motorbike and driving off with a roar. A plump middle-aged woman approached the gate. She wore a cheap nylon sari with a dirty green print, tucked in high at her waist as if to keep the hem from soiling. Her oiled black hair was pulled into an untidy bun.

She dawdled nearby for a moment, and then moved towards Shanti.

'I've been watching you. You seem okay.' She stared at Shanti through eyes that were as black and stony as the pavement. There was a small gold stud on the side of her wide nose. She spoke as if paying Shanti a compliment. 'Want to make some extra money?'

Shanti frowned and turned to retreat into the building, but stopped when the woman said, 'Before you, there was Nurse Julie. We know all about the old man. Your job is just to keep a small parcel for me now and then. He will never know.'

'What kind of parcel?' said Shanti, making no attempt at hiding her suspicion of the woman.

'A small one. Don't try to look inside. I will come and collect it after one day or three days or a week.'

An admirably simple idea, using a decrepit old man's flat as a half-way house for illicit goods. It seemed an easy enough thing to do. 'How much are you paying?'

'A daily rate for each day you keep the parcel,' said the woman, smirking at the look on Shanti's face when she named the amount. 'Work well and better things can come your way.'

'But you can't come up,' said Shanti. 'There are people on the first floor, they will see you.'

'I know about that couple,' said the woman. 'They are as harmless as corncobs. That boy works in a news channel, comes on TV, but doesn't know what is happening under his nose. And that mem of his comes back at all kinds of timings, comes home with strange men. Forget about them. Now, when I want to meet you, I will tie a cloth to that railing there.' She pointed to a litter-filled corner of the road with an old railing that ran behind two municipal rubbish bins. 'The cloth means that I will come the same night or the next night, at 11 o'clock. To give or collect a parcel.'

'Why not just give me a missed call?' said Shanti.

'No phones, no numbers,' said the woman. 'And you can call me Auntieji.'

Shanti considered this for a moment. Her heart had started beating fast. Who was this woman?

'Nurse Julie used to stand at the balcony every day, looking for the cloth.' The woman's brown lips parted in a paan-stained smile. 'Every day. Combing her long black hair.'

'What happened to Julie?' said Shanti, suddenly curious about the nurse who had looked after Maneckshaw before she arrived.

The woman shrugged, staring hard at Shanti. 'She left.'

'Listen,' said Shanti, nervously, the full weight of embarking on this new path suddenly descending on her. 'Don't try coming before eleven at night. Nothing before eleven.'

'I know,' said the woman. She waddled off slowly, as if her knees hurt, but tossed a few more words over her shoulder.

'Don't bother telling me anything, white-sari-girl. I already know everything.' The words were meant to put Shanti in her place, but they were not unfriendly words either.

Shanti felt as if Julie was not a person but an institution she had entered. Where was Julie now? In Dubai? In Singapore?

She thought long and hard about the woman called Auntieji, lying on her bed in her bare room, gazing through her window at the back of a building where water dripped from furry air conditioning units. They looked like small, black cages. She felt she ought to be afraid of the woman—she had emerged from the bowels of the city, knew the workings of its inner labyrinthine lanes. Shanti felt as if she was wandering on the edges of a dark space. As if the city itself, oblivious in its dome of bright lights, was teetering at the edge of the dark sea.

But in Maneckshaw's apartment, she felt safe. As long as she operated out of here, and interacted only with that woman, she would be alright. And she could always stop the arrangement if it didn't suit her.

The more Shanti thought about it, the more brazen she felt, ready to take on anything. If she stepped off the roof of this building, she would fly. Straight to Dubai. Straight to the city of dirhams and wide, clean roads and glittering open-top cars and rich families who would pay more for a nurse than she could dream of earning in Mumbai. She'd heard that in Dubai people ate dates and pistachios as casually as she snacked on glucose biscuits here.

As the days went by, Auntieji's parcels appeared and disappeared at a steady rate, no larger than a small bundle of books, always wrapped in a plastic bag, heavily sealed with broad black strips of tape. Only once was there a large, heavy cardboard box. She assumed the parcels contained pieces of stolen jewellery or cash. Perhaps a gun or some drugs. She didn't care. She was anonymous, safe, a demure woman in white, a nurse's cap pinned to her hair. Soon she would have enough money to disappear like Julie.

The name Julie sounded like a heroine's, in a film. Julie with long, black hair. She'd cared for Maneckshaw, slept in Shanti's bed, run up a huge bill making dozens of calls to someone—was it a lover? Shanti imagined him to be a steward or chef in a big hotel somewhere, bringing Julie all the things not served to the people in diamond earrings and gold watches: a box of pulao, pieces of chicken from the tandoor, creamy cakes decorated with fruit. Perhaps they had left together—the lover and the clever nurse—to build a life.

Under her mattress, Shanti found a large, zippered pouch decorated with a pattern of pink and white flowers. That must have been where Julie kept her salary and the earnings received from Auntieji. Shanti decided to use it for the same purpose. But she hid it under Maneckshaw's mattress. She could think of no safer place. It was easy to quickly lift up the mattress and add some money to the pouch while he was having a shower.

She took great care of Maneckshaw. She needed him alive and well for the moment, though in truth she did not see him dying any time soon—he was like a dried fruit, withered but stubbornly alive in its own somnolent fashion. When the wad of notes under the mattress started building up to a good sum, Shanti messaged the agent. She would need to pay an advance, he said, there were good openings coming up. She didn't have enough yet, she told him, but she would, soon.

Initially, Maneckshaw barely noticed her. Apparently, she was simply two hands and two legs that heated up his tiffin, opened the door for the sweeper, took in the newspaper, laid out a daily array of coloured pills and escorted him to the club. He had a small bookcase filled with hardbound books that looked decades old. Occasionally she would pull one out to hand to him, but it was usually too heavy for the old man to hold for long. The contents appeared as dusty and weary to her as the books themselves, with names like *Maratha Battles in the 18th Century*, *The Heroic War: 1965*, *A General for All Times*, and so on. He refused to use his mobile phone, becoming increasingly irritated when he tried to decipher the screen or jab at it with his finger. It usually lay with its battery discharged. 'Anyone who wants to talk to me can use the bloody landline,' he said once, when Mrs Presswala called to complain about it. Nobody really phoned anyway, apart from his son who called on the landline every few weeks.

Maneckshaw was usually silent, making little effort at eye-contact with Shanti, simply acquiescing to the fact of a new nurse. His mind seemed to be directed inwards, his eyes taking in mainly the things immediately related to his person—his hands, his bath towel, the plate he held on his lap. Even the newspaper and the television were simply ways of ignoring the world. The only time of day when he perked up was at the club.

Over time, though, Shanti felt a change coming over him. His eyes began showing a certain pleasure on seeing her first thing in the morning. When something on television amused him, he chuckled and looked at her as she sat on a chair nearby, as if inviting her to share in the joke. He began giving her crotchety scoldings when something wasn't up to his standards. A collar not ironed properly: 'Did you iron this or just sit on it with your behind?' Or once, when she sat at the wrong angle behind his chair at the club, he said, 'You want me to break my neck, looking for you? You think I'm an owl who can turn his bloody head round and round?' His friends had cackled at this, and the conversation moved on to the habits of owls, Shanti forgotten entirely. He made her laugh sometimes at his crusty manner of speaking, and he seemed to enjoy having this effect on her. The corner of his mouth would twitch as she raised a palm to hide her smile and brought out a few words to soothe his peevishness. It was not a feeling she was used to, being liked. She never presumed to overstep her boundaries, would never have dreamed of trying to say something witty to him in return. She ensured that she remained professional, self-contained. And yet, there were moments tinged with a mutual feeling of fellowship, as they passed their days together.

'What are you doing?' asked Maneckshaw one afternoon.

'Nothing, sir,' she said, startled. She was seated on the wooden chest at the foot of his bed, staring out at the balcony while he slept. On the balcony lay lemon-yellow puddles of sunlight, fallen through a grey sky that hung low over the city. 'Just waiting for you to wake up.'

'No, you are not,' he said. 'You are looking at the shapes formed by the sunlight.'

'Yes, sir.'

'Why?'

'No reason, sir.' She smiled as she stood up to fetch his clothes for the club.

'I am not an old fool,' he said. 'There is no reason why you cannot talk to me now and then.'

'No, sir,' said Shanti. 'I like to look at the sun. It reminds me of something.'

'Of what?' he asked, looking at her with a crabby stare.

'I am not sure what it reminds me of,' she said. 'Of something good.'

'I see,' said Maneckshaw. He sat back, leaning on his pillow, not crabby anymore, also staring out at the sunlight on the floor. 'I like it too,' he said. 'It reminds me of something good too.' He raised his head and looked at Shanti. She felt a sudden pity for him, this lonely, shrivelled man, gazing out at the pools of sunshine, the weak curve of his back resting on the white pillow behind him.

Perhaps it was a result of the slow unfolding within her, like a tightly folded capsule of paper unwrapped; or perhaps she had simply been staring at the sun for too long and was in a soporific state of mind; but suddenly she saw an unexpected picture in her mind's eye—she was looking down into Maneckshaw's apartment, as if into a roofless doll's house. She saw the quiet rooms devoid of movement and life, save for two human specks in a corner, close together. They seemed small and abandoned. And nearby, the sun and its shifting shapes of light.

She was kinder to Maneckshaw after that. She did not do anything drastically different, perhaps, but she began to water the plants on the balcony, imagining a life for the plants and for Maneckshaw beyond her own departure. One morning, as he tottered about outside on his stick-legs, he paused before the gnarled bougainvillea and gently touched the white flower at the centre of a newly arrived crimson bloom. A sparrow descended on a branch and sat there, pecking. Maneckshaw looked silently and with knotted brow at this scene of new life on his balcony, and then turned to look at Shanti, who sat on the wooden chest, watching him. He lifted a bony finger to show her the sparrow. The next day, Shanti strewed a few grains on a small stainless steel plate and put it on the floor next to the potted bougainvillea. The sparrow returned to resume its pecking, setting off a small clattering on the stone floor as its tiny bird feet clawed their way over the plate. The bird began to come every morning. After a few days, some pigeons started to descend onto the balcony as well, but Maneckshaw always said, 'Where's that rascal of a sparrow? The pigeons are eating everything.' He would say this even when the sparrow was in plain view in the midst of the pigeons, calmly eating its fill. Maneckshaw had taken to sitting on the wooden chest in the early morning, watching the birds gather around his newly greening plants.

There came an afternoon, many weeks later, when she found her mind at peace. It was as if a game of Patience had been solved and she had simply to wait for the cards to slide into place and reveal four aces on top. She stopped thinking incessantly about the wad of notes building up under Maneckshaw's mattress. When Maneckshaw fell asleep that strange and brilliant afternoon, and the only sound to be heard was the distant knocking of a workman's hammer weaving through the strident staccato call of a bird, she found herself wandering into the vastness of the living room and noticing her own breathing. It was steady, tranquil. She had never noticed her own breathing before. Nor had she noticed how the cool, large-windowed apartment kept out the haze of midday heat and allowed the sea breeze to gently roll through the rooms. She looked at the tall, intricately carved wooden screen that stood near a window. It was a thing of beauty to see the sun glancing through it and laying out delicate mango and cherry patterns on the speckled-cream floor tiles.

A series of rain showers over the next few days prompted some more of the brown plants on the terrace to revive, and she had the leisure to observe a snail gnawing at a newly sprouted leaf. She liked the orderliness of the stainless steel jars rowed in the kitchen filled with tea, coffee, sugar, salt, a few spices. Many had been empty, and she had filled them up slowly with a few pulses and grains for her own use and felt a novelty in being mistress of a kitchen.

She had never lived in such tranquil surroundings. At first, she caught herself panicking when she slipped into a reverie, her heart giving a jolt as if there were things to be done, plans to be made. But slowly, in the silence of the long warm afternoons, the sound of Maneckshaw breathing turned into a kind of meditation. There was so little to do, and yet she felt herself expanding into the crevices and corners of the time available to her, filling her days with rest.

She was sorry that she would be leaving soon. She had almost built up the total she needed to give to the agent. I will remember Maneckshaw when I am in Dubai, she thought. I will think back on this interlude of quiet breath and still mind. Unexpectedly, the foolish thought gripped her that she didn't want to leave after all. A profound reluctance came over her, a reluctance to throw aside the golden carapace of this flat and toil once more among strangers.

II

The rag appeared at the railing after a gap of several days. Shanti sat by the door at eleven that night and waited. When she heard footsteps on the stairs, she opened the door a crack and gave a start—the woman's face was so close to the door that all she could see at first were the black stone-like eyes. From behind her emerged a young man.

'What's this?' said Shanti, angry. She staggered a little, losing her balance as the woman pushed the door open against her.

'The package is a little different tonight,' said the woman, her mouth parted in an apologetic smile.

'This?' said Shanti, pointing to the man.

'Just for a while.'

The young man strolled through the door as if he had a right to do so. A wave of alarm came over Shanti.

'This is not a package,' she said to the woman roughly. 'I cannot keep this boy here.'

'Packages come in all shapes and sizes,' shrugged the woman in an affable tone.

'Are you out of your mind?' Shanti whispered, frightened that Maneckshaw would wake up. 'Tell that fool to stop bumping into the furniture at least!'

The young man was wandering about the living room, examining it, unmindful of the scrapes and creaks the furniture made as he brushed past and pushed it out of the way. A blunderer who is used to nothing but bare rooms and the chaos of the footpaths, she thought with disgust.

'Shanti ... Shanti ...' Maneckshaw's voice floated out faintly.

They all froze. The man stepped back quickly from a coffee table which he had bent down to inspect. Shanti gestured at them to not move or make a sound and walked efficiently to the bedroom. The heels of her sandals echoed through the still flat, unnaturally loud. She found Maneckshaw sitting on the edge of his bed, his feet partially in his slippers. The ceiling light was on.

'Where were you?' he said, his grey eyes looking accusingly at her.

'I thought you were asleep, sir. Toilet, sir?' Her breath came quick and fast. She smiled an odd, wide smile at him, and had the unnerving sensation that her tongue was too wide for her mouth.

Maneckshaw stared at her, confused. She couldn't tell whether he was planning to get out of bed, or get back in. 'Did you already go to the toilet on your own, sir?'

He looked uncertainly at his feet, as if he wasn't quite sure himself. The large old-fashioned alarm clock on his bedside table ticked loudly on.

Beads of perspiration broke out on her upper lip as she thought of the man and woman standing in the living room outside. She had been in here too long.

'I wanted to tell you,' said Maneckshaw in a sleepy voice, 'that I found my pistol.'

For god's sake, not this again, not now, thought Shanti. She bustled forward and began laying him back down, saying, 'Yes sir, very good sir,' struggling to keep her voice soft and soothing.

'It was right there,' continued Maneckshaw, as she drew the sheets over him. 'I'd forgotten it was right there in that drawer …' His voice trailed off as his head came to rest on the soft pillow, and he sighed, closing his eyes.

Shanti switched off the ceiling light for the second time that night and hurried back to the living room. The man and woman looked at her, tense and watchful.

'He's about to fall asleep,' said Shanti. She strode to the main door and yanked it wide open. 'Get out,' she hissed. But the man didn't move.

The woman began sidling towards the door, saying, 'I'll take him off your hands at exactly five in the morning. You'll get a bonus for this. What's that second bedroom used for anyway?'

'I give a damn about your bonus,' began Shanti in anger, but the woman had gone. For a moment Shanti felt a prickling in her heels as if her legs might fly after the woman in panic. Then she shut the door and walked quickly back to the living room. She stood in the doorway watching the young man. It was as if the dark back alleys of the city had snaked their way up into the apartment. She felt light-headed.

He was a nondescript fellow, with oily hair, wearing shabby brown trousers and a loose checked shirt. He had a short nose on a greasy face. He was the kind of man that peopled the streets in their hundreds, a man who could have been anyone, a peon, a waiter, a taxi driver. His face was instantly forgettable. That is why he is dangerous, she thought.

His head lolled to one side as he observed her. Then he looked about him critically and said, 'Why is it so quiet here?' His eyes fell on the TV remote control, and he reached for it, but with quick, strong strides, Shanti advanced and snatched it away. He grinned insolently. He'd never meant to take it. He was toying with her.

This man would think nothing of placing a pillow on Maneckshaw's face to suffocate him, she thought. He looked greedy, cocksure. However, she did not think he would harm her. He thought of her simply as an accomplice, on the same criminal level as him.

'Look,' she told him, 'if you want this arrangement to work, go into that room and go to sleep. Don't come out till the woman returns for you. I will bring you whatever food and water you need.' She made as if to leave the living room, expecting him to follow her.

Instead, he sat down on the plump armchair opposite the television, and hung his leg over its arm, looking at her, sucking in his thin cheeks. His air of menace had gone. He was now merely arrogant. That is the chair in which Maneckshaw has his lunch, Shanti thought, with a surprising sense of indignation on behalf of the old man. It was revolting that Maneckshaw's crisply ironed shirt and trousers would touch the same seat as this filthy goon.

'Do you know what is in the packages this woman leaves with you?' he asked her in an amused voice.

'No,' she said. 'She told me not to open them.'

'And you never opened them.'

'No.'

He began a silent giggle that showed uneven teeth and shook his skinny chest. 'So you're that kind of criminal.'

She said nothing.

'What else is here in this flat?' he said, looking around.

'Nothing. Just an old man who is sleeping.'

'An old man who is sleeping is not nothing. How old is he?'

Shanti remained silent, trying to think of a way to exit this conversation over which she had no control.

'A big secret, his age?'

'Eighty-one. Do you want any food? I'll bring it to the room.'

'Plenty of time for that,' he said, his head falling to one side and then the other as he stretched his neck. 'This is an interesting situation. Here is an old man, with this superb apartment, living all by himself, and too old to enjoy anything of it. Where is his safe?'

'There is no safe. I told you, he is just an old man who sleeps all day. There is nothing here of value.'

'There is the TV.'

'You can't find a safe place to sleep in, and you want to run with a TV. Are you going to carry it on your back like a donkey?'

'Is there a DVD player?' he asked, ignoring her. 'Computer? Music system?'

'No.'

'So,' said the man thoughtfully, getting up and taking a few steps around the room, 'there is just the old man and there are the clothes on his back. I don't believe a fucking word. Does he have children?'

'A son.'

The man stood still for a moment, tense, and asked, 'Where is he?'

'America.'

He burst into uproarious laughing. 'The motherfucker has a son in America, and you say there is nothing of value in the house?'

'Yes, yes, that is what I say, there is nothing of value in this house, okay? Now get into that damn room and stay there till 5 o'clock! Don't make a sound!' Shanti's voice shook with fury, her mind racing over options to defuse the man's manic train of thought.

'Why, are you afraid he might wake up?' he said, in an ugly stage whisper. He walked further into the apartment, towards Maneckshaw's bedroom, looking over his shoulder at Shanti as she followed him, enjoying her helplessness.

He opened the door to Maneckshaw's bedroom very quietly and stepped in. The light from the door illuminated the old man's shape, a small hill covered in blankets. He walked up to the bed and looked down at Maneckshaw who lay on his back. His chin was sprinkled with scraggly white stubble; he was unshaven because he had started a cold and lain in bed for longer than usual this morning. His cheeks sank loosely against his gums. He lay so still, he might have been dead. Shanti watched the young man, her breath quick and shallow, partly from anger and partly from fear that he was too foolish and too greedy to understand that if he harmed Maneckshaw, the arrangement was at an end. He reminded her of an unwieldy winged insect, the kind that whirred about drunkenly with no apparent control of its direction.

'Is he senile or is he all there?' he asked.

'He's not senile,' said Shanti in a low voice. 'He is capable,' she added, 'of calling the police, so be quiet.' By now, she had resigned herself to this man looting all he could find in the apartment.

The man walked to the telephone on the bedside table and yanked the wire out of its socket. He tossed the phone into the laundry basket, on top of the pyjamas Maneckshaw had worn earlier in the day, and strolled back to the foot of the bed to observe the old man.

Maneckshaw woke up at the noise and sat up in bed, switching on the bedside lamp with surprising alacrity. A yellow light fell on the room, as if a yellow moon had risen inside the lampshade. The three stared at each other. Shanti suddenly realized that Maneckshaw did not wear glasses. He did not even wear them for reading or watching television. It was an extraordinary detail that had escaped her, dawning on her now, as he fixed a piercing gaze on the young man. She saw, also, that Maneckshaw's hands were lying limp and relaxed on his blanket, and something about that bothered her. She found herself staring fixedly at his hands.

'Who the hell are you?' said Maneckshaw in a rough, authoritative voice. And then, turning to Shanti, he asked, 'Is this your boyfriend?'

She shook her head, and Maneckshaw turned his attention back to the man.

The man bent over in a mocking manner, his palms joined in a namaskar, his shoulders shaking in a silent snigger. 'Calm down, old man, I'm just having a look around. And I am so sorry, but I am going to take advantage of your hospitality for the night ... thanks to this ... *nurse* of yours.'

'Get out,' said Maneckshaw.

The man's eyes fell on the heavy wooden chest at the foot of the bed, and his expression changed. As if he expected it to hold something of value. His hand went towards its latch.

'Take care, I have a pistol,' said Maneckshaw.

The man stood upright in surprise. 'What?' he said.

'Bang! Bang!' said Maneckshaw, miming a gun with his hand. He pointed two fingers at the man, like a child playing a shooting game. 'Bang-bang!' he said again.

The man stared at Maneckshaw in astonishment and then burst into uncontrolled laughter. Maneckshaw began chuckling too, his eyes crinkling up and a grin spreading across his face. His mind has slipped, thought Shanti in panic. She watched in stunned silence, horrified at Maneckshaw's descent into pathetic spectacle.

The man's high-pitched laugh filled the room as he looked from Shanti to Maneckshaw, wiping the tears from his eyes, shaking his head both in appreciation of the joke and in disbelief that Maneckshaw was chortling along.

In that moment, Maneckshaw pulled out a pistol from under his pillow and aimed it at the man. This was so unexpected that Shanti gave a mad shout of laughter. The man looked at the pistol, open-mouthed, the hilarity draining out of his eyes.

'Colonel F.J. Maneckshaw, retired,' said Maneckshaw with contempt.

Then he shot him.

The man fell to the floor like a rock. Blood seeped across his chest, soaking the front of his shirt to a dark hue, and started forming a small puddle on the floor. Shanti stood immobilized by the thunderous crack of the pistol and the sharp, shocking smell that filled the room.

It was as if the resounding blast of the bullet had exploded the wrinkles off Maneckshaw's face. He looked twenty years younger. 'Now if you will kindly plug in my phone so that I can call the estimable Inspector Dubash,' said Maneckshaw. 'The blighter can't be bothered to come and see me except on Navroze. But I think he might make an exception tonight.'

Shanti turned numb, her head pounding. How did Maneckshaw know a police inspector?

Maneckshaw smiled soberly at her. 'Don't worry, my dear,' he said. 'Kaizaad's father and I served in the same regiment for years. He'll sort this out.'

Shanti took a deep breath and then another, her mind galloping. Now was the time to simply abandon this house and run. But the man was dead. He couldn't tell the police anything. She was safe there. Besides, Maneckshaw was literally sitting on top of her money. If she forcibly removed it now, her guilt would be as clear as day, and the police would hunt her down. But if she stayed, nobody would think of looking for anything under Maneckshaw's mattress. When the police questioned her, she would say it had been a forcible entry; she was a lone woman, after all, frightened for her own and Maneckshaw's life. Within a few days, she would hand in her notice, saying that she was too afraid to remain here any longer. All she had to do was to stay calm. Stay calm, and she would come through this unscathed.

She started breathing more easily. If the police were coming in the form of an old friend's son, Maneckshaw would make it alright. He would vouch for her. With trembling steps, she advanced and plugged the phone in.

'You bloody son of a gun,' croaked Maneckshaw into the phone, 'I have a cold and probably a chest infection coming on, and I have been wakened in the middle of the night by a bounder who entered my apartment by force. I've shot the bugger.'

The inspector arrived with some constables within fifteen minutes, a short, lumbering man with a square jowl and a black moustache. He looked down at the prone body of the man and gave him an incensed kick in the stomach. The man groaned.

Shanti felt the room sway as blood rushed up her face to her head. 'He's alive!' she gasped.

Maneckshaw, still sitting in bed, looked at her in surprise. 'Of course he's alive. I'm not a ruddy murderer.' He turned to the inspector, who was watching his men drag the young man into the living room. 'I have to admit that I wanted to shoot the bastard in the chest, but then I thought better of it. I aimed at his shoulder.' The inspector looked at Maneckshaw with exasperation, while the constables were clearly gazing at the old man in unabashed admiration.

More uniformed men seemed to be arriving every five minutes. Then she heard the young man's voice screaming out something incomprehensible. He subsided into sobs and then screamed again. Shanti watched the proceedings through a grey fog clouding her eyes and her brain, the pace of events outstripping her thought process.

A woman constable approached her, smiling, and Shanti managed to return the smile. A little flower of relief began to bloom within her. Of course, they'd ask her a few questions, but Maneckshaw would assure the inspector of her reliability. Instead, she felt her hands pulled behind her back and her wrists enclosed in cold steel. Confused, she looked at Maneckshaw. 'Sir? But you said not to worry. You said, "Don't worry, my dear."'

'You had better tell Inspector Dubash all that,' he replied, staring at her.

She felt her gut shrivel in fright as the constable began leading her out. Through the door she caught a glimpse of the bloodied man being dragged towards the stairs. She thought she heard mutterings of '5 o'clock' among the men in the next room.

'Julie did the same thing,' she said, tearfully. 'No harm done, sir. Haven't I looked after you all these months?'

For a slow, elongated second, she found herself looking deep into Maneckshaw's face, and the enormity of her days in his apartment came upon her. He would forgive her. The hours they had spent in each other's company, the seeds they had scattered for the sparrow on the sun-dappled balcony, the taxi rides to the club in the cool of the evenings, the domesticity they had established together. He would remember it all, she knew, and he would tell the police to let her go. She would look after him as she had always done, sharing with him the freshness of the green-leaved mornings and the peace that settled on the flat in the long, hot afternoons. She'd cook for him and tell Mrs Presswala, enough of the tiffinwalla, ma'am, sir deserves good, homemade food.

'Let me stay with you, sir,' she whispered. She could read his ancient face now, after all these months. He would make everything alright. 'I won't leave you like Julie. I'll stay here and look after you.' The grey fog swarmed across her eyes.

'I haven't the faintest idea who Julie is,' she heard Maneckshaw say. 'My biggest headache at the moment is that Mrs Presswala will no doubt be arriving shortly.'

TATA HITACHI

Where the Lights Never Go Out

JAIRAJ SINGH

Someone I met on an online dating app, shortly after I moved to Bombay, told me that if you live here long enough, the sea will start to disappear. 'You will stop even taking notice of it,' P said. 'You'll always be too busy, chasing after some pay cheque, some bit of a dream.'

I didn't believe her, of course. How could it even be possible to stop seeing something as vast as the sea?

P was a lawyer who had been living in the city for seven years at the time. She worked six days a week, almost ten hours a day. The extent of her social life, she said, was either cocktails after work with colleagues at a bar near her workplace in Fort, or listening to her roommate talk about a boy who was great in bed, 'beautiful even', but not ready for commitment.

One evening, she confessed she was lonely. 'The city really teaches you to be alone,' she said. 'It's not for everyone. You have to constantly struggle and hustle. Only then will it be home to you, the outsider.'

The things she would say often didn't make much sense. But somehow, they stayed with me. Over time they even began to haunt me a little, as though her musings over DMs held profound kernels of truth. I would roll her words in my mind when I would go on walks. I would look for her—or the image I had from her display picture—in the faces of people in the crowd and wonder if they felt the same way about the city. If everyone was lonely.

We never met, P and I. We never even tried to meet. We chatted for a few weeks and then she gradually stopped replying to my messages. Shortly afterwards, she either unmatched me, or I uninstalled the app. I can't quite remember. The conversations came to a grinding halt.

This was also my introduction to the city. At the time, I lived in a small apartment in Versova with two roommates, a couple always on the verge of a breakup. I had moved in my mid-twenties to work with an advertising agency, but switched to writing for films soon after.

I won't lie. At first, I used to feel like a complete stranger in the field, but one project always led to another. Even though most of what I worked on didn't materialize, there was always a steady stream of projects, and in time, the city became more and more of a home to me.

A few years later, I moved into an apartment by myself in an old, elevator-less, four-storeyed building in Mahim, not very far from the station. There was an empty lot next to it, which was a garbage dump of sorts, and my windowsill was a den for crows that would leave bits of rotting food there, but I didn't mind the company.

Around that time, I met someone at a party of a work friend. She was a photographer, wore a nose ring, had tattoos covering an entire arm, and had bewitching pixie-like eyes. She was seeing someone when we hooked up. We saw each other for about three months, but almost always at night.

Sometimes she would land up at my door at around midnight, after I knew she had been with him, and she would ask me for a drink. Her life, she said, had been hard. She had been a victim of serial abuse since childhood and was also a product of a broken home.

Sometimes she would talk until the wee hours of the morning about the pain she nursed, and I would listen. I was young, but she was younger than me. Needless to say, I was quite smitten by her—by the way she spoke about gender, oppression, even the shame she felt about her privilege. The entire world was always on trial for her.

I also loved looking at Bombay through her eyes. She would speak about different stations as though they were vortices to travel back in time and of old eateries as lost treasures. I became lost in the haze of her beauty, alcohol and the written word, and slowly, unbeknownst to me, the sea began to recede from the shores of my mind.

Then, one day, she vanished from my life.

Was I late? I was waiting for Rishabh and Asif, the two other screenwriters I was teaming up with, to meet Anil Kante at Anchor Bar and Restaurant in Andheri East—a dive that makes even Janata in Bandra West look posh. Lately, I had lost my sense of time.

The three of us were part of a writers' room that a production house had put together for a crime show about an ex-con—he worked in a dance bar and chaperoned girls to influential people in the city—and the troubles he found himself in. The project was meant to be a straight-up action thriller when we were signed on, but midway, we got a new showrunner, an early 2000s indie filmmaker, who started making us rewrite scene after scene, saying he wanted more authenticity.

'Everything is just more of the same.' 'The underbelly of Bombay is its biggest trope.' 'Can you really write about a world you haven't seen or sampled?' He would go on and on, and at some point, we began to lose all faith in the draft we were working on.

To prove a point, Asif—who was at least a decade younger than us and chiefly assisting us with research—had taken an auto around midnight one weekday to Juhu, right outside the once famous Sea Dolly Hotel, to see if he could speak to a sex worker. The street was deserted when he reached. He ambled into a by-lane, towards the beach. It was high tide and windy. He noticed women and trans people, lurking in the shadows in pairs or standing aloof, some in heavy makeup. Even though there were quite a few people milling about, something didn't sit right. His heart began to pound so hard that his ears hurt. He left.

We had reached an impasse. One day, the showrunner told us to meet Anil Kante—a contact of a producer who once had 'dealings' with the underworld. 'Get him to show you the entrails of the city,' he said. 'It's your only hope now.'

Not far from where I stood outside the bar, a cobbler was working under a blue tarp, the small enclosure barely four feet tall. He was stitching the seams of a pair of white sandals with a black thread and swollen needle. It was a warm evening, and his skin gleamed like polished leather. He noticed me looking at him and nodded with a wan smile. As I waved back, Rishabh tapped me on the shoulder and said that Kante was already inside, waiting for us.

'Bhai, this place sucks,' he said.

Anchor was dank and poorly lit; it smelled of frustration and despair. It was filled with cigarette smoke and men drinking hard liquor. The floor looked grimy, despite a boy tasked with mopping it routinely.

A short man in his fifties, Kante did not look imposing as a gangster in his neatly pressed cream-coloured half-sleeve shirt. His wide, heavy-set shoulders perhaps gave him away. He was already down a whiskey quarter and was helping himself to a plate of sliced-open boiled eggs and masala peanuts for chakna.

'Health is important,' he grinned.

It was only after a few rounds of drinks and listening to him drone on about his newfound interest in fitness that we got down to business.

'What is your film about?' he asked, resting his elbows on the grease-smeared table.

'It's a show about women who work in dance bars and on the streets,' Rishabh said, barely suppressing his irritation. 'Who they are, how they got into this line of work, what they …'

'Charge?' he asked.

'We want to get a sense of how it all works,' I said.

'These days everything is on a website. You can order a girl home like chow mein. Why do you need me?'

'What about brothels?' Rishabh asked.

'You are saying you have not been to the beauty parlours outside Khar and Mira Road stations?'

'What are those?'

'Mmm, it is all a business, is what it really is,' he said, peeling the skin of an egg. 'It is the same everywhere. Some girls work in kothas, some have dealers, and some freelance. Some come willingly into this line of work, some do it to earn extra or to make ends meet, and some are dragged into it from birth. There are all kinds for all sorts. It depends on what you're looking for and how much you can spend.'

'Kante sir, how do you know so much about this …' Asif said.

'Ya, you must have surely had a few on the side in your time,' Rishabh sniggered.

'Ay, motherfucker, do you think I'm a bhadva?' Kante looked suddenly incredulous. 'You see this?' He was lifting his shirt from his waist. 'These scars don't come from randi-bazi, from being a whoremonger. Bombay runs on business, and I know how business runs … I was born in Dadar East. My father was a communist, who worked in the mills—that poor sod lost his job and drank himself to death. I had to do everything I could to feed my family. I worked the streets day and night. And I survived. I survived the bloody riots, the gang wars, and even two murder attempts in jail. You fuckers should be writing about me.' Exhausted by his own outburst, Kante suddenly went quiet and pensive. 'Doctor says anger is not good for health,' he said, lighting a cigarette. Kante then looked at me and asked the rest, 'Is he always this quiet?'

I began to stammer.

'Tell you what,' Kante said, watching the unease in my eyes. 'Have you at least been to a dance bar?'

'Didn't they shut twenty-five years ago? Do they even exist?' Rishabh asked.

'Drink up, there's one close by,' he said, looking at his metal watch, which had no dial. It was 11.30 p.m.

It took me three weeks to realize that I was being 'ghosted'. The last evening we spent together was unlike any other. I was already in bed after having brushed my teeth—watching a Korean film about a woman in her sixties searching for the meaning of poetry—when she messaged she was coming over. I was exhausted, but a text from her was always exciting.

She was out drinking with friends and asked me to have three shots of anything strong before she arrived. I followed her instructions. When she reached mine, however, she was not in the mood to drink more but hungry. I made her an omelette, cut some cheese, and layered a toast with marmite. She had never had marmite before. We then settled into the sofa. I put on a playlist of old Hindi film music that she liked. She stubbed her pencil-thin cigarette in an empty teacup and asked me how my writing was coming along.

At the time, I was working on a short feature about a vampire—the last of his kind—imprisoned since Partition in a bungalow in Khar by three generations of a Sindhi family. In order to keep him alive, they would feed him rats and stray cats, guarding him like some family heirloom. They sought to exploit his powers—until one day, the vampire stirred from his slumber, sensing the presence of another like him, lurking in the western suburbs.

While talking, we went from holding hands to kissing and soon moved to the bedroom to have sex. The young and excitable kind. Our bodies were still new to each other. When we were done, she slid her body next to mine and asked if I loved her.

'Only with all my heart.'

'But you know I'm seeing someone else?'

I nodded.

'How can you be okay with it?'

'I'm happy just being here with you.'

'It's okay, even women can compartmentalize sex.'

The next morning, she left earlier than usual. It was a beautiful January day, with warm sunlight generously pouring in through the windows. The crows, too, were quiet. I made coffee. The apartment smelled of her and cigarettes.

I never saw her again. It hurt just how much time it took for this to dawn on me. Anyone who has had their heart broken knows that it doesn't, in fact, break—it just wilts. When I sensed that she was withdrawing , I began to feel, perhaps for the first time since I moved to the city, how alone I was.

The loss of the relationship soon festered into an abscess in my soul. While I would try and drown the days out with work and banter and the humdrum company of colleagues, the nights would be long, soulless and empty. My anxieties about life, those dormant demons that lay deep within me, would come tearing out to feast on me. I began to lose sleep. Even alcohol failed to have any effect on me.

I started turning down plans to meet friends. The incredible thing about this city is that if you say no often enough, it takes you quite literally and leaves you alone. For some time, my only link to the outside world was when the lights would come on in the apartments in the building next to mine at dusk. I would watch life playing out in other rooms while mine had come to a standstill.

One day, a few months after the relationship ended, she messaged out of the blue, wanting to return the books she had borrowed. She said she was sorry for the way she had ended things. 'It was the only way I could do it,' she wrote. 'I am messaging you because I have decided to choose love and would like to provide you closure … I want you to wish me luck.'

I remember the day clearly because, a few hours before, my landlord, a retired chartered accountant, rang my bell to inform me that the building was likely headed for redevelopment. He said I may have to move out soon. The cook had brought some kharvas from her village to celebrate her son clearing the class ten exams. And then, as if someone had pulled back the curtains, light poured in—and just like that, the sadness lifted. I was just broken. I remember having the urge to go on a walk to Dadar Chowpatty to watch the lights come on along the Sea Link.

Was this the city's way of asking me to leave?

The night should have ended at the dance bar. We shouldn't have drunk the amount we had. Kante should have shown some restraint while regaling us with stories of how he once ruled the city's corners. In fact, he should have never taken us to Lamington Road.

Let's rewind a little. The dance bar that Kante took us to was no seedy discotheque. It was housed on the mezzanine floor of an LED-lit building that operated as a watering hole with cabaret shows. When Kante walked in, the staff gravitated towards him to lunge at his feet. 'This boy has grown up in front of my eyes,' he said, introducing us to Ravi Kant, a wiry man in a shiny, large grey suit. 'He was just a waiter at Topaz, now look how his moustache has grown,' he said, patting his cheek.

The dance bars, which had shut almost overnight in 2005, had somehow slid their way back into Mumbai's nightlife like some open secret. 'You definitely need to know somebody to get an entry though,' Asif said. 'Someone you can call beforehand.'

We were sitting in a large hall with a DJ console in one corner belting out '90s Hindi film pop numbers, a dance floor in the middle, and plush seating at the other end, pushed against the wall. Kante ordered a few bundles of twenty-rupee bills—these were served to us on plates by liveried waiters. Rishabh ordered our drinks. It was clear, we were being ripped off. Everything was priced about three times the amount we would pay anywhere else—but we were at a dance bar.

The lights began to dim. Dry ice slithered on the floor, only to rise like a mist, as laser lights began to draw mad patterns across the hall. Women began to materialize from the haze, standing a short distance from one another, aloof, gently gyrating to the music.

It's impossible to explain, but no matter which woman we settled our eyes on, it felt like she was looking back at us, desperate to make a connection, with desire and a hint of mischief.

'You like anyone?' Kante asked, while Ravi Kant stood obediently next to him.

Rishabh pointed to a woman, and said, 'Man, she looks like Ahana Dubey, the actress.'

'Pakka, her name will be Ahana,' Kante said.

Egged on by the former gangster, Rishabh signalled to the woman to come towards him.

'What's your name?' he asked.

'I am Ahana,' she said, in English. 'Nice to meet you.'

'Ahana? No way! You really look like Ahana Dubey.'

'Yes, people tell me that,' she smiled.

Kante turned towards the waiter, who promptly picked up a stack of notes and showered the money over her, while she looked deep into Rishabh's eyes and started to slowly dance for him.

'She's so beautiful,' Rishabh said, after she had drifted back to the dance floor. 'I don't think anyone has ever looked at me like that.'

'Be careful or you'll slip,' Kante chuckled.

'These are not ordinary-looking women,' Asif said. 'If you met them in a mall, you would rate them a solid nine. You wouldn't be able to tell they work here.'

'Some of them are regular college-going girls and aspiring actors,' Kante added. 'Of course, this was not always the case ...'

He was interrupted by some excitement at the next table, which seated an elderly man all by himself with large piles of money on the table and a bevy of dancers around, vying for his attention.

'Obviously, he is in real estate,' Kante said, with a tinge of envy.

We must have been there for an hour-and-a-half when the lights came on abruptly, as though the venue was about to witness a midnight raid. There were cops swarming the main area where we were sitting.

'Relax, they do this every night,' Ravi Kant said, as he got us to clear the bill, while a bunch of hangers-on started clamouring around us for tips.

Outside the precincts of the bar, we were still in a bit of a daze.

'This was truly incredible, but we didn't get to talk much to the girls,' Rishabh whined. 'Do you think I can meet Ahana again?'

'Forget her,' Kante said. 'I know just the place where we can see a mujra right now. The girls will be even more beautiful, and we can drink as much as we please.'

There was plenty of commotion outside the bar as people were beginning to trickle out on the street and cops were asking the crowd to disperse. Rishabh claimed that he saw one of the dancers drive out in a Mercedes.

'This night can go for as long as you like,' Kante pulled me aside and gently said.

My head was swimming.

We hailed a kaali-peeli, and before we knew it, we were crossing the Sea Link, hurtling towards the heart of the city.

As the taxi turned left from Pedder Road towards Nana Chowk, Asif, who was sitting next to me and Rishabh, began to shudder. 'Bro, he's taking us to a brothel. Are you sure this is where we want to go?'

By now, Kante, sitting next to the taxi driver in front, was drunkenly babbling to himself about some lost love, Janaki.

The car dropped us off, per his instructions, at the mouth of a lonely, dark stretch. Not far from where we were, a man in a hoodie was sitting at the bottom of a metal staircase, keeping an eye out on the road. In the flickering light of a streetlamp, it was not easy to sight him.

'There was a time when a very beautiful girl used to live right here,' Kante said, pointing to a shuttered window. 'Come evening, the city's biggest businessmen would line their cars here to pick her up ...'

'What happened to her?' Asif asked.

But Kante had already sped towards the stairs. 'See, Janaki, I've returned!' he kept repeating to himself.

We walked past the man taking refuge in the shadows, up the stairs, to a hall, which had a rexine sofa set and an empty aquarium lit by a dull orange light; on the wall sat an idol of Ganesha with a stub of incense burning in front of it.

'This whole place has changed,' Kante said in disbelief, as if he was about to cry, and disappeared behind a curtained door. Meanwhile, we sat there, unsure of what was happening. Two men appeared from a hallway and welcomed us as if they had been expecting us all evening.

'If you're okay with the price,' one of them said, 'I can start showing the girls to you.'

There was soon a line of women of all ages standing in front of us. Most plainly dressed. Some even looked bored or unslept.

'They won't do,' Rishabh said.

While the man who had not yet spoken went to collect more women, the other one stayed back and reassured us that these girls would do *anything* we liked. 'If you want to drink, we can arrange for that in the room as well,' he added.

There was something deeply sad about the place. A dank sense of gloom—or maybe one hundred years of exhaustion—began to loom over us.

Asif suddenly got up and darted for the exit. He didn't even turn to say bye. Why was I still here when I had no intention of paying for sex?

'You wouldn't mind if I stay?' Rishabh asked softly, as if he were reading my thoughts.

Before I could answer, more women stood in front of us, staring vacantly. After studying them, he pointed to one in a yellow sari and cyan blouse, with brightly painted fingernails.

'Just please wait for me,' he said, as he followed her.

Now, as the remaining women turned to me, I pushed past them towards the curtained door, in search of Kante, only to land in a makeshift kitchenette, strewn with cups of half-drunk tea and what looked like raw meat in a bowl. It led to a tiny room bathed in dim light.

'You're not supposed to be here,' said a woman—spectral, luminous—seated calmly in a chair.

The room began to slowly take form. Kante was crouched next to her on the floor, head between his knees, looking frail, as though he had aged considerably in a short span of time.

'You ...' I said, pointing a finger at him.

'Forget about him, why haven't you selected a girl yet?' she asked.

The man, who had followed me from the sitting area, was now at the doorway, peeling the calluses off his hands. 'He didn't like anyone we showed him,' he said. 'His friend went with Mona.'

'Leave us,' she instructed him.

The woman got up from her chair and went to a corner of the room—where a wooden dressing table stood—and pulled out what looked like a small hand-rolled cigarette from a drawer. She lit it.

'Do you run this place?' I asked.

'You don't belong here,' she said, exhaling a column of blue smoke. 'You have strayed into a place where broken men come to exorcise their demons and cauterize their wounds. They drift in to lick the flames of pleasure, only to be burnt and consumed.'

She didn't seem angry. But the hiss in her voice, and her petite frame in that small room, lit by an errant lantern in a corner, and the sweet, heady smell of what she was smoking, made her seem terrifying.

'Just let him go,' Kante softly moaned, as though rousing from deep sleep.

'Shut up,' she shouted. 'Why did you bring them here?'

'Anna told me Janaki has returned ...'

'Anna told you?' she hissed. 'Anna has not stepped into this place for over thirty years, and Janaki is probably dead because of you.'

'Please, please don't say that, Aapa,' Kante pleaded.

'*You*,' she said, looking at me. 'You think this is a place for stories? Do you not know what your heart wants? Let me tell you why the crows have been leaving chicken bones at your window ...'

A cold chill swept over me.

I woke up in a state of panic, as though I had tumbled down a flight of stairs, only to find myself back on the rexine sofa.

The room was submerged in darkness. Even though I was alone, it felt like the old woman was still next to me, staring at me. I was terrified by the thought that I was trapped in this room, in this building, in this city waiting to be swallowed by the sea, like smoke in an upturned glass.

But somehow, the panic gave way to relief, as though I had been spared by a force beyond mere good and evil.

I remember morning had broken by the time I reached Grant Road Station. The sky was overcast. A rat was gnawing at the carcass of a pigeon. I was at the platform just in time to catch a Borivali Slow. I was out of breath for some reason; my hands on my arched knees, as though I was about to dive onto the tracks before the oncoming train, in a city where the lights never go out.

Strays

LINDSAY PEREIRA

TUESDAY TERROR: Six Blasts Rock Mumbai Railway Stations
19:15 hrs IST

A series of blasts took place at Matunga, Khar, Santacruz, Jogeshwari, Borivali and Bhayandar suburban railway stations on Tuesday.

All the explosions took place in first-class compartments of trains at a time when a majority of Mumbaikars were returning home from office, railway control sources said. Eyewitnesses said a large number of people were seriously injured, and all trains on the Western line route had been suspended.

Witnesses described seeing body parts strewn about the blast sites. More than 209 people were killed and around 700 injured, a police inspector said.

—*The Times of India*, 11 July 2006

He appeared the way so many did, absent one morning and present the next, like those mushrooms that come to life in the empty hours when no one is looking. He couldn't have been more than a few years old, as he slowly claimed a vacant spot of dirt near the railway overbridge at Grant

Road station. No attention was paid, nor was his presence questioned, because Bombay was long inured to the appearance of unaccompanied children. They washed up daily—some abandoned on trains coming in from small towns, others left behind by mothers and fathers who had never wanted them. So, he appeared, and stayed, and that was just how things were.

The locals grew used to the sight of him. Among the more sympathetic ones were cleaners and dishwashers at food stalls, and a few municipal workers employed to desultorily sweep the streets outside every railway station. They gave him names he didn't understand, or perhaps he chose not to, but he would always respond to offers of food—stale vada pav left unsold at the end of the day or half-full glasses of tepid chai. He accepted it all, keenly aware, as if by virtue of memory from an earlier life, that there could be other times when no meals would appear.

A year passed, then two, and he survived where others failed. He knew nothing of those who didn't make it, their emaciated bodies disappearing into the city's blanketing veneer of dust as if they had never existed. Those who could stay alive, did, and that was all that mattered. So, he ate what he was given and learned to move faster, propelled by the waves of activity that thrummed through everything in this insomniac city by the sea.

His was a world whose boundaries were shaped by the railway station with its two sides, East and West, connected by two overbridges. On the left lay remnants of an older Bombay, a place of narrow lanes carved by two- and three-storey buildings with staircases of wood, their foundations sinking into the ground an inch at a time with every raging monsoon. This was also where the big movie theatres were, Apsara and Naaz, Nishat and Royal Talkies, Jamuna, and the one he liked best, Minerva.

To the station's right was a bazaar, a place of chaos and commerce where brown sacks of lentils and rice leaned against each other, and where ground masalas of every colour rose in tiny, heaped mounds outside kirana stores, sharing counterspace with jars of pickled mango and khadi sakhar. He would spend hours on the street, his eyes and ears taking in everything, from the haggling of Gujarati housewives to the abuse of shopkeepers directed towards their young helpers—all minors trafficked into lifelong employment until they gathered the courage to run away towards something worse.

Like an unruly scrawl, it was a shapeless world populated by people who had lived there for generations and by nomads like him—boys and girls of indiscriminate age, a throng that could assemble or scatter like birds. They accepted him as one of their own and taught him their hybrid tongue, a curious mix of Hindi cuss words with regional dialects and snatches of dialogue from popular movies. When he was five, or six, or seven—for who is to say how children age when they are left to their own devices?—he learned to do more for food or money. He would dance, or smile, or pretend to weep for a few coins. He got better at reading faces, at noticing how some travellers could walk away without a glance, and others couldn't without handing over a rupee to soothe their conscience.

On some nights, after the stations had emptied and the last trains to Virar had rattled past, he would go with a few other drifters to the weight-checking machines, standing and stepping off to watch the tiny lights blink, until they were chased away by railway constables. Then, the children would huddle in corners outside and share what they had gathered, feeding the youngest among them first. He would listen to everything with half-closed eyes, taking in the day's accumulated wisdom: reports of who had been assaulted, which streets were to be avoided, and where leaky taps could provide water. When it rained, they would gather in narrow spaces between large municipal dustbins, with sheets of plastic torn from advertisement posters held above their heads, their wet bodies steaming in the dark.

From the other children he learned that questions were not welcome in public. They were a privilege, given or earned, but never for the unwashed or unemployed. He also saw that it was difficult for most people to grasp that one critical lesson: how to expect nothing from Bombay despite its relentless promise of everything. He saw how even dreams in this city came with a price tag, and how they were only for those who had something to offer in return. He saw that those who gave everything could still be turned away, their lives and bodies hollowed out like the food wrappers and plastic bottles that clogged every gutter.

When Grant Road slept, he would lie awake amid the skittering of mice and try to imagine where he came from. He wondered if there was a mother who had loved him and if it were possible that she was still around. Had she misplaced him, and was she still out there searching? He would then stumble into sleep, restlessly, and dream of nothing.

There were also things the city taught him about survival. He saw that there were other ways of earning money and tried as many as he could, sweeping the grungy floors of trains, or wiping down the windshields of taxis with a washcloth. He learned to blend into the shadows of buildings in the late hours when drunks would stumble towards the station from Lal Bazaar and Falkland Road, the darkness allowing him to pick their pockets as they fell.

There were rare days of plenty when leftovers from weddings were handed out, or when chicken pulao was distributed by local politicians looking for crowds to attend rallies before an election. Rich ladies from Malabar Hill or Pedder Road would come bearing packaged meals in disposable boxes—acts of charity to bribe their gods. They would ask the homeless for blessings, for prayers that the diamond merchants they were married to would live a while longer (or not for too long). He and the others would swallow as much as they could, ghee running down their grubby arms and staining their clothes, so they could smell the biryani for days after. He learned to bow in gratitude, touching the feet of those who didn't want to be touched, and saw how their eyes would never meet his; how he was a presence to them, never a person.

He sometimes stopped outside clothing stores to catch a glimpse of himself in their tall mirrors. He would see a begrimed face of indeterminate features, one that looked like many others around him, framed by unkempt hair that glinted a shade of dirty blonde in the dim light. He'd see ill-fitting pants around a scrawny waist propped up by pieces of string, and bones pushing their way out as if his skin was struggling to hold them in. When he could afford it, he would buy a T-shirt from vendors who traded in cast-offs. He would then preen outside store windows until he was shouted at—staring at his reflection as if it could teach him something about who he was, an elusive piece of information just beyond the tips of his begrimed fingernails.

He could never tell if the people he shared the streets with were happy, even though so many of them had more material things than he did. He would look at faces as they walked past, their eyes invariably on something in the distance. He'd think of what it meant to always know where one was coming from or going towards, and what it meant to have no answers to either question. Then he would feel lost, like a piece of driftwood, and get up and walk quickly in any direction until his feet and mind slowed down. He'd also look at the faces of children who hadn't been abandoned, as if for signs about the homes they inhabited.

He would look at women, especially the ones who seemed old for their years, the ones marked by something dark and inscrutable. He could sometimes tell if they were among the many thousands who poured into Bombay daily in the hope of becoming rich or famous, until they ended up here, outside this railway station, on their way to unhappy homes or soulless brothels.

To survive meant recognizing that safety was an illusion; that there were lines even in his seemingly unfettered world that could not be crossed. He saw those who did, and how they were adopted by older men who called themselves Dadas. Some of the children would hand over everything they earned in exchange for a semblance of protection. He heard of a boy whose eyes were gouged out before he was sent away to beg, and of babies handed to older girls who would pretend to be their mothers as they sang songs with outstretched palms on trains from Churchgate to Borivali.

But he judged nothing and no one.

He was ignored on most days, and beaten on some, waking up with his blood pooled around him. Men in khaki would push him up against walls and take his money, cheap liquor on their breath while they swore at him and the mother who had birthed him. He learned about his body, how it could be used or abused, and that there was always something that could be taken even from those who had little. He remembered a man who held him down on the broken tiles of a toilet at one end of the platform, his ragged cotton shorts down to his knees, his cheek pressed onto a floor sticky with urine. He remembered dragging himself out by his elbows and sleeping on his stomach for days, worthless tears leaking from the corners of his eyes.

The world sometimes grew larger, if only for a while, like the time Anil Kapoor and Sridevi stopped the trains for a few hours so they could shoot a film song on his overbridge. The station's children were shooed off, then called back to add authenticity to the singing and dancing. They all preened for the camera, thrusting their hips, running muddy hands suggestively through their hair. He watched all the movies that year, waiting every Friday for one magical image of himself alongside those two famous stars, but the song never appeared.

He liked sitting on the footpath outside Minerva on some Thursday nights when, after the last show, the week's cardboard cutouts were replaced with new faces and titles. He would watch as hand-painted figures of Aamir Khan or Madhuri Dixit rose, one giant piece at a time, their mouths open in lust or anger or defiance. He'd imagine snapping his fingers like Salman Khan to attract the attention of girls, and the possibility of some woman on a train recognizing him as her lost son by a scar on his forehead. He'd look for old men he could protect from thieves, who would then take him under their wing and introduce him to their families as a deserving heir. He understood, too, that these things didn't exist outside the gloom of cinema halls.

Like him, the station changed, an animal eating itself and regurgitating the parts it chewed off. Walls were painted over or demolished, and empty spaces were claimed by stalls that were then absorbed by the building. He accepted how the city neither welcomed him nor objected to his presence, leaving him to fend for himself as if to say that it had given him space and that was enough. He took nothing at face value, not even the shallow words of kindness offered by well-meaning college girls from St. Xavier's and Sophia's, who turned up at the station to teach the homeless how to read. He preferred the blunt honesty of rage instead, as his childhood fell away from him. Walking to Bombay Central and beyond, he kept to the corners, stopping in front of open windows to see couples sitting in silence or old women watching television, and he once stood for half an hour watching a man rock a baby to sleep. For those moments, something restless within him would die down a little.

In time, he met a girl who appeared to be as old as he was, who came from a railway station further north, beyond Mira Road and Bhayandar. She said little too, and he could sense that this was not because she didn't have the words. Neither could articulate how they slipped into an arrangement, but it was the only way they knew, the tenuous scaffolding of a relationship that could either last years or just a couple of nights. But she stayed, and he grew used to her, and they would walk the streets after midnight, their journeys soundtracked by the barking of dogs.

They would stop at Marine Drive or climb up an overbridge to see how Bombay spilled away into the horizon far beyond the tracks, and she would listen as he'd speak of movies he had watched, or what he heard the homes of rich people were like. He told her about the underworld dons, and how one-time murderers from Grant Road had whitewashed their reputations to become government ministers. He told her of a vendor outside Dadar's flower market who sold the tastiest mutton samosas in the city, until he was arrested after a customer found a mouse's foot in the minced meat. And the lassi seller at Colaba caught thickening his milk with blotting paper. She would accept his tales with awe, and over days and months, he began to understand what it meant to have someone to come back to. He tasted something new and grew to recognize it as hope.

On the night a few policemen from Charni Road took her, he had leapt at them even as they beat him back with lathis, striking him across the head and spitting at him as he lay on the street, his blood mixing with the dirt. He had wanted to walk to Haji Ali because she had never seen it, and because he had wanted to be the one to show her that inscrutable shrine in the sea. He had watched her laugh with pleasure at the thought of the mosque they could walk to through the waves by day, and wanted her to see what it looked like by the light of a full moon when its walls glimmered in the distance against a dark expanse of water.

But the police stopped them on the way back and brushed him aside as they pulled her into a van, driving away as he struggled to push himself up, his legs slipping under him. He remembered screaming, a guttural sound rising from somewhere deep, running down the road they had taken and turning back because he had no idea where to go. He screamed at passing taxis and wept until he reached Grant Road, sitting down in the gap between two dustbins that she had turned into a space of their own. He lay awake as long as he could, until the pain in his head pulled him under.

She wasn't there the next morning, and he walked the backstreets of Gaiwadi and Girgaum in agony, his eyes sweeping past shadows cast by abandoned odds and ends. There was no one he could ask because she was like him, a woman of no identity, an indistinguishable question mark. He walked without stopping or eating, observing every face, afraid of any flash of colour that resembled the faded pink salwar kameez she had been wearing. Sweat poured off him as he cursed everyone and everything, abusing their mothers and fathers, while whispering her name like a prayer.

She didn't return that evening, but was back the following afternoon. When he had ended the day's search, he found her sitting where she used to. He tried holding her, but they both felt the futility of his embrace, how his frail arms encircled insubstantial flesh and bone, neither providing nor receiving anything of warmth. So, he let go and shared his food with her, watching her swallow a few morsels listlessly before she lay down and slept.

He would bring her jalebis, glistening in their orange plumpness, or gulab jamuns swimming in sugar, but she would swallow them without tasting. They no longer walked together, so he would imagine her presence beside him as he made his way down the street towards the Tardeo AC Market, stopping to watch an obese bridegroom on a horse, or a chain-snatcher being assaulted by a mob. He would return to tell her of these things and wait for her to ask questions. But she had none.

And then, one day, she was gone, her straw mat beside his own empty, except for the comb with which she would brush the lice out of his hair. Something inside him broke, surprising him because he had not known of its existence, even as he understood why she had chosen to leave. He spent the following months watching policemen as they made their rounds, imagining them all dying, their bodies twisting in fires that would engulf him too.

Years later, his hair began to thin. His body started rebelling at the smallest of tasks as he sang on trains or begged outside the station. He muttered to himself often, a litany of furious words and empty vows of vengeance. It felt as if the city was starting to fall apart too; old buildings were replaced by structures taller than the tallest trees but brittle with their glass facades. The movie theatres he loved were torn down for malls that would not let him enter, and even the sea at Marine Drive began to recede as if in disgust, its view from the street erased by ugly flyovers or roads dotted with cement mixers. He no longer walked alone after sunset, afraid as if for the first time, of what he would encounter, for it felt as if the people of Bombay had lost something as well. There was now a nakedness in their yearning for more than they could stomach, and goods they once cast away with abandon were now held tightly to their chests, out of spite, or greed, or both. It was a place of exhaustion and anxiety, and where he had once found beauty in its wood and stone, there was only plastic and naked metal.

On the evening before he decided to leave the only home he had ever known, he sat on the overbridge, leaning against a wall midway between the East and West platforms. It was after 5 p.m.—the offices were starting to empty—and the crowds rushing past appeared to surge and thicken like a river in flood. No one stopped, and the dirty handkerchief by his feet saw no coins other than the few rupees he had placed on it to entice some wayward acts of charity.

He watched the trousers and salwars as they passed, the jeans and saris, until he was distracted by a man who stumbled in front of him, dropping his bag as he fell. Young and clean-shaven, he appeared to be part of a small group of others like him, all dressed in unassuming shirts and dark trousers. One of them helped the fallen man up, then swore, picking up the heavy bag that had slipped off his shoulders. Its zipper had come undone, and there was a sparkle of metal in the fading light before it was pulled shut. It looked like a pressure cooker, but there were also wires inside the bag, red and blue, or green. Every other man in the group carried a similar bag, and they all sweated with the weight. They looked at each other and then at him, pausing for a few seconds as if to gauge if he was a threat. He glanced away, and then they were gone, pushing their way downstairs towards a train that would take them past Dadar, to Bandra and Andheri or Borivali.

He thought about what he had seen, running his fingers through his dirty beard. There was something about the men that fascinated him, but he couldn't say what it was. He had read faces all his life, and what he found in their eyes resonated with some hidden part of him. It was the way they had looked around, in fear as well as anger, and the more he thought about it, the easier he began to breathe. He didn't know where they were going or what they intended to do, but he knew it would not be good, and that pleased him. For the first time in what felt like years, his chapped lips curled upwards, and he felt a lightening in his chest, as if something placed there a long time ago had just been lifted. He began to giggle, stopping abruptly when a passing policeman idly swung a lathi on the ground by his handkerchief, prodding him to move away.

Struck on the calves by the lathi's second stroke, he picked up his handkerchief and stood up, making his way down the stairs. The policeman didn't follow as he walked across the platform and out of the station, giggling again. He returned to his place by the dustbins and began to hum a song, the tune dying on his lips when he realized it was one he used to sing to her.

Leaning back against the bins, he stretched out his legs and watched as commuters continued rushing into the station. After half an hour, he rubbed his face vigorously and stood up, walking to a tiny tea stall at a corner where the station road tipped into a larger one. He paid the vendor four rupees for a cutting chai and sipped it. It was hot and sweet—its steam infused with the scent of cardamom and ginger.

There was a shout behind him, and a flurry of activity; he turned to see people run out of the station. Above the honking of cars, he heard a burst of static followed by the crackle of an announcement made by the station master. Looking up, he saw windows opening in the buildings around him and people stepping out onto their balconies. There were rushed conversations on cell phones around him, and he heard a passer-by mention an explosion on a train at Matunga. A bomb had detonated, and there were rumours of a terrorist attack. There was more shouting and talk of blasts at other stations.

Turning his back to the crowd, he breathed in deeply and closed his eyes. Then, he took another sip.

Silver Clouds

DHARINI BHASKAR

Mik and I had no good reason to house his second cousin. But then, we had no good reason to snub him either. Which I suppose is another way of saying: this was as fine a decision as any.

We should've been home alone. Or in a restaurant.

But the moment we pictured it—wedding anniversary #8; the two of us; sharing a table (or not), holding hands (or not), speaking (of what exactly, Mik's boss, so not)—the precariousness of the day, the fact that it asked for definitude or for lavish acts of coupledom, pressed down on us. We grew jittery.

I grew jittery.

It was prolonged post-pandemic stress, that's what our therapist, Noor, had deduced. Six months together in a three-bedroom apartment had robbed both of us of anticipation, of the wait and the want, of being apart just long enough as to yearn for touch.

We were apprehensive.

We were bored.

The therapist wasn't wrong. The therapist wasn't correct either.

What I'm saying is that her analysis proved sufficient. It seemed to explain everything.

Which is why, two days before anniversary #8, when Mik suggested booking a table at Neuma—its decor was all the rage, gram-worthy and swish—an answer came easy.

'I don't know if a restaurant's a good idea, Mik.'

'But why?'

'Noor told us to take it easy if either of us was stressed. And, you know, crowds stress me out.'

'Since when?'

'Since … I don't know … the pandemic.'

'The pandemic is ancient history …'

'It's not …'

'Anyway, it's Neuma, Shibs … where are the crowds?'

'There's always a crowd. It's buzzy.'

'Come on …'

'Let me think it over.'

That's where the night should've ended. With a no that wasn't a yes.

But just then Mik, who had been tinkering with his phone, muttered, 'Fuck.'

'What's wrong?'

'Neev's in town. And he's asking if he can crash at our place on Sunday.'

'This Sunday?'

'Yeah.'

'Two days from now Sunday?'

'Yeah.'

There's a term the Greeks have coined for it. Deus ex machina. A god from the machine. An actor falling headlong, sky to earth, to abruptly resolve that which to mortals seems unsolvable.

Hear me. Neev was an emissary of the gods.

One must welcome the gods' emissaries.

'Let him stay over.'

'Shibs ...'

'It's only polite. He's your cousin.'

'Second cousin.'

'And he's visiting Bombay after—how long?—eight years? Our wedding?'

'Shibs, it's our anniver ...'

'It is. And there will be others.'

I wasn't like this. I wasn't one to take wedding anniversaries lightly. I recognized their significance, the fact that they were a reminder of our worst mistake or of our best decision; that, no matter the verdict, we had given ourselves another year to feast or recover.

That we hadn't as yet fallen to pieces.

For our first wedding anniversary, Mik and I had re-enacted our first date, or what we perceived as being our first date. I caught bus 108 at VT, Mik hopped on at Ballard Pier. We shared a seat.

Back then, Mik and I, fresh out of college, had been travelling to work—Mik to a law firm in the Express Towers, and I to a newspaper's features desk in the exact building. We didn't know it, of course—that we were headed the same way, or that we had crossed paths at Xavier's, or that we had common acquaintances, or one exactly, Neev. We didn't know any of this.

What we did know was that we were sufficiently intrigued to start a conversation.

I was intrigued by Mik's scent, by the high notes of myrrh, but also by something else, less obvious, by Mik's South Bombay hauteur, so even when he sat in a rickety bus, he seemed above all of it, the fumes and the talk and the conductor's trenchant call. Mik later told me that he was intrigued by my manner; that I seemed—and I quote him—'untouched'. Which, I suppose, is the SoBo way of saying that I was laughably naive.

Naive enough to speak to a stranger.

'So, you live around here?' Mik began.

'Not exactly. Sion.'

'Interesting.'

'I wouldn't call it that. How about you?'

'Kapur Mahal.'

'Ah, Marine Drive?'

'It has its uses. For instance, I get to see India's cricket matches live from my balcony.'

'Much of the nation will be envious.'

Later, Mik told me that he had been to Ballard Pier for a breakfast meeting. Still later, he told me that he had no idea where I lived, and that he hoped Sion was in Bombay, though who knew, it could be outside of it, in whatever city or state that lurked beyond Byculla.

'I'm Mikhail, by the way.'

'Shibani.'

'Nice to meet you.'

'Nice to meet you, too.'

'Okay, I know it's an odd question to ask, but are you free this evening?'

'Excuse me?'

'See, I mistakenly purchased two tickets instead of one. For a play. NCPA. You know … that Kenneth Branagh thing. And I'm … well, I'm happy to give away the second ticket. That is, if you're interested.'

'I'm not sure I …'

'I'm sorry ... that sounded strange. But I saw you had a book with you, that Booker thing. So, I thought you may be into theatre.'

'I'll take the ticket. Thank you.'

'I'll pass it on at the venue. Seven p.m.?'

'Seven p.m.'

The 'Booker thing' was *Aerogrammes* by Tania James, a writer who is but rarely confused with James Kelman. The 'Kenneth Branagh thing' was *Macbeth*.

Mik later told me he didn't have spare tickets. He had palmed off his second cousin Neev's ticket to me.

Neev later told me that he was livid with Mik. Mik was not in the least bit interested in Shakespeare. Neev was. The idea had been Neev's all along. His date had ditched him. He had invited Mik as an afterthought. 'And the bastard took everything.'

Neev promised to forgive Mik for his dumb move if Mik became a true gentleman and married me.

Mik was forgiven. It took three years.

It was when we got off the 108, and I accused Mik of stalking me, and he became defensive and flashed his visiting card as proof that he had no desire to stalk, that we realized we spent sixty hours a week in the same building.

Later that evening, Mik and I shared a cab to the NCPA. We stopped at Mondy's after for drinks. We walked to Bayview, the sea a string of fairy lights, and ordered too much spaghetti. We caught the last bus to Kapur Mahal.

I texted Neev from the bus. 'I hope you catch Branagh's *Macbeth*. It's crazy-wonderful. It makes me believe that tonight will never end.'

'That fucking idiot stole my ticket,' Neev replied.

We left it there.

We may have continued the exchange had the driver not announced our stop. Or had I known that Neev was, in fact, referring to Mik.

It was my first visit to Kapur Mahal. To Mik's residence. It came with mahogany doors and bubble-glass windows and black-and-white photographs of men in sharp clothes.

I felt it then, most strongly, that I'd live there forever. In this home that carried a fraying gentility.

I kissed Mik.

We re-enacted all of this, like I said, for our first wedding anniversary, maybe not my text to Neev or the short walk to our former offices—Mik by now was on partner track in an up-and-coming Worli law firm; I had made it to features editor, the magazine office was in Fort—but the rest of it, the pub and the buses and the late-night kiss.

It had been careless, the kiss. I don't think I was in love with Mik—no—so much as the idea of Mik, or more specifically, the idea of Bombay when I was with Mik. He knew all the cool places, the hottest items on the menu, the waiters who were 'boss'—how smoothly he said 'boss', the word all brandy ...

The city parted to make way for him, and thus, for the both of us.

Mik's Bombay was unlike my own, the one I returned to after work, the one I spent most nights in. Mine was a Bombay that was careworn, without histories I knew of, or was invested in, without that frisson of glamour. It slept too soon. It woke to temple bells at dawn. It had precisely one restaurant of snob-value. I joke. Peninsula: Pure Veg. The plastic chairs lined up in a row, always taken.

What I'm getting at is this. Mine was a Bombay without a sea.

When then did I fall in love with Mik?

I believe it was in Neev's presence.

The day I bumped into Mik, I had known Neev about a month. My first meeting with Neev was at Gallery Chemould, where he was to help curate an exhibition; I had been commissioned by my editor to cover it. I was meant to interview Neev about Geeta Kapur's oeuvre, and maybe I did, but what I recall most distinctly is speaking to him of everything else sun-under—of his fondness for F1 and my indifference to dessert and our combined love for Sofia Carmena Coppola. Our favourite film, for god's sake, was *Somewhere.*

What I'm saying is that Neev and I hit it off.

We promised to meet again, and soon, and (expectedly) didn't, sending sporadic text messages instead that laid bare our hearts. I learnt, via text, that Neev was not one for commitment, that he judged those who were indifferent to the colour grey, and that his favourite word was curmudgeonly; the world to him was swarming with curmudgeonly souls. I told Neev, in turn, of my tendency to overcommit, that I judged those who used text-speak, and that I longed to inhabit 'whimsy'—it was a manic pixie dream word.

It was on my second date with Mik, just a week after our first, that I met Neev again. It happened by accident. Mik had snagged a table at Wasabi. The date was meant to be fancy, unlike our first, with miso-marinated black cod and mini tofu cheesecakes. And ceiling lights so damn yellow they meant business. We had just about seated ourselves when Mik suggested we go elsewhere.

'But why?' I protested.

Before Mik could furnish a convincing reply, Neev walked up. 'Hey there,' he said.

Mik assumed that he was being addressed. I assumed I was. 'Such a small world,' we said as one—my statement buoyant (I was happy, beyond happy, to see Neev); Mik's perhaps too effusive, straining to sound good-natured.

'You know each other?' Again, Mik and I spoke as one.

'Listen, if you go on like this—speaking in a single voice—you may as well marry.' This was Neev.

'Shut up, Neev.' This was Mik.

'In fact'—Neev looked pointedly at Mik—'if you become a true gentleman and promise to marry Sheeba, I may consider forgiving you for last week.'

Neev always called me Sheeba. Right from the day we met. Sheeba of a thousand riddles.

Mik glared.

'Forgive Mik for what?' I had to ask.

Mik turned pale.

Neev laughed. 'It's a long story, Sheeba, much too long for today. I'll regale you with the details another time. It's scintillating, I promise, rich in …'

'What are you doing here anyway? And don't you have a date or something to be with?' Mik interrupted.

'Unfortunately, this date ditched as well. Actually it's the same girl. That's two in a row. Third time lucky, it's what they say.'

'Go the fuck home then …'

'Nah. I'm here. I may as well join you. The tab's on you, Mik.' Neev asked a waiter to pull an extra chair to our table and ordered wine by the glass and sushi and more sushi.

Neev was excellent company, with careless gossip and trivia and wild storytelling.

He always had a comeback.

His date was an idiot.

By the end of the night this much was clear—Mik and Neev were related; I was Neev's friend; I was Mik's whoknowswhat.

This, too, was clear. That in Neev's company, Mik was more than he otherwise was. He remained a doorway to the city, the most exciting one—we traipsed, the three of us, post Wasabi, to Gateway, tried bribing a drunken boatman, setting sail. But, now, Mik was also jealous and watchful. He was quick on the uptake. For Mik, wit was hard work. With Neev, he was committed to putting in the hours.

I laughed more than I ever had. It was a belly-aching, heart-exploding kind of laugh.

It was fleeting.

It was addictive.

We returned to Mik's at dawn.

Perhaps Mik sensed his capacity to shape-shift in Neev's presence. More likely, Neev was utterly bored and found delight in Mik's flailing attempts at keeping pace. Either way, for the next three years, my dates with Mik had Neev around somewhere—background, foreground, with a new girl, with two, or none.

'Bachelor's next weekend?' Mik asked, as the sky turned purple. He was watching me.

'Sure,' Neev said, before I could.

I shrugged.

We went to Bachelor's the next weekend, Mik in the driver's seat, Neev sprawled across the backseat, reading. Now and again, he'd reveal a sentence—it was Hanif Kureishi, it was *Intimacy*.

'*You have to find the right distance between people. Too close, and they overwhelm you, too far and they abandon you.*'

'Yup.' This was Mik.

'I think the backseat is about the ideal distance, no, Sheeba?' This was Neev.

'More like clawingly close.' Mik again.

'Is that your way of saying that Neev overwhelms you?' Me. To Mik.

'About time, too. Eloquence is overwhelming.' Neev. The laughter. So light. Like a pocketful of coins.

'As is stupidity.' Mik.

'I love that you qualify that as a riposte.' Neev.

'I love that both of you think you amuse.' Me.

'But we do, darling. Admit it.' Mik kissed my cheek. The swagger. The damned swagger.

I think I fancied him right then.

Neev reading in the backseat.

I returned to Kapur Mahal that night, sans Neev. Wanting. Wanting all of it—the sentence that had turned the evening over, the laughter, so easy, it windchimed.

I wanted to hold all the world's swagger close.

And I did.

I admit, I was partly to blame for Neev's abiding presence, dropping a text here, a DM there, suggesting, always suggesting, come-along-why-don't-you. I did it, I now think, because it had started terrifying me a little, not the grander intimacies or the loitering, but this—the idea of sustaining a conversation in a restaurant with Mik-sans-Neev.

What I told myself though was something quite else. That this was temporary. That I was trying to make the most of my days with Neev before he packed up and left.

Neev had made it clear—the day we had bypassed Geeta Kapur's oeuvre he had made it abundantly clear—that he was leaving. It was a matter of time, that's all; a question of bureaucratic readiness; of when the Americans would permit him to join his parents and their business in Pasadena.

He hadn't wished to leave, Neev informed me, that was never the plan. After boarding school, he had every intention of living alone in his grandparents' vacant flat in Cuffe Parade. He didn't quite know what he'd do in life, he had no reason to know, but this much was definite—he'd get a degree in Bombay, and find a job in Bombay, and live the good life he was born to live in Bombay. The plan was solid.

And then it wasn't.

Neev blamed a relationship gone sour—the only relationship he had sustained long enough to go sour—and the fact that its failure portended the collapse of all else that he had been sure of: a future and a life. A life in this city.

It was a good reason. It was one good reason of two.

1993 was the year Neev was left broken-hearted. And here's the thing—in 1993, a great many of us in the city were left broken-hearted. We blamed the colleges and schools we were tethered to, the families we had inherited, those fleet, will-o'-the-wisp, fly-by-night love affairs. And sure, they pricked. But what, I suspect, we really ached over was something wholly other, the fact that the island we had believed to be stable, the island we had anchored ourselves to, was drifting away.

In three years, Bombay would become Mumbai.

Once: Bom Bahia to the Portuguese. Decent bay. Home to wanderer and vagrant. Sufi and mussafir and miscreant and trader and peddler.

It was no longer in the mood to welcome.

And so, I suppose, we did what we had to. Some—this was Mik—immersed themselves in the city's shimmer, as though shimmer were all. And some—this was Neev—chose to walk away.

Two-and-a-half years into my association with Mik—Mik and I were now officially a couple—Neev mentioned that he'd be leaving in six months. I recall everything about that moment. Leo's, the lights bouncing off a mirror; Mik seated by my side, his hair gelled and with frosted tips; Neev before me, his skin almost golden.

It's the moment after that I struggle to remember, what I felt, what precisely, panic or pain or indifference (never indifference). Whether I commanded Neev that he had bloody well stay, whether I didn't.

What I do know is this. When Neev left Leo's—he had to leave early, he wouldn't say why—Mik and I became inhabitants of that murky nation between lust and banter. I think it's why Mik asked.

'Shibs, will you marry me?'

I think I said yes.

I think I texted Neev from the car; I planned to tell him of the proposal, of Mik's you've-made-me-so-happy, of my yes-why-not-yes-yes-and-yes.

Instead, I told him: 'I love you, Neev.'

Six minutes later, Neev replied: 'I love you too much to say I do too.'

Mik, Neev and I continued hanging out—as though nothing had altered, nothing monumental; as though the texts we had exchanged had never been sent; as though Mik's proposal, now sealed with a blooming ring, were insignificant.

Insignificant. And compared to what?

I suppose, dinner.

Our last night together, Mik, Neev and I didn't do dinner. I told Neev that my parents were expecting me at home—wedding prep. Neev told Mik that his parents were expecting him on a call—moving prep. Mik—and this left Mik, and Mik's parents were no more (that's a story for another day)—told the both of us that he had a job interview. This was, in fact, accurate.

Neev attended our wedding a month later, we knew he would, we knew he would be gone twenty-eight days exactly (I counted). I hugged Neev the moment I saw him on Day 29. He seemed younger—how was this even possible?—and jauntier. And quicker than ever with his comebacks. And now, he chose to deliver a speech, Kenneth Branagh and Shakespeare in starring roles.

When shall we three meet again
In thunder, lightning, or in rain?

When the hurly-burly's done,
When the battle's lost and won.

Mik burst out laughing, I'm not sure why, maybe because he thought it hilarious, the weird sisters' song and dance, their crackling double-speak. More likely, he laughed because he was drunk, and everything tickled Mik when he was drunk. He forgot he had to be sharp.

And this, I think, is when everything unspooled, though, of course, it didn't, we played our parts, the masquerade feeling not completely depleting, not even like a masquerade. Neev's existence had touched our lives just enough that the after-effects would outlive his presence or absence.

But the unspooling, like I said—it started the day we made our vows, the day Neev decamped with no visible date of return.

So, here's what I did not tell the couples' therapist—that, once, I had known Neev.

A day before wedding anniversary #8, Mik made his peace with Neev's impending visit. 'There's nothing to be done,' he shrugged. He accepted the stuff he felt unable to change.

It made him good at being married.

I cut my hair.

This made me think that I was good at being married, too.

Besides, it made me feel eight years younger, which I told myself was all that I needed to become the person I once was, seated by Mik, laughing, telling backseat-Neev to cut it out.

As I looked into the salon mirror, I could see the three of us—Mik, Neev, me—outside Bachelor's, in the car. I could hear my voice. 'Neev, seriously, stop.'

'But I haven't got to the best part ...'

'God, I can't laugh anymore.'

'Alright, alright ... moving on. Hear this, Sheeba ...' I could see Neev, sprawled carelessly, the book in his hands.

'I'm incapable of hearing anything ...' Tears, mad tears, rolled down my cheeks. What had Neev said, what outrageous hysterical thing? I couldn't recall.

'I'm reading it out anyway ...'

'Neev, no . . .'

'*You can protect and encourage the most delicate of gifts—love, affection, creativity, sexual desire, inspiration—but you cannot requisition them. You cannot will love, but only ask why you have put it aside for the time being.*'

The laughter all at once tied by the reins.

Intimacy isn't at all a funny book.

I snatched Neev's copy the next week. I refused to give it back.

'Sheeba, you haven't grown a day older, it's almost criminal.' It's the first thing Neev said when I opened the door on anniversary #8.

I had done well with the haircut.

It was eight on a Sunday morning, I was still in pjs. Mik, always an early riser, was through with morning yoga and whatever else he did to walk the way he did, like nothing in the world could throw him off; like he owned a chunk of it. Neev wasn't an early riser—how do I know this?—but it didn't matter, because whatever the time, he seemed alive, like something leaping out of a page.

'Neev!' I squealed.

'There are people who are actually pleased to meet you, Neev.' Mik. With a swagger, but grumpy.

'I missed you, too, Mik.'

Neev threw himself on a floor cushion, and began, in media res, as though we had spoken only the night before—and I could wager we had—about the fact that he had no choice but to flee a friend's wedding in Delhi.

Neev was meant to be in Delhi, he was meant to raise a toast. But then, he remembered a book, and it was an important book, and he had to catch a flight to claim the book ...

'In short, Sheeba, I want back my copy of *Intimacy*.'

'You flew to Bombay for a book?'

'I only ever fly for books. Even Pasadena. My mother claimed to have secured *How Late It Was, How Late*. Autographed. A lie.'

'Never heard of Amazon, Neev?' This was Mik.

'Too plebeian even for you, my friend.'

'Never claimed ...'

Mik didn't get to finish the sentence he had obviously laboured over. Neev had moved on to other matters, the bloody humid weather, and that he abhorred air conditioning, and that he abhorred even more the lack of it.

'I've turned into a curmudgeonly old man.'

'You have, Neev.' This, of course, was Mik.

'On the bright side, you occupy a favourite word.' Me.

'I grow more curmudgeonly and more seductive. Now give me the damned book, Sheeba.'

'On the condition that you read none of it. You're not being a damp squib.'

Neev read out a whole page.

As a passage, it felt like the most devastating one I had heard in years; the words collapsing into themselves.

'*Soon we will be like strangers. No, we can never be that. Hurting someone is an act of reluctant intimacy. We will be dangerous acquaintances with a history. The first time I put my hand on her arm—I wish I had turned away. Why didn't I?*'

Like Kureishi, I was 'in three minds' about this and most other questions.

'Well, on that cheery note,' Neev got up, 'it's time we grabbed breakfast. And lunch. And maybe ...'

'You do know you're gatecrashing?' Mik. So sullen.

'I always gatecrash. Invitations are boring. Though, to be fair, I did inform you ...'

'It's our anniversary, Neev. Thanks for asking.' Mik. Still damnably sullen.

'Really? How long have you suffered this man for, Sheeba?'

'I'd rather not tell. It's depressing.'

'Well, let's try allaying some of your suffering. I know just the place.'

We left an hour later. I had changed out of my pjs. Mik was still in a sulk, but less so; it was impossible to remain testy when Neev was in his element. Besides, Mik's competitive streak had now been stoked; Neev was too much himself.

We did breakfast at Sassanian. We lay in a park. We did lunch at an eatery by the park, I forget its name, but it was new, the linen spotless, the waiters alert.

It was like nothing had altered, as though the eight wide years between us—between Neev's meandering wedding speech, and this instant, when the sun shone, and Mik griped, and Neev let slip a comment about the problem with whiners, and I laughed, and it was laughter I believed I had been estranged from—had condensed into a single heartbeat.

Then, Neev suggested we catch a cab, he had planned a surprise, and the surprise took us to a part of the city Mik frequented only if he had to. A gallery, of course a gallery, but not Chemould. It was something newer, swisher, larger. Vainer.

And we climbed up the stairs, past the silkscreen rendition of Monroe, past Indiana's *Love*, past ...

Till we reached a room, on the face of it so ordinary, transom, door, threshold, and slipped in, and slipped really into a discrete atmospheric layer, where up and down, hovering, were pillows of tinsel and of light, fuller, more buoyant than anything I had known. A docent in the background kept talking: '... the metallic pillows hold regular air and pure helium ...'

'Warhol. You know that, don't you, Sheeba?'

I was in the midst of silver clouds, floating, and away from it all—Kapur Mahal and Mik and we've-been-married-eight-years.

How faraway the voice sounded, the words no longer words, no longer even sound, *Shibs-it's-our-anniver* ...

It is. And there will be others.

I was no longer of the earth, a broken earth, but sky.

And in the sky, in the sky

anything is possible.

I reached for Neev's hand.

Hoodbhoy House

PRAYAAG AKBAR

'Sorry we had to bring her,' her mother called out. 'There was no one at home. We've already let our servants go.'

'Don't be silly, Namita,' the bearded man said, walking towards them from a way down the brightly lit hall. The servant who had let them in, wearing a green smock that made him look to Shirley Kalra like a hospital nurse, retreated on light feet. The host looked the girl up and down without real interest and turned back to her mother. Shirley, on the other hand, was very interested as her parents had talked about the bearded man nonstop for the two-hour drive from Andheri. His fine beard was brown, almost orange. The shirt was tucked in and open to the waist, narrow chest and a few fibrous hairs showing. 'Abhay mentioned. When are you guys off? Looking forward to it?'

'A bit nervous,' Namita said. Shirley watched her mother blink a few times in rapid succession in that slightly stupid way she did when she was nervous. 'We're so used to the pace of life here. The work. End of the week we're leaving.'

The house was fancy. There were many paintings on the walls in the hall itself, and even other things you don't usually see strung up, like brass shields and swords and wooden masks, plenty of photographs of the city from British times. There were flowers in vases and pink petals floating in a large stone basin by the entrance. Shirley had once seen a post on Instagram that showed how all the really old apartments in Malabar Hill had very high ceilings. This house was just like that.

Abhay was parking the car. Namita and Shirley walked carefully through the gleaming foyer and into the living room, the young girl noting the couches of different bright colours and a few people, six or seven, occupying various seats.

'I need you to sit here quietly,' Namita whispered, pointing to a chair in a corner of the room. 'Ari and Rahul don't have any kids.' Shirley did not need reminding. Namita handed her daughter a tablet, which she opened to Roblox, a game she'd started playing in the car that involved colour-matching and then shooting down balloons before others could. When she next looked up, her mother was at the bar with the host. Soon, the doorbell rang, and her father came into the room, and he also began to chat with people and drink whiskey from the glass he was given, as if Shirley wasn't there. In some time, the servant brought her something to drink that she hadn't ever tasted, something floral and fruity, though with a sharp, bubbly taste. She sipped it slowly at first.

When the balloons began to jump into one another and the game started to sizzle her eyes, Shirley looked up once again. A group of the older people were laughing in that free, loud way they do once they've had some drinks. Her father was standing not too far away, talking to a short woman, very fit, in a tight blue dress, with a face that seemed not to move as she spoke.

'We've thought about it ourselves quite often,' the woman said. She had a compressed way of speaking, like her mouth could not open wide. 'The city was so tough during the pandemic. And Goa can be great fun. Cyrus's family has a house there, in Bambolim. But what about work? That's what Cyrus always says.'

'I'll be running my production house from there,' Abhay said. 'We've got some exciting work lined up. I'm even pitching for a feature. Wrote it myself.'

'I don't know anything about your world,' the lady smiled. 'Goa must be a lovely place to shoot.'

'Oh yes, gorgeous,' Abhay said. He had adopted the loud, direct voice that always made Shirley squirm. 'There's not a lot of work there, of course. I'm planning to be in and out of Bombay all the time.' He leant slightly towards the woman, and when he used a lower tone, his daughter felt sure immediately that she could tell what he would say, that she'd heard it already. 'You see, we have to move because of our daughter. She's having a tough time adjusting at school.' He took a sip of his drink and leant in closer. There was some difference of height, but it still seemed like they were nearly touching foreheads. 'Getting bullied.'

Shirley could feel her ears growing very hot. She usually didn't mind her parents talking about her. But all that horrible rubbish had started in school only this year, after the winter break. Her parents had been talking about moving to Goa at least a few months before that.

'I'm sorry to hear this,' the lady said. 'The change might be good. She'll have more space to run around.' The woman glanced in Shirley's direction, and when she saw the young girl looking back, she smiled thinly at the father and walked on. Abhay stood there looking a bit lost, handsome, studying the other faces, until finally he saw his daughter staring at him. He produced a grin and walked over.

'If you think this is nice,' he said, eyeballs darting to each corner to indicate the swirl of glamour around them, 'you should've seen the family place, Hoodbhoy House. Massive bungalow right on Cuffe Parade. Imagine. Lawns that looked out onto the ocean. Souzas and Razas on every wall.' Abhay turned suddenly to one side, then watched the host as he moved across the party floor towards the bar. He hurried off in the same direction.

Shirley knew not to be sad about what her father said to the lady because this was an important night for him. It was all her parents had talked about on the drive over here and through the last few days. A few years ago, her dad had shot an ad for this Rahul guy's textile business. It was a name that had been mentioned many times in their house: Rahul Hoodbhoy. Her parents would go to parties at his house and talk about the evening for weeks. Then they started referring to a couple, Rahul and Ari. But Shirley hadn't heard either name in quite some time now. She was surprised when her parents told her they would be coming here for dinner—that too right before they left the city for good.

The legend in the family, the story she'd heard related by either parent over dinner and at family gatherings so many times, was that Rahul loved the first ad so much that he insisted his company's garment ads would all be shot by Abhay. This was no ordinary company. No ordinary Rahul. The family was known throughout the country, Rahul directly in line to inherit Mumbai's largest textile mill and property beyond imagination all over the city, all over Maharashtra. There was a distant Hoodbhoy cousin two years above Shirley in school, and even he showed off like anything. Shirley had heard the lore of her father's ad and its popularity so many times, but this evening, just a few hours ago, when they were stuck in the traffic along Haji Ali, as she watched the headlights of the SUVs and the yellow blinkers of the construction cranes, and her mother and father argued in a low tone about something or the other, she caught one remark, Mummy's voice turning snide, acidic, 'Of course it was all very easy when Rahul wanted to get in your pants.' Shirley didn't understand quite what her mother meant, though she felt a sudden flutter of warmth in her stomach and was a little fidgety after.

The production house Abhay worked for had grown very fast. Abhay insisted it was all because of his work, because of these suit ads in particular; he fought with the guy who owned the production house and decided to set up his own. But for some reason the textile ads stopped. That was when he began to spend a lot more time at home, sitting in front of the massive iMac screen in the living room until very late every night, rum and cigarettes by his side.

There was a little brown fizz left in Shirley's glass, so she drank it down. The last bit tasted very tart, and she noticed now there were some funny seed-like things at the bottom. It was a little unfair, what her father had said to this woman. Firstly, it was her parents who had wanted her to shift schools. She was happy at St. Anthony's. It took them weeks to convince her. To Shirley, it felt they were a bit weird about it. They would sit her down at the dining table with a Frooti or Coke, and they'd have these unnerving smiles attached to their faces, and they'd try to explain how important it was, how crucial to her future, how they'd heard from a friend about all the great facilities. But the thing they were most excited about—she could tell, she could always tell—was that this new school would plug her, and plug them, plug all three of them into some kind of amazing, unbeatable network. Shirley couldn't understand it at first—like what was she, their daughter or a router. But she got it now. She got it as soon as she walked into that rich-snot school.

The servant must have come through again, because her glass was gone, and in its place had appeared a plate of tarts filled with a foamy blue paste, topped with tiny marbles of translucent green. Shirley had been looking at the art on the walls, some of it very different from one another, but now, boring of this, she began to study the many beautiful things on the tables around her. On a side table in the corner there was a cute little hedgehog, its cast-iron bristles sticking out in bubbles like a custard apple. She reached for a tart. It was delicious. On one side of the long bar was a wooden Buddha and on the other a marble Ganesha. There was an old and kind of dirty metal fireplace, which was puzzling, for Bombay. And all the way in the corner over by the doorway there was an antique cherry-red rotary phone with handles of gold or brass inlay. Shirley wasn't sure if it was the first time she'd seen a rotary phone. She couldn't stop staring.

Shirley had already forgiven her father. He was trying his best. She had a sense that he had been quite stressed about work for the last year or two. Her parents had also been fighting a lot, about the shift and so on. That was expected before such a big change. Her mother had explained that to her. Shirley was thinking about the worst fight she'd witnessed, each screaming from the opposite side of the dining table, when she became conscious of a tightness in her belly, just underneath her stomach. The long drive and then that tall fizzy drink had left her needing to use the bathroom. She stood up, trying not to scrape the legs of the chair, though the murmur that emanated from the party had turned noticeably louder, a low clamour. As she walked out of the room, she paused for a bit to look properly at that perfectly polished phone, its thick layer of red, like the paint on a car, the floral engraving patterns wrapped around the earpiece on the golden handle. She now noticed something strange. The rotary dial had a smooth clear-crystal lid cover, completely transparent, so you could see all the numerals in their circular cages. Set to one side of the crystal lid was a metal plate with a tiny golden key slotted into a keyhole. It was very puzzling. She couldn't understand why anyone would make a key and a keyhole to lock up the dial of a rotary phone. But then she thought about how everyone locks their phones even now, just that they use a password instead. It probably made sense in olden times too.

Out in the hall, one door was left open at a discreet crack, telling her the bathroom lay beyond. The servant in his green smock was standing there too, a little way down the hall, unsmiling, not looking at her or at anything, it seemed. For a few months, things had been fine at the new school. Not totally fine, but pretty much okay. She'd made a couple of friends. It's not like everyone at the school was mean or money-minded. And there were quite a few kids who weren't loaded. But some of the rich kids would let you know when you wore cheap shoes or a cringey bracelet. Even the rest, the ones who had been taught that it wasn't right to openly show off, would talk in class about the trip they took to Europe over Diwali because their parents couldn't stand the pollution. Things like that. Everyone knew, as if by instinct, who stood where.

There was a pretty girl in her class, Anamika, who occupied one of these positions near the front of the parade. She had the right hair, knew the right kids from outside school hours, *through our families*, as they liked to say. Every day Anamika brought a new bottle of Prime to school (800 rupees per bottle). She usually ignored Shirley, but one time during lunch break they had a tense moment—Shirley cracked a joke to a couple of girls about how Anamika had pronounced a certain word in English class and Anamika heard. For some weeks, there was no response. But then she got wind of the fact that Shirley was one of two girls, along with four boys, who wouldn't be going on this year's school trip. Over winter break, the class was visiting Verbier, a ski town in Switzerland, for an eight-day camp where they would learn or improve their skiing and snowboarding. Shirley did not inform her parents about the school trip. There had been some fights that month about credit card bills.

In January, on the first day of school, just before class, Anamika and two of her friends went up to Nita, the other girl who had not gone to Switzerland. Nita was a scholarship student, captain of the U-13 volleyball league, dark, but not too dark, a bit like Zendaya. She came from the Prem Nagar chawl. That morning, Anamika and her friends made a big deal of Nita, telling her, *we missed you so much when we were there, we all chipped in to get you this, it's made from 100 per cent sustainable materials,* and they presented her with this multicoloured backpack from a company called Namuk. They ignored Shirley completely. And only then did she notice, because she turned around now and looked to the back of the classroom where they hung their schoolbags, that all the girls in class had bought one of these backpacks in Switzerland. Some of the bags came in different colours and sizes, but each had this distinctive style and branding. Shirley could not control herself. She started to cry. And now it had become a thing in their class, a funny running joke, to leave her out of stuff. To leave her out of everything, basically. Nita did it too. Shirley didn't blame her.

Still, she'd never asked her parents to move out of Bombay. Not even to take her out of the school.

The hallway bathroom was enormous, mirrors everywhere, and smelled amazing. Shirley peed slowly and washed her hands in the pink sink. When she entered the party room again, she saw that one of the male guests had climbed on to the couch and was snaking his hips about to the music, as Ari, whom she had identified through the photographs on the walls, laughed and pretended to pull him off. Shirley looked around the room. Her father seemed to have finally got the quiet moment he needed with Rahul. Her mother was sitting on a couch with that same frozen-face woman Papa had been talking to. She felt a surge of emotion. Mummy was crying, though not in a dramatic way. She wanted to go to her, to help. But she felt sure her mother did not want her there. 'There was some bad timing, that's for sure,' Shirley heard her mother say. 'Just as Abhay had the company rolling, all the ad spend seemed to shift to social media. He just couldn't get any projects.'

Shirley didn't want to listen anymore, so she thought she would check out the antique telephone again. Her father was leaning against a pillar in that part of the living room. Rahul was standing just in front of him, his hand on Papa's shoulder, squeezing it gently from time to time. She couldn't hear what they were saying. Shirley walked up to the phone now and squatted next to it, studying the crystal lid, the rotary dial underneath it, the numerals one to nine housed in their neat circular cells. She stared at the key. It seemed to get bigger as she looked at it. She still couldn't understand why the numbers needed to be locked up like this, locked out of all the fun, the fresh air, the people and conversations, just sitting there, locked out as forces and fires of every kind swirled around them.

A twist of panic. Her father's voice suddenly crying out. 'So that's it, then? You're absolutely sure?' he said, his voice loud in dismay. Shirley wondered if other people at the party could hear. She wondered if her mother could hear.

The host shook his head sadly. Her father shrugged off his hand with a start, as if he'd suddenly realized it was there. Rahul did not like this. Shirley could see it on his face. He'd been looking up at Abhay. Suddenly his eyes turned narrow.

'It's not in my control, Abhay,' he said. 'Things are different since the IPO. It's not a family business anymore. We've hired an outside CEO, there's a team that makes these decisions. I've taken a step back—in fact, I'm hardly involved now.'

Shirley was supposed to take the key. Suddenly she was certain of this. It was important—more than that, crucial—to liberate those elegant numerals. How did it matter, amid this profusion and splendour, it was only a tiny key, not even real gold. There was no way anyone would miss it. She looked around the room. Her mother was still on the couch. Her father was by the pillar. Like everyone else, they were locked in conversation. No one paid any attention to her. All she had to do was unlock the lid and slip the key into her pocket. Her hand began to shake, but she raised it all the same. Placed her fingers upon the shining oblong bow of the key. Turned it, checked to see if the lid actually opened. It did. Immediately, she felt a wave of relief, like some weight had been taken off her head. Again, she scanned the room. No one was looking at her. She drew the key out of its hole and slipped it into her pocket. It felt amazing. Perhaps she had stopped breathing for a bit, because suddenly she took in air in big gulps. She turned around casually, no longer with her back to the party, and was about to go back to her chair, when she saw the servant staring directly at her through the open doorway.

She froze. Her brain seemed frozen too. Or the thoughts were rushing in too fast, a cascading river, she couldn't hold on to just one. The servant stared at Shirley with no expression on his face. Could she detect the beginning of a smile? A smile of knowledge, of control, of power. More than anything else in the world, she did not want him coming into the living room and confronting her there, in front of her parents, in front of all these fancy guests. Instead of going to her chair, she pretended to herself, maybe no one else had noticed, that she needed to use the bathroom again, and walked out of the door. The servant was standing by the bathroom door. It was natural to walk in his direction. She wanted to explain about the numerals, wanted to show him it was just a trifle. But as she approached him, she lost her nerve. It was his face—she could not tell if he was impassive, oblivious, or if that was indeed the hint of an evil smile. She walked by him, unable to utter a word. He did not even nod at her. But as soon as Shirley put her hand on the bathroom door handle, he said in Hindi, 'Madam, what did you take from the table?'

Suddenly a new courage. 'What are you talking about?' she asked in her iciest tone. She answered in English, to emphasize the difference in status. So he would remember his place. His expression did not flicker, still curious, suggestive, indeterminate.

'Madam, from the table,' he continued in Hindi. 'I saw you take something and put it in your pocket. Was it one of those jade figures? The ceramic bowl? Everything in this house is expensive.'

'I didn't take anything,' Shirley said. She tried to keep her voice firm. 'Leave me alone.'

'Yes, you did. I saw. Give it back. Don't make me look for it.'

'If you touch me, I'll scream,' she whispered.

'You're right,' he said. He started towards the living room. 'Better to tell sir.'

'Wait!' she whispered again. What a rotten, mad impulse. A mess of a moment. Her mother and father to be mortified in front of all these people. Just imagining it made her panic. 'Please,' she said. 'Don't go.' She put her hand in her pocket, feeling the key between her fingers, rolling it into her palm. She clenched her fist tight around it. Took her hand out of her pocket and opened her palm. For a second the servant looked stupefied. He gazed at the brass key in her open palm and then at her face, the key again and back at her, surprise and confusion written all over him.

'What is that?' he asked.

'From the old phone,' she said.

'Why would you …' he began. Then went silent. He extended his hand.

She did not want to return the key. She considered dashing to the door, waiting by the car for her parents. She dropped the key into his hand and rushed into the living room.

Twenty minutes later, they were in the car on the way home.

'I don't understand why she couldn't use the loo there,' Abhay said. He looked at his daughter in the rearview mirror. 'She doesn't look so bad.'

'I did go,' Shirley said. 'My tummy still hurts. Hurts very badly.' Out of the window the nondescript buildings of Pedder Road rolled by. She put a hand on her stomach in case her father was still watching in the mirror.

'We didn't even get to eat,' her mother said, turning to look at her. 'I'll have to see what we have at home. Did you eat any snacks there?'

'Not hungry,' Shirley said. And she wasn't. She was desperately on edge. Any moment, Rahul or Ari would be calling. The servant would have told them by now what she'd done, hopefully as an aside, not in front of all the guests, though she could imagine that scene too, the servant's public denouncement, their familial humiliation. They were almost at the Sea Link and still no call came. When they picked up speed on the enormous bridge, her mother suddenly made a sound.

'Oh, Abhay,' she said, 'how did it go with Rahul? Completely forgot to ask. Was he keen?'

Her father concentrated on the road for some moments. She saw his Adam's apple bob into sight and then disappear. Lights flashed by. A Porsche SUV too. 'I didn't get a chance to ask him,' he said.

'I thought I saw you guys chatting,' her mother said.

'We were catching up. I was building up to it.' She saw Papa eyeing her in the rearview mirror again. 'But then our baby had to go home. What to do?' he said. 'You know she's the priority.'

MARG

The Hon. Secy

KERSI KHAMBATTA

Mr Parikshit Kothari stood at the threshold of his front door, staring down at something six inches away from his feet, something shockingly alien. It looked like a swirl of chocolate ice cream emerging out of a cone, spiralling upwards and ending in a perfect perky point, except it was on the hard tile of the corridor outside, and it wasn't ice cream, was it, and that is what filled Parikshit Kothari with a quantum of anger he had never experienced before—*this was a violation*, this deserved a thermonuclear rage that would sear eyebrows for a hundred miles.

He sipped short breaths. *Inconceivable. In … in …* but he could not think of another word starting with 'in'. *Out*rageous. *Un …* un*conscionable.* He threw quick glances up and down the empty corridor, gratified that there was no one to witness this—this *in*vasion of his sacred space. Moreover, there was no one to witness how rattled he was by it—he, the honorary secretary of Ashok Niwas, Nepean Sea Road, a man as naturally inclined to lead as to breathe, now weakened by this abomination. How could it even be possible in a civilized world, in a building with one of the most coveted addresses in this island city, that the Hon. Secy would open his front door and be confronted by freshly dropped animal shit right on his fucking doorstep? From the eye-watering, nostril-searing stench, he also had a pretty good idea of what animal it was.

He went back in, and on shaky legs walked to the kitchen counter and pulled out a large garbage bag; only a pathological hatred for procrastination could trump the revulsion he felt. Straddling the open doorway, he turned the bag inside out, shoved his hand in and picked up that thing, almost weeping when he felt an evil squish, *eeeuuuurrrrggggbhh*, *hold it in, hold it in, Parikshit!*, then turning the bag right side out again, knowing that this was, quite simply, up there with the hardest things he had ever done in his life, harder than breaking it to his wife that they were done and battling her for equal time with his daughter, harder than even getting through his first four years of college with an unfortunate first name like Prick-Shit in that cruel, jeering nation far to the west.

He walked down one floor with that thing swinging next to his leg. The searing heat of the late-afternoon sun lanced him as he crossed the parking lot and opened the big dumpster stacked against the far wall. Fighting a gag reflex as it blew out garbage breath, he dumped his disgusting load and slammed the lid shut. Done! Although he could still scarcely believe what had just happened. He felt a shooting spasm in his lower belly, probably an ulcer forming there, he was sure of it.

As he staggered back into the cool of the hallway, a low, plaintive wail startled him out of his thoughts. He whirled around in time to see a big white and black tomcat emerge from No. 2 and eye him with disdain, like it knew him—*did you like the gift I left for you?*—then, in a flash, scurry past him out into the open, making him yelp and skip backward.

Flat No. 2! Miss Nair! He should've known it!

Alright then, he snarled, no time like the present.

He thumped the door of No. 2 three times with the flat of his palm. He jutted out his jaw at the peephole and thumped three more times, the third time almost slapping his palm into Miss Nair's nose. She was greying, medium-sized and wiry, with a stone-carved face and a body language that hinted she could throw a good punch if pushed to it. 'What do you want?' she barked, obviously peeved at Mr Kothari's stormtrooper-like manner. 'Do you see this doorbell?'

The tone of voice, talking to him like that! He pointed. 'The cat that just emerged from here. Do you feed it?'

She looked at where he was pointing, that is to say, in the direction the cat had disappeared. 'What cat?' she snapped.

Ah, a sense of humour. How droll.

'The filthy animal that just ran out of here and which I presume you let out, unless it can operate a Godrej latch, *that* cat.' No, sarcasm was beyond her. Mallus don't get sarcasm. 'Are you aware,' he continued with gravitas, 'that it does its toilet inside the building? Right outside my front door, in fact?' She started to shake her head, and he held up a finger. 'No, don't shake your head. You are merely a tenant, not even an owner. Are you aware of the anti-pet clauses in the building's bylaws?'

Obviously, she could not be aware, because Mr Kothari had just made that up on the spot.

'I don't know what you're talking about,' she said curtly, and started to shut the door on him. The ... audacity! He slammed his hand on it. 'Madam, you listen to me!' His voice squeaked in rage. 'This is your first and last warning ...' He stopped, stunned. Another cat, a striped tabby, sauntered out of a back room in her flat and leapt nimbly into her arms. She nuzzled its head and cooed at it. He gaped in disgust. 'How many are there?' he shrieked. Behind her, he saw yet another jump onto a chair and stare at him malevolently. His eyeballs bulged. 'What is this, a cat-shelter? Oh, I'm going to have a word with the society about ...'

She shut the door in his face, leaving him limp and stunned, dismissed like he was five years old. He seethed, feeling tears of incandescent rage prick at his eyes. He stood there for quite a while and then abruptly stomped outside into the parking lot, where the cries of little kids playing sounded like shrieking birds being mass murdered. His eyes spotted an unlikely ally far away. 'Ravindra!' he roared. Kothari blazed a warpath towards him, storing it away that the security guard just stood in the tree shade in his crisp brown uniform and tinted spectacles, stroking his movie-star moustache insolently. When Kothari was ten feet away and closing rapidly, he saluted, 'Namaskar, sir!'—which Kothari ignored and got straight to the point. 'Are you allowing stray cats to enter the compound? There seem to be three of four of them!'

Ravindra hadn't been a security guard for twenty years without knowing that the only way to face an irate honorary secretary was to look and act like he had the lowest passable IQ required to open and close a gate and nothing more. 'How do you stop a cat, sir?' he grinned. 'They just jump over walls and go where they please.'

Kothari pointed in the direction of Flat No. 2 on the ground floor. 'Does that lady, Miss Nair, feed them?'

Ravindra shrugged, although he knew the answer. 'Maybe, sir.'

'What maybe? If people don't feed stray cats, then they'll stop coming, no? They'll go somewhere else, am I right or not?'

'They've been here long time, sir, as kittens, long before you ...' Ravindra stopped, wondering if he had been spotted feeding them as well. He liked their furry company in the guard post.

'I don't care! One of these cats shat right outside my door!' Mr Kothari howled.

'Outside your door, sir?'

'And that bitch just ignored me. Just ignored me!'

'O-ho. Tch, tch, tch.'

Kothari glared at Ravindra, looking for signs of mockery, but Ravindra was a veteran. 'I'm going to get her thrown out,' Kothari snarled viciously. 'You watch. Just like those two ...' He didn't know the word for homosexual in Hindi. 'Those two in No. 42, know who I'm talking about?'

'Oh, those. Yes,' said Ravindra, wondering what they had done to piss off the secretary.

'Yes! They think they can fool me. Noticed anything odd about them?'

Ravindra wisely (and unfairly) made up the only answer that would suit Mr Kothari's mood. 'They're snooty. Look at me and talk to me like I'm beneath them.'

Kothari didn't care much for injured self-pity from a security guard. 'Get out your cell phone,' he ordered.

Ravindra looked pained. Kothari wiggled his fingers. With exaggerated reluctance, Ravindra poked first his front pocket and then his back pocket, and then eventually came around to the front again and slowly pulled out a new smartphone. Kothari sneered. 'Fancy, Ravindra.'

'EMI, sir,' Ravindra said, showing him his teeth.

'Looks like you have a few side hustles going, eh?'

'No, sir,' said Ravindra, looking hurt and defensive.

Mr Kothari pulled out his phone. 'What's your number?'

Ravindra uttered each digit as though he were selling his kidney in bits and pieces. Mr Kothari dialled the number and Ravindra's phone rang. 'Good,' he said grimly. 'Because you never answer the intercom! I want those cats out of here. All of them. Taken somewhere so far away that they never find their way back. Understood?'

'Taken … where, sir?'

'You don't understand what faraway means? Malad, Borivali, I don't care!'

Ravindra's eyes flicked this way and that. 'Can be done,' he said uncertainly, hinting that this would be Mr Kothari's cue to stick a five-hunner in his hand immediately.

'Tonight!'

Ravindra looked grave. 'Tonight won't be possible, sir.'

'Why not?'

'You can't catch cats so easily. You need carry-boxes, and food to lure them in, and …' Ravindra licked his lips.

Mr Kothari waited.

'And all together is impossible, sir. One maybe tonight, another on another night, like that.' Ravindra, the cat-lover, knew of a perfectly good cat-shelter. Question was—how much could he get this miser to cough up?

'They have to go all at once.'

Ravindra's eyes flickered shiftily. 'It'll cost money, sir.'

'How much?'

Just the slightest hesitation, and then: 'About … five thousand rupees.'

Mr Kothari reeled. 'Five thousand rupees for what?'

'For the carry-boxes,' Ravindra rattled off, his eyes deadpan. 'For bait food.'

Mr Kothari boiled and frothed. The ulcer gave a pang. Ravindra waited, watching the secretary squirm. And then immediately regretted it, because Mr Kothari had spotted something else now. 'What is Mr Prabhudesai's scooter still doing there?' he demanded, summoning a fresh rage.

'Sir, I told him,' Ravindra said weakly. 'He doesn't listen, and ...'

'So, then you do what I told you to do, no? Pick up that damned scooter and get it out of my parking space. Then he'll learn.'

'Sir, please tell him yourself. He is, after all, a senior person, and he's your neighbour.'

'I have told him,' Kothari lied. 'But he pretends to be deaf. Go and move it, now.' Ravindra waited patiently—surely this, now, was the secretary's cue to dip his hand in his pocket, but Mr Kothari just crossed his arms. 'You know I can stop all your side hustles like this, yes?'—snap of fingers. 'Never at your post when needed. Twenty years on the job won't protect you, my friend, if the committee and I decide otherwise. Go!'

Ah! The sheer hatred that shone through those tinted lenses as Ravindra waddled out of the shade. Kothari shouted after him, 'Don't scratch my car.'

He watched as Ravindra tried the scooter handle in the hope that it was not locked, for then it would be a simple matter of wheeling it out. But of course, it was locked—the fastidious Mr Prabhudesai would have it no other way. Ravindra beckoned to Chandu and Dilip who were having a smoke by the compound wall; they swept and swabbed the hallways of Ashok Niwas twice daily and cleared out the garbage for the BMC. When they walked up, Ravindra said something to them with a surly pout, and then all three looked at Mr Kothari, who felt their lower-class hatred waft towards him.

They bent over and hefted up the heavy Lambretta that was parked right next to Mr Kothari's shiny Škoda. Ravindra looked like his heart would explode out of his mouth. Sweat gushed down his face, making his moustache dye run down his lips and chin. The three men shambled and shuffled, sucking in air, as they lugged away the Lambretta from its sheltered spot towards the row of two-wheelers parked out in the open. By the time they set it down, the watchman's brown uniform was black with sweat. This satisfied Mr Kothari tremendously—somehow, in small measure, even balanced out the indignities he had suffered so far today. He walked back through the squalling children into the dimly lit stairwell of the four-storey walk-up that would soon be redeveloped into a shiny, phallic tower standing with the other giants on Nepean Sea Road.

Back in his flat, Mr Kothari flipped open the lid to his weapon of mass destruction and started firing away. First email, to the committee members.

> *... on the issue of Flat No. 42, it remains to be seen if the owner is just blithely uncurious about the nature of the relationship between the tenants who occupy his flat as long as he gets his rent. I mean, this Rajdeep Singh, an ex-sailor (calls himself a marine consultant), sharing a flat with this Mr Gidwani who owns a chain of hair salons?? Two single men in their 30s sharing a flat?? A sailor and a hairdresser?? What is this, some ridiculous YMCA cliché?? Do they have any shame??*

He imagined the four-member committee swaying mesmerized in front of their screens, their sheep-eyes sucking in the words and their sheep-will being yoked to his—here he was, the new sheriff in town with compelling pop-culture references and forceful rhetoric. He signed off: *The Hon. Secy*. Thumped the send key. And the email flew to the intended targets. No. 42—as good as done. His mood improved considerably; he banged out the next one.

> *... it is abundantly obvious to the more clear-headed members of this society that the future is glass and steel and marble lobbies and three elevators zooming up twenty floors, not squat, ugly, four-storey eyesores and chawl-style flats lined up next to each other ...*

He stopped typing. Too much unintended poetry? Would the Top Suits at Agarwal Builders appreciate his literary flair and the breezy informality in what should be an official email? Of course, they would; they were only human. Plus, it let them know they were dealing with a renaissance man.

Just twenty poky flats, he pounded on, *sprawled horizontal, when you could have one hundred piled vertical. People ready to pay top dollar and solve the deepening housing crisis*. Ah, a renaissance man with a solid eye for facts and practicality. *It has gotten so bad, I almost got locked out of my flat the other day as the front door just swung shut, the floors are warped so badly ...*

He lifted his fingers and let them cool off or they would go on doing the frilly word dance around the main point of this email. *We are almost there; there is just one intractable flat owner, No. 11, a certain Mr Prabhudesai, who is influencing the others against redevelopment. He just needs a push in the right direction*—'Straight into oncoming traffic,' he said aloud and snickered, as his fingers played on—*and it will be sorted in time for the next SGBM when we will put it to a vote. On behalf of the members of Ashok Niwas, The Hon. Secy.*

Send. He unkinked his neck, and his eye caught an unread mail in his inbox. Sender: utkarsh.prabhudesai@ashokniwaschs.co.in. Speak of the devil! It was copied to every other committee member. He wondered what Utkarsh meant, probably something noble and inspiring in Sanskrit—'He Who is Anti-Progress,' he spoke aloud again, amused by his own wit. He opened the mail and read the half-wit babble. *I strongly urge you'll to check the financials of said builder for the redevelopment project as I believe your being too trusting on word alone ...*

He thumped back a reply-to-all entirely unassisted by his brain. A veteran of countless emails, his fingers just knew where to fall. *Mr Prabhudesai, I strongly urge you to never use 'you'll' when you mean 'you all'. And 'your' instead of 'you're'??? Did you go to school or are you just too lazy to use apostrophes in the right places?*

Ah, too harsh? Well, he was eighty or something, wasn't he? Old enough to take it on the chin. He hit send.

On a roll now, he immediately dialled the landlord of No. 42, who lived elsewhere but rented out his Ashok Niwas flat to—'Fags,' Kothari said aloud, a word he could never have used in New York, he thought sourly. It was after six in the evening now, and the landlord got snotty about the sanctity of work-call timings, but Mr Kothari got straight to the point, and in the next ten seconds the landlord of No. 42 was spitting and sputtering. 'The committee has unanimously decided what? How dare they ... how, how, what, what ...' Mr Kothari waited for the man to try and finish at least one sentence and then cut him short. 'It has already been decided. And in future, when the new building comes up, please screen your tenants properly so that the society does not become a den of debauchery …' He hung up.

Later that evening, at precisely 9 p.m., he called his ex-wife, discussed alimony and daughter-sharing, zoned out the second she got bitter about this and that—'Everything is about you, even what time we speak on the phone, you just manipulate the whole world into thinking that you are somehow more important'—yadda, yadda, yadda—until he cut her short with—'We can discuss the final arrangements again on Thursday at this same time'—and then hung up.

He watched television for a bit, not really concentrating, aware that the ulcer pain in his lower gut was not coming in waves anymore but was more of a steady low moan, the dial at, say, two. He popped the last two paracetamols in the strip and the low moan went away. Must call a doc tomorrow about this ulcer, he told himself.

The next day, after a leisurely afternoon nap, Mr Kothari drove his gleaming Škoda to Foodland, barely a kilometre away, to stock up on provisions. He strolled through its air-conditioned aisles, plucking this and that, humming to the soothing elevator music. It had a tiny pharmacy section—throat lozenges, antacid pills, the ubiquitous paracetamol. He grabbed three strips of the latter. The dial on his gut pain was still at two, but ulcers only got worse if you let them, didn't they?

When he returned, Ravindra was absent from the gatepost, as always. Never mind; he'd catch him later, that cut-throat tariff to dispose of the cats requiring some serious renegotiating, oh yes. As he drove in through the unmanned gate and beheld the squat and ugly building of his birth and childhood, he grimaced with revulsion.

The very first day he had come home after twenty years and gazed upon it, instead of nostalgia, it depressingly reminded him of the tiny walk-up on Lex Avenue in NYC he had now abandoned forever. It had reminded him of—he couldn't say the words, but they flitted across his mind—mediocrity and failure. His failure in New York after twenty years, despite doing everything to conform—mastering the accent, voting Republican. In the end, he lived on a street called Curry Hill with other … mediocre failures. The stench of grilling kebabs and rotting flesh in day-old garbage bags outside the Indian and Pakistani restaurants—oh, the ignominy of it. Mediocrity and failure, two words he would never use again. Ever.

Soon, Ashok Niwas would be Ashoka Apartments, the newest jewel of Nepean Sea Road, and with the right pushes and nudges, an all-vegetarian haven. His top-floor penthouse would command the finest view in the whole of the island city.

He drove past Mr Prabhudesai, who was looking down miserably at his Lambretta scooter slowly grilling under the sun. Kothari was in no mood to listen to that croaky, whiny voice but, of course, he had barely boop-booped the car doors shut when the old fool walked up, all twisted with age. 'Good evening, sir,' Mr Prabhudesai said, never forgetting his manners.

Kothari turned a cold eye upon him. 'Yes?'

The old man gave a world-weary sigh. 'You know what this is about. We had this conversation four months ago when you moved in, after your brother … passed. I requested you if I could …'

'Yes, your scooter. What about it?'

'You said I could continue to park it in your space. You see, outside in the sun, the seat gets so hot, I can't even sit on it. And the paint just fades away.'

'Well, your scooter scratched my car door. My parking space is not wide enough for both vehicles.'

'Scratched your door?'

'Just got it fixed,' snapped the Hon. Secy, running his fingers randomly over gleaming steel. A sad and amused smile drifted across Mr Prabhudesai's face. 'That is just not true, sir. But it is so, I suppose, if you say it, because who has the time or patience to go up against you?'

Mr Kothari shivered with annoyance. 'I really don't understand people like you. Why are you so … anti-progress? And riling up other members as well? I just don't get it.'

'Are you talking about my scooter now or …'

'Forget your bloody scooter! Or wait. Let's use your stupid scooter as an example, maybe that will help you understand. Say, I offer you a twenty-lakh motorcycle in its stead, with … I don't know …' His hand waved in the air because he really didn't know anything about the subject and was improvising. 'A turbocharged engine and … and … a music system and speakers and … and … better brakes and … whatnot. What about that, huh? Would you or would you not take it?'

Mr Prabhudesai gave him a pitying look. 'Mr Kothari,' he said patiently. 'This builder you have chosen to redevelop Ashok Niwas is not a reliable one. There's a history of corruption, shady dealings, cutting corners, talking big and not delivering and …'

'And you know this how?' Mr Kothari raged.

Again, that look of aggravating condescension. 'Why, the trade papers, the business news. It's all out there, their track record, and I am merely drawing your attention and the society's to it …'

'Utter rubbish! I can find dirt on the cleanest businessman on the internet if I choose to. I could find dirt on Mr Ratan Tata if I wished.' He held up his hand as the old man opened his mouth. 'Mr Prabhudesai, there's no such thing as a free lunch. Understand? Everything is give and take. Actual work on redevelopment is at least six months away, and you are holding it up with your ill-lettered emails to other society members. You want favours, you give in return, and don't be difficult and … contrarian. Do you understand what I'm saying? Do you?'

Of course he understood, thought the secretary with relish.

Mr Kothari was thirsty, and the paracetamols were in his shopping bag when they should've been already calming his lower digestive tract. He swivelled on his feet and left the old man standing next to his stupid scooter whose seat was too hot to sit on and whose paint was already fading in increments. Why do they even call them *cooperative* housing societies, he wondered in disgust as he walked up to his first-floor flat, when you have imbeciles like …

He stopped dead in his tracks.

There, in the geometric centre of his doorway, was a little pile of steaming fresh excrement, like it had just been dropped seconds ago. Mr Kothari felt the blood drain from his limbs. He tightened his grip on the shopping bags lest they fall. He could not put names to the feelings that coursed through his soul as he unlatched his door, stepped over that freshly laid thing of horror and dashed into his house, letting the front door shut on its own. He dropped the shopping bags and leaned on the kitchen counter. Bullied—that's how he felt. The universe was bullying him. He popped two paracetamols and poured a stiff vodka, added soda, drank it slowly, then poured another, and then a third.

He called the gatepost on the intercom, quite drunk, and felt his temper soar as it rang on and on. He called Ravindra's newly acquired cell number, and he could picture Ravindra eyeing the Truecaller ID and ignoring it …

He poured a fourth drink and thought of innovative ways to castrate Ravindra when he met him next. He looked out of the window to see if he could spot Chandu or Dilip somewhere and yell at them to come up and remove that ghastliness outside his door. No sign of them. He realized that he was as good as trapped in this flat, trapped until that abomination outside had been cleared, because he could not bear to open the door and repeat yesterday's ghastly process again. There may well have been, instead of mere faecal matter, a coiled viper waiting outside for him.

He poured himself another vodka, opened his laptop and drunkenly tapped out a succinct set of keywords—*cat shitting outside my front door*—and speed-read the results. Before he knew it, he was down a Reddit and Quora rabbit hole of opinions on likely causes and hokey homegrown solutions, which he devoured as he drank two more vodkas. When three hours later—it was almost 9 p.m.—he was plastered completely, he once again transformed into a man of action. All squeamishness was gone, drowned dead in Absolut. He felt tigerish.

He grabbed his house keys and an old *Vogue*—the magazine amused him sometimes—and tore off its thick, glossy cover. He grabbed a *GQ* as well—he read those avidly—and did the same. Armed with two resilient Condé Nast magazine covers and half a bottle of 40 proof alcohol churning his brain, he opened the front door. It was still there, of course, with those gazillion invisible germs swarming all over. He bent and scooped the pile of shit with the *GQ* cover pressed onto the *Vogue* cover. He walked down the corridor, holding the *Vogue* cover horizontal, the noxious hors d'oeuvre weighing it down. He walked down one floor and stood outside No. 2, waiting and listening. He heard domestic sounds of television and crockery from within. He entertained a delicious vision of ringing the doorbell and flinging the cat shit at Miss Nair's stupid bolshie face, but quickly dismissed the idea because the vodka hadn't given him courage enough to deal with the full-blown fistfight that would most certainly ensue afterwards with the enraged, shit-spattered Mallu harridan.

So, he transferred the *Vogue* cover to his throwing arm and flung its cargo at the door of No. 2. It made the softest *flup* as the cat shit streaked across her door, some of it sliding down to the tiled corridor. And then Mr Kothari dropped both magazine covers and darted like a frightened meerkat upstairs, back to his flat, giggling like a loon. Once safely behind his door, he let out a sigh of rapture—oh, that had felt so good. Tit for tat, Miss Nair, try waking up to that tomorrow morning. To celebrate, he poured one more drink and slept like a baby through the night.

'Bleach?' The bai looked at Mr Kothari for three seconds longer to wrap her head around what he was saying.

'Bleach,' he confirmed, his head heavy and wobbly with a crushing hangover.

'And that will make this cat stop?'

'Yes, it will!' He offered all that he had read on the Internet last night. 'Their nose … the smell … brings them back to the same place every time. Bleach will remove all past traces, plus add in the harsh, new bleach smell. The stupid cat will simply go elsewhere, find a new place.'

'Someone else's doorstep?' grinned the bai, who liked a little stir-up in her otherwise mundane day.

'Not my problem,' Mr Kothari said curtly, ending the conversation. And so, the bai assiduously poured the bleach into the bucket, and then applied the swab cloth to the floor, covering a large area on both sides of the door, which also included the floor outside Mr Prabhudesai's door. Mr Kothari inhaled, and his eyes watered—*take that, you cat.*

Later, when he stepped out looking for Ravindra to unleash hell on him, he paused outside No. 2 downstairs, smitten by a hazy memory of last night. Had he actually…? Everything was spotlessly clean now, of course, but he had, hadn't he …? And of course, she must have known it was him. Good.

He could not find Ravindra anywhere. He did find a substitute watchman in his place, a dull-looking, washed-out old man. Apparently, Ravindra was unwell and had taken a few days off. Furious at having had his gratification delayed (because he now had another plan, way more devilish and one that would not cost 5,000 rupees), he felt his ulcer stab at him as he walked back to his flat. He told himself, *I must call that doctor*. But he forgot as soon as he let himself in.

'Is this bleach?' inquired a bewildered Mr Prabhudesai, standing by his doorway, looking down at the floor.

'Should've been done right after the very first time. And you can thank me for taking care of the area outside your door as well.'

Mr Prabhudesai did not look thankful at all. 'The colour of the tiles …'

Mr Kothari looked—yes, the art deco tiles with their dramatic geometric patterns, all the vibrant magentas, blues and yellows, they were now …

'Bleached,' gasped Mr Prabhudesai. 'Almost gone.'

Mr Kothari had to admit that yes, this was indeed in stark contrast to the rest of the corridor that still shone in multihued splendour. All in just three days.

'A bit like your scooter in the sun, perhaps?' he riposted with a cruel sneer. 'Ten days to the SGBM! I hope you're using your powers of persuasion for the greater good!' He slammed his door in Mr Prabhudesai's face.

Later, much later, during his scheduled 9 p.m. conversation with his wife, she said, 'Pepper. Cats run a mile from it. It hurts their delicate noses.'

'Pepper?'

'Yes, ground pepper. You should try that. Don't be frugal. Build up a perimeter, like a Lakshman Rekha, and then sprinkle the inside liberally as well.'

'Hmm. That is a good idea!' That probably being the nicest thing he had said to her lately, as he sipped his third drink of the night. This was something new, drinking every night, but it felt good. The ulcer had gone away as well these past few days, good riddance, and he credited the booze in some measure for that.

'You'll have to do it every day. Two-three hundred grams.'

'Look at you, suddenly the expert on cats and pepper.'

'Weird, huh,' she said.

After he hung up, he went to bed, two more drinks down and in a good mood. And so did his wife, wondering what other bright idea she could give him tomorrow so he would make an even bigger ass of himself, all of this nothing more than tiny sips of revenge for the way he was treating her.

'Pepper now?' Mr Prabhudesai almost wailed, his eyes and nose red from itching.

Mr Kothari shrugged. 'Just hold your breath entering and leaving your house. Common sense.'

'But why?'

'Because it's working! Or haven't you noticed? Five whole days, not one incident! But of course, why would you notice? It's not your doorstep the cat had chosen.'

'Where do you get these ... odd ideas?' said an anguished Mr Prabhudesai, wiping his watering eyes.

'The internet. And from experts,' sniffed the Hon. Secy.

Mr Prabhudesai shook his head wearily. 'Your brother, he loved cats. Did you know?'

Mr Kothari did not particularly care to know, but the old man clearly had more to say. 'Before Miss Nair used to feed them, he used to feed them. They would come here and wait patiently. And then, after he passed away, one of them, the black-and-white one, would come back regularly and just sit here, sad and forlorn, do nothing but just sit here with the saddest eyes, waiting for him to return. This was before you moved in.'

Mr Kothari started to get annoyed with all this sentimental imagery. 'Sad and forlorn,' he mimicked. 'Waiting for him to return, oh boo-hoo. And then what, it suddenly decides to shit here instead?'

Mr Prabhudesai just shrugged. 'Animals are strange. Who can understand them? But they always have good reasons for doing things.' And with a very pointed look at the Hon. Secy, he disappeared inside and shut his door before a furious Mr Kothari could ask him just what the hell he meant by that.

Two more days passed in this fashion. Kothari's doorway stayed resolutely undefiled—the damn internet had got it right, hadn't it, or maybe it was the pepper, for which he did not thank his wife because she was back to being a pain in his ass. Ravindra would return tomorrow, he was told. And then—yeah, he'd like to be around as Miss Nair wailed and tore out her hair when his new diabolical plan had been set in motion.

Just one ugly incident marred those two days. It was inevitable, you might say.

It was 7 p.m., the summer sun still visible over the horizon. His carry bag clinked with two bottles of Absolut and a dozen bottles of tonic water, as he locked his Škoda and started towards the entrance. He did not see a huddle of three men standing next to a large tempo laden with luggage. He was only thinking that an hour from now would be a good time to pour his first drink and …

'Oi! You … you! Mr Secretary!' Mr Kothari turned and his stomach clenched in fear as Mr Rajdeep Singh, ex-sailor and now marine consultant, barrelled right into him 'Did you make this happen? Did you?'

'Made … made what happen? I'm sorry, I … I don't know what …'

Mr Singh turned around. 'Yo, Ash. This is the fucker responsible.'

And then the other guy—the chain-of-hair-salons CEO—marched up, fists clenched and forearms wriggling with veins. 'What the fuck is wrong with you?' he asked.

'He's a cunt, that's what he is,' offered the marine consultant.

'I'm … what, sorry? No, no, I'm … I … I have no idea what …'

'Did you rile up the committee to have us kicked out?' asked the hair salon CEO.

'I … no. No, that's not …'

'What about us made you think we were gay, you stupid meddling cocksucker?'

'Do you know how hard it is to find a decent flat to rent in this city, you motherfucker?'

Mr Kothari babbled. 'I … I did not … I … I …'

'I … I … I … I …' sneered the unrelenting marine consultant. 'You fucking choot!'

Salon CEO stepped closer, and Mr Kothari cringed. This guy looked fluent in violence. 'Are you a closet fag?' he hissed. 'A frightened little bumbandit yourself hiding in plain sight in this uptight society?' And he jabbed four fingers painfully in Mr Kothari's chest. It was only with Herculean effort that the secretary did not burst into tears. This was uni all over again, so many years ago—the sign stuck on his back with a drawing of a penis next to a pile of shit, *my name is Prick-Shit, come say hi.*

Mercifully, the landlord of No. 42, who had only watched so far, walked over and put a hand on Hair Salon's arm. 'Let it go. Idiots like him exist, sadly. My broker will find you a better place to live.'

But the young men were not fully done yet. 'Kothari, huh? What is that, some cult of baniya cunts? Fucking Nazis,' spat the hairdresser.

'Slimy little worm. Coward. Shit-stirrer.'

Mr Parikshit Kothari just looked down and did not say a word.

That night, he slept a broken man, his tortured dreams looping the same humiliation and failure over and over again.

The sharp pain in his lower gut was now dialled up to a four and stayed with him despite two doses of paracetamol.

If Ravindra, back from his unannounced 'sick' leave, had hoped that time would have somehow miraculously mellowed the rampaging secretary …

For five minutes, Parikshit Kothari railed at Ravindra's sudden 'sick' leave. Then he held up his phone to Ravindra's face, the screen alive with information. 'Here. The price of one carry-box. One thousand rupees. Go and buy it now. Trap one. Drown it there,' pointing towards the Arabian Sea just beyond Ashok Niwas, whose dirty waters lapped against the shore of Nepean Sea Road. 'Come back for the other three. Plan it efficiently. Maybe hundred rupees for bait food. And because I know you'll want a fee as well, that's 1,500 rupees, rounded off.'

Mr Kothari fished out three crumpled five-hundred-rupee notes and jammed them into Ravindra's sweaty palm. 'Tomorrow morning if I see any of the cats here, I'll make sure this is your last day, and good luck getting hired anywhere near.'

'You want me to kill them, sir?' Ravindra was almost weeping.

'It's called pest control,' snapped the secretary and stomped away.

Ravindra stared at the currency notes, his chest heaving with emotion. This bastard had him cornered and fucked. He knew he could not possibly trap all four and take them somewhere safe, all in the same night. Full of shame, he pocketed the 1,500 rupees.

That night, Mr Kothari drank his Absolut slowly and in a civilized way, with lime slices. He was determined to forget all the unpleasantness in his life recently. The ulcer pain was gone. Tomorrow onwards, the universe would start aligning his way, he was sure, the cat problem perennially solved and the SGBM in the bag because he had firmly put that old fool Prabhudesai in his place. He opted for mood lighting in his flat and listened to Kishori Amonkar via a YouTube playlist of her Jaipur Gharana ragas. Hmm, he reflected as her third raga on the playlist started up, he had never really tried Hindustani classical before, definitely an acquired taste, but he had more than sufficient time to acquire it, hadn't he? He saw it clearly through the lens of three vodka tonics, hosting soirées in his top floor penthouse in the new tower, surrounded by fellow gourmands and aesthetes—wholesome god-fearing vegetarians, all, and swaying to La Amonkar …

By the time the raga playlist ran its course, he was six down, drunk, bored and zoned out. ''Slike a workout, this Gharana music. Gotta do it over and over,' he resolved.

He saw it was 1 a.m. and wondered if the first of the cats would be going underwater by now, trapped and yowling and kicking up a fuss and Ravindra weeping boohoo but doing it anyway.

He staggered to bed and fell in it. He barely had time to switch off the light before the six V&Ts yanked him under.

Around 4 a.m., Mr Kothari jerked upright. What had brought him to the surface was the pain. Oooooh, he gasped, that ulcer, that fucking ulcer …

Pain like he had never experienced before, pain that obliterated all thought. He sat and gasped. Then he started getting vicious acid reflux. Then he felt a vague stir and made it to the toilet bowl where he sat for eight sweaty minutes trying to coax his bowels … no luck.

He washed up and staggered around the flat, bent over in unrelenting agony, the acid reflux something terrible, as if he were trying to belch out burning lumps of coal.

A little after 5 a.m., the taxi rattled towards St. Elizabeth's Hospital, and ejected him outside the entrance to the ER. The surly night doctor, who had been awakened almost at the end of his shift, greeted this pale-skinned and sunken-eyed human with scepticism when it said, 'I thought it was ulcers, but now I think it's my appendix!'

'Are you sure?' asked the night doc, instantly scorning WebMD self-diagnosis, that too from someone whose breath reeked of alcohol. 'Had a wild night?' he asked, somewhat jealous that he was pulling night shifts while Bombay partied.

'No, not really,' gasped Mr Kothari. 'Just a few drinks.'

'Hmm. Something disagreed with you clearly. What did you eat?'

'Eat?' He remembered that he had eaten nothing at all, just drunk himself legless. 'Nothing really.'

'That figures,' said the doc. 'Could be just a strong gut allergy to all that alcohol, and your digestion has gone into shock.'

'Look,' Mr Kothari pleaded, 'can you just rule out appendicitis, please? Because that's dangerous.'

The doc scoffed. 'The MRI tech comes in at 10. I can do a 2D scan right now, though, if you like.'

'And that will tell you enough?'

'An inflamed appendix will stick out like a sore thumb in the scan.'

'Okay,' Kothari gasped. 'Do it.'

The doc nodded. 'First, let's give you something for the pain, anti-inflammation drugs and something to soothe the gut.'

'Oh, god, yes,' sobbed the pain-ravaged Hon. Secy.

The needle went in, and it may have been a placebo effect, but Mr Kothari could swear the relief was almost instantaneous. He barely registered the sensual glide of the 2D scanner over the cooling gel applied to his lower abdomen. By the time the scan came through, Mr Kothari was so unbelievably pain-free that he almost thought it was a bad dream he'd had. He sat up feeling just slightly sleep-deprived, but otherwise like a million bucks. The doc showed him: 'Look, nothing here. No inflammation of the appendix. All is quiet and dormant down there.'

Mr Kothari looked but could not make out anything apart from light and dark shadows.

'Told you,' said the wise night doc. 'Just a bad reaction to something you ate or drank.'

In excess, he didn't say—it felt unnecessary, given the sour booze breath that wafted out of the patient's mouth.

Kothari got chatty. 'I suspected ulcers a week ago when the pain started, but that was very mild compared to this.'

'Hmm,' said the night doc, not really interested. 'You have a stressful job?'

'Oh boy, you could say that,' laughed Mr Kothari.

'Right. Good luck then,' said the doc, nodding at him with the briefest of smiles and vanishing back into his quarters to change into his day clothes.

When Mr Kothari got back to Ashok Niwas, it was almost 7 a.m., the start of the day cool and fuzzy, with a liar's promise that the sun would not make a living furnace of the city a few hours from now. Nobody at the gatepost to report on the fate of four cats who had been summarily despatched to the afterlife.

As he walked through the parking lot, all was right with the world, cars parked neatly in their slots and Mr Prabhudesai's scooter out in the open and awaiting the sun's assault. He marched towards his flat, the doorway smelling of bleach and spices, but untouched and undefiled, *ten whole days now*. His bed beckoned. He needed sleep, maybe a few hours to set right the ravages of the night. Then he'd wake up and get back to doing what he did best.

Win.

He awoke at noon, his body awash with fever. The pain had returned with a monstrous ferocity; it was like a blunt, red-hot knife slowly being turned in his flesh. Not his appendix, the doc had said, but then what was this? What manner of ulcer was it that bubbled like a molten lava pool in his gut? Back to the goddamned ER, but this time nothing less than a thorough MRI scan would do and a solicitous physician with an alert bedside manner—not some night jockey awaiting the end of his shift.

Mr Kothari dressed with great difficulty, barely able to get his pants on. Courage, Parikshit, courage, he told himself. It's just another short taxi ride to St. Elizabeth's, and all will be well. He packed a bag with extra clothes—most certainly there would be an overnight stay for observation this time, and maybe a quick palliative surgery. Resolved to get on with it, he strapped the bag to his shoulder, stepped to the front door and opened it.

Right there at his doorstep, squatting comfortably, was the large white and black tomcat with flanks quivering and in the process of ejecting several three-inch-long glistening goobers of fresh cat shit right over the ground pepper and bleached tiles. Mr Kothari gasped, a hundred unfinished thoughts streaking through his head—all for nothing, doesn't work, the bleach, the pepper … CAT STILL ALIVE … RAVINDRA!!! I'll … I'll …

Something snapped. With a bellow of rage, Kothari swung one leg back and aimed for the animal's backside just as the last of the shit-goobers was emerging. Except he was no footy-player and all the cat might have felt was a slight breeze as the foot whizzed past it and continued on its upward arc, up and up, and Kothari suddenly realized he was falling backwards, weighed down by his shoulder bag. He fell on his back with a thump, and as nobody had ever taught him to tuck in his chin, cracked his head soundly on the floor tiles of his house. He was rendered temporarily unconscious. The front door firmly latched shut on its own.

It was in that brief spell of unconsciousness that Mr Kothari's appendix exploded like a swollen piñata, the same appendix that had eluded the lazy 2D scan of the night doctor by turning up and around and hiding itself nicely behind the colon. Mr Kothari briefly came to just in time to realize the terrible truth of his situation—sepsis was blazing a molten-hot warpath through his lower abdomen. 'Help,' he screamed. 'Help!' But he couldn't be sure if it was a scream or a whimper.

Across the landing, Mr Prabhudesai, who was just sitting down to lunch, clearly heard the bellow of an angry human and then a resounding thump. He calmly finished his lunch, and only then did he open his door. He saw the steaming, reeking failure of his neighbour's cat-repellent plans. From behind the door of No. 12, he heard a weak cry. It seemed to say *help*. Mr Prabhudesai leaned against his doorway and waited. Another cry, more a croak this time, yes, it definitely said *help*. He waited a while longer, then stepped back and shut the door to his house.

Later that afternoon, he peeped though his spyhole when he heard Mr Kothari's doorbell ring. It was the bai, who was never given a set of keys. She rang twice, huffed in annoyance and left. Mr Prabhudesai passed the afternoon writing emails to the committee and other society members once more asking them for discretion in the appointment of the redevelopment builder. There was no caustic reply all of that day from Mr Kothari.

The next morning, Mr Prabhudesai summoned Chandu and Dilip to clean up the pepper and cat shit in the corridor. He tipped both 500 rupees each for their trouble. Then he sauntered over to the gatepost and had a long chat with Ravindra, and later, Ravindra helped Mr Prabhudesai wheel his Lambretta back in the shade of the No. 12 parking space, right next to the Hon. Secy's shiny Škoda. Mr Prabhudesai tipped Ravindra 500 rupees for his help.

For the next three days, Mr Prabhudesai and Ravindra went about their lives, faces deadpan, when they heard other committee members mention that it was most odd that Mr Kothari wasn't answering his phone, door or emails so close to the SGBM. On the fourth day, Mr Prabhudesai dutifully reported a foul smell emanating from No. 12. As the gurney with the covered sheet was wheeled out into the parking lot, four beady-eyed cats, all nine lives intact, plus a bunch of solemn but dry-eyed humans, including Miss Nair, blanched and turned away from the awful odour. Ravindra, the watchman, with his hero shades and movie-star moustache waved to the hearse driver and shut the gate, marvelling at this thing called fate and wondering how many more instances of sheer dumb luck life would award him with, and concluded probably *not too many*, probably *not ever again*. He did, however, take Chandu and Dilip for a rollicking piss-up at Joy's Country Liquor Bar at

Grant Road, and still had a few bucks left over from the 1,500 blood money.

After all of this, it is rather anti-climactic that Ashok Niwas still stands untouched on Nepean Sea Road, a four-storey walk-up amongst towers of glass and steel, because its new Hon. Secy, Mr Utkarsh Prabhudesai, is yet to find a scrupulous builder for redevelopment.

The Girls of Visty Villa

NAMITA DEVIDAYAL

Every evening, when the grandfather clock in Visty Villa chimed six times, Bindiya would walk up to the bungalow. The stairs were gloriously gleamingly wooden. Sometimes, she had a flash-thought about how the steps could be chopped and transformed into an eight-seater dining table. Bindiya could not help herself. Her mind compulsively conjured up possibilities, an eternal tango between what is and what could be.

Today she was a little early. Bindiya muted her imagination. She checked herself quickly in a liver-spotted mirror near the door and smiled with satisfaction at the short girl bulging out of a poly-cotton shirt, before turning the key in the latch.

'Good evening, Aunty Fa!' The cheery sing-song greeting was as predictable as a doorbell. 'Good evening, Felly and Freny.'

'Good evening, Binky Winky. Come, come! The girls are waiting for you, dear,' said Farah Batliwala or Aunty Fa. She was seated on a beige and gold chintz sofa. On either side of her, at the two ends, sat two girls, one dressed in a red chequered seersucker dress, with matching closed shoes; the other in a green, similarly chequered dress and white canvas Bata sneakers. Both wore ankle-length socks that had lost their elastic, so flopped slightly, but Aunty Fa felt that the socks could survive one more season.

The vast living room was surrounded by mirrors, paintings and ancestral portraits. On the south side, floor to ceiling, French windows opened onto a small garden. A silver tea set had been laid on the table. On the tray sat four blue and gold Limoges cups, as poised as their mistress.

'Freny won't be drinking tea today as she has a weak tummy. The jam biscuits seem to be over. Perhaps you could pick some up for me next time, Binky? Felicia loves those, don't you, dikri?'

The girl next to her did not respond.

Aunty Fa enunciated her words as if she were perpetually on stage. Fair, frail, she sat erect, her legs crossed with insouciant elegance. On the wall behind her was a distant echo from her past. Frozen into a gold frame was a porcelain-complexioned Farah Baby sitting at the feet of her grandfather, the imperious Sir Vistasp (Visty) Batliwala, whose upward curling moustache seemed to dismiss gravity and anyone who questioned his authority.

Sixty years later, Farah Batliwala was wearing a similar high-necked white lace top with ruby silk trousers. Her silver hair was twisted into a low knot secured by a tortoiseshell barrette. In her ears, classic diamond and ruby drops sparkled lightly when she moved her head. They matched the rings on her fingers which now held a teacup that quivered ever so slightly as it travelled to her lips. Her wrists were delicate and slim. Perfectly manicured fuchsia pink fingernails matched her lip colour. Farah, or Aunty Fa, was the most well-groomed Parsi dowager this side of the Tower of Silence.

'Very few know how to slice bread thin enough for cucumber sandwiches,' she said. 'And why are there such few Ambassadors on the road ...?'

'Bo-oy!' Aunty Fa shouted in a delicate bellow.

An elderly, myopic Nepali man shuffled out of the kitchen, slipping on frayed white gloves. Ram Singh Tamang's name had long been obscured and replaced by Boy. He had spent forty-odd years in the service of the Batliwalas. At some point, this colonial bungalow became his home while the small house near Bagdogra, filled with sniveling, snotty, indifferent children, and then grandchildren, faded out. Visty Villa was familiar, comforting. And then, there was Farah Baby. White. Pristine. Eternally vulnerable.

'Yes, Baby.' He stood in front of her with his hands behind his back, his head slightly bowed. He looked briefly at Bindiya, with undisguised disapproval, convinced that she was too dark-skinned and too poor to be sitting in the same parlour as Farah Baby.

Bindiya's inner cinematographer instantly made Ram Singh have a heart attack and fall with a dull thud. Then, her camera moved to the teapot and melted the silver in slow motion, repurposing it into a pair of earrings. Or maybe bangles, many bangles and necklaces, she thought, like those worn by their rich neighbour in her mother's village. Who even uses silver teapots anymore, she thought. A mug with your own photo lasered onto it would be more practical, no? Her round face flickered into a Mona Lisa half-smile before returning to impenetrable neutrality.

'Please take all this away. I am done. Felly and Freny are not eating anything,' said Aunty Fa to Ram Singh, waving her hand over the silver tray.

She reached out and tenderly pushed a strand of Felly's brownish silky hair behind her ear. Felly's hair was in a ponytail while Freny had two thick black braids that came down her shoulders. They had pallid complexions. Their startlingly blue-green eyes stared straight in front of them. Their lips were pink. They were almost pretty.

Felicia and Freny were life-sized dolls.

It was a sight to behold—three women in a vast, powder-pink parlour, seated with symmetrical precision as though embalmed.

Horrifying. Beautiful.

Horrifyingly beautiful.

And one woman who was palpably different, in her poly-cotton shirt and platform heels. Yet, Bindiya behaved as if she were spending her evening in the most normal way possible, sipping tea and discussing things that were happening in the city of Bombay. (Although the government had officially changed the name of the city just a year earlier, people like Aunty Fa thought that Mumbai sounded decidedly vernacular. And Bindiya, of course, agreed.)

Their chats were mostly a monologue by Aunty Fa. She jumped from topic to topic with alarming alacrity, unleashing a series of non sequiturs, as if someone above was mindlessly flipping channels. Today, the fanciful flights went from art to sandwiches to cars, somewhere between being charmingly child-like and absurdly unhinged. But within that mishmash was embedded a thread of astute intelligence.

'How can anyone auction art? How utterly philistine. I mean really ...'

Bindiya had no idea what philistine meant, but she nodded sagely. Some decades back, the Batliwalas had donated their phenomenal art collection (which included Impressionist paintings) to a relative who owned a gallery in Fort. It was meant to be on permanent display for the public. Recently,

Aunty Fa had learned that the paintings were being valued with many absurd zeroes attached to them. Evidently, some uncouth forces had started turning art into real estate, every square inch translating into a few lakh rupees.

'Now why are there hardly any Ambassadors on the roads these days? What is this Mr Singh doing? He is so elegant in his cerulean blue turban, but I wish he would just leave things the way they were.'

Bindiya gently picked up Felly and Freny and took them into their room, laying them on their twin beds which had pink hearts embroidered on the pillows. She shut the door and glided silently to the next room—the room once redolent with Sir Vistasp's cigars that now gave in to a cloying feminine scent. She sat for a few minutes on a rocking chair and played with the black mole on her chin, distracted, allowing her imagination to turn Freny into her friend, her companion, with whom she could sit giggling in the garden on the white cast iron chairs whose seats resembled doilies. She then got up, opened the cupboard and pulled out a nightie. Over the last few years, Bindiya had slithered into Visty Villa and become the stoic companion of a woman who was not of sane mind—or so she thought.

Bindiya was not born Bindiya. For the first five years of her life she had been Miriam, the illegitimate daughter of a Muslim fisherman from coastal Raigad, and a Mangalorean Christian domestic worker. The young Bindiya may or may not have seen her father beat her mother unconscious, but it didn't matter. He had long been abbreviated into a black-and-white photograph that hung on the wall next to Mother Mary in the staff quarters where she lived. She wasn't sure of her name or surname, until her mother's employers, the munificent Moolabhoys, registered her in St. Joseph's Convent School in Colaba a few lanes away, near the Afghan Church. That was when her mother decided to baptize her Bindiya D'Souza, a vaguely cosmopolitan name that would melt safely into Mumbai's hybrid crowds.

As she grew older, she would hear her mother mutter about what a good man her father was, but Bindiya suspected that her mother fell in love with him only after he had vanished from her life and could be re-configured through the charitable filter of nostalgia. She imagined her father back in the coastal village of Mora, across Bombay's eastern harbour, living in a small mint green house with three or four children and a wife who held the nylon thread which he pulled and knotted into fishing nets clasped deftly between his curled toes. Or maybe he was dead. Or he had become a terrorist supporter who allowed boats from Pakistan to harbour by the city's coast.

Bindiya grew up with the Moolabhoys' daughters, a year older and a year younger than her. She went to the same neighbourhood parks where they sat on rusty swings, and she joined them for Sunday morning movie screenings at Eros Cinema. They watched *Chitty Chitty Bang Bang* twice. She sometimes accompanied them at the dinner table on special occasions like Christmas or a birthday. But, in the end, she would always retreat to her small windowless room, where flies and humidity would besiege her sleep, and she would be woken up by her mother snoring or crying or praying.

Bindiya felt suffocated and mostly miserable. She never invited her school friends over. No one knew that she was a housemaid's daughter. On annual day, she told her mother what to wear—only Sunday church saris, no housework clothes. She was grateful that the school principal, Sister Meena, always treated her mother with respect, especially in front of others.

It was in her mid-teens, when an atavistic crustacean survivor instinct emerged from deep within to help shield her from the painful assault of reality, that her imagination began conjuring up an alternate compliant world. She became the director, the actor and the viewer. Sometimes, she was being driven to school in the Moolabhoys' air-conditioned Ambassador, giving instructions to the driver; or she would be strolling in Paris in red high heels round and round the Eiffel Tower—her only visual reference.

The first time the reel in her head unspooled, and took her into her private Happyland, she felt really, *really* good. Soon, it became an addiction. She needed it. Any spare time and she would be flying. Once, her inner screenplay had the Moolabhoys' handsome nephew Tarik asking her to marry him, kneeling in front of her like a gentleman from a '50s film she had just watched, and she fell asleep twisting a phantom eternity band on her finger.

But reality was a persistent, relentless downer.

A few days after the betrothal daydream, the bell rang, and she opened the door to the real Tarik who, instead of kissing her lightly on the cheek, walked breezily past her as if she didn't exist. He was back from Cambridge, a bar at law.

'A glass of cold water with lots of ice, please,' he said, without even looking at her. 'Is aunty at home?'

She knew he probably didn't remember her name even though he had been in and out of the house all his life. Tarik pulled off his lavender tie and flopped down on a chair with his leg slung over the armrest. Bindiya thought she saw a flicker of interest in his eyes when he put the glass back on the tray. She knew she had grown into a reasonably attractive dusky eighteen-year-old—even if a little plump, a little compromised on height—and she had seen that look before. In fact, she picked her clothes carefully to accentuate her breasts just enough to catch the attention of men like Tarik.

He mumbled a distracted thank you and picked up *The Times of India* whose front page had an enormous picture of the politician Bal Thackeray dominating the newsprint, his hand raised like a führer. Bindiya retreated into the room where her mother was fast asleep, snoring so loudly that it sounded like the monsoon high tide crashing against the tetrapods that bordered the city. Asthma and possible depression had begun to take over, and she would sometimes sleep through the day, leaving her daughter to do the dishes and clean up the kitchen. Bindiya could never manicure and paint her nails because they got ruined within two days.

The Moolabhoy girls left for London to pursue higher studies and to discreetly seduce eligible young bachelors, and Bindiya stayed on in Colaba. She enrolled in a good Christian college with the help of her parish priest and a year later, started working part-time at the Marine Drive clinic of a vet who specialized in putting chronically ill animals to rest. She spoke perfect English and dressed well, often in designer hand-me-downs that came from her employers, one size too big.

As she saw hopeless poverty loom like a permanent penumbra around her, Bindiya's fantasies became more feral. They featured imported cars with leather seats, vast rooms with sea views, and handsome men whom she had seen in the clinic or college canteen. Her dreams often had Tarik pop in and out, an intermittent lover who took her to the rooftop restaurant of the Taj Mahal Hotel or for a drive down Marine Drive in an open Dodge.

One afternoon, Mrs Moolabhoy put down the telephone receiver and called out for Bindiya, using the new wireless bell. When the device rang shrilly in the quarters, Bindiya was inside an airplane on her way to some faraway place, sipping a glass of white wine. She slipped on the pants she had taken off to beat the heat and came out.

'Darling, would you consider spending time with my classmate Farah Batliwala? I've just got off the phone with their family solicitor who said that she could do with some adult company, for she is terribly, terribly lonely. You can read to her or just drink tea with her and chit-chat. Poor little girl,' she said, shaking her head.

Bindiya's mother had also come out and stood behind her employer, clearly pleased with this new career prospect for her daughter.

'Bindiya baby, you must do,' she said. 'Thank you, madam.'

'From where to where life takes us, only the lord knows, Mashallah,' continued Mrs Moolabhoy, waving off the thank you. 'Faroo used to be the life of the party, and boy, could she cha-cha-cha. But after she lost her parents on the *Queen Mary* ship, everything changed. It was rumoured that her mother had killed her father before drowning herself. And they were first cousins.' Mrs Moolabhoy sighed, now almost talking to herself. 'No one knows what really happened there ... but Sir Vistasp raised our Faroo like a precious doll and never let her leave the house. After we finished school, we hardly saw her. There was talk about her getting married, but I think he felt that no suitor was good enough. On the first of every month, she would go with her cat and those two dolls that her grandpa had got her, for a round through Marine Drive in her pink Ambassador. After some time, I think even that stopped.'

Bindiya stood in front of her benefactor, vaguely processing the prospect of adding a senile Parsi woman to her life already populated by an irksomely chirpy employer, a depressive mother and many sick animals.

'Sure, madam,' she replied, robotically.

'Oh, and of course you'll be paid for your time. We can build up enough for your dowry,' said Mrs Moolabhoy with a little giggle, turning around and looking at her old helper, who had become her abiding almost-friend. For Mr Moolabhoy was so laconic that he may as well have not been there.

The very next day, a sealed envelope arrived from one Doshi & Doshi Esq. Typed across the cover:

MISS BINDIYA D'SOUZA
c/o MRS M. MOOLABHOY

That was ten years ago.

'Mashed potatoes and roast chicken, my absolute favourites,' squealed Farah Batliwala to the plate that was placed in front of her at the dining table. This had been her staple supper with variable desserts for the longest time. On Sundays, the meal changed to minced meat cutlets, a side of green beans and hot buns. This would be followed by Josephine, a rich chocolate custard pudding. Wednesday was the only day there was Indian fare—mutton dhansak with rice and vegetable cutlets, followed by a sugary sweet raspberry pink jelly. This was the menu that Ram Singh had followed with clockwork precision while Farah Baby grew into Aunty Fa and then tipped over to the other side of the curve to decline into doll-like oblivion. Having retired Freny and Felicia to their bedroom, Bindiya now sat opposite

Aunty Fa, watching her wield knife and fork with cultivated ease; Bindiya struggled, hoping that the chicken leg would not fly off the plate as she gingerly forked it and tried to slice off bits and chew slowly.

Only one caramel custard arrived from the kitchen. Aunty Fa did not offer Bindiya a bite.

'Sorry, Farah Baby. I didn't know that Bindiya madam was staying for dinner tonight,' said Ram Singh sullenly. Food was his weapon against the perceived enemy.

'Binky will not mind. She is such an understanding young woman. I have a special embroidered hanky for you, my dear. It belonged to my granny. I hope you are staying on this evening. Will you read to me from *David Copperfield*?'

The doorbell rang. It was Kevin, a man with a trim white goatee, who had managed the household ever since Sir Vistasp had passed on. Kevin was not a lawyer (though he understood the law). He was the grandson of Sir Vistasp's ship's loyal captain and his connection with Farah Batliwala was deeper than the North China Sea. His loyalty was faultless. For the past twenty years, he had coordinated between Doshi & Doshi and Farah Batliwala, handling the family's personal matters, bringing a plumber when needed, sometimes gently counselling Aunty Fa who was the same age—and of similar temperament—as his mother. He did the monthly groceries and paid the vendors who delivered to the door—meat, chicken, eggs, milk. He was the one who suggested to the solicitors that she could do with a companion.

'Farah-bai, please sign the document that you asked me to prepare,' he said. He looked at Bindiya with a gentle, polite smile.

Bindiya noted that this was a private conversation, so got up and walked into the bedroom that she had now transformed into an extension of herself. Her footwear stood like plastic ducklings in a row; a big canary yellow teddy bear that she had picked up in Colaba Market sat by the bed, one glass eye missing. A bamboo plant, wrapped in red ribbon, sat on the windowsill, her talisman against evil. Over the last two years, she had spent more than half the week here, going home on weekends so that she could attend church with her mother.

Aunty Fa put on her glasses and spent a good ten minutes reading and rereading the document. She then held her hand out for a pen without raising her eyes and signed it. She clasped her hands and shut her eyes for a few minutes, as if praying. Kevin waited in deference. He then took the pen and signed below her. He slipped the document into his briefcase and kissed Aunty Fa's hand.

'Thank you for doing this, Kevin,' she said, sounding different, astonishingly normal. The demented edge in her voice was absent. Then, as if it were a mask she could slip on, it came right back.

'Binky-Winky,' she sang out loud. Bindiya came out wearing a purple satin men's dressing gown covered with white embroidered Chinese clouds. They both moved to the sofa, and Bindiya started reading aloud to her. She hated these books. She found her own stories far more compelling than tales of Hobbits and impoverished Victorian boys.

Aunty Fa played with her ruby ring, pushing it back and forth on her finger, then pulled it off and left it with a plink on the coffee table. She got up and glided away.

'Good night darling,' she said. 'Remember to shut the window. There are some naughty fairies floating around. Let's go to the well tomorrow. I need to pray for the girls. We will leave in the morning after breakfast.'

Aunty Fa disappeared into her room.

Bindiya picked up the ring and slipped it into the pocket of her dressing gown. A few minutes later, she thought better of it and put it back on the table. This was not the first time that she had engaged in casual larceny. Over the years, she had filched multiple small objects that no one would ever notice—not the fading Farah, nor her near-blind valet, nor the goateed Kevin. Trinkets, small silver bowls, a crystal jug, an ivory comb with little green flowers, these kinds of things slowly evaporated out of Visty Villa. She had sold the comb to a pawn shop on Colaba Causeway to buy a new pair of high heels; the silver bowls had fetched enough for her first trip to Goa with her mother.

But Bindiya's ambitions were far more audacious. In her head, it was a matter of time before her biggest fantasy would merge into reality.

That summer, everything changed.

Aunty Fa seemed to get more and more disoriented. She would prattle—the non sequiturs moving in rapid fire now—and then lapse into a long silence. Her lipstick had become a smear, no longer defining the delicate bow-and-arrow lips.

One evening, Aunty Fa was sitting on the sofa staring straight ahead of her. She then bent over sideways and lay her head on Felicia's lap, and stayed there for several hours, not speaking a word. She suddenly sprang up.

'Annabell. Where have you gone? Anna-*bell*! It's time for your supper, darling. Where could she have gone? Felicia, please do look under the sofa ... Bellaaaa!' Her voice rose like a soprano—she was soliciting a Persian cat that had long been dead and buried in the garden under the banyan tree—and then suddenly, she went silent.

Aunty Fa started moaning softly like a child, looking bewildered. She stared into the distance, and her eyes seemed to lose focus. She quietly got up and, as if on cue, her loyal retainer appeared and led her to the bedroom, gently aligning his pace with her sleepwalker gait.

A month later, in the Bombay monsoon, Aunty Fa, not yet eighty, finished her usual fare of roast chicken, mashed potatoes and caramel custard in silence, while Bindiya sat across from her, now eating with her hands with a recently acquired careless confidence. Aunty Fa dabbed her lips with a napkin, got up, and picked up Felicia and Freny from the sofa in either arm. She went into her room, lay them on the bed and crawled between them without changing her clothes, one hand clutching each of theirs. Sometime after midnight, she passed away, lying flat on her back, her eyes shut. Freny lay next to her, her blue-green eyes wide open; Felicia had rolled over and fallen on the carpet near the bed, her leg contorted in an impossible twist.

Farah Batliwala was taken to the Tower of Silence. Present at the funeral was a distant relative from Udvada, Kevin, the recently widowed Mrs Moolabhoy, a very weepy Ram Singh Tamang, and the stoic Bindiya. The priests rendered the prayers in Gregorian unison, and when they asked for the names of her descendants, Mrs Moolabhoy said, 'There's no one left.'

Bindiya clung on to Visty Villa like a barnacle. This was going to be the beginning of her new life. She would find some concoction from the clinic to put Ram Singh to sleep forever, so he could join his beloved Farah Baby. She started adding more and more things to her room. No one questioned her. Ram Singh was in a daze. Kevin had disappeared—his daughter was getting married in Melbourne. Mrs Moolabhoy was still grieving. And Bindiya's mother had long embedded herself in a state of zombied melancholy, abetted by wads of tobacco that she housed in the corner of her gums.

For the first time in her life, Bindiya felt calm and happy—not the kind of happiness that she experienced in her daydreams, but a genuine relaxation that comes from having money and, with it, freedom. One day, she decided to invite her old school friend Tisha to Visty Villa for tea. She was now thirty-three years old. She had invested ten years in a career that was finally going to yield dividends. She was entertaining for the first time in her life. The doorbell rang, and she went almost skipping to the door.

But the person at the door was not Tisha. It was Kevin.

'Oh, I didn't think I would still find you here, Miss Bindiya,' he said with his polite smile. 'I was away in Australia, so have not been able to come and check on things since Farah-bai's sad demise. I wanted to give Ram Singh news about the will.'

He looked at Bindiya with a hint of surprise. She seemed to be inadvertently guarding the door. She realized that she had been blocking the entrance and quickly stepped out onto the wooden landing, leaving the door open. He stepped in and made a quick survey of the changes in the living room. There were bright new cushions on the sofa. A couple of portraits were missing from the wall.

'Farah-bai has left the house to Freny and Felicia,' said Kevin.

Bindiya stared at him, and her brain slowly froze.

'The girls will continue to live in Visty Villa. Ram Singh will look after them until his death. They will go for a spin around Marine Drive once a month, which I will organize. Miss Bindiya, she has left you her Basra pearl earrings, all the books you so kindly read to her and an antique ivory comb with inlaid emerald flowers that is quite priceless.'

Bindiya continued to stare at Kevin and then turned around to see a taxi that had driven up the long driveway with her friend Tisha in it. Tisha seemed wonderstruck at the imposing beauty of Visty Villa.

'I can help you get the antique comb valued through an international auction house,' said Kevin. 'I suspect, with that money, you may be able to buy yourself a small flat in the suburbs. Miss Bindiya! Miss Bindiya, are you okay?'

Bindiya was staring at the liver-spotted mirror. There was no one looking back at her.

PHILLIPS
Estd 1860
फिलीप्स

Sufficient Magic

MANU JOSEPH

I remember a day when I was twenty-six; I had finished all my assignments, done all my chores and paid all my bills. For the first time I was not in the middle of something. I had nothing to do in the future.

I lived on the ninth floor, in a small room that had its own ledge, where I usually sat half-naked in a bean bag and gaped at Beach Towers. Now and then, when some curtains of Beach Towers parted, I could see right through the homes to the Arabian Sea.

Far below, on the narrow road, a girl walked in the drizzle. She walked slowly with her hands in the back pockets of her jeans. She was slender, her hair was in a ponytail. Even from that height, there were signs that she was pretty. I only needed an inch of any side of a woman's head to deduce that, as though there was a fractal quality to beauty. She was wearing boots—not rain boots but a kind of masculine black leather boots. Yet she seemed like a girl who would have painted toenails and a tissue in the fist. When she removed her hands from her jeans pockets, a folded paper fell on the pavement. She didn't notice. She just kept walking. Most girls never use their pockets; they probably don't even know they have back pockets.

She vanished into a building. The paper lay in the drizzle. No one took it. If it were one rupee, it would have gone by now. I put on a vest and ran down. In less than a minute I reached the folded paper. It was very wet but otherwise intact. It was a printout of an internal email of the Tata Institute of Fundamental Research. My heart was racing because I had hurtled down from my perch, but it felt right that it should beat so fast.

Finally, a proof of magic. Could that be possible? Was this the sign, was the whole dance meant for me—the girl, the way the paper fell from her?

I knew there was magic. I had once seen its contours. I craved to see more, but it is in the nature of magic that it usually offers only signs.

It began to rain heavily. I put the paper in my pocket and decided to go for a walk. I could turn left or I could turn right. Was it preordained which way I would go? It was. This was the sort of supernatural thing I knew was true. Now a scientist at the Tata Institute of Fundamental Research said he could prove it, he could prove that every little movement was predestined.

Four hours later, I was on my motorcycle. As usual, in the rains, I was riding in my shorts, no shirt, no helmet, no shoes. I carried dry clothes and shoes in a backpack. The wind tried to lift the bike off the road. In places it howled. All around me were signs of magic. The hollow in a banyan tree. So many swastikas. Bells, temples, domes and chants from antiquity that could not have come from a happy place.

The city was in a rush as always, which fooled everyone into thinking that Bombay had something called 'pace', that people here were short on time, that they worked hard, that they did some great stuff, which was bullshit. You make a guy run behind a train or a bus, it'd look like the city has 'pace'.

I parked in Colaba and changed in a damp taxi. I went to the very edge of Bombay, into the long thin finger by the roaring sea. You can go on living in Bombay without ever seeing soil, but when it rained the whole city smelled of wet earth, like the more ancient town I came from.

When I reached the Tata Institute of Fundamental Research, I showed my press card and lied that I was there to meet a professor. I had been there many times. It was the best place in Bombay. There was an L-shaped building, the only thing Indians had built in the city that was not ugly. There were ten acres of lawns that disappeared into wet black rocks, and then there was the grey sea in a tumult. The Arabian Sea in the monsoon is a lot of drama, but it is by nature a placid sea, unlike the Bay of Bengal, which is pure death. Never trust all the beautiful things the Bay of Bengal says.

In the past I had come here to listen to public lectures in theoretical physics, which was a sort of magic. I came hoping the old bastards would shake my being and stun me. Some three hundred people turned up for such talks, probably for the same reason. To be shaken and stunned. We were the lonely, the truly lonely, because only this kind of mystical thing could complete us. Like the temples drew a sort of people, this place drew its own seekers, most of whom were also the temple crowd.

But what I was attending today was not a public lecture for lay people. I was not supposed to be here. It was a guest lecture for the institute's research scholars. It had begun by the time I walked into the small classroom. The blackboard said, 'The science of determinism and the impossibility of free will'. There were only about two dozen people in the room. One of them surely was the girl I had spotted in the morning. She was wearing the same clothes. I could see only half her face. She was bird-like but in a pretty bird way. She evidently was a scholar here.

The man who was talking was in corduroy pants, but old. He looked like one of those megalomaniacs in science who pointed at Voyager's image of earth as a speck of dust and said, 'We are so insignificant.' I listened carefully to him. There was a lot of physics and maths and biology, but I could understand half of what he was saying. And what he was saying was that emotions were not random, they were entirely created by subatomic particles, hence human decisions were not random. And the fates of the particles were decided at the beginning of time. So, there was no scope for free will. I was disappointed with him. To explain the mystical through subatomic particles is dumber than explaining subatomic particles through the mystical. I saw the girl rise and slink away. I must have been staring at her, she threw a look at me.

I stayed until the man finished. Maybe something towards the end would blow me away. But nothing of that sort happened, and I felt very lonely again. I had been on the high of anticipation and the gloom of losing it hit me. I had nothing else to live for that day and nowhere to go. I had no friends. No girl. There were no plans in the world that involved me.

She was standing by a bus stop, smoking. The rains had stopped, and a faint evening light seemed to have lit her face. I walked to her; said I was predestined to speak to her. She laughed. She said she saw me at the class. Was I a student? She had never seen me.

I told her I was a journalist.

Science reporter?

I did a bit of everything, I said. I told her I had come hoping there would be a confirmation of magic. She did not say anything. It was as though I had spoken to her in her mother tongue and she feared that if she responded it would be too intimate. But she certainly had a view about the supernatural; all girls were mystical.

She asked me what I meant by magic.

There are three kinds of magic, I said.

For some reason that made her laugh. She removed her glasses and tied her hair tighter. Somehow that made her prettier.

'Go on,' she said.

Grade A magic is god, ghosts and afterlife. Mind-blowing stuff. If they turn out to be true, nothing can be the same after that.

But they don't exist, she said.

They don't.

That's sad, she said.

But there is something else that is Grade A, I said, which exists. The sky. It is the proof of infinite space, so proof that the supernatural does exist.

But space could be finite, she said.

That doesn't make sense, I replied.

Doesn't matter, she said. We're not sure either. We're working on it.

What is Grade B?

Grade B, I said, is destiny, premonition, a machine achieving self-awareness, mystical things that can have a logical explanation.

Alright, she said.

Grade C is the appearance of an advanced alien civilization, all the weird stuff quantum physics says, things that are very probable, very easily explained by science, but amazing stuff.

She nodded. Her hair collapsed from its own knot and fell on her face. How hard can it be to tie up some hair in a fierce knot?

I did not tell her everything—that I knew one more example of Grade A magic. It was as evident as the sky, but no one paid much attention to it. It was not that I knew it completely, but I had seen something of it.

'Three grades of magic,' she said, and nodded in an exaggerated way, as posh girls do sometimes.

Her name was Sabena. She lived in Bandra, like all girls. So, this morning she must have been visiting a friend in Prabhadevi.

I stopped a cab and offered to drop her, even though it was going to be very expensive to do that. She did not ask where I lived. We sat at the two far ends of the backseat, but when the rain returned and became severe, water sprayed through the windows, and she had to inch a bit towards me.

She asked why someone as young as me was so … she then said she was trying to find the word. 'So philosophical', she said.

I was glad she didn't use the word 'spiritual'. 'Philosophical' was manly.

Did something happen, she asked.

Nothing, I said, I had a normal life.

One night, when I was seventeen, my drunk father was screaming at my mother as he had done every night in my memory. But he stopped without finishing his regular abuse. There was quiet, then he called out to me. That had never happened before. There was no panic in his voice, but he just kept calling my name. I stepped out from the bedroom I shared with my sister, and saw my mother standing in the kitchen. She had doused herself in kerosene. She was holding a lit matchstick. And she was trembling in the fear of a very painful death. I leapt at her and put out the match.

If your mother tried to burn herself at night, what would you do the next morning?

I went to college.

I did sit with her the next morning, put my arms around her, hug her sideways and coerce her into saying what I wanted to hear. She said it would never happen again. She said, 'You don't worry. I am fine.'

I didn't want to be in that house, so I went away. I don't know why I didn't sit with her the whole day, why I didn't stand guard. Why, less than twelve hours after she tried to immolate herself, I would just leave her alone.

I don't remember what I was thinking that day in class. I remember I was very sad and alone.That evening, as I approached home, I finally grew very scared. In Madras, those days, when you got home and found a lot of slippers outside the door, it usually meant your dad had died of a heart attack. Mothers never died in Madras.

The rain crashed into our taxi even though the windows were rolled up. We were sweating. Once you're in a yellow-and-black with a person, you are automatically in a relationship. Sabena had been studying string theory—for five years. My pursuit of magic made me read all sorts of things, and I had read four books on string theory. Everything is made of vibrations—what is not to love about that.

Tell me something, she said. How did you know about the lecture today? It was not a public lecture. They don't call the press for something like this ...

I saw a piece of paper on the road, I replied.

She was not sure I was serious.

I showed it to her.

Where do you live? she asked.

Prabhadevi, I said.

She nodded and looked away, in disbelief.

What?

I was there this morning. This is mine ... I had lost it.

I didn't want to ham anymore. I kept quiet. There was a chance we would become friends. Then I would have to tell her the truth.

Why are you dropping me then, she said, it's way out.

I have nothing to do.

I could not tell if she liked me, there were no signs. The universe was filled with mystical clues to an astounding reality, but there was not one hint girls saw anything in me.

I was not going to tell her about my mother. You should never tell girls about your misery, or 'humble origins'. They find it unattractive. I was not going to tell her about Somen Pillai either, because then she would know everything there is to know about me. Maybe that is all there is to a person—a past epiphany.

My mother was alive when I got home. She said she would never do it again. About a week later, I told Somen Pillai about my mother. I also told him that the morning after her attempt, I went to college leaving her alone the whole day, and now I knew I was a second-rate person. He said that if his mother had immolated herself, he would not have felt anything, even as he watched. She was a lovely mother, he said. And I knew that was true as I had known Somen's family since I was a child. Yet, he said, he could watch her burn and not be affected. I asked him, how. But he refused to say anything at all.

Sabena and I rode in silence, looking in opposite directions. I finally decided to try the question.

Can I tell you something? It might startle you.

About?

About everything, everything around us.

She didn't get a sense of danger. She, in fact, wanted to laugh. She was like the other eight people I had tried it on.

What? She asked. What is it?

I was just messing with you, I told her. And we laughed.

I had known Somen Pillai since third standard. Throughout school, he had been a silent, unremarkable boy with a feminine face. When we were kids, he had played the role of my daughter in a play. 'Edith'—I still remember. Now he had a lot of muscles; many of us were building muscles.

Somen lived close to my house. And because his parents went to work, he was alone all day. He did some computer course somewhere, but for the most part he was home.

After what he said about his mother, I kept returning to his home to find out more. But he wouldn't elaborate beyond sharing that I was focusing on the least important part of what he had said. That confused me more. One day, he said, I'm ready to tell you something, but I don't know how you will react.

I said, what?

He was quiet for a while. That was not unusual; he was an inarticulate person in all the three languages we used to speak. Then, he said, maybe it'll scare you; actually, it will scare you. But control.

The sensation I remember distinctly is a sick sense of danger. There was nobody in the house, and Somen was between me and the door. I don't know why I was thinking any of this. Somen had only said that he wanted to convey something. Besides, he was a bit smaller than me. I could take him on—unless there was someone else in the house.

Then, he told me. He seemed nervous as the words came out of his mouth. He said, this whole thing, this whole thing, what you see around you, is not real. There's something totally different underneath it. Something else is going on.

That was all.

But in that moment, I completely understood what he was telling me. And I sat in shock.

He probably did not expect this.

He had narrated the story to several people, but only I was stunned. Only I quietly walked away.

The thing about an epiphany is: it may have been said to other people a million times and not moved anyone. But to you it is a bolt. Besides, the words through which the epiphany has come is simply a gist of what needed to be said. But you alone see the colossal message in its entirety. And your life is not the same again.

I almost saw what Somen saw. I had transformed.

Incidentally, when he told me these things, he was not speaking in English anymore. He had switched to Tamil. I would have never imagined that anything in Tamil could alter my life.

When I dropped Sabena off, she didn't offer to give me her number. I did not ask because I never asked for the numbers of girls. In a preordained universe ...

Okay, maybe I was just not a very smart young man.

I went back to my life where nothing much ever happened, and I almost never spoke to anyone. I walked without aim. No matter how much I worked, I had enough time to feel a deep boredom.

Then, one night, my phone rang. It was Sabena. She said she had called the newspaper several times and eventually found my residence number. I could feel raw happiness fill my chest. I said I had two press tickets for the late evening show of *Mission: Impossible 2* tomorrow. Did she want to go. She said yes, but she would confirm in the morning.

I didn't ask for her number. And she just hung up without giving it to me. Maybe she forgot.

In the morning, I waited for her call. I tried to fast, because if I stepped out for breakfast, I could miss her. But then, I got hungry. I was out for just ten minutes. I don't know if she called while I was away. In any case, I didn't get her call. Maybe she would just land up straight at the theatre.

I waited on the steps of Sterling.

This, by the way, has happened many times. Me standing alone on the steps of Sterling, surrounded by groups of friends and their happy murmurs. How did people find so many people to like them? It was 7.30 p.m. She was yet to come. Everyone around me started to walk in, and soon it was just me waiting. Another second, and I would have turned to go in, but then I saw her a hundred metres away, walking fast, looking anxious. She couldn't see me. She was in blue jeans and a black top, which surely had a posh name. Her clothes were two sizes smaller than what I had thought was her style. Suddenly, everything fit her snug. She was not a baggy girl. She wore her hair long and it bounced.

This apparition—I would think of it a thousand times, throughout the rest of my life. A pretty girl hurrying to meet me. That never happened again. Only because of what was required for that to happen. A girl had to be late, and walking towards me as I stood in a place from where I could see her and she couldn't see me.

Somen Pillai struggled to explain. He was in a bad way. Something was very wrong with him, or maybe something was too right. He clearly wanted to communicate something specific, but the idea was so abstract it was beyond his means to convey it. He did not have the words or the way of speaking. We hear people talk and we think they know how to talk. But most people get by with maybe a hundred words, and those are not enough sometimes to say what you want to say.

He was also very scared. Whatever it was that had possessed him was very powerful.

One day, he said that there was evil in this world, primordial evil, and its touch was exactly like a burn. Not figuratively, but exactly. And there was a way to escape it, but that involved seeing through the charade laid out by the senses. All ancient religions and cults were occult signs that some seers had left behind, which were later misunderstood by spiritual clerks. Very few could receive and decipher these signs; and even the few who could had to be ready.

The signs, when received, were powerful, Somen said. They did things to the brain, they changed it physically. Something imploded inside, some structures fell apart, and that was when one saw 'the whole thing'. After that, most 'receivers' didn't survive; the act of seeing reality killed them.

If at all they survived, they lived very very long in extraordinary health. So long that to escape detection they vanished from their homes and wandered for decades.

You don't be scared, Somen said, you know nothing yet. You're not ready.

What about you, Somen?

He didn't say anything.

What is it that you know, what is it that you have seen?

I figured out after some weeks that he was inflicting pain on himself, chiefly small burns. Once, he took me to a place where a new road was being laid and he walked on the hot tar. I had to bring him home, like pale mothers who take their sons home from the police station after torture. Somen said the path to receiving his vision involved mortifying the flesh in every way. He plucked his own hair, starved for weeks. His parents went mad trying to understand. They came to me, seeking help. Once, his mother held my hand and cried. 'Save him,' she said. 'Say something to him.'

It never occurred to me that even I could try to inflict pain on myself. I was starving anyway, but not for spiritual reasons. I could see a sliver of what he was seeing, and I wanted to see the whole thing—but I was just not into pain.

For the next three years, Somen and I spoke about his most wondrous discovery. We spoke about the magic that hid in plain sight.

Then, just like that, Somen stopped meeting me. He said, the next stage of his evolution needed him to be entirely solitary.

I was twenty back then. I found a job as a reporter in Bombay. I could finally escape home. I would work hard and one day make a movie. I had plans. I tried to meet Somen to say goodbye, but he wouldn't meet me, he wouldn't come out of his room.

On the day I was to leave, I got a call from him. I went to his house. He was still the same, but very quiet and very dreamy.

He said he had asked me to come because he didn't want to meet ever again. There were things I wouldn't understand, and I was bothering him with my 'foolish, basic questions'.

I told him, I am going away to Bombay today anyway.

Good, he said, that is a relief. Just never get in touch with me. You will hear from me in some way or the other, at some point in your life, just once, and that will be important. But before that, never get in touch with me.

He hugged me and didn't let go. Then, he punched me on the shoulder and in a good-natured way asked me to get lost.

He stood at his gate watching me leave. I never saw him again. I kept my word.

When Sabena finally saw me, she was relieved. She smiled, and we waved, and in that moment, I was just like anybody else, any twenty-six-year-old guy waving to a twenty-six-year-old girl, and we were going to go watch a movie, and we would have popcorn, and we would have coffee, and we would have a meal and ice cream.

This was too much happiness. How could this moment be a lie, an illusion?

Yet it was.

But can any man deny himself this? Even if he knew that the purpose of this uncontainable joy was for a dark force to hide something it did not want anyone to see?

Since the epiphany in Somen Pillai's house, I had seen the edge of truth. But I did not test it. I had only watched another boy go to extreme lengths to be something.

I went down the steps of the theatre and began to walk away from Sabena. If I could do this, at this moment, I was the ascetic that I hoped I was. If I stood with her in her fragrance, it would be hard to leave.

But then I stopped walking. Maybe the mechanics of my action made me feel I was fleeing. And I did not like to flee.

Sabena came to me looking confused. I gave her the tickets and told her I had to leave and that I would explain some day.

I walked away.

For the first time in my life, I was doing something difficult to understand the true nature of reality, and it felt like I had done something violent—to a girl and to myself.

Still, to walk away was to prove that I had enough strength in me. So, I walked, at first telling myself that once this madness ended, maybe in a minute or two, I would just jog back and find her. I could make it look like a prank.

But I kept walking, and I grew more and more resolute. The enormity of my sacrifice made me feel that I was on to something.

I walked all the way home, for three hours.

Next morning, there were apocalyptic rains. I ran into it. I was enjoying it too much for it to be an ascetic act. I ran all the way to Sabena's institute, which was about 15 kilometres away, but I was used to that distance. I hoped to torture myself. I ran back, and after 30 kilometres, I felt the pain, strangely only in my neck. I was now suffering, but I kept on going. I paused for a banana. I stopped after about 50 kilometres.

Next morning, I ran the same distance again. I had to stop several times. Midway, I threw my shoes away. But they were expensive, by my standards. I felt small when I returned to collect them.

Every day, after that, I would wake up at 4 a.m. and run 50 kilometres barefoot. I went to work too. After ten days of this, I had to stop because my knees were swollen and I could barely walk.

So, I decided to stop eating. On the first two days of the indefinite fast, I went to work, but the third day I was too weak to rise from my floor mattress. I was also hearing voices, which were incoherent. Maybe that was a good sign. My brain was changing form perhaps.

I moved out of my house with a backpack filled with water bottles, and I sat on the filthy floor of Parel station. I spent the night there and the next morning.

This was not the first time I was sleeping in a train station. I had done it once when I was sixteen to escape my drunk father.

The act did not seem either tough or heroic; the hunger did not feel like hunger anymore but like an excruciating headache.

On the fifth day of the fast, I had to give up. I went home and ate a cake that was lying in the fridge. I was not ashamed. This was a good start.

I would soon resume the mortification of the flesh, and one day I would see the whole structure of magic.

When I resumed work, a senior assigned a story to me. I had to solve a mystery. Bombay was suddenly filled with wandering mad men; then they vanished; then they filled the streets again. It was a good mystery. I solved it in two days. Apparently, ward officers picked mad people off the streets and put them in an asylum, but when the asylum filled up, they just released them.

Opened the doors and let the men run out. Then they picked them up again. It was unsafe on the roads for mad women; so, they were usually never released.

The psychiatrist who told me this was a very serious and bored woman. I was in her dismal office. She had no curiosity about me. This was the first time I was meeting a psychiatrist, and she seemed like any plump elderly woman. I wanted her to make my story interesting. I asked if she had met unusual homeless mad men? And were mad men very different from mad women?

She spoke of some mad men who did not seem all that odd to me. But, then, she said that the previous week she had met a wandering teenager; maybe he was eighteen or so. He was striking because he was from an affluent family. And he was very scared. He told her that the whole world was a lie; there was something else underneath it. People were not supposed to know the truth, they would not be able to bear what they saw. She said, 'This is classic schizophrenia.' Then I heard her ask, 'Are you alright?'

I just left. As I walked out, I understood everything, the whole history of magic from the beginning of time.

Mysticism is primordial schizophrenia. All of it. A glitch in the human brain, that's all.

It's why the defining aspect of our most powerful ideas is that we will always fall short of comprehending them. They are the visions of the mad. The sane trying to see what the insane see—all our tumults come from that.

Somen Pillai was schizophrenic. There was no magic.

That life didn't have a purpose—I didn't consider that philosophy; it was the opposite of philosophy, it was the opposite of art, it was the opposite of all beautiful things. But that was all there was to the whole business.

I called Sabena several times and finally got through. I said that I wanted to meet. She said she was done with weird men. I told her I used to be weird but was not anymore. There was no magic, now I knew. She said she did hope for magic. Yes, yes, darling, we will search for moderate magic. Nothing so potent that men have to do weird things, but nothing so ordinary that it is reduced to science.

It was when I stopped believing in magic that I realized how much of my day it used to fill. I stopped going to temples and churches and science lectures.

But I went to the Japanese temple in Worli, only because I liked it for non-mystical reasons. On the way, a group of women carrying yoga mats emerged from a taxi. Once the art of wandering seers, yoga is now stretching exercises for unhappy people. Anywhere in the world, a person in lotus position has no clue what he is doing, absolutely no clue. There is no such thing as meditation. It is all a misunderstanding, all primordial schizophrenia. If people must make a mistake—maybe they should go in search of magic at seventeen and be done with it within a decade. If they go in search of magic at fifty, they will only find complicated ways of having tea.

As always, in the temple, there was an old Japanese monk. He was in lotus position, his eyes shut. I tapped his shoulder. I no longer respected meditation. When he opened his eyes, I asked the Worli Zen monk, 'What's meditation?'

This backfired, because the old man turned out to be so lonely, he rejoiced upon finding someone to reform, and he spoke spiritual nonsense for the next one hour.

I tried to call Somen. He was just another mad man in this world and I had no reason to respect his instructions to keep away. But his number had changed. And I did not persist.

Sabena and I met a few times. What was there not to like in me. Just another wise young man in the world who knew there was no meaning to life. She didn't like the change. She tried to appear interested, but I know the subconscious minds of girls more than they themselves do. She was not sure what to do with me.

One night, I was on Internet Messenger with an old schoolmate who was in the US.

Remember Somen? I said.

Oh yes, Balki said. We used to have very deep chats.

You too? What about?

Spiritual stuff, deep stuff.

I wonder what he is doing now, I said, it would be funny if he was a Eureka Forbes salesman or something.

You didn't know? said Balki, Somen died years ago.

How many years exactly?

Five, six.

Five or six?

Six. Yes, six.

How?

Brain haemorrhage.

He was too young for that.

Yes.

You know the date of his death?

No.

I made some calls and found the date. It was the day I left Madras. He probably died an hour after. It was as though he had been waiting to meet me. He had prophesied this. That he wouldn't survive, he had seen too much. His brain had to implode.

No one can make their brain implode or know if that is even coming.

But Somen knew.

This was paranormal. I felt an old force return to me.

This was sufficient magic. This would do. This was enough to keep looking.

Snakeskin

SHUBHANGI SWARUP

The baby snake moves on the human palm, in various shapes of infinity. It has brown and black stripes and can be mistaken for a large earthworm. But the hand that rescued it from the disorientation of a busy highway, lifting it gently by the tail, knows better. This hand knows its species and sub-species, and has an insight into its tiny, reptilian mindset. The wildlife rescuer claims it is lost. As the pockets of green vanish, these animals turn homeless overnight, seeking their way back to safety. 'All creatures search for a way back home. They know the way, in their DNA,' says the caption on the Instagram feed. The girl pauses from scrolling. The words hit her. Even a snake knows things she doesn't.

The city that breathes fumes, waits outside the doorless auto to ingest her whole. She ignores the heckles and tugs, the curses and thugs, to stare at her phone. She messages her parents: 'I'm leaving.'

'At least pick up your phone,' her mother texts.

'No' she texts back. No to three healthy meals a day and three litres of water. No to cognitive behavioural therapy. The girl has been diagnosed with a body dysmorphia, and she refuses to let her quest be reduced to a disorder. In a city that operates in chaos, she has been singled out for being out of order.

She slips on her headphones and switches to the noise cancellation mode. Surrounded by an artificial silence, she closes her eyes. What is it like, she wonders, to be a snake in this city?

The girl's dad had trained her to stomp her feet on monsoon treks. Snakes were deaf and relied on vibrations, he'd said. But the vibrations here are hell. The auto trembles with the driver's frustration as he accelerates and brakes, all while stuck in traffic. Concrete spews into the sky above. It erupts from a layer of smoke, filth and clamour. There are no roots. This city has no roots, only noise.

If she were a reptile, she would have simply slithered away, brushing against the roughness of pavements and rust of the gates till she bled. She would have found a small, abrasive opening to squeeze through, encouraging the skin to moult. Snakes, textbooks say, shed skin to accommodate their growing selves. Her need is more basic. She is in search of a different skin.

The girl graduated with average marks a week before her twenty-second birthday. It was nothing to celebrate, but nothing to cry over either. On her birthday, she drew her face close to her mother's and confided in her. She told her of the open pores that dotted her cheeks, the blackheads on her nose ...

'No one can see it,' her mother said, 'only you.'

She grazed her face with her fingers, bringing the uneven terrain of micro-peaks and pores of her skin to life. Her mother was right, even she knew it. But what was worse, she wondered, to be seen or unseen?

The girl is on her way to a small room at the island's edge. She prefers to call the city an island. It makes fantasies possible. As she moves away from her sheltered existence in the south to the western suburbs, there is a shift in intensity. Everything is multiplying—the skyscrapers, the slums, the flyovers, the roads, the people ... even the noise, the traffic and the fumes! She peers at the skyline, bold in its palette. Shades of the setting sun reflect on all the glass facades, magnifying the intensity. The essence of her city, she is relieved to see, remains.

She arrives at her destination in the dark. Someone found ten fingers worth of space under a tree and built a solitary shanty. A small shrine at the trunk's base prevents the neighbours—a garage on one side and an obscene bungalow on the other—from encroaching. The board on the door screams, PROPERTY OF DEVI TEMPLE. DEMOLISHERS WILL BE CURSED, in loud, red lettering.

The room belongs to her friend, an influencer of minor proportions. Her social media handle is a mix of manifesting and wellness, celebrating inconsistencies in thought and lifestyle. The influencer has sublet the room from a man who rented it from a woman who claimed to have sublet it from someone who rented it from the owner's grandchildren or some such lineage. No one knows who the original owners are, and the only way to secure possession of the shanty is to occupy it.

Everything about it is illegal and temporary. The construction, the water and electricity, even the sand, illegally quarried from the beach to reinforce the mud it stands on. The shanty itself is a squatter here, like the temple and the god it houses. Everyone, except for the tree.

Exhausted, the girl enters the shanty. All she can do is move restlessly amidst the smelly, humid sheets she's spread over the futon. A lifetime of fears, suppressed and buried, begin to resurface. Fear of nails scratching against a blackboard. Fear of something wet, slow and sticky, crawling over her foot. Fear of ghosts and unicorns, roses and thorns. Fear of being raped and mugged, beaten and drugged.

The sea breeze brings with it the smell of shrimp and prawns left out to dry. It makes her nauseous. Intensely nauseous. She rushes to the toilet in the room's corner, an Indian style commode and basin, separated by a frayed curtain. A sulphuric stench emanates from the yellowed, cracked bowl. She can see bottle caps and polythene entangled in hairballs and dust clumps, floating in the black hole at the elongated edge.

A warm liquid trickles down her groin, wetting her chappals. A reminder that she hasn't used the toilet since she left her home twelve hours ago. Here she is, on the first day of the first decision she made all by herself, independent of reason and elderly counsel. Here she is, wetting her pants.

She slowly undresses herself and rinses her underwear and sweatpants with water. She goes to open the window and hang it over the frame. The sound of waves floods in. Rhythmic. Calm. Persistent. It is only now, at 2 a.m., that she can hear the waves.

At 2 a.m., the city is a forest of sounds. It comes to life as the high tide that drowns the constant clamour of construction. It comes to life as the eager songs of a cricket wooing the air-conditioner, mistaking its gentle hum for a mating call. It comes to life as the growls of a leopard, startled by headlights, somewhere at the edge of the national park. If the city is home to millions of humans, it is also home to billions of other creatures. Emboldened by the dark, they speak up and hope to be heard.

The girl also hears the loud gush of a man relieving himself on the wall. She confuses it for a water tap, left half-open.

The man urinates on the compound wall of a forty-crore bungalow. No one can stop him, for it is his home. A decrepit old woman, wrapped in wrinkles and rags, stands right behind him. She has a way of finding him, be it two in the afternoon or two at night. He could be on his way to work or returning wasted—she appears from nowhere and hisses at him in her toothless dialect. It has taken him months to piece the words together. And he has tried to ease her confusion.

'Ajji,' he says, 'my grandparents built this bungalow eighty years ago. My family, and only my family, has been living here since then.'

She nods like she comprehends his broken Hindi, pounded with words from Marathi, Gujarati and English. But the fact that she shows up means she doesn't. She is here to convince him that she once lived here, when it was all a mangrove. She has seen a leopard attacking a hen, and the hen flying away in fright, where his garden now stands. She has seen dozens of herons and egrets shitting from the branches that surround. This has given way to pigeon shit now. It wasn't the best dwelling place, this spot. But it was home. It is home.

'It is my home!' The man shouts in exasperation. 'This is my inheritance! Didn't you hear the lawyers this morning? The banks don't stand a chance. They are the fools, and the man who fooled them is dead. My dad is dead!'

He is exhausted. He's lost money in the stock market and his mind to a cocktail of chemicals. He wipes his hands with sanitizer and walks ahead. He punches the security code on his gate and wishes it could all be quicker. For he, a mass of protein, testosterone and credit cards, is afraid. He's afraid of the frail, homeless woman accusing him of crimes he isn't guilty of. He's afraid of the infections lurking on all surfaces in the great outdoors. He's afraid of the night for turning him into a petulant child.

He enters the safety of his porch, only to realize the relief is short-lived. He is sinking into an emotion, as heavy and sticky as sugar syrup. He can't help it. He feels regret. He shouldn't have shouted at her like that. So what if she's a stalker, she's also old and frail. He removes a hundred-rupee note from his wallet and makes his way out. He will hand her the note and call it charity, not truce.

She isn't around. Barely a minute has passed, and this hunchbacked, hobbling creature has disappeared from the scene! Except for the rain trees, he is all alone. A Devi shrine blocks the lane, deeming it a dead end. It protects them all from the chaotic crowds thronging to the beach, on the other side.

He is about to turn back, when he halts mid-step. A huge shadow has caught his eye, coiled on his car's bonnet. His limbs, like his mind, freeze at the sight. His brain swells with fear, even as the heart feels awe.

There is no fight, let alone flight.

The texture of sweat in Bombay is the smell of armpit and groin, mixed with samosas and cutting chai, the girl muses. She laughs at her own thoughts as she walks at dusk, with two bars of chocolate and chips. She has been here for less than a week, and she is already getting used to it. One bar is for her, and one for her friend, the little boy who lives in the garage. He spends his day playing with spare tyres, pebbles and plastic, while his father works.

A vulgar honk nudges for her attention. A man noses his car into her personal space, like a dog sniffing her out. He rolls down his window and asks: 'You live in the slum next to the temple, right?'

She nods, trying not to take offence.

'Be careful, the other night I saw a cobra on my bonnet. It was huge, coiled up and ready to attack ... scary, right?'

Mistaking her discomfort for disbelief, he trails her in his car.

'You don't believe me? A whole ton of cobras, pythons, kraits and vipers are showing up in the city! The government is mowing down the mangroves and they have nowhere to go! The other day, they discovered a fat, fourteen-foot python living in the police station. The cops knew about it, but did nothing. They believe it's the ghost of a dead colleague. Google it, it's all there. Quite a horror story, no?'

'I'm scared of creeps, not snakes,' she replies.

'I'm sorry! I, I, I'm not trying to ...' The man brakes his car abruptly.

The girl looks up to see an old woman blocking the road. She is walking zigzag, disoriented. Her saree, a faded piece of blue and green, barely hides the flesh, pale and swollen. Yet threads of gold, frayed as they are, glisten in the headlight.

The woman looks up. Her eyes—in an advanced stage of cataract—are blurred. She breaks her spell of ghostly blue with a toothless smile. The girl recognizes her.

'She's a stalker!' The man blurts out. 'She was there on the night of the snake! She does black magic, I'm convinced she put it onto me!'

The girl can see the globes of sweat on his brow and shirt. There is something about it, its liquid and involuntary nature, that sticks with her. It brings the incident back, later that night, as she sits all alone on a crowded beach. It is possible to hear her thoughts, even amidst the clamour and laughter, drama and clutter. It is possible to survive on a bar of chocolate.

She cannot separate the man from his fears, the trembling and sweat from the air-conditioned interiors of his sports car. But why would he fear that old woman?

On her first night in the shanty, when the nausea had swallowed her whole, she had hurried to open the window.

She had opened it and begun to cry. A cry without words and thoughts. A cry without hope and a cry without despair. She had cried silently by the window, till she had seen something move by the tree.

She had seen the old woman resting her head on its trunk. She was muttering something under her breath. It was a strange sound that books love to describe as a hiss—books written by people who divide the world into noise and silence, and classify this moment as silent because they are unable to hear their own heartbeat, loud and urgent as an ambulance siren, or the swish of the palm fronds, grazing against the wall. The girl gently shut the window and returned to her bed. She had found the solace she needed.

At dawn, the girl dreamt a dream she had never had before. A jungle came alive to all her senses, as she stood in complete darkness. Her feet were sinking into mud as the rain gently fell onto her skin. Sounds of insects, frogs and crickets filled the air; sounds of small splashes and branches grazing against each other. The smell of freshly wet earth sifted through a cold breeze. And then the clouds parted. Under the moonlight, she saw a pond at her feet, probably rain-born and rain-fed. Dragonflies and fireflies hovered all around, drawing her attention up up up, to the branches above her. A frog croaked at the edge of one. Green and red, with blue bulging eyes. Painted in the colours of a flower.

Something else shifted, almost imperceptibly. It moved in spirals, as it coiled around the branch. It glowed with an iridescent blue …

She had slept through the day and had woken up, consumed by the spiral of the turquoise blue snake. She didn't know that she was capable of such beauty, even in her dreams. She brushed her teeth and strolled down to the spot where the woman had sat. She rested her head on the trunk and looked up at the vastness. She surrendered to the web of branches, the many lives it nurtured, the many dreams it sheltered. She too, was one of them.

The small boy accompanies his father to work in the garage. The girl avoids asking, 'Why don't you go to school?' or 'Why don't you find a job?' to the homeless. It is only the outsiders, the affluent and the truly disconnected, who indulge in such rhetoric. He must be around five, she reckons. For, when she asks him, he says he's a hundred years old. He wears his worn-out shorts and vest as if it were a uniform, day in and day out.

She shares her food with him, and he shares his world—filled with old tyres, broken pipes, made-up games and the occasional dance to a Bhojpuri tune. He insists on cricket and she on goti. Sometimes, they settle on a game of hide-and-seek.

He has hidden his face against the tree trunk and is counting out loud. She runs to a corner in the compound and pushes the tin drum aside. She's about to crawl behind it when she sees a hole at the bottom of the wall. It is stuffed with a frayed rag of gold, blue and green. Threads of gold glisten in the sunlight, creating diamond-shaped patterns. She has seen the design somewhere. It is all too familiar in this neighbourhood of strangers.

'Can I tell you a secret?' the boy asks her. He has found her staring at the hole and senses a pause in their game. 'A baby snake used to play here.'

'Are you scared someone will hurt it?' she asks. 'Is that why it's a secret?'

'No. that's not the secret. You know it. If you have seen the old woman, you have seen the snake too.'

'What?' she says. 'I don't follow.'

'She is a snake spirit. She haunts this place because it used to be her home.'

The girl musters the courage to reach out on her last day in the shanty. She owes the man a conversation, if not an explanation. So, she invites him to a coffee shop just outside the shared world of their lane. They sit across each other in awkward politeness.

His cold coffee has arrived again. He returned the previous order on account of it being too cold. He told the staff to reduce the ice to just one cube and reduce the sugar to a pinch.

'I'm sorry,' he says. 'I'm not good with small talk. I have social anxiety. And while I appreciate you taking time off to tell me all this, why should I believe the theories of a small kid who doesn't even go to school?'

She's lost to the world outside the glass window. The cars have begun to crawl after a complete halt in traffic. She can sense the commuters' relief.

'I would rather believe in the wisdom of a child than the fears of an adult,' she replies.

She excuses herself under the pretext of using the restroom. She goes to the counter instead and pays up. He hasn't noticed. His hands twitch in silence when she returns.

'I haven't told anyone about the cobra ... but you,' he tells her.

'Why?'

'You are a stranger, I guess?'

Both know it's a lie. Loneliness is a language that seeks conversation, if not connection. The girl is a misfit, just like him, in search of something that those, fitted at the seams, won't understand.

'Why does she appear as different snakes to different people?' he asks, scrutinizing her face through his sunglasses.

The girl has reflected on this too. The conversation with the little boy led to questions left unhinged and creaking in the doorways of her mind. They made her desperate and delirious. She had called her mother that night.

'I saw a snake,' she had told her. She had gone home soon after the confession. She ate an omelette cooked by her father and went to sleep in her own bed. She had got her own room only when she was fifteen, when her mother got a promotion, and her father threw a party. Till then, they had lived in a miniature apartment, where she slept in the living room. Her bedroom was a blessing, not an entitlement.

The answer to his question came to her after a cup of tea, one among the many, that her father so proudly brewed at home. He would mix two brands of tea leaves, cheaply sourced from the local kirana store, brew it with adrak and pudina, and call it their very own five-star chai.

'The form it takes is a reflection. The snake is a mirror to what we hold within.'

The boy holds innocence, the man holds fear. And what about her?

Beauty, she realized. Through all the despair and disorder, she held on to it, the connection that she shared with snakes and trees, the old and young. What was her dream, if not a reflection of all that she carried within?

His hands twitch, but he ignores the urge to itch. He is embarrassed by the bright pink patches of psoriasis that dot his elbow. He tries to distract himself. He thinks of something else.

He thinks of snakeskin.

He has never seen a discarded one, even in passing. He wonders how it would be? Would a snake itch, if it slithered from a pavement, burning at forty-two degrees, to a coffee shop, artificially cooled to eighteen degrees, such as this one? Would its skin explode with sweat and dryness, the way his does?

The girl too, is daydreaming. Above them, sunlight is an artist, creating patterns on the coffee shop's ceiling. Circles of light expand and shrink. Shapes cut through the emptiness and contain it. Lines crisscross, crisscross with such intensity, they create a mesh. They give rise to form and set it apart from nothingness. They become skin.

Is this how it is, she wonders.

For a fleeting moment, the entire world is lost to the same thought. Is this how it feels, to shed old skin and grow anew?

A few nights have passed since then. Full moon, or no moon, it makes no difference to the city, an ostentatious display of neon and flashes. A balloon seller cycles back after long hours at the beach. The noise of the city is down to a low hum, and he moves in silence. He glides.

It is 2 a.m., and no one respects the traffic signal at this hour. Yet, the cyclist halts.

An old lady stands naked under the traffic light, her hair like a mop. She has shed her rags for the wrinkles adorning her skin. He can't help but stare. Her body has a smooth and sinuous contour. Her skin has an odd glow. It is ominous. It appears as if something is about to happen. There is something in the moment, perhaps it is the serenity of the old woman, that makes him pause.

The balloon seller closes his eyes. He is lost to the vision. He is in his village once again, holding on to his newborn. The baby's skin is pale, soft and shrivelled. And her eyes are new. He is with his wife and daughter. He is whole.

Meanwhile, the woman begins to shed. Like all snakes, she seeks shelter when her vision blurs, when the skin over her eyes congeals. She seeks her home.

Now that her skin has transitioned from a bluish hue, the time has come. Human beings will never understand this moment. This moment of clarity, when the skin is crystal clear like still water. It is the moment before the layer slips off and gives way to a new one.

The traffic continues, in fits and starts. Some think she is smiling, others think she is frowning, in the way old people with drooping skin tend to. Horrified by her nakedness, by the game time plays on all, no one has the courage to understand her story. Without a signal to obey, they halt, then shift gears and drive away.

Your Meat in My Hands

JEET THAYIL

She felt her brother's craving in her own belly. They were alike, reliably alike, she always sensed what was going on inside him. Right now, nausea, a scooped-out feeling in the chest.

She hurried across the platform, took a seat on the bench farthest from the central ticket and reservations hall. Battery had said to be there at seven, and she'd rushed, and now she was early. Once seated, she was immediately uncomfortable, as if someone was watching from the platform opposite. It was a mistake to be early. When had the old, owl-eyed dealer ever been on time? She'd been buying from him for more than a year now, and she knew nothing about him, not his name or where he lived. His customers called him Battery because he wore high-power prescription spectacles, lenses so thick his other name was Soda Bottle.

All across Platform Five, in the heavy November heat, huddled bodies waited for the night train to Kurla. Giant fans spun overhead, circulating warm air, but the sleeping figures lay under blankets. To Luz, they looked dead. Motionless humanoid figures wrapped up in the heat, too many to count. Not one showed a sign of life, not a sneeze or a snore. There were no stray dogs to be seen (they'd disappeared two years earlier). As on the street, so in the station. No cows, no goats, no birds, no cats.

Meat. Every living thing was meat.

Playing with the sleeves of her flesh-coloured rain slicker, she went over everything that could go wrong. Police. Vigilantes. Spies. Battery might have been caught, might have been forced to turn on his clients and lure them to disaster. If she were detained what would happen to Rene, impatiently waiting, getting more and more jittery as the hours passed? Bastard Battery, she whispered to herself. Son of a bitch of a bastard Battery.

'Sorry, what?'

A woman had taken a seat on the other side of the bench, a young woman in hijab, who lit a Capstan and sent a blue stream of smoke to the tiled roof of the station. She spoke without seeming to move her lips, and somehow the noise on the platform amplified her voice.

'Waiting for someone? Could be we're waiting for the same person.'

Luz turned over the sleeve of her slicker and felt goosebumps rise on her arms. Then she took a closer look at the woman and her pulse settled. It was okay. She had the look, the sunken eyes and caved-in cheeks, that oily sheen on the forehead, those empty eyes and the way she sucked at the cigarette. Like she'd never get enough.

Oh, yes, no question. It was definitely okay.

An announcement came through, singsong English in a robotic Maharashtrian accent. *The future's coming for you. Report suspicious persons to the Comptroller window. Our non-human brethren are not for eating. Thank you, don't mention.* Then came a list of offenders apprehended that day. Her brother's name was not among them. She could stop worrying.

But for how long?

She watched a group of kachra-pickers wearing the uniform of jute overalls and black canvas boots, trailing those loathsome foil-lined sacks. The uniform filled her with dread. You never knew when they would be in your neighbourhood, invading your building, picking carefully through bins and trash buckets for bones, eggshells, fish scales, or traces thereof. If you were foolish enough to leave these items in your trash, well, you deserved what would surely come, the bleeding red X on the door, arrest followed by torture and moral correction, the medical procedures they had all heard about, execution.

She had nothing to fear, not today. Her garbage was clean.

The woman spoke again, tapping non-existent ash from her cigarette. 'He told me to wait on the farthest bench on Platform Five, and here I am. Obediently waiting.'

'Same, same,' said Luz. 'That's what we do, people like us. We wait.'

'People like what?'

'People like us, people with plans.'

'I've seen you before.'

'No. I don't go out so much.'

'I've seen you before.'

'I doubt it. Like, seriously, I'd remember.'

'This is the advantage of hijab. It's a superpower. Makes you invisible.'

'So it isn't for religious reasons, your hijab?'

'No,' said the woman, with a touch of pride. 'In point of fact, I was born into a Christian family.'

'Hallelujah.'

'Here, take my number,' said the woman.

'Your number.'

'We should stick together. You never know when you may need to borrow a hijab.'

It was true. The woman took up no space at all, slender and dead-eyed, with a sly mousiness about her, something unremarkable and troubling at the same time. Luz didn't want to give the woman her number. For what hellish or earthly purpose? She used her phone almost purely for work, and at the moment she was not working, hadn't worked since they shut down the restaurants that served meat, fish and eggs. That was the end of her life as head chef at a Bandra-Dharavi ramen shop. She got by on her savings and the occasional pay cheque Rene brought in as algorithm engineer of interactive websites for some offshore multinational or the other. No, she didn't want to give the woman her number. Then she did. Because the woman took out her phone and introduced herself. Amara.

Passengers rose all along the platform, an uprising of the undead, unkempt sleepwalkers who gathered bags and scattered belongings, then shuffled perilously close to the platform's edge. Luz saw the train advance towards them. An old man took a seat in the middle of the bench and took off his glasses and polished them on his T-shirt, his pouched eyes unblinking and suddenly naked. A black plastic bag appeared on either side of him. Battery had arrived at last. There should have been real hallelujahs, a heavenly choir, hymns of thanks and praise. The curses she'd aimed his way a moment ago were forgotten, replaced by pre-oxytocin hormone rush fuzziness. Good old Battery, always there when you needed him most. Just as you were about to give up, there he was, such a sweetheart.

'Hurry up,' he said. 'That's my train.'

Amara placed money on the bench, looking straight ahead. Luz did the same. The train stopped, metallic screech shredding off the tiled roof. The doors opened to a sudden crash of human heat and smoke. The old man who called himself Battery pocketed the cash and carefully boarded. Immediately, Amara disappeared with one of the bags. Luz, uncomfortable again, saw a camera nestled into a corner of the roof. Then she thought of Rene. She picked up the bag and checked to see no train approached and crossed the tracks to the great slum of Bandra-Dharavi, the city within the city, a humming network that its inhabitants claimed, with justifiable pride, as the densest and most civilized slum this side of New York City.

Just beyond the exit to Bandra-Dharavi East, she found the regulated scatter of the night market, deserted now, punctuated by burned-out stalls, carefully destroyed squares of melted tarpaulin and wood. Who had done this and how had they managed such a fine job? She was struck by the meticulousness of the work. They were like artists, great artists who knew beforehand what the piece would look like, before anyone else had an inkling. It was brilliant, really, quietly brilliant and visionary. Only the butchers' shops, long shut, had been burned. The other businesses were untouched, the flower seller, the vegetable vendors, the grocery and provision stores. The guy selling used gas cylinders and rubber slippers from a piece of cut tarpaulin, even his wares were fine, there wasn't a lick of damage. She thought of it as a marvel of precision engineering. If only it were applied to the city's infrastructure.

The plastic bag in her hand felt unaccountably heavy as she passed the police outpost at the main junction. She checked to see that it wasn't dripping. That it was as innocuous as any bag carried by a lone commuter on her way home after an endless day at the wage cells. As she made her way into the building, past the big-bellied father deities that framed the front entrance, she checked the street and thought she saw a group of men loitering at the temple crossroads. Then she caught the gleam of a cigarette flicked to the gutter, and the skin on her arms prickled. She didn't see the spectral figures waiting under an awning on the dead-end side of the street, their soiled uniforms colourless in the murky light.

From a third-floor window Rene watched Luz enter the building and knew from her stride that she'd scored. He wheeled to the front door and held it open for his sister.

'What?' he said, dizzy with anticipation.

'Late as usual, Battery.'

Rene waited in his wheelchair and didn't say a thing. He was afraid of discovering that Luz wasn't there at all and that the heat and dizziness had begun to affect him.

In the second bedroom, Luz took the slabs of meat out of the foil envelope and placed them on a greased iron pan. A flick of a switch powered up the induction grill and custom air filtration unit, a homemade vacuum funnel that led all the way to the roof of the adjoining building. She was cooking the wet slabs of liver when the commotion began. It was a sound they'd anticipated many times, so intrusive that it overwhelmed the instinct for caution. She thanked the gods that the front door was made of reinforced wood and wire, and stayed where she was, adding into the pan a snip of rosemary and a quick glug of Shaoxing wine.

Rene had already started to eat the half-cooked liver meat, scooping chunks of it straight from the pan into his mouth, gasping, his lips wet and his eyes glazed with pleasure. The banging outside continued as he chewed and swallowed, and swallowed without chewing. He'd waited two days for the blessed metallic taste that was flooding his mouth with saliva and gratitude. The transformation was immediate, and for the first time in twenty-four hours he fell asleep for a few seconds and opened his eyes as another crash hit the front door. Luz watched his face, pale in the fluorescent light, floating above the rubberized wheels of his silent new wheelchair. A shiny piece of liver stained his lap. One hand lay protectively across the dark meat. With the other he wheeled steadily to the door and squinted through the recessed peephole. A crowd of men. There were hunting knives and sticks. There was an electric battering ram. A man with a sickle checked the time on his smartwatch. And still Luz stood at her spot by the stove.

'Run,' Rene told his sister. 'To the roof like we practised.'

'What?'

'Don't come back.'

'Rene.'

'Go. We planned for this.'

Luz saw the look in her brother's eyes and obeyed. She propped a metal deck chair against the door, for whatever good it would do, and hopped on the bedroom counter from where she scrambled up the filtration unit's exhaust tube to the roof. They'd rehearsed it enough, and she carried out each part of her escape without thinking about her brother.

On the roof, a skylight opened. Luz's tall figure emerged into the moonlight, preceded by the gleam of a Japanese blade, her favourite kitchen tool, an instrument designed for slicing through tough joints of meat. She'd used it to cut the liver and never thought to put it down. As she stepped to the adjoining roof, there was an explosion of noise and light from the floor below, the place she'd called home for three years and more.

In the sparsely-furnished apartment downstairs, wood splintered as the battering ram finally crashed through the door's reinforced panels, and a uniformed boy in a helmet and knee pads stepped in and grabbed Rene by the mouth, not allowing him to chew, forcing him to spit out the bit of liver he was trying to swallow. A bespectacled man in plainclothes put the half-chewed meat into a glassine bag and filled in the date, the name of the perpetrator, and the quantity and type of meat that had been confiscated. In a separate bag, he put what little evidence still remained in the pan. Someone marked a red X on the door with enough paint to make the letter leak, to make it look like it was bleeding.

Two days later, Rene's trial (eight minutes, his guilt determined on the spot by a jury of three) and his execution (fourteen minutes) took place in the public square outside the Hanging Gardens, whose name had come to mean something its founders could not have anticipated. On a high stage, trapdoor hinges newly oiled, the jury introduced itself, member Deep T, member Akhil R and jury foreperson Amara H. Each read a version of the charges against Rene. That he was a consumer of meat and therefore a lawbreaker and recidivist offender, according to Deep. That he was an addict and therefore a habitual threat to the well-being of the state and its citizens, said Akhil, adding that no such criminal could be rehabilitated. That he was a non-functioning member of society and as such he was a drain on the resources and tax burdens of respectable citizens, said the foreperson, who held up a leaf scroll on which someone had scribbled incomprehensible red markings.

'Guilty,' she said. 'Filthy as charged.'

The crowd roared in approval.

'Hang him,' someone shouted, and the chant was taken up by the audience that stretched from one end of the square all the way down the street to the curve that dropped towards Chowpatty.

In the crowd was Luz, the hoodie of her rain slicker pulled low, watching from behind a roast corn vendor doing the fastest business of his career. She stepped closer to the stage and saw the jury forewoman for the first time. It took a minute because the woman was not wearing a hijab but a black double-breasted suit. Amara, the meat addict. Luz hid her face as Amara stepped behind Rene, placed a rope around his neck with the deft touch of an expert, and turned to face the cameras.

'For all of you here and all of you watching at home sweet home, here's our gift for this wonderful Sunday,' she said. 'A reminder of the fate awaiting any and all meat-eaters. You are the past. The future is coming for you.'

Another roar from the audience, louder now, more joyful and unhinged.

Amara leaned in close and whispered in Rene's ear. 'You poor filthy boy, have you any last words?'

Pulled out of his wheelchair by two municipal workers, Rene was trying to stand upright. He wore the dungarees he'd had on when Luz saw him two days earlier. Somehow, he'd managed to lose his sneakers. His feet were wet and dirty.

It was the sight of his dirty feet that shocked Luz.

'Yes,' said Rene. 'But only one or two.'

'If you have any words now is the time,' said Amara, her smile fading, in a hurry to let the trapdoor fall and conclude this weekend's attraction.

'I'm going home,' said Rene, loud, a little hysterical. 'I can't wait.'

Shouts rang out. 'Hang him!' 'Filth gets justice!'

Then a slow chant began, 'The future's coming.'

'Fuck the future,' said Rene, as a piece of cabbage hit his eye and slid down his face. A ripe egg followed, its yolk leaving a red stain in his long hair.

Luz caught a sharp chemical stink of sweat, rot, testosterone. A man lifted his young son to his shoulders. 'Hang him,' cried the happy boy. 'Hang him, Papa.'

As if she had heard the boy's request and wanted nothing more than to grant it, Amara pressed a lever and the trapdoor swung open with a crash. When the municipal men let go, Rene dropped fast and stopped, like he'd been yanked upward. The coarse rope bit deep into his neck. The blessed iron taste of meat flooded his mouth, and Rene's wide eyes met the wide eyes of his twin. Luz saw his mouth open to form a word, and then she saw the light and worry drain from his face as if a curtain had dropped between them.

For that day and the next, she went about the city with the expression of a person woken from a deep sleep, dull, without interest, her mind elsewhere, trying to still the panic moths that had taken up residence in her chest and throat. The first night, she slept on a bench near the koi pond at the children's park in Juhu. She watched the torpedo-like fish, but it was her brother's eyes that lingered in her mind, the look on his face, the exact moment at which his neck had broken and life had left him.

On the fifth day, she made her way on foot across a patch of mangrove rot to the banks of the Mahim Creek where a caved-in Fiat stood sunk into the earth, tires shredded, rims warped, dinner plates stacked in the broken trunk, roof peeled to reveal baby clothes drying on the seats, and after she took in these details of domesticity, the casual attempt at homemaking in what was little more than a mini jungle, and noted the other vehicular skeletons that sprouted from unexpected corners of the lot, the early Marutis and Ambassador taxis and muscle

Škodas, she had the strangest sensation of peril, one of those premonitions from the future, or a doom-laden catapult from the past, from when they were children about to be taken to task by a teacher or member of the kitchen staff, any one of the myriad adult vectors who knew they were orphans and had gleaned the boats of information that sailed the dusty air of the classrooms and staff quarters, information that rode above the giant thermals of the corridors, above the smell of disinfectant and nail varnish, and it was as if her brother was beside her, breathing into her lungs the fear that had taken over at the last moment, as if it was he who propelled her to an old Hyundai van under a spreading banyan at the outer edge of the dealership, a van so ordinary it might have been designed for her.

Not that she intended to dwell in the ordinary.

The dealer noted her stained hoodie and slicker, the scuff marks on her dress shoes, the dirt under her nails, and he adjusted the price of the car, took it down a couple of hundred. It had been parked on the premises for more than two months now. The dents on the roof, the caved-in passenger side door, the rust, all of it made the van a liability. You'd have to be crazy to pick it. His best offer, he said, was thirty-five thousand.

'My best offer is twenty-five,' said Luz. Seeing him hesitate, she added, 'Cash.'

'Here at Auto Mart? We don't take anything else,' said the dealer, rubbing together thumb and forefinger in the universal sign of money.

She counted a sheaf of new notes into his damp hand and drove the van to the market next door and bought toiletries, underwear, a mattress she installed in the rusted space at the back. At a phone repair kiosk, she picked up a secondhand cell phone and a pair of plastic ties. At a provisions store, two tins of kerosene. She paid cash for everything. The dilapidated old van, parked in public places around the city, attracted no attention. She lay there in the dark and fell into long spells of dazed thought. Words played in her mind, mainly the word *filth*, so terse and onomatopoeic. Her brother Rene, obsessive about order and hygiene, was anything but filthy. Even during the worst days of isolation, he took care to shave and shower and keep his clothes clean. Late at night, in his memory, she bathed at a hammam near Dadar station. A hundred rupees for a slice of soap, a towel and the use of a toilet. She wore the slicker's hoodie low on her face and sprawled on a bench outside Mumbai Hindu University and kept abreast of the news on her cheap new smartphone.

She learned that the world's largest statue, a gold and rhinestone likeness of a former prime minister installed in the sea near the Gateway of India, had been swept away in a minor tsunami. Now that year-long monsoons were a fact of city life, as were tsunamis, they were easy to adjust to, said a commentator with a million-and-a-half followers. The pricey seafront properties of Bandstand and Juhu were already worthless, the girl said. In a matter of months, not years, they would be undersea. 'You Can't Give Them Away' was the title of an opinion piece in the *Colaba Times*. A plane had stayed in the air for fifty-four hours without refuelling. Another, a Boeing, had crashed on take-off in the Maldives. The next public hanging was on the weekend, on Maha Shivaratri, the fourteenth day of the lunar month of Phalguna—two simultaneous executions at the Hanging Gardens, the state government's preferred site for termination by rope. The official reason was solid: 'The Gardens' picturesque battlements and lustrous landscaping make for urgent, edge-of-the-seat television'.

In the rain, the Gardens seemed overrun by ghosts, misted through and dead still. The same trio of judges on stage, Amara, Deep and Akhil. Amara in a black pinstripe suit, the two men in ochre robes. The crowd was standing-room only. Viewers had pushed into the balconies of the buildings that looked on to the square. Others clambered on top of buses and rain-slick pavilions. Luz parked nearby and walked into the thick of the crowd, where she watched as the condemned and soon-to-die were paraded. She saw Battery, looking old and wretched, beaten about the head. His glasses were missing. He wouldn't stop crying. The other condemned prisoner was a girl of no more than fifteen who was trying to smile at a group of weeping women in the front of the crowd. The foreperson read the charges (meat-dealer, meat-eater), said something about the pernicious nature of carnivores, and then came the highlight, the moment the crowd had been waiting for. Amara told the girl she was filth, irrelevant filth, at which the women in front wept louder. But Battery, she said, was true filth, responsible for so many broken lives. She didn't ask if he had any last words. When he tried to say something, she made a municipal worker gag him. She placed the ropes around their necks at the same time. The weekend attraction ended hastily and efficiently. Afterwards, as the crowd applauded, Amara bowed and smiled and applauded in return.

People began to disperse. Some went to the vendors to satiate other cravings—tutti-frutti ice cream, kulfi, roasted corn on the cob, Bombay sandwiches made with white bread from which the crust had been removed, filled with sliced cheese, boiled potato, fresh tomato and cucumber, hot green chilli chutney and sweet pumpkin chutney. Others went to Chowpatty Beach to walk along the expanding waterline. Amara took her time to emerge from the green room at the back of the hanging stage, in hijab, the suit gone. As she picked her way past the small hills of garbage and went towards Walkeshwar in search of a taxi, her phone rang. She answered eagerly, expecting to hear from a new dealer.

'Look behind you,' said a voice. It was Luz, smiling from the driver's seat of a rusted old van that hit Amara on the side, hard enough to send her a few inches into the air. She landed in a small heap in the middle of the road. Luz helped her into the back of the van. When Amara opened her eyes, they were parked on a deserted by-lane somewhere near Wilson College or Bharatiya Vidya Bhavan. She saw the sign for a guesthouse, Sea Face, and a defunct streetlamp. She saw Luz in the front seat, reading something on her phone. She tried to move. Her hand was fastened to the van's dirty floor.

'Please,' she said.

There was no reply.

'Please.'

'Stop talking.'

'What are you doing?'

Luz sighed and looked up from the phone. She noted the occasional pedestrian headed down the street towards the beach or up to Malabar Hill.

'I'm waiting for the dark,' she said, holding up her phone. On the screen was the image of a long-haired young man with haunted eyes. 'My brother, you hanged him.'

'I'm sorry,' said Amara. 'I didn't know. I had no choice.'

She felt the need to talk. She couldn't sit still. She was very thirsty, and she needed to pee, both at the same time.

'Please, I have to pee.'

'So, pee.'

'I can't. Through my clothes? I can't.'

'So, don't.'

'I didn't know he was your brother.'

Silence. Amara considered the question of sitting in a puddle of pee, her clothes wet. It would be uncomfortable but not unbearable. Holding it in was unbearable. After some time, a few minutes or longer, she wasn't sure, she let go with a sigh. She felt the mattress get wet under her as the smell of urea and coffee filled the van.

'I prayed,' she said softly. 'I swear I did. I didn't want to do it, they made me. Please. Please let me go. I won't say anything.'

Luz turned around to face her.

'He was only twenty-two, my brother,' she said. 'He isn't filth. He's the one who named me. Luz, Our Lady of Light.'

'I think about it every day. I would change it if I could,' Amara said, sobbing freely.

'It won't change anything,' said Luz. 'Your thoughts and prayers.'

New silence. Then Amara said, 'I'm pregnant. Two months. You'll be killing an unborn child. I know you don't want to do it.'

Luz put her phone away and looked at the deserted street and imagined the baby, little more than a foetus, though already possessed of hands and feet and a ticking heart, like the black heart of her mother. She heard the woman's sobs, the smell of urine sharp in her nostrils, and she picked a sample bottle out of her bag and dabbed a bit of perfume on her upper lip. Pregnant. Pregnant, of all things.

'Please.'

'Shut up.'

She got out of the van, went to the back and opened the door. She took the knife out and cut the plastic tie that bound Amara to the floor. She held it up, her favourite kitchen implement, with its scalloped Japanese blade.

'Go on,' she said. 'Don't make me change my mind.'

'Can you drop me to my car?'

'Yeah, I don't think so.'

She went to the driver's seat and watched the woman limp forward, humming softly, her robe wet. What was she actually humming? She thought of their first meeting. *We should stick together*. The way she'd smiled at Rene as she broke his neck. Luz thought of the foetus ticking inside her, of Rene's eyes as the life left them. What was she humming? Their anthem. *The future's coming for you*. Luz ran the woman over once, twice, a third time to make sure. Then, working quickly, she cut away Amara's clothes and stripped the meat from her bones, the knife doing its work on its own. All she had to do was guide the blade, the slightest correction and the tempered steel obeyed as if flesh were butter or wagyu. She worked by moonlight, quickly, pleasure working its way into her blood like a drug. If her brother was addicted to meat, she was addicted to dressing it. After the initial rush of blood, there wasn't as much as she had expected, and in minutes she was done. The white flesh lay furled in long strips, attached to the body by an inch or two of skin. Dead Amara had become a phosphorescent jungle flower, open to the world and dripping with light, more appealing at that moment than she had ever been in life.

Luz went to the back of the van and soaked the mattress and interiors with kerosene and set it all on fire. When the trucks arrived, they'd find a smoldering hulk of metal near a jury foreperson flayed and dressed like meat in a fine-dining restaurant. By then Our Lady of Light would be on the top deck of a BEST bus, in the front seat, enjoying the unaccustomed feel of wind in her hair.

The Sound of Silence

YOGESH MAITREYA

1.

It is not that you cease to exist when you die. The problem with death is that the world gets a free hand to distort your story. It defines you in a way you never wished to be defined. It makes its own version of your story in which you simply appear lifeless. Of course, I did not know this. How are you to know unless you stand at the threshold of death?

2.

The tale of lost dreams also dies when its dreamer does. But if you are reading this story, I can assure you that neither the dream nor the dreamer is lost. Because it is here. I am here. I escaped from a small town in India, to arrive in Mumbai and weave the quilt of my dream of being a writer—totally unaware of the fact that Mumbai is the graveyard of many, many dreams—dreams that dare to create a fusion of love and justice, not just love, not just justice, but a symphony of both.

3.

I cannot remember the last time I listened to my own voice. I lived in Mumbai, where one's voice is submerged in the sounds of conflict—of people, of dreams, of desires, of needs, which are at times incomprehensible. When you lose your voice, you lose the map to your dreams. It is difficult to put in words what it means to lose your dream—no matter how small or trivial that dream may be—and then live, transporting your body from one place to another, from one pair of arms to another, either high on marijuana or drunk. The intention is to dissolve, like salt or sugar in water, to numb the pain, to get lost from the eyes of the world. You hope that tomorrow, somehow, you will come to grips with your life and find your voice. And once you find it, you will find your way to your dreams.

But the problem with losing the map to your dreams is that you can only hope to regain it. And while that happens, you sink deeper into the complexities of desire. It is at this brittle juncture of life that one can feel the arrival of death. It is at this unbearable moment that the distance between life and death becomes the distance between what you once had aspired to be and what you are becoming.

4.

I am sitting in a place—a small public library in the city of Hamburg—where silence is the norm. I think it exists to allow each person to be in contact with their thoughts. When I came here to attend university, I found that not all silences were violent in nature. Silence in some places, at times, can be a canvas on which you draw the map of your dreams, with the colours of your thoughts. I feel the silence of this place is that silence. I can see people coming and going, browsing, working on their laptops, a few seemingly lost in the books they are reading. There are people here, strangers, but nobody seems to be invading my thoughts. The struggle to be in touch with your thoughts—the first step to reaching your dream—is a direct battle between the world and you. Well, not all of us can afford to be in touch with our thoughts—or I must say, dreams—especially when we have almost touched death.

From here, I will walk back to my place. On the way, I will stop by for a beer at a sports bar, run by people of Turkish origin. They know very little English, and I speak neither German nor Turkish. But it is fine. Being a frequent visitor to this place, people know my face and I know theirs. Sometimes, all that matters is just to recognize each other, without developing the desire to understand each other.

I get to walk a great deal here. My life is simple at this place: I read, I walk, I write, I drink my beer and I sleep, knowing that if not for this simple life, I would have been dead.

5.

If you think this is my story, and only my story, you are grossly mistaken. Not everyone survives to tell their stories, and even if some survive, they can hardly lay bare their vulnerabilities for the world. Hence, life consists of two things—surviving and exercising the courage to be who we are. When I arrived in Mumbai for the first time, I lacked life. To acquire a bit of life, I had to follow my desires and, thus, expose myself to fear—for, who knows where our desires can possibly take us?

6.

'Can I kiss you?' I said, looking into her eyes, which were drunk like mine.

'My lips are dry from smoking, are you sure?' she said, with a tone of nervousness in her voice.

I met her (let's call her Susan) because I wanted to meet strangers. Because known people who seemed vulnerable like me, scared me, always. They reminded me of my own lack of courage to expose myself to the world.

But meeting strangers is risky, too. Of course, I did not know it then, and to taste a bit of life, I was simply following my desires. What followed after that first kiss was the insatiable need, ever growing, to feel the warmth and wetness of flesh, floating in life without the weight of fear of any kind. A hunter does not follow the prey; he primarily follows his own desire to kill. The secret the hunter does not know is that eventually he becomes prey to his own desire, simply because he does not know how to deal with it as he gets blood on his hands, a lot of blood.

Can you decipher the metaphor here? Well, you will, as you follow this story. You'll have to navigate with me from moment to moment, from place to place, to be with this story.

7.

Outside the double-glazed window of my room, people pass less frequently. It is cold outside, which appears romantic and, at the same time, hauntingly intense. Cars pass by on the cobblestoned road without honking—unlike the past, when honking was a way to inform the world of your dominance. If you know how hierarchies are manifested in Indian society, you will understand what I am saying here. In Hamburg, I am used to this scene repeating itself every evening, when the darkness is darker than one can imagine. But what is the use of the light outside, when people constantly push you into isolation, like in Mumbai, where you cannot even find your own voice? Feeling a little bit of loneliness here is better than being abandoned amid a sea of people. I've made a just choice—I choose to navigate loneliness rather than live in a darkness that is powerful enough to swallow my voice, lethal enough to swallow me. Here, in Hamburg, despite the recurrence of spells of loneliness, I am able to listen to the voice of my thoughts. This is enough—to live one day at a time.

8.

Susan left one day, after two years. I was ghosted. It was like waking up, exasperated, from a dream, good or bad, no one knows, but it was troublesome; it was emotionally gut-wrenching. Have you ever been ghosted by someone with whom you have been naked for a great deal of time, in all senses of the term? Well, it is like you want to throw up, but you cannot. This happens when your body and mind do not work in harmony. When the communication between body and mind is broken, the space of this communication is replaced by darkness; the possibility of light ceases to exist. This darkness, so slyly, is replaced by pain you don't know how to deal with.

9.

As a child, I saw men shouting, being angry all the time, and one day, in a moment of anger, some of them got cardiac arrests. It was attributed to their alcoholism, but that is only partly true. Born in certain social conditions, and made to believe they were victims of it, they developed anger as a defence mechanism, as a way of expression, as a way to speak; this anger, over a period of time, worked like a fatal drug. Not to mention, anger is also addictive. No one talks about it. Some of them, at a young age, in order to tolerate ruthless working conditions at factories, or while doing menial jobs, got drunk every day, and one day, met with an accident at work and died. Death was a widespread reality in my childhood, rather than a celebration of life. Before I came to understand this truth, self-harm became the default mode of function in my life. I mention this here because the past is never irrelevant, especially when you are on the brink of repeating it.

10.

The night is getting darker and calmer. I do not feel the need to lose myself with substances anymore. I do not feel the need to shut out the sound or the silence of the world around me. Now, in Hamburg, after many years, I can see the stars. While living in Mumbai for a decade, I had actually forgotten to see stars amidst the debilitating glitter of city lights. In Hamburg, I am mesmerized by the gleaming stars above, the chill in the wind, this grey but comforting landscape of the night. To me, this is no less than an achievement—that I have retained the ability to be mesmerized by the monotonous simplicity of the life around me. I do not feel held by the life I am breathing in, or by the people I meet here. Just a year ago, amidst the colours, the sounds and the crowds of Mumbai, I had begun to feel suffocated. Why? I am trying to find the reasons.

11.

I lost a great deal of appetite four months after Susan disappeared. A friend suggested that I see a doctor. I consulted a psychiatrist. To relieve me of my pain, I was prescribed oxycodone once a day. It was my first interaction with something called medication. I felt slightly euphoric after consuming it. I wanted this feeling to last long, as I was experiencing it after months, or, to tell you the truth, years. I wanted more of it, maybe because I had not felt it before with such intensity. Marijuana helped extend this feeling. Things such as the sound of traffic, people's gaze and uncomfortable situations ceased to bother me. I began to talk to those who had scared me.

Once, in the university, for a course on social systems, we were asked to write an assignment on 'social conditions and its impacts on people'. I wrote an essay about men from my basti who had died of alcoholism. I related their condition to caste, loneliness and their experiences against the world. I had written it from the vantage point of what I had seen before my eyes. I had managed to reflect on my experiences and observations. I had written the assignment as though I were shouting out something that I had wished to tell the world for a long time. I did not pass the assignment. The professor said that it was not academic enough, and that it needed more sociological references. 'It sounds like a monologue,' he told me. Men about whom I had written were not only absent from academic reflection, but were essentially rendered absent by society as a whole. If they were considered, they were viewed as delinquents, as beings unworthy of human attention. People who are historically absent as thinking minds in our collective cultural and social imagination—how could they land in academic treatises or be part of the 'intellectual' pursuits of university pundits?

I felt terribly depressed. One dose of oxycodone and marijuana brought me out of it. I began to perceive this as a remedy for pain.

12.

I am waiting for a train at Heimfeld station. It takes about forty minutes to go to the university. Life here is cold and slow, but it buys me enough time to look around, to make sense of how people live across different cultures. In Mumbai, it is so challenging to find time, to reflect amidst the rush of people and their anxieties.

The train is approaching. At a particular spot in the station, a woman in a wheelchair is waiting for the train. The train stops. Doors open. Some passengers get out and some get in. The driver of the train comes out of his cabin, spins the key so the door won't close until he commands it to. He comes to the woman in the wheelchair, takes her to the passenger carriage, unfolds a metal plank to bridge the small gap between the station platform and the train carriage. He moves her inside. Then he comes out, goes back to his cabin, looks around, looks in the mirror, locks the door. It all takes about five minutes. Life is not rushed.

Where I escaped from, I am not used to this—to valuing individuals and their needs, to perceiving them as being worthy of human dignity. When I saw this for the first time, it took me to a past where I had seen bright young students dying by suicide because of discrimination, because of indifference and because of loneliness. I could not help but to revisit a time when they were forced to either die early or lose their way in life—not much of a difference between these two. I know of a Dalit PhD student who broke up with his girlfriend, and failed to recover from it. Now, he roams around the city, barefoot, asking people for change to buy tobacco or cigarettes.

Hundreds of Dalit students die by suicide in Indian universities every year—institutionalized murders. The exact number of victims of caste as an institution is hardly known.

I draw a correlation here between victimhood and choices. You can be a victim of society, its institutions. You can be a victim perennially, or you can make a choice not to be one and alter things. When the world does not seem to be even slightly empathetic towards you, it takes courage to kill yourself, because you have already forgiven the world for its cruelty; it's just that you cannot bear the ugliness of society anymore and want to free yourself from it. But it takes far greater courage, effort and determination to live, to change the course of your life, to fill the space around your existence with a kind of love that has been taken away by the world's hate towards you.

13.

I developed an indifference towards the university I was studying in, after they failed me for writing the assignment—an assignment in which I wrote about my life as and what it was, instead of making it an 'academic' piece. I met a couple of girls after that who were either victims of sexual harassment in the past or who had inherited a life that was starkly different to mine. If you are hurt, it is possible for that hurt to extend to the lives of those around you. Two people who were hurt in their individual pasts, when they get together, unfortunately, blame each other in the present. This is a vicious cycle. It is incredibly difficult for them to develop the language of love and forgiveness, and then move ahead. In the couple of relationships I had around then, when difficult situations occurred, I blamed the girls for my hurt and they blamed me for their own hurt. Respite came in the form of marijuana, medication or getting so drunk that I had blackouts. The more difficult an emotional tangle, the more I relied on substances. This is how, I presume, dependence on substances begins.

14.

My weekends in Mumbai were spent with my friend (let's call him Isaac). Isaac was someone with whom I could explore the many hues of literature and words and stories.

One weekend, we got drunk in the afternoon. 'Now I need to see a friend, so I will jump on,' he told me. I did not want to feel alone, so I said, 'Can I also tag along?' He smiled. We met his friend near his house in Sakinaka. She was his classmate from the university he hated so much now. 'Universities kill your imagination,' he often said. The three of us went for a drink. Isaac and I were already drunk. When drunk, the body does not function the way it should, but the mind challenges this reality. In truth, the mind wishes to escape reality, and it seeks a little bit of pleasure as a means of escape. Isaac and the girl began kissing as we were about to leave the bar. Then, he went to the toilet. She came to me while we were waiting for him. She held my hand and kissed me too. It was late in the night. We walked out of the bar, drunk and seemingly lost. We were looking for an auto. Two bikes passed; the bikers passed comments while looking at us. Isaac shouted back. The boys on the bike returned and started manhandling Isaac. They got into a fight and Isaac suffered a head injury. His friend and I shouted at them to stop and leave Isaac alone. Some other people rushed in to intervene. We took Isaac to the nearby hospital. While he was being examined and bandaged, she and I were making out in the corner. This was surreal. 'You can't do this in the hospital, what kind of people are you … doing this when your friend is hurt,' the doctor said, seemingly confused about how to react.

All three of us came back to Isaac's house, still drunk. Again, at his house, while Isaac cleaned his hands, she came and kissed me. Then, she kissed Isaac. We made out, drunk or not drunk, I do not know, but I remember all of it. Sometimes, the most surreal moment in life is the one that reflects the most naked reality of our being.

Later, I dropped her home. Then, I went to catch a train. It was 4 a.m. and there were two hours still to go for train services to be resumed. I did not have enough money for an auto and was not in a position to walk home from the station. I slept there on the platform. I woke up to the sounds of people and a couple of dogs around me. I could not hide my shame. In that moment, I felt I was a wrecked ship drifting in the sea without an anchor and a destination to be arrived at. I think, in such a moment, you can see your loneliness in perspective. And seeing it is extremely scary.

15.

For a week afterwards, I kept myself inside my room in the hostel. It became impossible to make sense of my life, and as an introvert, it was even more difficult for me to speak out.

One evening, my phone rang. I did not pick up. It rang again, and again, and again. I answered. 'Check out the news, Rohith has gone.' Isaac's voice was at the other end of the phone. Then, he messaged me the letter Rohith Vemula had written before dying. It seemed like institutional murder. I read Rohith's letter, I don't know how many times. I cried, I do not know why. I sobbed. Then, I read his letter again. Those hundred-odd words were powerful enough to shake me, wake me up from my own pain. The letter did two things—it made my own pain appear trivial, and it rescued me. While reading it, I was reminded of my own dream—of writing, of becoming a writer.

When I escaped my childhood home to come to Mumbai, my dream was to become a writer. I lost my dream while navigating life in university. I gathered courage to look at the fan, to which I had tied a rope a day before, thinking death would free me from the pain that seemed impossible to overcome. Now, I stood on a chair and cut the rope at once. I packed all my books, my clothes, and took a train straight home. All I did, after that, was write every day, without any expectation attached to it. It helped me regain my voice. For a year, I kept applying to universities in Germany.

Almost a year and a half later, I secured admission.

I left for Germany, carrying my dream with me and the determination not to allow anything to take it away again. Rohith's words were so potent that they completely radicalized my vision. Through his words, I began to regain a passion for life.

Sometimes you don't need to fight people or society. You just need to distance yourself, so that you can see life in perspective, so that you can create a little bit of beauty elsewhere, despite the ugliness you were forced to witness and consume. This is also another way of making life worth living, and making death a story of how you lived with the beauty you found within yourself.

You are no more significant than a flower that, in its lifetime, spreads fragrance, and adds beauty to the world, and then transforms into a form of energy that makes a place livable.

16.

Surrounded by the sound of silence, I am still fighting, because I am writing. I bear you witness in this.

The Painter's Last Stop

RANJIT HOSKOTE

I've been dead about eighty years. More or less. Fortunately, no one's noticed. Even to myself, I'm visible only in flashes. Things go on as they always have, and that's what people notice. They notice that things get done, not who's doing them. They attune themselves to rhythms and patterns, the habitual architecture of days and weeks. Best to leave them undisturbed. Day after day, I come down and set up my easel and lay out my brushes, arrange my palette. Most mornings, the aroma of linseed oil sings through my studio, and the heavier smell of turpentine hangs over it, until I've opened the French windows that are the pride of the house and give onto my garden.

Other mornings, the rank smell of drying fish sweeps across my studio from the Danda shore. That's a spring tide no one can push back or escape. Unlike my neighbours, who complain bitterly—in the old days, they would have wasted vials of precious eau de cologne on ineffectual handkerchiefs—I simply open my nostrils to the incoming flood. I enjoy that nose-prickling stench, even if it gives me a long, lingering, eye-watering headache afterwards. Sometimes, a price is worth paying.

For a week now—or perhaps longer, I lose track of time easily these days—my canvas has stood blank. Acharya used to labour that tedious metaphor every chance he got. '*Bara ka Vasudeva, agdi shanta, agdi nirmal, agdi amurta. Sadaiva asach asava chitralekhanacha arambha*,' I can hear him intone. I didn't throw that verb in to sound clever. Acharya never talked. He always intoned. 'I say, Vasudeva, utterly tranquil, utterly pure, utterly without image. Ever thus should pictorial art be inaugurated.' Something like that. As if pictorial art—the whole of pictorial art from the Attic amphorae and the Sanchi bas-reliefs to Turner's seascapes and my own lovingly detailed panoramas of the Mahabharata, all of it—was nothing more than the annual salon of the Bombay Art Society, with the governor cutting a silly silk ribbon.

Never say anything clearly and simply if you can bundle it up in pompous Sanskrit—that was Acharya's motto. His verbosity impressed the half-wits who gathered around him at Gladstone Hall, to be bamboozled by his quotations from the Upanishads—always the same old Ishopanishad, I doubt he'd read the other seventeen—and the Gita. How that acrobatic text manages to bend in every reader's chosen direction is beyond me. The South African barrister called it a song of peace, the Bengali bomb-thrower called it an anthem of war, and Lokmanya thought it was the patriot's creed. Acharya liked the image of Sri Krishna preaching on a chariot. He must have seen it as a self-portrait.

Acharya loved all the attention, and the reputation it brought him as a scholar, a philosopher. *Kasle thor vidvaan*, they would marvel to each other, his acolytes. I could see them cluster around him as his voice rose and fell in practised cadence. I would watch them from my deserted corner at the other end of the school's vast, windy studios. I had a clean line of sight to the circus across the heaped skulls and Platonic solids and the busts of sundry Roman emperors, each looking like it could do with a stiff drink.

The lectures that Acharya gave twice a month were attended by the city's great and glorious, the Parsi baronets and the Marwari merchant-princes clip-clopping up to the museum in their buggies, to be hypnotized by his magic lantern. The boring articles on the Ajanta murals and Pre-Raphaelite paintings that he contributed to *Bhutam*, I don't know who read them but everyone praised them. Never mind the hideous colours he used in his urban vistas, with a Bombay monsoon shitwater ochre slopped all over delicate turquoise hints of wall, dull gamboge pitched against hysterical magenta, wispy cerulean skies murdered by swaying trees done in madder, the impasto piled high. But I digress, I digress, and I really have to do something about this. Death doesn't remedy one's foibles, I've learnt.

Now, unlike Acharya, I don't deal in metaphor. I say what I mean, and I mean what I say. My canvas has stood empty, absolutely 100 per cent vacant, untouched by tint, unaltered by graphite or pigment since I set it up last Sunday. I was hoping an image might make the leap from one of my sketchbooks to the easel. But those sketchbooks lie open on my grandfather's rosewood table—silent, sullen, unhelpful. But let me be Acharya, dear lord, for once let me be Acharya. Utterly tranquil, I should say, utterly pure, these fine-grained sheets of mine, utterly and gently reluctant to hand over their images.

No one had stopped me from painting the grand umbrellas of the rain trees that someone had brought across from Brazil many years ago and planted along the avenue around the corner from my house. Such a feathery canopy, already! No one had stopped me from painting the parakeets that screech in the mango trees in my own garden, had they? Why couldn't I paint the whiplash of waves on the shore road at high tide? I love walking there, down the avenue of rain trees to Danda, when the first showers come. The tang of salt, the roll of thunder, how do I paint that taste, that sound? The church bells of Bandra, ringing through the air, how do I reach out and hold their high, sailing notes?

Someone lovingly playing a Chopin nocturne on the piano one evening, as I walked through Chuim. Very early one morning, from another house, closer to Ghodbunder Road, carrying across salt pans and coconut groves, a voice shaping a bol-taan into raag Ahir Bhairav. These glories, these amazements! The lamps of the lighthouse, far away in the harbour, glowing through drizzle and torrent. The spreading sickle of sweat in each armpit of a fisherwoman's blouse, the glint of her fillet knife as it goes through silver scales and grey belly, splash of pink on stone. In my mind, I was always escaping the heat, the sweat, the mud, the sand. I was always trying to paint these scenes and figures as if they would never wilt in the tropical swelter, as if they would never die.

In those early days, when we were friends, Acharya would cheer me on. 'Look at this fine, muscular boatman putting out to sea, Vasu! He's the Guha of our times, the boatman who will take Sri Rama across the river into exile. This Koli girl with her sari tucked up around her thighs, striding into the water, she's Matsyagandha, mother and grandmother of kings! And that maidan there, down by the hill, that's where the Kauravas and the Pandavas will meet in battle array. *Dharmaksetre kuruksetre samaveta yuyutsavah / mamakah pandavascaiva kimakurvata sanjaya.*'

In those days, I would take Acharya seriously, I would go by his advice. He knew his epics alright and he meant well, but even he couldn't build me a bridge of rocks. To connect the mainland of what I was seeing in front of me to the island of what I was seeing inside my head.

When the Great War began, I wasn't sure I would ever get to see another jar of Prussian blue. Ships were being bombed in the night. Armies were crossing deserts and mountains. Railway tracks were being blown up. Our own men, Sikhs and Rajputs, Marathas and Madras Sappers were being sent off to fight in Mesopotamia and France. The Prussians had taken many of them prisoners. And here in Bombay, in India, we were imprisoned in a cage of rations. Rice in short supply. Dal in short supply. No onions. Rotting potatoes. The meat, slim pickings. I couldn't do without my mutton curry on Sundays. The vegetables seemed to have dried up. Luckily, there was no shortage of bombil fry and minced prawn. How my wife managed during that time, I have no way of knowing. In truth, I never asked. I noticed that things got done, not who was doing them. I kept at my life's work, the panels of marouflage that wound all the way up the staircase of my home. If I couldn't go out, if school hours were going to be erratic and foghorns were going to be going off like banshees at odd times, I would lock myself in my house and turn my house into my studio, my museum, my temple.

You would find me in front of those panels in my studio, at any hour of day and many hours of night. Or else I would be overseeing some of my assistants—the few who remained—as they carried the panels up to the staircase, set them against the wall, fitted them in. One by one, all the way to the door that gave onto the terrace. Each panel was a canvas panorama crowded with figures—the kings and princes gathered at Draupadi's swayamvara, watching Arjuna look into the pool and shoot his arrow at the ceiling, or the sages gathered around Yudhishthira's Ashwamedha sacrifice, their eyes fixed on the fine horse at the centre of the composition, everywhere clouds and jewels and luxuriant trees in bloom—and each one had to be plastered to the wall, until the last one pointed to the sky. I began to think of these stairs as my Stairway to Heaven.

I read in the newspapers that the Prussians had used a strange chemical gas in the early battles, and that soldiers were coming back from the trenches dazed, poisoned, half-dead, paralyzed. Nursed back to life, they turned into skeletons going through the basic animal motions of life. The figures of the vanaras that I was painting—relying on some of the exquisite folios from the Punjab hills that Coomaraswamy had just discovered in Lahore—were more real to me than the Great War. They were right in front of my nose, in their fine tawny fur, gold-bound armbands and spiky steel armour, lying as if dead under Indrajit's spell. I heard the Red Baron had been shot down, his famous triplane a wreck. I didn't pay too much attention. The kettledrums of Lanka's rakshasas were beating in my head. How was I going to paint Jatayu, his wings hacked off by Ravana, brought low from the skies and impaled on a peak? I read that the Czar of all the Russias had been murdered by the Bolsheviks, and that people in every country were dying of the Spanish flu. How would I paint the Pushpaka Vimana? Should it look like a ship floating through the upper air? It couldn't look like an ocean liner, though. Or a galleon. Better to give it clean lines, as if Leonardo had drawn it in a codex of his. Or should I wrap it in a curtain of exuberant gargoyles and yakshas and apsaras, as if a Madurai gopuram had taken wing?

You do know what marouflage is, don't you? Did they teach you anything about it at art school? Why would they? Your teachers think it's old-fashioned, don't they? Out of date, out of step, out of tune with the times. And what do the times say you should do instead? Splash a single colour on a canvas and give it the name of a Hindustani raga? Turn a man into a stick figure and say it's a portrait of the human condition? Tear up vanishing-point perspective, show a scene from three points of view and tell everyone how much more of the world it brings in? If I wanted more of the world, I would go and sit in the dress circle at Regal Cinema and watch all the newsreels.

Take off that stupid beret and stop pretending you're in Paris. You're in Bombay. Wake up and smell the bombil drying in the wind. And yes, you'd be right to tell me that I should have taken my own advice.

After the War, the authorities at school decided that my record was patchy. Best to assign me the duties of the taskmaster, they felt. In their eyes, I was no intellectual. For the next few years, I kept up my routine of horse carriage and tram to the school and back, sketching and making notes along the way. I presided over the students as they went about their life classes, reducing living models to volume and shading. I could correct the angle of the pencil, temper girth and stature, sharpen perspective and demonstrate landscape, talk about impasto and glazing and scumbling. For all this, I was *the right man for the job*, as the principal put it in his jovial, fatherly way, patting me on the back. But not when it came to writing the textbooks on aesthetics. Someone else would be the author. Or when it came to chairing committees. Someone else was the right man for that job. Or the school's annual celebrations, which would be planned and organized by someone else. Demands rained on my roof, favours rained on Acharya's.

Fatherly, did I say? Was that how I described the principal's way of speaking? Yes, if your father was Yayati and you were Puru, and he wanted to squeeze the juice of your youth and gulp it down. If he cast you aside and never grew old, while you shrank and withered away into the shadows. Principal David showed up spry as ever to the morning meetings. Acharya processed through the studios and the sculpture gallery, his entourage of students and young teachers in attendance. The first grey streaks appeared in my hair. If I left my chin unshaved, the stubble would be a scatter of white. Don't get me wrong. I'm not complaining. I didn't care much about David or Acharya. My mind was fixed on my Stairway to Heaven. I was creating a world there, into which I could disappear.

After the War, I took any work I could get.

The Gujarati newspapers wanted illustrations for their 'Sensationals', their amateur detective stories peopled by runaway daughters, gold-digger sons-in-law, elegant detectives and villains in gilt masks. How would you know someone was a villain if he didn't walk around Bhuleshwar in a gilt mask? I didn't ask the Gujarati editors any questions. I was their man.

The publicity agencies wanted to picture the Perfect Indian Woman. At home in the world, cautiously. Bringing the world home, in small doses. Anatomically implausible, in a sari, holding a copy of one or another of the latest women's magazines from Britain. Again, who was I to ask questions? I was their Perfect Indian Artist.

And then, all of a sudden, with the durbars and the princely conferences and the secret meetings about India's future—which everyone found out about through the gossip columns—the maharajas and the nawabs wanted their portraits done in a way that would put back all the grandeur they had lost to their British overlords. For this, I was the ideal society painter. I, that is, and Antonio Piedade da Cruz and Jehangir Lalkaka. The three of us gave our patrons what they wanted. AP removed their sagging jawlines and the bags under their eyes, played up the highlights on their pips and gongs, the insignia bestowed on them by a gracious sovereign. Lalkaka hid their paunches behind broad cummerbunds, raised their height and burnished them with chiaroscuro dignity. I encased them in silk robes, turned up the highlights on their diamond cravat pins, the emerald pench ornaments in their turbans. The maharajas of Kashmir and Travancore, Gwalior and Bikaner sat quietly like tame cats in our studios. Governor Brabourne and Field Marshal Chetwode stood like mannequins, holding their pose for hours. Sir Cowasjee Jehanghier Bart—now he would start tapping at the silver handle of his cane and mutter under his breath about how long we took, but even he consoled himself that it was worth the trouble. With the Birlas and Premchands, reserved men in their austere white kurtas, we didn't know what to do. We made them look far-sighted, with a touch of ivory around the eyelids, a discreet speckle of grey-blue in the iris. We made the judges look like rishis, turned the merchants into lions.

Good Catholic and nationalist that he was, AP secretly painted a cycle of events in Gandhi's life. The Mahatma as Buddha, as Christ, as Saint of Labour, as Friend of the Poor. These paintings he kept to himself. Just as I kept my marouflage panels to myself. Not a day passed when I didn't work at my readings of the Mahabharata and the Ramayana, my scale drawings of Nala and Damayanti, Rama and Sita, Bhishma and Shantanu, Arjuna and Subhadra, Krishna and Balarama.

'Have you lost your mind, Vasu?' barked Acharya one day, standing at the door of my studio at school. This time he did not intone. 'You have surrendered your soul to the Goddess of Commerce.' I smiled at him, without saying a word. I had not told him, and would not tell him, about my Stairway to Heaven. How was I supposed to build it, without help from the Goddess of Commerce?

'What have you been saying to people behind my back, Acharya?' I asked him, the day after a student told me, hesitantly, how he had been concluding his museum lectures for several months after he had exploded at me.

'Behind your back, Vasu? What do you mean?'

'You've been telling your audience of grandees at the museum that they shouldn't have their portraits done by Indian painters?'

'Who has been misleading you with these half-truths? What I have been telling them is that they should find nobler ways of ensuring that they are remembered for posterity. As connoisseurs, as patrons. By supporting our art schools and our museums here in Western India. By donating their collections to our museum. Why do you object to that?'

'But you haven't been stopping on that high note, from what I hear.'

'Well, I may have said that they should not waste their time and money on getting portraits made. Especially when that genre is properly the preserve of the European artist, born and bred in northern climes, trained from birth in the ways of the Renaissance and the Baroque, in the manner of Titian and Velázquez, Van Eyck and Van Dyck.'

'I'm not Sir Sohrab Tata and this isn't one of your museum lectures, Acharya. What you're really saying is that we in India are coolies of the brush. Punkah-wallahs who shouldn't aspire to the palette. So why do *you* paint? Why do you teach painting? Why do you play the local pope of the arts? Why are you here?'

'I don't cheapen myself at the altar of the Goddess of Commerce, Vasudeva. I don't forget who I am and where I come from. I paint and I teach to uphold my own tradition, my parampara!'

'Really? And we had oil paints during the Mauryan period, did we? The sculptors who created the Bharhut stupa knew Renaissance perspective? The Tanjore glass painters were such perfect naturalists that they pumped their baby Krishnas full of air and floated them in a green haze?'

'Not a green haze—how dare you? It's the Ocean of Infinity! I am not talking about the means, which may change from yuga to yuga. I am talking about the spirit, the ideas, which are eternal. That is what I am talking about. And that is what you are betraying when you waste your talent, your gift, in this bazaar of ahamkara!'

'You have no idea why I am doing this, or how deeply steeped I am in the parampara. And do you think a tradition remains frozen? That the spirit never changes? Go away and impress someone else with your rhetoric!'

'What do you know of the tradition and its eternal spirit, and the sacrifices it demands of the individual, you *salon artist*?'

'Is that a term of abuse now, to be spat out? What you see before you is someone who is eagerly sought after by the same people that you eagerly run after. You see a rival, whom you'd written off, and you don't like it.'

'What I see before me is a man who sat on his hands during the Great War and was too terrified to stir out of his house. Were they fighting with bayonets at your doorstep? Were the bombs going off in your garden? And after the Great War, you ran out to do anything you could to find a foothold in society again. First, you sketched for the public prints. You cheapened your pencil and brush in the service of advertising. Why? To see your work in every broadsheet and magazine. And for nearly twenty years now, your only aim has been to gain prestige and accumulate wealth by flattering your sitters. At least you aren't hiding from this new World War that is raging around us, thank god. Too busy with your mincing princes and viziers, I suppose. Yours is the way of pandering, conceit and deceit. You have fallen very low, Vasudeva. I had such great hopes for you, once.'

And what do you think you're doing at your museum soirées, I should have asked the hypocrite, if not pandering to the rich? I'd never asked him that. What about the patrons who pay for your travels in the Central Provinces and the bazaars of Shimla and Lahore, Acharya, where you go poking and prodding for broken bits of ancient statuary? Where you rifle through jewelled albums with their unfaded, unfading portraits of princes, sages, women walking in forests lit up by lightning. Albums and statues that you hug to your chest, talking about them in words a mile long but rarely allowing any of us the slightest glimpse.

One late summer day that year—how well I remember the pink and green of the watermelon that lay sliced on a plate in my studio—Acharya went too far. I had moved my easel to one of the grand windows for which the school was justly famous, with the light that poured through it sharpening every line and filling every colour with resurgent energy. I was painting a langur, scaling it in the manner of a single portrait, testing out a brushwork technique for a Hanuman in one of my Ramayana panels at home.

'Why don't you tie a big silk safa around his head, Sir Vasoodeo Juggernaut Kirtikar?' asked the sage of the school, mangling my name in high Oriental Library oratorial style. His acolytes tittered. Dutifully, I noted with gratitude. 'Or better still, since he looks like quite an intelligent specimen, why not crown him with a nice red Puneri pagdi and put a bhikbali in his ear?' That one landed much better. The laughter exploded all around me and came from the heart.

For a month and more after this encounter with Acharya, I kept to myself, avoiding my students, not spending time over tea with the other professors in the common room. Acharya, too, was away on his expeditions in the countryside, I gathered. Somewhere in the Deccan, with an archaeologist and a Buddhist monk, studying a row of fifth century caves that had just been discovered in a heavily forested gorge.

I took on fewer commissions that season. The sardars and rajahs and dewans of princely states were served as before, but I decided to space them out on my calendar. Even a society painter has a right to his periods of rest. I began to go down to the shore every evening, sketching what I saw and sensed by available light. The years dropped away. I felt like a boy again, looking up at the moon, tracing the tides, judging the mood of the currents.

Some evenings, as the hours deepened into night, I walked up and down, studying the boats that had been drawn high up the sand to their mooring posts. I checked their oars. I had learned a thing or two about handling boats, from the tandels who had taught me to swim as a boy. These walks by the Arabian Sea—my cradle, my escape—would cure me, I was certain.

As May melted into June and the monsoon clouds began to gather on the horizon, Acharya returned from his travels, his journals overflowing with drawings of dvarapalas and shalabhanjikas, frottage rubbings of friezes and pediments.

I went over to his studio at the school, paused to remark on a gandharva here and a bodhisattva there, and suggested we meet and talk, and make our peace. We had known each other too long to fall out like this, I told him. He weighed my words carefully. A walk along the Danda shore, perhaps, as in the old days? A boat ride on the night sea?

I don't think I'll ever forget that dog. Its eyes made of burning amber, staring out of a coal-black face, its ears serrated and drawn back like two knives about to be hurled, its teeth bared in a snarl that must have been heard all the way to the fort.

It had watched us as we walked down to the water's edge. It had watched me as I unmoored a boat that I'd marked for the purpose and pushed it out into the water. It had looked on with curiosity as Acharya and I climbed into the boat and rowed out. Was it still watching when I allowed the boat to stall? There was no moon in the sky that night, no moonlight to shimmer and scatter along the waves. Still, Acharya looked out over the dark waters and burst into song. Could the dog see us, as I struck Acharya hard on the back of the head with a short truncheon I pulled from my satchel? Did it continue to watch as I struck him again and again, until all the music had drained out of him? And when I strapped iron weights around his legs and struggled to push him off the boat, upsetting its balance and going half overboard myself?

Acharya bobbed, slipped under, bobbed up again, was carried away. I had read the currents correctly. A line of bubbles twitching along the sea's skin showed where he was drifting away. By the time the boat came back to shore, the night was slipping towards dawn. The dog stood squarely on the sea wall, as if it had been standing there and snarling since the beginning of time.

I don't know who it saw, though, jumping out of the boat and hauling its draggled, seaweed-garlanded length up the sand, to leash it to its mooring post again, just as the rain came down in torrents.

No one missed Acharya for some weeks. It was assumed that he had gone off on one of his mysterious journeys into the countryside. Usually, he would whisper the names of villages, mouth the names of dealers, let drop the address he might be found at, a haveli here or a wada there. This time, he had not left word with anyone. Occasionally, he would send postcards to some favoured recipients on the faculty. He lived alone, the school was his family. This time, no postcard.

If there were any policemen or detectives on the case, they would have been swept up in the currents of the agitation that exploded through the city. The trains had stopped running, the trams had come to a halt, crowds larger than any you could have imagined swelled up in the streets. The Mahatma had demanded that our British overlords leave at once. The 'Quit India!' agitators were everywhere.

It's all a bit hazy now, but I recall reading about the V2 bombs that hit London, and have some recollection of the camps into which the Nazis herded Jews and murdered them. I've been mixing them up lately with the camps into which refugees from Punjab and Sindh were herded after the Partition and the camps into which I've seen Palestinians being driven in Gaza, and everywhere, mud, shrouds, and the bodies of children. I can't tell if it was then or now. So many people without a roof over their heads, wondering when death will claim them, while I sit here trying to think of what to paint.

Finally, they put Acharya on a list of Missing Persons and got on with their lives. They forgot about me too, soon enough, once they'd put my name on that list. My tram had come to its last stop. Eighty years have passed since. I think. You don't have to take my word for it, of course. To be honest, I may have lost my grip on time.

The houses around mine have been coming down at a frightening rate. There are more earthmovers and bulldozers in Khar than houses. Instead of the twang of the cotton-carder's bow, the whirr of pneumatic drills. Instead of the chirping of sparrows, the drone of air-conditioner plants. Instead of the cries of street children during an eclipse of the moon, the tinsel din of film music. Rain at the wrong time, the tides missing the clock, the coasts bereft of fish.

All I hear is the language of parasites and scavengers. Everything you have ever collected and treasured is excess baggage, to be thrown away, dismissed as—that crass expression, it's always grated on my nerves!—raddi-bangar. Sooner or later, everything becomes bangar in this anxious, restless city that wants to travel light. My grandfather's fornicator, his carved rosewood table, my rare French chess set crafted in wood and bone, my easel with its chipped dowels, my brushes and palettes.

Luckily, my house has been spared. My daughter hasn't given in to the moneybags. She's preserved my Stairway to Heaven. Last week—it was late afternoon, around the time she sits down with her students and begins to teach them what colour really means, that it's a song in the eye—a young woman brought her ten-year-old son to meet Radhika. Or Radhika-bai, as they call her now, the neighbours and their children.

This boy couldn't sit still. One of those rare, strange boys who runs around the house, taking books down from their shelves; stops to look at the paintings on the walls, the bronzes in their alcoves, the high Chinese vases on their pedestals; and passes into a dream as he walks around the garden. 'This is a *white* hibiscus!' he announced to his mother. 'And look at the *orange* bougainvillea!' While his mother had tea with Radhika, he explored the house. And soon enough, he came to the foot of my Stairway to Heaven. And he couldn't stop. He kept calling out the names of the characters, the episodes. Where was this boy when I needed clever pupils?

'Amma, there's Vibhishana, bowing to Rama! Isn't this Ghatotkacha, killed by Karna? Look at these creepers, how they turn into canopies! See how many people there are, standing on Rama's Pushpaka Vimana!' His mother had a hard time keeping up. They were nearly at the door that led to the terrace. The boy had stopped talking and was tracing patterns in tune with the paintings. He stopped and pointed excitedly, 'Amma, there's a *painter* in this painting! You can see the foot of his easel behind this pillar. Why does he have his back to us? Is he laughing at us? He's turning to look at us, he has a brush in his hand ...'

'But his canvas is blank,' said the mother. 'He hasn't painted anything yet.'

'Why?'

'Maybe he's waiting for the right subject?'

I did say I'd like to disappear into this world of my own making, didn't I?

Acknowledgements

This book, as it is now, exists because of the faith and participation of the contributing writers: Raghu Karnad, Amrita Mahale, Diksha Basu, Prathyush Parasuraman, Shanta Gokhale, Tejaswini Apte-Rahm, Jairaj Singh, Lindsay Pereira, Dharini Bhaskar, Prayaag Akbar, Kersi Khambatta, Namita Devidayal, Manu Joseph, Shubhangi Swarup, Jeet Thayil, Yogesh Maitreya and Ranjit Hoskote.

One writer in this list has a greater role in the materialization of this anthology. Dharini had already sent in her story when I learnt she was joining HarperCollins and—wonders of wonders—was assigned to work with me on this book. Dharini and I met as bloggers in our late teens and were part of a group of 'aspiring writers' called The Writers' Game. The blogging platform (Xanga.com if you must know) no longer exists, but she and I have published our own novels, and now this book, together.

I'm grateful to my agent Hemali Sodhi of *A Suitable Agency* who has the uncanny ability to shapeshift between being an enabler of wild ideas and a guardian of common sense. I'm thankful to Udayan Mitra, Ananth Padmanabhan, Naiyya Singh and Kartik Chauhan of HarperCollins India for enriching this book with their expertise and conviction. Both *The Only City* and I are lucky to have the singular eye of Bonita Vaz-Shimray to design and dress this book.

I'd reached out to Chirodeep Chaudhuri, whose photography I've long admired, for a cover image. I'm thrilled that our conversations, and his abiding love for the city, led to a deeper engagement, with his photographs providing a canvas for the characters colouring the book.

I owe a great debt to Sooni Taraporevala, Suketu Mehta, Jayant Kaikini and Sonia Faleiro for being early readers and reinforcing the book with their considered feedback and endorsement. And to Naseeruddin Shah for offering his support.

Many thanks to Manu for arriving at the book's title; to Ranjit for doing an SOS translation of the epigraph, and to Vidyagauri Gokhale (my friend Tanya Naik's grandmother) for her wise counsel on it. I must thank Jane Borges who was part of the book from the very beginning, but had to withdraw. My friend Rashi Jhunjhunwala for her perceptive and annoyingly detailed notes. And Supriya Nair, who flatly refused to be part of the book, but has been witness to rollercoaster weekly updates—I tend to swing between jubilation and despair—more than anyone else.

It is impossible to name every person and institution that has shaped and continues to shape Bombay as *The Only City* for me, but I hold this space for all that inspired the idea of this anthology. Thank you, Bombay.

VIDEOCON
HD

videocon
videocon
videocon

About the Writers

About the Editor

ANINDITA GHOSE is a writer, journalist and communications consultant based in Bombay, where she arrived as a newborn and still lives. She is the author of the novel *The Illuminated*. Anindita was previously the editor of the Saturday magazine *Mint Lounge*, and led strategic communications for a global social impact consultancy. She studied journalism and linguistics at Columbia University and the University of Mumbai.

Anindita has conceived, commissioned and edited *The Only City*, which also features a short story by her.

AMRITA MAHALE is the author of the novels *Real Life* and *Milk Teeth*. She works in the space of AI for social impact (and spends a lot of time thinking about the impact of AI on society). She was born in Bombay, and while she grew up in towns across Gujarat, all her school vacations were spent in her city of birth, which remained a fixed point in her itinerant childhood. She currently lives in Mumbai.

DHARINI BHASKAR is the author of *These, Our Bodies, Possessed by Light* (shortlisted for the JCB Prize for Literature and the Literature Live! Award) and *Like Being Alive Twice*. She is also associate publisher, literary, at HarperCollins

India. A St. Xavier's College alumnus, she left Bombay in her twenties, only to find herself returning, year after year, to converse with the sea and with her parents. Her son was born in Bombay, as were all her dogs and cats.

DIKSHA BASU is the author of the novels *The Windfall* and *Destination Wedding*. Originally from New Delhi, Diksha first visited Mumbai in 2007 for what was meant to be a two-week holiday and then barely left until 2020. She currently lives in Brooklyn, New York.

JAIRAJ SINGH is a writer, editor and journalist. He has contributed essays to several books and authored two children's stories. Though Bombay has been home for only six years, the city by the sea—a place for all souls lost and found—now feels his own.

JEET THAYIL is a poet, novelist, librettist and musician. His novel *Narcopolis* was shortlisted for the Booker Prize and won the DSC Prize. His book of poems *These Errors are Correct* won the Sahitya Akademi Award. His latest collection of poetry *I'll Have it Here* won the Sarojini Naidu Award and the Kalinga Literary Award. His new novel is *The Elsewhereans*. Jeet Thayil is a Bombayite who no longer lives in Bombay.

KERSI KHAMBATTA wrote the screenplays for *Being Cyrus*, *Finding Fanny* and the Netflix series *Class*. His debut novel, *The Village of Pointless Conversation*, was shortlisted for the Literature Live! Award. His second work of fiction, out in early 2026, is an ode to Bombay, a city he calls home with an equal mix of adoration and loathing.

LINDSAY PEREIRA was born, raised and educated in Bombay. The city was the setting for his novels *Gods and Ends*, shortlisted for the JCB Prize for Literature, and *The Memoirs of Valmiki Rao*, which won the Literature Live! Award. Lindsay no longer identifies with the city but acknowledges that there is still a small corner of it that comes closest to what he thinks of as home.

MANU JOSEPH is a novelist, screenwriter and journalist. His works include the novels *Serious Men* and *The Illicit Happiness of Other People*, the Netflix series *Decoupled*, and his latest non-fiction book, *Why the Poor Don't Kill Us*. A migrant from Madras, he arrived in Bombay at a time when only certain kinds of people could be found here.

NAMITA DEVIDAYAL has lived all her life in Bombay, other than her time at Princeton University. She has spent most of her working life at *The Times of India*, chronicling the diverse worlds that coexist in this bottomless city—from the 'yummy mummies' of South Bombay to the old suburban music circles. Bombay has also been an abiding character in her books: *The Music Room*, *Aftertaste*, *The Sixth String of Vilayat Khan* and *Tangerine*.

PRATHYUSH PARASURAMAN moved to Bombay in 2019 to become a writer—by Bombay, he means the suburb Mulund, where he spent his childhood summers. Today, he is a critic and journalist at *The Hollywood Reporter India* and columnist for *Frontline* magazine. *On Beauty: The Cinema of Sanjay Leela Bhansali* is his debut book, the first of three film monographs. He also programmes films at G5A Foundation for Contemporary Culture. Despite the cratered roads, the crowded trains, the clogged streets, stratospheric prices and scummy air, Prathyush remains in Bombay—Mulund, really.

PRAYAAG AKBAR is the author of the novels *Mother India* and *Leila*. *Leila* won the Crossword Jury Prize and the Literature Live! Award. The novel was translated into Hindi, Marathi and Turkish and was the basis of a popular Netflix series. Prayaag teaches creative writing at Krea University. He spent many happy years in Bombay, living in a succession of apartments that seemed to shrink inch by inch as soon as the rental lease was signed.

RAGHU KARNAD was born in Bombay and grew up in other cities. He is a journalist and essayist, and the author of *Farthest Field: An Indian Story of the Second World War*. He also works on video, podcasts and documentary film, and was part of the founding team of *The Wire*. In 2022-23, he was a fellow at the New York Public Library's Cullman Center for Scholars and Writers.

RANJIT HOSKOTE is the author of eight collections of poetry, including *Jonahwhale*, *Hunchprose* and *Icelight*. He has translated a fourteenth-century Kashmiri mystic's work as *I, Lalla: The Poems of Lal Ded* and an eighteenth-century Urdu poet's work as *The Homeland's an Ocean: Mir Taqi Mir.* Hoskote lives in Mumbai, his birthplace, which he calls Bombay. When asked where he grew up, he has three answers: Khar, which has always been home; Mahim, where he attended the Bombay Scottish School; and Kala Ghoda, where he read for a degree in political science at the grand Gothic Revival edifice of Elphinstone College and embarked on a career as an art critic and curator.

SHANTA GOKHALE has lived in Bombay all her life. She went to school in Bombay, taught at a college in Bombay, worked in a leading pharmaceutical firm in Bombay and did a stint as arts editor at *The Times of India*, Bombay. Soon after she quit her job to become a full-time writer, Bombay became Mumbai. But whether Bombay or Mumbai, her piece of it has always been Shivaji Park. This is where she has walked, thought, dreamt and written her books, including the one *on* Shivaji Park.

SHUBHANGI SWARUP is the author of *Latitudes of Longing,* which has been translated into seventeen languages and won numerous awards, including the Sushila Devi Book Award and Literature Live! Award in India, the Émile Guimet Prize for Asian Literature in France and Openbook in Taiwan. She attributes her worldview to her upbringing in Bombay. In a city starved of nature and open spaces, she dreams of the time it was an untouched island, and takes solace in the city's barbets, snakes and seashells.

TEJASWINI APTE-RAHM is a writer from Mumbai. *The Secret of More*, her first novel, won the Literature Live! Award. The histories, moods and textures of Mumbai are closely woven together in her fiction—in her novel set in early twentieth-century Bombay; and in her short story collection *These Circuses That Sweep Through the Landscape*. She has worked as a journalist and environmental researcher, and written for *Screen* magazine and various newspapers. She currently lives in Germany.

YOGESH MAITREYA is the writer of *Singing Thinking Anti-Caste* and *Flowers on the Grave of Caste*. In 2023, his memoir *Water in a Broken Pot*—about Mumbai, literature, Ambedkar, love, academic life in India and being a publisher—was published. He spent about a decade in Mumbai before Covid, arriving in the city as a student wanting to follow the path of writing, and leaving during the Covid frenzy as a publisher. His history informs his stories and Mumbai is the language of it.

About the Photographer

CHIRODEEP CHAUDHURI was brought up in Bombay and has photographed the city for over three decades. His interest in photojournalism was triggered when he came across *Life* magazine at a streetside book vendor at Flora Fountain. He went on to join the photography teams of the *Sunday Observer* and *Outlook* magazine, and head the design and photography departments of *Time Out*'s India editions. Until recently, Chaudhuri was the editor-of-photography for *National Geographic Traveler*'s India chapter.

Often referred to as 'the chronicler of Bombay', Chaudhuri's work documents the urban landscape, straddling a range of genres, from documentary and architecture to portraiture. His Bombay projects include his three-decade-long search for the city's public clocks in 'Seeing Time: Public Clocks of Bombay' and 'The Commuters'. His photographs of the city's architectural heritage are part of seminal books such as *Bombay: The Cities Within*. He believes that the best way to observe Bombay is as a commuter on its suburban trains.

HarperCollins *Publishers* India

At HarperCollins India, we believe in telling the best stories and finding the widest readership for our books in every format possible. We started publishing in 1992; a great deal has changed since then, but what has remained constant is the passion with which our authors write their books, the love with which readers receive them, and the sheer joy and excitement that we as publishers feel in being a part of the publishing process.

Over the years, we've had the pleasure of publishing some of the finest writing from the subcontinent and around the world, including several award-winning titles and some of the biggest bestsellers in India's publishing history. But nothing has meant more to us than the fact that millions of people have read the books we published, and that somewhere, a book of ours might have made a difference.

As we look to the future, we go back to that one word—a word which has been a driving force for us all these years.

Read.

Harper Collins | 4th | HARPER FICTION | HARPER NON-FICTION | HARPER BUSINESS | HCCB HARPERCOLLINS CHILDREN'S BOOKS

HARPER DESIGN | Harper Sport | HARPER PERENNIAL | HARPER VANTAGE | हार्पर हिन्दी | BOOKTOPUS